Maggie Hope was born and raised in County Durham. She worked as a nurse for many years, before giving up her career to raise her family.

Also by Maggie Hope:

A Wartime Nurse
A Mother's Gift
A Nurse's Duty
A Daughter's Gift
Molly's War
The Servant Girl

Maggie Hope

A Daughter's Duty

EBURY
PRESS

1 3 5 7 9 10 8 6 4 2

First published as *When Morning Comes* in 1999 by Piatkus Books

This edition published in 2014 by Ebury Press,
an imprint of Ebury Publishing

A Random House Group Company

The Random House Group Limited Reg. No. 954009

Addresses for companies within the Random House Group can be found at:
www.randomhouse.co.uk

A CIP catalogue record for this book is
available from the British Library

The Random House Group Limited supports The Forest Stewardship
Council® (FSC®), the leading international forest certification organisation.
Our books carrying the FSC label are printed on FSC® certified paper. FSC
is the only forest certification scheme supported by the leading environmental
organisations, including Greenpeace. Our paper procurement policy
can be found at: www.randomhouse.co.uk/environment

MIX
Paper from
responsible sources
FSC® C016897

Printed and bound by CPI Group (UK) Ltd, Croydon, CR0 4YY

ISBN 9780091952921

To buy books by your favourite authors and register for offers visit:
www.randomhouse.co.uk

I am indebted to Keith Armstrong's
THE BIG MEETING for details of the Miners' Gala and
the quote by David Bean at the beginning of this book.

For Sue and Lol

On the first Durham Miners' Gala, 1871:

'One August night, ninety-three years ago, the good people of Durham barred their doors and windows, locked up their spoons and their daughters, called in police reinforcements – and waited for the worst. For the miners – those rough, savage men from the rural pits, who smashed machinery, said rude things to the gentry, beat their wives, ate their children, and squandered their spare time in drink, cock-fighting and gambling – were moving on the city. They were coming, it was whispered round the timid town "to get their reets".'

David Bean, 1964

Chapter One

'Howay, Marina. Don't drag your feet, man. Let's show them we can –' But the rest of what Rose was saying was lost to her friend as the band behind them, the Jordan Silver Band, started playing full blast and the colliery banner carried before them billowed in the wind, like a sail on a ship.

'It's my new wedgies,' Marina excused herself. Well, the shoes were a bit higher in the heel than she had been allowed to wear up to now. She glanced down at them, admiring the grown-up look of them. All the fashion they were.

Marina was fifteen years old and this was her first Big Meeting, for there had been none during the long years of the war. Her hazel eyes sparkled and her light brown hair swung out behind her as she threw herself into the dance. The line of girls in dirndl skirts and New Look jackets dipped and swooped in the Palais Glide even though the steps didn't exactly match the music. They'd come all the way from the station and now they were over Elvet bridge and there was the County Hotel and all the bigwigs on the balcony, grinning at them and waving.

'Think they're royalty,' said Rose, who took an instant dislike to anyone who thought they were something better, but the remark was automatic and she swung round as the line formed a circle and skipped around for a few minutes in front of the balcony, and a crowd of pitlads cheered as the girls' full skirts caught in the breeze and lifted to a height that wasn't exactly decent, and Rose squealed and let go of Marina's hand so as to hold down her skirt, and Marina went careering off to the side and fell into the gutter, bumping into a lad standing there and almost knocking him off his feet too. Her starched petticoat was practically over her head and showing her knickers, which were school regulation bottle green with elasticated legs. Glimpsing them, Marina was mortified. Why wouldn't Mam let her have cami-knickers like the other girls? And worse, the handbag which had been over her arm fell off and flew open, and lipstick and purse and sandwiches scattered over the pavement.

'Marina!' screamed Rose but she was borne away by the others, on their way now to the cricket field where just about all the pitfolk in the county were congregating. Bright red with embarrassment, Marina scrabbled for her belongings and was shoving the burst packet of sandwiches back in the bag when she saw her lipstick almost in the drain and she stretched out a hand for it. The lad she had bumped into was before her and fielded it neatly.

'Yours, I think?' he said. She straightened up and pushed her dark hair back, looking into his grinning face. He wasn't a lad, really, not a pitlad, more likely an undergraduate from the university, she reckoned, as she took the lipstick from him. His hands were too soft and the nails were manicured, for goodness' sake! In spite of his height and broad shoulders their Lance would call him a nancy boy with hands like that. The thought of her elder brother made her look behind her apprehensively. Lance was carrying the banner with Frank Pearson and if he had seen the lipstick roll out of her bag there would be war on. But the banner was gone, already turning down to the race course where the Big Meeting was held.

'Thank you,' said Marina, remembering her manners, and ran off after it, threading her way through the crowds until at last she was on the field. At first she couldn't see the folk from Jordan and stood looking about her uncertainly. One lad sitting on the grass with his mates, a half-full beer glass in his hand, shouted over to her, 'You looking for me, pet?'

She blushed and stared across the field to the opposite corner. The pubs were open all day for the gala and, as Mam said, some of the men properly showed themselves up. But thankfully she caught sight of their banner with the picture of Attlee painted on it and ran across to it.

'You might have waited for me,' she said, looking reproachfully at Rose.

'Aw, go on, you couldn't have got lost, you just had

to look for the banner.' Which was demonstrably true, all the banners were in full sight, with the people of their home villages milling around beneath them. Some of them were draped in black, denoting that lives had been lost in winning the coal but thankfully there had been no big disasters in the past year so on the whole people were happy and out to have a good time.

Rose flopped down on the grass and grinned at her friend, deep blue eyes twinkling with mischief. 'I knew you'd be all right,' she said. 'You are, aren't you? A good thing you weren't wearing any nylons, you might have laddered them.' Her face went solemn at the awful thought. Nylons were as rare as gold dust so soon after the war.

'I haven't got any nylons,' snapped Marina as she too sat down on the grass.

'There you are then, no harm done.'

'What do you think, Sam, as many here as before the war?' Frank Pearson was asking Marina's father.

'More, I'd say.'

Marina stared round. It was grand to have everything back to normal. She could hardly remember the last Big Meeting but so far this one was living up to everything she'd heard about the annual event. By, everything was exciting this year. Even though there were still shortages and rationing and everything, folk were happy and today especially as it was Durham Day. The race course was overflowing with people, a lot of them looking about for relatives from other collieries, some already beginning to congregate before the platform where the politicians and labour leaders would be making their speeches. And over to one side there were sideshows and roundabouts and shuggy boats, the first time she had seen them since the war an' all.

Rose jumped to her feet and caught Marina's arm. 'Let's get away,' she said.

'But we've just got here,' Marina protested. Then she saw Rose looking across the field and noticed Alf Sharpe, Rose's father, standing there. Rose must not want to speak to him. Marina and Rose had been friends for so long they almost always knew what the other was thinking.

'Righto,' she said, 'let's go.'

Rose caught Marina's mother's eye on them and called to her, 'It's all right if we go for a walk by the river, isn't it, Mrs Morland?' Kate Morland hesitated but Rose had already taken Marina's arm and was pulling her away.

'Not for long, mind,' Kate called after them but her voice was lost in the general hubbub. With an expression that said she didn't know what lasses were coming to nowadays she turned back to her sister Janie, who lived by the sea at Easington. They hadn't met since Christmas.

Most of the crowds had already come on to the race course so the two girls made their way back to Elvet bridge fairly easily. A lot of the shops were boarded up but they weren't interested in shops. They made their way down the steps to the left of the bridge and started to walk along the banks of the Wear. It was a warm day and after a while they climbed up the slope and sank down on the cool grass beneath some trees near the cathedral.

'By, it's nice,' said Rose. She delved into her bag and brought out a couple of apples, tossing one into Marina's lap. The two girls munched away at the ripe fruit as they watched the sun on the waters of the Wear. Rose flung her head back, running the fingers of one hand through her thick black hair which was much envied by Marina who considered her own to be mousy and far too fine. And Rose's skin, so white, almost translucent, set her hair off beautifully.

In the distance they could hear the murmur of the crowds on the race course; further along the banks of the river the sound was overlaid by the brassy tones of a speaker coming over the tannoy. But it was all in the distance, the city's noise muted from here, the traffic banished to the outskirts until the Big Meeting was ended and the bands and their followers marched out in the evening.

'Is something the matter, Rose?' asked Marina, who had been covertly watching her friend.

Rose sat up straighter. 'No, why should there be?'

'I just thought...you're all on edge, like. Are you in trouble with your dad?'

'No, I'm not.' Rose looked away across the river. She pulled back one arm and threw her apple core so that it skimmed across the water. 'He's a bonny lad, isn't he?' she said, changing the subject.

Marina looked across at her friend. 'Who?'

'You know as well as I do who I mean. Don't come that,' said Rose with a scathing glance. 'That student you bumped into.'

'He's all right. I didn't take very much notice. I'm not interested in boys. I want to get on in life, not be married and a have a kid on the way before I'm eighteen. I'm going to take my School Certificate and my Higher and go to university.' Marina took another bite of apple and nodded her head to emphasise her words, but Rose wasn't impressed.

'Hadaway wi' you! I saw the way you looked at the lad. You like boys just as much as I do, only I'm more honest. Anyroad, by the time you've done all that I'll have made my money at the clothing factory.'

Rose had started at the Council School the same day as Marina but she had stayed on there after her friend went to the Girls' Grammar School at Auckland and had left when she was fourteen to work on the band at the factory at West Auckland.

'Hoy there! What're you two doing sitting all by yourselves there? Howay along with us, we'll have a good time. What d'you say?'

The girls looked down at the two boys on the path. 'It's Jeff and Brian,' Rose said unnecessarily, for the two had been a couple of years ahead of Rose at the Council School and worked at the pit at Jordan. 'Come on, let's go with them, it'll be more exciting than sitting here.'

She jumped to her feet and took a few steps towards the path before looking back. 'Don't be such a wet blanket, Marina Morland.'

Marina remembered that Rose had always liked Jeff, who was tall and good-looking, his fair hair darkened with brilliantine and slicked back from his brow with a quiff in the front. His skin was clear, untroubled by the scourge of acne, unlike Brian's which was pitted with old scars. Marina felt a twinge of sympathy for him, perhaps the reason why she got to her feet.

'All right, I'm coming.' She followed her friend down to the path where Rose pushed her way between the boys so that Brian fell back, leaving her to walk with Jeff.

Jeff and Rose were talking and laughing close together and the couple behind watched in silence as Jeff bent his head to whisper something in Rose's ear, casually putting his arm around her waist. Rose glanced back at Marina with a smile which made Marina blush and stare down at the path in case Brian should have noticed. Not that he would care, she told herself. The lads probably thought she and Rose had been there by the river waiting for a couple of presentable boys to come along the path, ones they could have a harmless flirtation with, just for the afternoon. What else was there to do when the old folks were listening to boring old speeches or catching up on family gossip? But she was still a bit worried about Rose. She seemed frenetic somehow in her determination to enjoy herself today.

Marina glanced sideways at Brian and caught him look-ing at her. He grinned. 'How about going on the river?' he asked. 'The punts are just down there, past the bridge.' Without waiting for her reply he called to the other two, 'Hey, how d'you fancy taking a punt out?'

'Howay then,' shouted Jeff, and Brian caught hold of Marina's hand and all four of them began to hurry to where the punts were lined up in a row at the side of the water, a small crowd of young people waiting their turn to get in one and push the punt away from the bank with a long pole to glide away with the current.

'Are you sure you can use one of them poles?' Rose asked the boys. 'The water's awful deep, mind, and I've got me good clothes on.' She hitched up the neckline of her peasant blouse so that it covered her shoulders. 'Me mam'll give me what for if I get them spoiled, we have no clothes coupons left.'

'There's nowt to it,' Jeff asserted. 'What's to go wrong anyroad?' He grinned across at Brian, who was helping Marina into the punt, and his friend grinned back. 'You'll not get a spot on your clothes.'

'Have you done this before?' Marina asked nervously, wishing she hadn't been so keen to get in the boat. She thought about getting out again, but when she moved the punt rocked alarmingly and Rose, who was just stepping in, shrieked.

'Keep still, man!'

Marina looked at the punts already on the move. They

seemed to be doing all right, and by, it must be lovely just to sit back and glide around the bend in the river with the steep wooded bank to one side and the cathedral towering over the water. It was just like a picture she'd seen once with Robert Donat pretending to be a student in Oxford – or was it Cambridge? Anyway, he was poling away on the river there in a punt just like this one and it had looked as easy as pie. Besides it was too late now, the punt was moving and Jeff was standing there, showing off, pushing the pole into the water then suddenly they were into the middle of the Wear and across, almost to the opposite bank.

'The other side, you daft beggar! Turn it round or we'll be ganning nowhere,' shouted Brian. 'Here, let me have a go.' The punt swung round and Rose shrieked and fell off her seat.

'I knew we shouldn't have come with them,' she muttered to Marina, who decided it was a waste of time reminding her whose idea it had been as she helped Rose back on to the seat. The two girls hung on to the sides of the boat, just in case.

But they were travelling serenely down the Wear now. 'Hey, look, I'm getting the hang of this,' Brian shouted.

'Why aye, man.' Jeff nodded his head. 'Anything those bloody students can do, a pitman can do better.'

'If your mam heard you swearing like that she'd bat you round the ear,' Rose observed, but he didn't deign to hear.

There were a lot of punts and rowing boats on the river now, mostly navigated by young lads from the myriad pits of the country, and it wasn't long before the four from Jordan found themselves getting into the thick of them. Marina realised that she and Rose were the only two girls in this lot, but before she could warn her friend the cheerful insults the lads were shouting at each other turned into outright war.

They were starting a mock battle, their weapons poles used like lances. It was just as well there were no points on them.

'Howay, Brian, don't forget we have the lasses.' Jeff belatedly remembered their responsibilities. To give Brian his due, he tried to steer away from the battle but when the punt nearest them tipped over and splashed into the water after a particularly telling blow to the 'knight' at the helm, their own was almost overturned and there were Marina and Rose, swamped in dirty river water, choking and spluttering and spitting it out. Brian leaped about and the punt rocked even more dangerously and suddenly Rose found herself over the side, her movements restricted by the weight of water in her full skirt, with Marina clutching on to her and screaming.

'Give me your hand!' someone shouted, and Rose saw there was a rowing boat beside them with someone leaning towards them, holding out an oar. Then somehow or other she was hauled into the punt and Marina after her and they were moving away from the scene of the battle,

threading their way through overturned punts and pitlads
swimming in their best suits, and the two girls were being
helped out of the boat on to the grass of the race course
and Marina's mother was there, scolding and using the
tablecloth she'd brought to have a picnic on the grass as a
towel to dry Marina off.

'By heck, our Marina, I sometimes think you'll never
grow up. Making a show of me in front of all me relations
like that! Do you not know the Wear's a lot deeper here
than it is at Bishop? It would have served you right if
you'd drowned – then you'd have been sorry! It was a
good thing Charlie was there to save you. Now say thank
you to him.'

Marina looked over her shoulder and there was the lad
she had already bumped into once today. Charlie? She
coughed and spluttered, trying to get rid of the foul taste
of river water, and suddenly it came to her. It was Charlie
Hutchinson of course, from Yorkshire, the one Mam's
cousin had practically adopted. This was twice in one day
she had shown herself up before him and there he was, a
superior sort of smile playing about his lips. Well, blow
him, she thought and turned away, lifting her nose up in
the air and pretending a great interest in Brian, who was
standing to one side looking guilty.

'Oh, Brian,' she said, looking up into his face with
exaggerated concern. 'You didn't hurt yourself, did you?'

The only trouble was it was hard to get rid of him after
that. Kate invited him to share their picnic and everyone

pooled their sandwiches and sat around on the grass. The wind dried the wet patches on their clothes, leaving them only grubby, not half as bad as the lads who had had to swim for the bank in their thick suits. Charlie disappeared, probably gone off home disgusted with the behaviour of these common folk, Marina thought.

'There you are, Rose,' said a familiar voice. It was Alf Sharpe and Rose suddenly looked even more bedraggled and pale and sick to her stomach. No doubt she had swallowed some water, Marina thought, and then her friend was whisked away by her father without even being allowed time to say goodbye.

After Marina had spread her skirt and dried off a little bit it was time to wend their way up to the cathedral, following the three bands and banners which had been chosen for the service this year. They played 'Gresford', the miners' hymn, willed to the Union by the composer, and Marina was struck dumb by the solemnity of it and the grandeur of the great church of St Cuthbert.

'Cuthbert's people, we are,' asserted Dad, nodding his head. 'Aye, we're the real Cuddy's people, never forget it, lass. Never mind these university folk, it's the workers that count.'

Marina's dad was a great labour man. He never forgot the hardships of the depression years, the hard times of the twenties and thirties, and was always talking about them. And the fact that many of the undergraduates of the universities had gone against the workers in the general strike of 1926, rushing to man the buses and such. Not that any had gone so far as to go down the pits, he would add with a grin.

But Marina only half listened to him. She'd heard it so many times before and the thirties were just history now, weren't they?

Chapter Two

'I feel real bad, lass,' said Sarah Sharpe wearily. 'I haven't even been able to get up and give the bairns their dinner. And you know all the women were away, there was no one to see to them for me. They had to fend for themselves.' She lay back on a pillow damp with sweat and sighed.

Rose gazed at her mother guiltily. She really shouldn't have gone off to Durham, she knew that. But, oh, she had so wanted to have a break, a day out in Durham with everyone else. She glanced at the twins, Mary and Michael, standing together, thumbs stuck in their mouths, both with tear-streaked faces and runny noses, both with jam on their clothes where they had been digging into the jar. No longer crying now that Rose was home, they simply stared at their elder sister, waiting for her to make things better.

'All right, Mam, I'll see to them,' she said. 'I'll make some eggy toast. You like eggy toast, don't you, kids?'

The pair nodded. 'Can I have two, Rose?' asked Michael. 'And Mary wants two, an' all.'

'All right. But go and play while I see to our mam and I'll call you when supper is ready.'

The twins went out into the yard readily enough and Rose heated water and helped her mother to wash before changing her bed. She found a clean nightie for her, brushed her hair back from her forehead and wove it into a plait. Rose remembered it being as black and thick as her own but now it was streaked with grey and thinning rapidly. A wave of anxiety ran through her as she made her mother comfortable, turning her pillows and straightening out her sheets.

'I'll start on the supper now. At least I'll have the bairns to bed before he comes home,' she remarked. 'Then they might get off to sleep.'

'Eeh, Rose, don't talk about him like that. He loves you really, you know,' Sarah protested weakly. 'He is your dad after all.'

'I do know. The thing is, sometimes I wonder if he does,' Rose said grimly, but in an undertone to herself as she got out the iron frying pan and put a knob of dripping in it before setting it on the hob. There were four eggs and she considered using them all but Sarah seemed to know what she was thinking.

'Leave an egg for your dad, he'll be hungry when he gets in.'

Regretfully, Rose put one egg back in the bowl, though in fact she thought it more likely that her father would be too drunk to eat by the time he finally left the Club and staggered up the road. Weekends were the worst by far, she mused. At least during the week when he had his work at the pit to go to he didn't drink too much, though he still went down to the Club. But Saturday nights were hellish for her and her mam.

She beat the eggs with salt and pepper and dipped slices of bread in the mixture before frying them in the hot fat.

'By, it smells nice, mind.' Sarah's comment came through from the 'room', where her bed had been set up since she found it hard to climb the stairs.

'Yes, well, I hope you eat it, that's all,' Rose replied. She was encouraged, Mam didn't often show any interest in food these days. She glanced through the connecting door which led from the kitchen. By, her mother looked so white and frail, apart from that lump on her neck. If that was a goitre, like the doctor said, then she was a Dutchman. The feeling of anxiety which had begun rising in her the moment she had turned into the gate was heavy on her now but she smiled at her mother. 'I'll call the bairns in,' was all she said.

If she got them fed and washed and into bed she would be able to follow them upstairs herself before her dad came home, and all three of them would be out of the way of him and there would be no rows or anything else. It was the anything else which loomed before her, filling her with dread.

Lying in bed, tired out but unable to sleep, Rose

couldn't stop thinking about her dad. She remembered
how it was before the twins were born. She'd idolised him
then. Mam and Dad had been so different. He'd hardly
ever gone down to the Club apart from a Friday with his
mates and then only for a couple of pints. They'd played
games together, she riding on his shoulders when the three
of them had gone for a walk. Mam had always been small
and slim, like a girl, and had acted like a girl too, playing
games with her daughter. They would find a stick and play
cricket with Rose's painted rubber ball and Mam could
run like a hare after it. And laughing...she'd always been
laughing.

Had it been the twins that changed her? She was often
lying about after that, putting on weight, looking bloated
for a time. And then she'd gone thin, so thin. Rose turned
on to her side restlessly, pushing the sheet back from her
overheated body. What was the use of wondering what
had gone wrong? Probably things had always been as they
were now, she had just been too young to see it. She heard
unsteady footsteps coming up the yard, the back door
opening, and turned again in the big double bed to put out
a hand to her sister Mary, curled up in a ball beside her.
There was a sort of comfort in touching the small body.
In the tiny room opposite where Michael slept in a narrow
bed which nevertheless took up most of the floor space,
the boy coughed but didn't wake up.

Rose waited, her muscles tense, listening to the noises
from downstairs. After a while, the square of light which

showed on the landing from the kitchen below went out, the middle door downstairs closed softly. Rose relaxed slowly, for tonight at any rate her dad had gone to bed.

'I want to stay on at school,' Marina said to her mother. 'I want to go to university.' It was a few weeks later and almost the end of the school holidays.

'I had to leave school at fourteen and go away to a place in Lancashire,' replied Kate. She was standing at the table rubbing fat into flour for the pastry crust of the meat pie she was making for dinner, which was at five o'clock today, Sam and Lance being on back shift.

Marina sighed. She'd heard all about how her mother had to go away to work when she was only fourteen but that had been in the bad days of the twenties, for goodness' sake. She tried again.

'Mam, you were as pleased as punch when I passed for the grammar school. You knew it meant I would have to stay on longer at school.'

'You're staying 'til you're sixteen, aren't you? Why, man, you should be able to get a good job in an office then. No scrubbing floors or washing clothes for a living for you.'

Marina tried a different tack. 'I'd get a grant, you know, if I got into university.'

Kate picked up the jug of water and tipped a little into the pastry mixture. Marina stood by her side and watched as she mixed a while with a blunt knife then tipped more water into the bowl and mixed again. Eventually Kate reckoned she had the right consistency and put down the knife. She mixed and shaped the lump of pastry with her hands before flouring the board and picking up the rolling pin. Marina watched, diverted for a moment or two for when she tried to do it the dough was always too sticky or too dry. And when she asked her mother how much water, Kate never knew. 'Just 'til it's right,' she said. Still, Marina reckoned her mother used about a quarter of a pint. She would remember that next time she tried.

Forgetting about the pastry, Marina returned to the issue of her schooling. 'Grandma left school when she was nine and went out to work but she didn't make you do the same, did she, Mam?'

'Now, Marina, don't try to argue with me. I've told you, you don't have to leave on your birthday, you can stay on and try for your School Certificate. A lot of girls won't even be let do that.'

With an air of having said the last word she was going to on the subject, Kate deftly lifted the crust and laid it over the steak and kidney. Marina knew it was a waste of time arguing after that. Feeling frustrated, she began to clear up the baking things and took them into the large pantry, where Dad had recently had a white enamel sink installed. Mam had been so pleased with the sink, she thought as she sluiced the baking board down with cold water. The tap had been moved over from its former place on the back wall and though there was only cold water, it was a tremendous improvement. Before that the washing-up had had to be done in a dish on the kitchen table with an old tin tray for a draining board. The present draining board was just a piece of board put up by the plumber but at least it sloped into the sink.

Marina brought hot water from the boiler in the range and began the washing-up proper. By, she thought, it would be lovely to have a proper kitchen like the one in the pre-fab bungalow which Peggy up the street had been allocated by the council. The pre-fabs were from America and not only had proper kitchens and bathrooms but there was a refrigerator in the kitchen too. Oh, luxury! Peggy made ice cream with evaporated milk and had let Marina have a taste one time when she was baby-sitting little Clive, Peggy and Tony's asthmatic baby, the reason why Peggy had been allocated a pre-fab in the first place. Marina's tastebuds, starved by the long years of monotonous food in the war, had gone mad. She'd felt it was the nicest thing she had tasted in her life, for she couldn't remember what things were like before the war, not really. Dad sometimes brought ice cream home from the pit canteen but he worked at Leasingthorne and that was miles away and the ice cream was all runny by the time he got home.

Marina's sunny nature was restored by the time she had finished the washing-up and wiped down the board and sink. She rinsed out the cloth and hung it over the edge to dry, for though the day was cooler, heralding the coming of the autumn, it was still August and there were germs about, not least from the ash closet at the other end of the yard. She grimaced as she pictured in her mind's eye the wriggling germs on the slides they had taken turns to look at in science class. And they hadn't been anything special, either, just everyday germs which Miss Mather said were everywhere!

By, it must be grand to be able to study them in a real laboratory, not just the labs at school. To be able to spend all your days doing that and getting paid for it. Or learning to be a doctor maybe. She would love to be a doctor, though she had never breathed a word about that ambition to anyone, not even Rose. And now, since her friend was working, she seemed more grown up and distant somehow, passing Marina in the street-with only a word and not stopping for a chat as they had always done before. Big Meeting Day had been the exception, Rose had been her old self, then a few days later she'd answered her friend's greeting with only a mumbled hallo and looked away.

'How's your mother?' Marina had asked, determined to find out what was wrong.

'A bit better, thanks,' mumbled Rose, not looking at her. 'I have to go now, there's the twins...' And she had hurried off.

Marina sighed and filled the bucket with water, gathering the slab of yellow soap and scrubbing brush and floorcloth. It was her job to scrub the lavatory seat at the end of the yard and since seeing what germs looked like she tried to find time to do it most days. There'd be just time before the dinner was ready.

Rose did have to pick up Mary and Michael that day, they had to go to the school dentist in Auckland. She had had to take the afternoon off work.

'How often is this going to happen then?' Mr Jones had asked grumpily. He was the foreman and always looked grumpy. 'You know it'll come off your wages? And who am I going to put on the band in your place?'

'I'll work through the dinner hour,' she said. 'Anyroad, you know I'm faster than anybody else. I'll make it up, I promise. Only me mam's bad, I told you, and somebody has to take the twins to the dentist. I had to put oil of cloves on our Michael's tooth last night, the poor bairn was crying with it.'

Mr Jones shook his head, but still he let her go when the time came. He wasn't so bad, the girls on the band agreed.

So here she was running into the infants' school to pick up the kids and only five minutes to get to the bus to Bishop.

Sitting in the waiting room holding on to Mary so that she didn't go running into the surgery after her brother, Rose felt she had been running for half the day and the other half she had been sewing furiously, side seam after side seam, so she could get ahead and not have so much to make up tomorrow. Well, at least Mary had stopped struggling now and she could relax. 'Watch the trees, pet,' said Rose. 'Aren't they bonny now?'

Mary nodded her head and leaned against Rose's knee while they both watched the leaves, turning russet now, through the tall windows of the old mansion on the high ridge above Auckland. Ninefields, it was called, though it was surrounded by houses, but Rose supposed that when it was built by an ironmaster of long ago, it had been surrounded by fields. Marina had told her that Elgar had stayed there often, being a friend of the ironmaster, and by, she could almost hear his music in the rustle of those trees. She sat back in her chair and stroked Mary's fine, dark hair, thinking of that long ago time.

A wail from the surgery shattered the moment. Mary started to cry. She wanted to go in and see what the nasty man was doing to her brother, but then she didn't want to go in for the nurse came for her and it was her turn.

'It'll only be for a minute or two, Mary,' Rose promised. 'If you're a brave girl I'll buy you both a paper windmill on the way home. And we'll go into Rossi's and you can have lemonade and drink it through a straw.'

'Michael an' all?' the girl stipulated and Rose agreed. And before long they were walking down the hill into the town, the twins short of a back tooth each, but they were milk teeth and would grow again. The dentist had promised Mary they would before she agreed to sit in his chair and let him look in her mouth.

Rossi's, the coffee shop on the corner, was full of

the grammar-school crowd and Rose was lucky to find a booth. But she did and sat in a corner while the twins sucked noisily at their straws, all thoughts of the dentist forgotten. She saw Marina come in with her friends, the girls in bottle-green tunics and the boys in dark red blazers.

Rose felt herself shrink back in the booth instinctively. She didn't want to be seen in her old work coat for she hadn't had time to change and knew her hair was in need of washing. She felt decidedly scruffy before the grammar-school crowd. Marina looked like a stranger to her somehow and years younger than she herself, just a bairn really, laughing and carrying on with her mates. Though she came over to them readily as soon as she saw them, beaming a welcome.

'Hallo, Rose,' she said. 'You're all right, aren't you?' she went on, turning to the twins. 'The dentist isn't so bad.' And they looked at her with big eyes over the rims of their lemonade glasses and said nothing, taking their cue from Rose who couldn't think of anything to say anyway. Which was silly, Marina had been her friend for years, hadn't she? But now she seemed a world away. After an awkward minute, Marina rejoined her school friends. 'Well, I'll see you later, Rose,' she said. 'We'll catch up on the gossip, ah?'

'Yes, we will. See you later,' echoed Rose, and the gulf between her and her friend made her want to cry.

'Howay then, pets,' she said briskly, covering up the

moment of emotion. 'Drink up. We have to catch this bus.'

And they had gone out by the back door, and as far as Rose could see Marina never noticed them go. They ran for the bus, the twins holding out their windmills to catch the breeze and shouting with excitement as the coloured strips of paper whirled round.

Chapter Three

'Marina Morland, please.'

The woman stood back and tipped her head enquiringly and Marina stepped forward and through the door. The room was vast with a thick carpet on the floor and an enormous desk behind which sat the Treasurer and another man, his deputy, Marina supposed. The Treasurer was old, older than her dad, easily fifty. And he had rimless glasses which reflected the light so she couldn't see his eyes.

'Sit down, Miss Morland,' he said, kindly enough, so she sat down on the chair before the desk and tried to hide the fact that she wasn't wearing stockings or gloves by tucking her legs under her chair and her hands under her bag. She'd noticed while she was waiting that all the other candidates wore stockings *and* gloves.

The Treasurer was looking at a paper in front of him. He finished and handed it to the other man, nodding slightly.

'You wouldn't mind travelling from Bishop Auckland

to Durham every day, Miss Morland?' he asked.

'Miss Morland'. She had never been called that before;
it didn't sound as though he was actually addressing her
but her father's sister, whose intended had been killed at
Dunkirk and who swore she would never marry, though
Mam said she still saw that look in her eye whenever there
was an attractive man present.

'No.'

Ten minutes and a few searching questions later she
was running down the steps of Shire Hall, smiling with
relief at being released. She still didn't know if she'd got
the job or even if she wanted it, but if she had to go out to
work instead of taking her Higher she supposed Durham
City wasn't a bad place in which to work. She turned up
the road into the city centre, lingering by the steps leading down to the water from Elvet bridge, looking at the
line of punts and rowing boats drawn up by the boathouse
on the edge of the river. Further along, trees and bushes
framed the curve of the river and covered the steep bank
side below the cathedral.

The sun broke through the clouds and glinted on the
water and on the river a punt glided along smoothly, the
pole handled expertly by a boy, a student probably. A girl
sat quietly, her hand trailing through the water at the side
of the boat. She lifted her head, listening to something
the boy was saying, and Marina felt a momentary pang of
envy. Did she know how lucky she was? But Marina was
not one to be envious of anyone else for long and, after

all, what did she know of the girl's life? Good luck to her, whoever she was.

She climbed the steep hill into the market place and saw by the town hall clock that she had just missed a bus to Bishop Auckland, so she went into a cafe and got a cup of coffee, taking it to a table by the window where she could look out. She sipped the coffee slowly, making it last until the bus was due.

It was market day and watching the people crowding round the stalls, she didn't at first notice the lad pause at the window. When he tapped on the glass she looked at him, startled. It was that friend of her Yorkshire relatives, the one she had met at the Big Meeting. He waved and indicated he was coming in and the events of that day last summer flashed through Marina's mind. She flushed with embarrassment.

'Marina, isn't it? You remember me, don't you? Charlie Hutchinson, OK if I sit here?' Without waiting for answers he sat down opposite her and signalled to the waitress. 'You'd like another cup?' he said to Marina, and ordered for them both in spite of her demurral.

He was tall and gangling and his mop of dark hair fell into his eyes. He swept it away impatiently every few minutes, hardly noticing he was doing it. He had a quick, almost nervous way of moving and talking, which he did almost all the time, pausing only for Marina's replies. He drank his coffee black with three spoonfuls of sugar and leaned his elbows on the table, holding the cup in both hands as he talked. His hands were narrow with long lean fingers and clean nails cut straight across.

'What are you doing in Durham?' he asked, and not just politely, there was real interest showing in his eyes.

'I had an interview for a job at Shire Hall,' Marina answered, and found herself telling him all about the Treasurer.

'You'll get the job,' he told her confidently. 'If you want it, that is?'

Suddenly she knew she did want it, for after all, if she was honest with herself, she knew that Mam wasn't going to change her mind and let her stay on at school, and it wasn't really her fault either. Kate tried so hard to make the money go round and then, just when she thought she was on top of all her problems, she would get another nasty blow. As she had last night when a man up the street had told her that Dad had borrowed three pounds from him to bet on the outcome of a dominoes match and hadn't paid him back.

'I thought I had a good chance and the money would have come in useful if I'd won,' was all he had said when challenged. He had sat beside the fire in his pit black, looking hunted, so that Marina wanted to shout at her mother to leave him alone.

'And you were the one who wanted the lass to stay on at school!' Mam had said. 'Fat chance with you for a father.'

'Shut up, woman!' Dad had flared up but soon subsided

and got out his baccy and cigarette machine to roll himself a tab. So Mam was going to the Co-op today to take out the dividend she had been saving to buy Marina a new outfit for when she started work and use it to pay his debt.

'Marina? You look faraway, what are you thinking about?' asked Charlie.

Brought back to reality, she took a sip of coffee. 'Oh, nothing,' she said. 'Nothing important anyway. Do you know, I think I would really like to work in Durham.'

'It is a nice place,' said Charlie. 'I've enjoyed my time here. And now I'm doing post-graduate work, I think I'll enjoy it even more. When term starts –'

'Oh, of course, it's not term-time yet,' Marina exclaimed. So much for her envy of the young girl in the punt, she thought. She was probably just someone like Marina herself, out on her afternoon off and spending it with her boyfriend.

'No, not until October. I have a job though, I have to be here in the holidays.' He didn't elaborate on what his job was and Marina didn't ask.

'I have the afternoon off,' Charlie continued. 'Would you like to go for a walk? It's a nice day, there won't be many more like it this year.'

Marina was surprised and flattered. But she was being silly; he wasn't suggesting they start 'going out' together, of course he wasn't. Maybe he was just being polite because she was a relative of his friends? There was a dismal idea.

'I . . . I was just going to catch a bus home.'

'Oh, do you have to go?'

She should, really. Mam was still upset over Dad and this morning had started a migraine which would last for days if it was anything like her usual ones. No dinner would be prepared for the men coming in from the pit.

'No, I can stay for a while,' replied Marina, not even feeling guilty.

They walked down Silver Street and the steps leading to the river path there, following the wide loop of the river which surrounded the steep hill with the castle and cathedral on top. They talked as they walked, Marina finding herself telling him all about her family – except for Dad's gambling of course. And Charlie told her how his father was a miner too, an ironstone miner in North Yorkshire.

'My mother died years ago and Dad married again. I don't go home often now,' he said. 'Sometimes I stay at Fortune Hall with my aunt.' He smiled down at her as she took his arm impulsively from sympathy. 'It was a long time ago, you know.'

They walked along the towpath for a while, silent now. Marina kept her hand on his arm, feeling the warmth of him through the rough serge of his jacket. She hadn't felt like this about a boy before and found it slightly intoxicating. She peeped up at him through her lashes. Charlie was looking out over the river to where a family of ducks quacked quietly by the opposite bank, the ducklings almost full grown now. The path skirted the old woollen mill which stood by the side of the Wear and they went on round the loop of the river all the way to Elvet bridge and the row of punts and rowing boats.

Leaves were already falling on the damp earth, the grass at the side yellowing. Autumn comes early around here, she mused, but it wasn't a melancholy thought. She looked forward to the winter now, starting a new job at Shire Hall, with always the chance of meeting Charlie Hutchinson around the city. If she got the job, she reminded herself. Oh, how she wished she'd tried harder at the interview!

'Would you like to go on the river?' asked Charlie, and Marina blushed as she remembered again the drenching she and Rose had had on Big Meeting Day. But she nodded and he paid for a punt and they floated out on the water. Marina sat on a cushion and watched Charlie as he poled the boat out over the water, sailing back round the bend the way they had just walked. And she felt like a queen, or at least as good as Princess Margaret Rose.

It was on the way home that she met Rose again. Marina had got off the bus from Durham in Bishop market place and walked along to the bus stand for Jordan. Rose was huddled in a doorway there, her shoulders hunched as though she was cold though it was quite a mild evening. There was even a pale shaft of light from the setting sun lighting up the doorway and Marina could see that her friend was looking worse even than she had the last time she'd seen her. Her hair was lank and worn simply clipped back from her brow, which was bumpy with spots and whiteheads. But she wore a new coat of navy blue and a little velvet hat to match, one of those with a hairband inside so that it hugged the top of the head.

'Now then, Rose,' Marina greeted her. 'Waiting for the bus?'

'No, I'm just standing here 'cos I like it,' Rose replied, but she grinned as she said it and the grin transformed her face and for a moment she looked like the old Rose.

'Still making a fortune at the factory, are you?' Marina leaned against the wall. 'That's a new coat, isn't it?'

'Factory sale,' said Rose. 'You should go, there's some real bargains there. Mind, I get a discount.'

A picture of Dad giving her the money flashed vividly through Rose's mind. He had come into the house just as she was telling her mother about the factory sale. Mam liked to hear about things outside the house, always listened to her eldest child with great interest, so Rose saved up pieces of news to relate to her at the end of the day.

'Buy yourself something nice, pet,' Alf Sharpe had said, handing over three pounds. He'd smiled at her then, his glance going over her neat figure and lingering on her pert young breasts as they thrust against her blouse. Automatically she had hunched her back and turned away.

'You see, Rose?' Mam had said, pleased. 'You've got a good dad, haven't you?'

'How's your mam, Rose?' asked Marina now. 'Mine says the doctor's been again.'

It was as if shutters had come down on Rose's face,

she was all closed up again. 'She's bad,' she answered and turned away, looking up the street in search of the bus. She stood with her back to Marina, discouraging any further conversation. After a few minutes the bus did come and it happened that Marina got on first, fully expecting her friend to come and sit in the seat beside her. It was like a slap in the face when Rose walked past her and took a seat at the back of the bus. Righto, Rose Sharpe, Marina said under her breath. If you don't want me as a friend I can do without you. But what on earth was the matter with her?

'Did you say something, pet?' Eddie the conductor asked as he held out his hand for the fare.

'Just that I've got a return ticket,' Marina replied. She stared out of the opposite window when Rose got off at the stop before hers.

Rose knew exactly what Marina was thinking but she just couldn't help herself. She walked past her and got off the bus and trudged up John Street to her back gate before remembering she was supposed to get the rations from the Co-operative store, so she had to trail back along the street and down the main road. When she finally got back with both arms pulled down by the weight of the carrier bags, she stopped for a moment or two just outside the gate in spite of the string handles cutting into her fingers. She had to steel herself to go in.

'You're back then, pet,' said her father. He was kneeling before the tin bath in front of the fire, sluicing the coal dust from his upper body. He sat back from the bath, raising his arms and flexing his muscles, watching her out of the corner of his eye. 'By,' he remarked casually, 'I'm ready for my bed.' He took the towel from where it was hanging on the brass rail over the range and began rubbing himself dry, the upper half of his body gleaming white in the firelight.

'I'm back.' Rose put the bags down on the kitchen table and began to put the groceries away.

From the room her mother called, 'Rose? Rose, is it you?'

'Yes, Mam, I'll be in in a minute.'

'Oh, aye, do that,' her father said, his voice muffled by the towel. 'Never mind me and my dinner, I've only been working all day.'

Rose bit back a retort that so had she and went in to see to her mother. 'Have any of the neighbours been in, Mam?' she asked. For her mother was lying in a bed wet with sweat and her hair was sticking to her forehead. The grotesque lump on her neck loomed smooth and white, in contrast to the yellowish tinge of her face.

Sarah Sharpe took hold of Rose's arm and weakly pulled her close so she could whisper. 'Your dad told them to keep out, that we can manage on our own,' she confided, glancing at the door to the kitchen.

'But why?'

It was her father who spoke from behind her. Rose swung round and there he was, lounging in the doorway in his pit hoggers, the clean top half of his body in contrast to the coaly legs sticking out of the dust-caked shorts.

'Because we don't need anybody poking their nebs into our business.'

'But what are we going to do, man? Can't you see me mam needs somebody to look after her? Not to mention the bairns!'

'Aye, well, pet, we've got somebody, haven't we? You're big enough now, aren't you?'

'But I have to go to work!'

'No, you don't, you can give in your notice. In fact, I should think you won't have to go back, not if you explain how we're held, wi' your mam and the bairns and everything.'

'But the money?'

'Aye, the money.' Alf Sharpe was ready to give his big news. 'We don't need the money now, do we? 'Cos I've got the job of nightshift overman, that's why. I'm going to be making plenty of money!'

Rose could only stare at his grinning face, feeling like a trapped animal.

'There's a letter for you, pet,' said Mam as Marina came through the back door, a heavy shopping basket hooked over her arm. It was the Saturday following her interview in Durham and Marina's pulse did a funny little jump when she saw the long brown envelope propped up before the wedding picture of her brother Robson and his wife

Edna, which stood on top of the sewing machine. She put the basket on the kitchen table and turned to stare at the envelope. Durham County Council, it said along the top, Treasurer's Department. There wasn't a proper stamp, just 'postage paid' in the same red ink.

'Go on then, open it,' Mam encouraged her. 'I've been waiting for you to come in ever since the postman came.'

Which was a sign that she was now officially an adult in the Morland household, thought Marina. Her mam wouldn't have thought twice about opening her letters if she'd still been at school. She picked up the envelope and slid her thumbnail under the flap, tearing it along the top. She took out the single sheet of paper, it too headed 'Durham County Council'.

'Well?' demanded her mother.

'Mam,' said Marina, 'are you sure there's absolutely no chance of me going back to school? You know I'd get a grant from the county if I went to college?'

'Oh,' said Kate. 'Turned you down, have they? Never mind, pet, they'll be missing a good worker in you all right. And there's plenty more jobs –'

'Mam?'

Kate plunged her hands into the earthenware bowl and began rubbing lard and margarine into flour; Saturday morning was always baking morning. She didn't look at her daughter, keeping her head bent to her task. 'Marina, it's now we're short. Even if you get a grant for college, how are we going to get along in the two years before then? You're practically a woman now, it's time you were keeping yourself. Anyroad, what would I do if you went away to university? Why, man, you know you'd have to go away, miles away.'

Marina had heard it all before but she had wanted one more try. Girls in Jordan were expected not only to keep themselves, but also to contribute to the home.

'I got the job, Mam. I start on September the fifth.'

'Eeh, our Marina! Why did you let me go on? It's grand, it is. Nobody else has a daughter working at Shire Hall!' Kate rubbed her hands together to rid them of particles of fat and flour and held out her arms to her daughter. 'Come here, pet, give us a hug. By, I knew you could do it, I did!'

Marina moved over to her and hugged her. Mentally saying goodbye to her dream, she smiled at Kate. 'I'll mash the corned beef with the tatie and onion, will I, Mam? Dad'll be back in an hour and you know how he looks forward to his pies on a Saturday.'

When the pies were cooking in the oven at the side of the range, Marina began to take off her apron, thinking she would go along to see Rose, tell her the good news. Always, ever since they'd started school on the same day together, she had told Rose everything. Until these last few months, that is, when Rose had grown so strange. But the habit was a hard one to break. With Rose's growing distance from her, Marina felt as though something had gone missing from her life.

Chapter Four

That Christmas was plagued with shortages: electricity cuts, and no let-up in rationing. 'I blame this Labour government,' Kate said grimly on the Saturday morning before the holiday. 'Sold us out, they have. I don't see them walking to work in that Parliament. They're all the same, man. Once they have a morsel of power it goes to their heads.'

'Why, Mam, it's not their fault,' Marina tried to argue with her. 'The war left us bankrupt, that's what it was. Look how much worse it is on the continent. Think of all those poor displaced persons with no homes to go back to. Our government has to help out with them an' all.'

'Aye, well, I don't see why. God helps those who help themselves,' Kate stated firmly.

There were displaced persons, DPs as everyone called them, working on the farms all about and living in an old hall on the Durham road. They received a mixed reception from the locals. Mostly the pitfolk were welcoming, and some of the girls eyed these exotic-seeming young men with interest, but Kate, with a young daughter to protect, was instinctively against them.

Marina was getting ready to go to work. It was early on a bitterly cold Saturday morning and Kate had got out of bed to light the range and provide some warmth for the men when they got in after fore shift.

'You'll not be late the day, our Marina?' She watched as her daughter pulled on her rubber overboots and tied a scarf round her head and neck. It would be a cold hour before she got to the office in Old Elvet and even then the heating might be cut off.

'I'll try not to, Mam. But you never know if the bus will be put off, do you?'

Sometimes Charlie met her out of work and they went to a restaurant frequented by students and had beans on toast. Marina felt a little thrill of anticipation at the thought. He might do that today, she hadn't seen him for almost a week. She finished tying her scarf to her satisfaction and tucked a lock of mid-brown hair under it before picking up her handbag.

'Got your sandwich?' asked Kate. 'It's a long morning before you get home for your dinner.'

'Yes, Mam,' Marina answered patiently. After all, it had been her mother who had tucked it into the capacious handbag. 'I'm off now, TTFN.' And she closed the door behind her and ran off up the yard and along James Street to the main road. There was a little knot of people at the bus stop outside the newsagent's, waiting for the bus into town. Marina bought a *Daily Mirror* so she could do the crossword on the bus to Durham, and joined the queue.

Later that morning, in the old house opposite the imposing Shire Hall, one of the many which took the overspill of the County Council offices, Marina sat at her punch-card machine, right hand flying over the keys as she punched in the hours and wages for the roadmen, ready for the tabulator. Only ten minutes and she would be free to go. The minute-hand on the clock on the end wall moved with agonising slowness round to midday. She finished her stack of cards and took them over to the sorting machine which was operated by Jean Morton, a girl from Crook.

'No mistakes in this lot, I hope,' said Jean as she took the bundle and slotted them into the machine. 'I have my Christmas shopping to do before I go home, I want to be away on time.' But everything was fine and when the clock struck twelve there was a sudden bustle as the girls covered their machines and made for the door.

There had been no let-up in the weather, there were icy patches underfoot in the street and the cold pinched the chins and noses of the girls and men as they streamed away from the offices. Marina felt a sense of sickening disappointment as she looked around and there was no Charlie lounging in a doorway waiting for her. She hesitated for a moment, having to step back against the wall to avoid the scurrying crowds, but no, there was no tall, rangy figure with a college scarf wound round and round his neck making his way against the tide. Oh, well, she thought, might as well join the queue at the bus station.

Durham was crowded with pre-Christmas shoppers and Marina had to watch two buses pull away before she managed to get on one, and it seemed to take hours to lurch its way through the villages on its roundabout way to Bishop Auckland. She was thoroughly depressed by the time she alighted in the market place. She still had Charlie on her mind. He must have gone home to Yorkshire, she thought. There was nothing to look forward to until after the holidays now, unless he had another job in Durham until term started again.

'Now then, Marina Morland. Too stuck up to speak to us, are you?'

Marina had been gazing into Doggart's window. Not really seeing anything as she walked to the corner, she'd almost bumped into Jeff Monroe. As usual he was with Brian Wearmouth. The pair of them must have been buying Christmas presents as both had brown-paper bundles in their arms.

'Oh, Jeff, I didn't see you there,' she said. She stopped in her stride and smiled at him, more tall and handsome than ever, a cheeky grin on his face. 'Hallo, Brian.' She tipped back her head to speak to him, standing behind Jeff, fumbling with the string on a parcel.

He blushed and looked at her. 'How are you doing, Marina?' he said. His eyes were a rich dark brown, she'd forgotten how nice they were, and his complexion had cleared up. He seemed almost as good-looking as his friend, she saw, perhaps more so with his dark hair. And he had a lovely smile.

'Are you off home?' Jeff was asking.

'Mmm.' Marina nodded. 'I finished at twelve but it's a long ride from Durham.'

'We're off now an' all,' said Jeff. 'We might as well keep you company.' All three of them set off down Newgate Street for the bus to Jordan.

'How's Rose getting on?' asked Jeff casually, but Marina could see by his eyes that he wasn't feeling very casual. He liked Rose, she reminded herself, always had.

'I haven't seen her lately,' she admitted. And thought of the time she had last seen Rose, hanging out the washing in the back yard. They hadn't spoken. 'Her mother's bad, and getting worse,' she added, feeling a wave of sympathy for her friend, for Rose still was her friend, wasn't she?

'Aye. She's had to leave the factory to look after her, so her dad says,' Jeff replied. 'He's the new night shift overman, you know.' He sighed. Alf Sharpe was making his job purgatory. Jeff didn't know why but the older man seemed to hold a grudge against him.

Oh, yes, Marina thought, she knew all right. Hadn't Kate taken umbrage about it when she had offered to help Sarah and been rebuffed? She could talk about nothing else for days afterwards. 'The man's a brute,' she had told Marina, full of indignation.

Jeff seemed to have forgotten about Rose for the

minute; he was whispering something to Brian, grinning slyly. Somehow, and Marina was well aware that he was doing it, Jeff managed to nudge Brian forward so that he was walking with Marina while he himself trailed behind. Brian cleared his throat and looked sideways at her.

'You going to the rink the night?' he blurted out suddenly. 'Because we could go – together I mean. There's a few of us going.'

Marina shot him a startled glance. The rink was a dance hall with a sprung floor. Once it had been a roller-skating rink but now some of the big bands played there and it attracted dancers from miles around. Its real name was the Clarence Ballroom, but everyone still called it 'the rink'. She shook her head. 'Oh, no…' she began, and Brian flushed again and fell back a step.

'I just thought I'd ask,' he muttered, and began fiddling with the string of his parcel again. Thankfully, when they turned the corner there was a bus for Jordan, and Marina sat in a front seat, the boys going further back.

Now why had she said that? she wondered. There was no chance of her seeing Charlie, and it would be a dull Christmas for her if she wasn't going dancing at all. There would be nothing to look forward to except the carol concert on Christmas Eve, and she was going there with her mam and her mam's friend, Edie Brown, from up the street. And she and Charlie weren't exactly going out together, were they? He knew she liked dancing but never took her to a dance. In fact, now she thought about it, he never took her anywhere except for walks and maybe the coffee bars in Durham. Yes, she argued with herself, but he was a student, wasn't he? He hadn't much money.

Still, when the bus stopped at Jordan and they all piled off into the bitter wind which swept up the rows of colliery houses, 'with nowt to stop it, that bleak this place is in the winter', as her mother complained so often, Marina waited for Brian and Jeff.

'Look, Brian,' she said, trying to keep her voice low so that the people throwing them curious glances couldn't hear, 'I think I would like to go to the rink tonight. If that's all right?'

Jeff grinned and Brian stammered, 'Emm...yes. Why aye, of course, it's champion. We'll gan on the half-past-seven bus then? That's the one we all catch. Can you make it?'

'I will,' Marina assured him, and wondered why he spoke so broad sometimes, not so much pitmatic but a bit like the old miners.

'Right then, I'll watch for you at the stop.'

'I'll be there,' she promised and turned up James Street for home.

Rose swept the film of ash from the hearth plate in the front room. It was of enamelled tin and tiles with roses painted on them and was surrounded by a brass rail which sparkled in the firelight. Though the room was suffocatingly hot, she added a small shovel of coal to the flames before rising to her feet and turning to her mother.

'You warm enough now, Mam?'

'Aye, I'm fine, flower.'

Sarah Sharpe smiled faintly at her daughter and Rose sat down on the edge of the bed, carefully, so as not to cause the least disturbance. She was bone-weary. After her father had come in from work at one o'clock in the morning, she had hardly slept. She had heard her mother moaning downstairs. At least it had meant Sarah was asleep; she always moaned in her sleep now. But then there came her father's step on the stairs and Rose had known he was standing just outside the bedroom door. Her hand had tightened around Mary and her sister had whimpered in protest and moved away.

'Rose?'

His voice was soft, little more than a whisper. She lay absolutely still, not answering. It came again, a little louder this time. 'Rose?' And again. She couldn't stand it any longer. After all, Mam *might* need her.

'What is it, Da?'

'Come here a minute, pet, I want you.'

'What do you want? Is Mam worse?'

He was silent for a moment. 'No, it's not that...' Then, 'Just come out a minute. We don't want to wake the little 'uns, do we?'

Rose lay rigid, feeling her mind had seized up along with her body.

'Will I come in, Rose?'

'No! No, don't, Dad. Don't!' She sat up in bed. 'What about the twins?'

'Rose, I'm not going to hurt you, honest I'm not,' he pleaded. 'It's just I feel so badly about your mam. Can you remember how we used to cuddle each other when you were little? Can you remember, Rose?'

'Please...' she began, but at last the talking woke Mary and Michael and the boy started to wail for Rose and from downstairs she could hear her mother calling weakly, 'Is anything the matter, Rose? Alf? Alf, are you in bed yet? Will you come down here to bed? You won't disturb me but you are disturbing the bairns. Anyroad I'm cold, you can build the fire up.'

He muttered something under his breath but after a moment turned and went back down the stairs. Rose had let out a sigh of relief.

'Come on in bed with us, Michael,' she'd called through to him. 'Move up, Mary, make room for him.' She'd spent the rest of the night between the twins, one arm around each of them. But not before she had placed a chair under the door handle. Around about dawn she fell into an exhausted sleep.

'Your dad doesn't touch you, does he not,' said Sarah now and it was a statement rather than a question. 'He doesn't hurt you.'

Rose stood up from her seat on the edge of her mother's bed and walked to the window, looking out across the street to the row opposite. She looked up. Behind the houses the trees were brown and bare against the cloud-laden sky. He didn't hurt her. He'd never lifted a hand to her, no, but it was the look in his eyes, the note in his voice. She tried to analyse what he had said last night. He hadn't actually said anything wrong, maybe had just wanted comfort after all, when her mam was so bad...

'He doesn't hurt me, Mam. Why should he? And why should he touch me? What do you mean?' Touching could mean so many things, she thought dumbly. He didn't touch her, not to hurt her, no, but sometimes his hand brushed against her breast and she wasn't sure if it was an accident; sometimes when she was going out of the room into the kitchen he stood in the doorway and she had to brush past him, he didn't give way.

She heard a sigh from the bed and turned round quickly but Sarah was all right, she was smiling. 'You know, pet, he's not a bad man. You could have worse for a dad. I know he likes a drink but he works hard and gets tired, you know. He's done well an' all, getting this new job.'

Rose said nothing. He was out at the Club now, had got out of Sarah's bed and gone upstairs without a word when Rose had knocked on the door of the room at nine o'clock to take in her mother's tea and help her prepare for the day. At eleven he'd come down again and gone out dressed in his good suit.

'Will I do you some breakfast, Dad?' Rose had asked him but Alf hadn't looked at her, just grunted something and gone. The atmosphere in the house seemed to lighten after that.

The twins were out of it for today at least, they were asked to a birthday party over in James Street and Rose had dressed Mary up in a green pleated skirt she had made for her and a Fair Isle jumper on top. For Michael, she'd made a red velvet bow-tie and he looked a real treat in his blue suit. She was proud of them both. At least working at the factory had taught her how to sew and it was amazing what could be done with remnants off the market. Not that Dad kept them short of money, no, he was fair with the housekeeping.

Rose felt a twinge of regret for the factory, the other girls on the band, how they'd laughed and joked and had a good time. It seemed like another life, so far away.

'Rose, I worry about you,' her mother said, and Rose looked at her, thinking she meant about *him*.

'Don't, Mam, I'm fine.'

'Aye, but you shouldn't be tied in here all the time with an invalid, never getting anywhere but the shops. You're just a young lass. You used to love to go to the rink, didn't you?'

'I did.' Oh, yes, the rink, she had liked the rink. She could quickstep with the best of them and the lads knew it, she'd never lacked for partners. She used to go with Marina, she thought, though she hardly saw her friend now. 'But I don't mind, Mam, honest I don't. I like to stay in with you.'

'Well, you could go out tonight. There's nothing to stop you. I feel better tonight so it's a good chance for you.'

'But what about the twins?' Rose was torn. By, it would be lovely to get out, but no, it wasn't possible. She couldn't leave her mam for all those hours, she couldn't. 'No, Mam, I'll not go.'

Sarah sighed. To be honest she didn't know how she would manage with Mary and Michael, and even if Alf came back, which was unlikely before midnight, he was no sort of help. 'I'm sorry, Rose, I really am. I'm a right burden to you.' Sarah's lower lip trembled as she said it.

'Look, Mam, if you're sure you're all right for an hour, I'll just go for a walk. That's all I need, some fresh air,' said Rose. 'I'll go to the library, it's still open. I'll get a nice romance and read it to you. And later on we can listen to Saturday Night Theatre on the wireless. That'll be grand, won't it?'

Sarah nodded, though she turned her face to the wall to hide her tears. She was dying, she knew it and didn't care for herself. But what was going to become of her bairns she didn't know. Not just the little ones but Rose, her beautiful daughter. Oh, God, was it really as she suspected? Was Alf interfering with her? Oh, no, surely not? It was just her own nasty mind, that was all it was, her illness, this terrible thing growing in her neck, this parasite sucking away her life's blood. It was just that which was making her imagine things. Dear Lord in Heaven, it must be.

Chapter Five

As Marina turned into the main road she saw Jeff and Brian already waiting for the United bus which went to Spennymoor and the rink. Brian's face lit up; he was so obviously pleased to see her it went some way to easing her feelings, bruised from Charlie's neglect. But Brian said nothing, simply nodding his head to her, and it was Jeff who spoke.

'Now then, Marina. By, you put Lana Turner in the shade, you do. Did anyone tell you you could have been a film star? Your hair looks a treat done up like that.' As it was a black dark evening and the only light was from a dim old gas lamp which was on the opposite side of the road, and since she had the shawl collar of her coat up around her head, Marina just grinned.

A few more people joined the queue. They stood silently waiting, hands stuffed into pockets, chins tucked down in their coats. It was bitterly cold, frost forming on the road. Only the irrepressible Jeff larked about, repeating jokes from the wireless, laughing his rich belly laugh until some of the queue relaxed too and laughed with him.

'...an' so Bobby Thompson said he knocked on the door of Buckingham Palace and Mrs Queen opened the door and she said, "Why, it's little Bobby. How are you, Bobby?". An' I said, "Nicely thanks, Lizzie, is your Geordie in? Only I was in London to see Montgomery and I thought I'd call".'

'"He's round the back building a pigeon cree, Bobby. Just go round, he'll be that pleased to see you –"'

Jeff broke off suddenly as he caught sight of Rose over the road by the light of the street lamp and forgot all about the joke as he gazed over at her.

'Rose?' Marina called. 'Rose? Is that you?'

Rose, who carried a basket over her arm with a library book in it and a newspaper-wrapped parcel redolent of fish and chips, paused and looked over to the bus stop. 'Oh, hallo, Marina. Hi, Jeff. Brian,' she said and nodded to the boys. She felt as though they were from a different world, a younger world somehow.

Marina glanced at Jeff, who for a change seemed lost for words. He was sweet on Rose, why hadn't she realised it before? 'Come on over a minute,' she said. 'We're just going to the dance at the rink only the bus is late as usual.'

'Well, I have the supper in the basket,' Rose answered hesitantly.

'Come on, a few minutes won't make much difference to it. Anyway, you can shove it in the oven for a minute or two,' Marina encouraged her. Seeing Rose had brought back the good times they used to have together. She didn't know what had gone wrong and wanted to build bridges. She felt a small surge of triumph when her friend crossed the road.

'You should have been coming with us, man,' Marina said. 'It's Saturday night after all.'

'Aye,' said Jeff, recovering somewhat and assuming an American accent. 'You and me could cut a rug, baby. We'd show them all how to jive.'

'I can't, Mam's poorly, I can't leave her for long,' Rose answered. She gazed at him and even in the darkness looked forlorn, but only for a moment. Then she threw up her head and grinned, determined to be cheerful. 'Anyroad, if we were going to jive I'd have to teach you first!'

'Why you –' Jeff advanced on her and took hold of her arm, lifting his fist in mock threat. She leaned back.

'Mind, man, I'll drop the supper!' she warned. The bus, ten minutes late by now, was coming at last, and the headlights picked out the four of them, laughing and jostling each other, set apart from the queue as it surged forward to meet the bus.

'Rose! What the hell are you doing? Get yourself over here this minute unless you want a belt on the ear!'

Jeff dropped his hand and all four of them turned to see Alf Sharpe standing on the corner, under the light. They could tell he was raging mad. Rose seemed frozen into immobility for a long second, the grin still on her face.

Then, 'I have to go,' she muttered and walked across the road to her father, head down, chin buried in her collar.

'If I catch you with your hands on my lass again, I'll swing for you!' shouted Alf as he grabbed her arm and pulled her behind him. Rose, aflame with embarrassment, realised he was just drunk enough not to care who heard him and felt like sinking into the ground with mortification as her friends, forgetting the bus now, stared at her and her father in consternation and the rest of the queue muttered to each other.

'We weren't doing anything!' Jeff burst out. 'Leave her alone!'

'No, you randy beggar, *you* leave her alone!' shouted Alf.

'Come on, Jeff,' said Brian, catching hold of his arm as though he feared his friend was going to start across the road to confront Alf Sharpe. 'Come away, he won't touch her. The bus'll go, man. Look, let's just go.'

Jeff allowed himself to be drawn on to the bus at the tail end of the queue, his face red, while Alf stood there under the street light and simply glared at him the whole time.

'Come on, Dad,' Rose said, 'the fish'll be cold for me mam's supper.' But he kept on standing there and all the passengers watched them as the bus pulled away from the stop and set off along the main road, springs groaning and with a loud grating of gears. Jeff and Brian had turned round in their seats; Brian was saying something to his friend who looked suddenly like a young schoolboy whipped for something he didn't do. Rose looked away. She couldn't bear his humiliation, let alone her own.

'You never thought about that when you were carrying on with that lad, did you?' her father was saying.

'Oh, Dad, I wasn't carrying on, I was just talking to Marina and the boys. They were at school with us, that's all.'

'Oh, aye. I know who they are, them two, they work at the pit. Useless an' all, the lot of them. I have to watch them young lads like a hawk. Do you know, I caught one of them taking a cigarette and a couple of matches in the other week? And do you think I don't hear them, with their filthy talk and jokes about the lasses? Why, if you heard them you wouldn't speak to them again, I'm telling you. No, howay. How you could have left your mam on her own, I don't know.' He grabbed hold of her arm again and hustled her up the street, his grip biting into her soft flesh.

'You're hurting me, Dad! Leave me be, I'm coming,' she protested, though what she really wanted to do was shout, 'What do you care about Mam?'

'Aye, an' I'll hurt you a lot more if you shame the family with one of those lads,' he replied, nodding his head grimly as he pushed her up the yard and flung her into the kitchen.

'Is that you, Rose?' called her mother and Rose, regaining her balance, realised that her father had not come in himself but was stumping off down the yard again. She put the basket down on the kitchen table.

'It's me, Mam,' she answered and unwrapped the fish and chips, putting them on a plate and into the oven to heat up a little while she pushed the kettle on to boil and spooned tea into the pot, all the while fighting back tears of anger and humiliation.

'Did I hear your dad?'

'No, Mam, he's not here,' Rose replied, and only then did she rub her arm, wincing as she felt the extent of the bruise.

'Have you brought us chips, our Rose?' Michael and Mary rushed out of the room where they had been playing on the mat beside Sarah's bed.

'Aw, I thought you would both be full up with birthday cake,' said Rose. Their faces fell. 'I'm only kidding, of course I brought you some chips. Now come on, you'll get them when you're both washed and in your pyjamas, ready for bed.'

'Just a cup of tea for me, Rose,' Sarah called, and Rose put her head round the door. Her mother lay back on the pillow, face white and exhausted, eyes red-rimmed.

'Will I make you a cup of hot cocoa instead of the tea?' Rose coaxed.

'Anything you like, pet.' Sarah closed her eyes as though the short conversation had been too much for her. She felt so deathly tired.

*

'He's a right blooming tyrant!' Jeff was saying. It was half-time at the rink and he was sitting with Brian and Marina at the coffee bar which was tacked on to the end of the dance floor.

'Forget about Alf Sharpe, Jeff,' Brian advised. 'Don't let him spoil the night for you, man.'

'But you know what he's like at work! We can do nowt right for him. He's just not normal…'

'He's all right with the others, they reckon he's fair.' Brian looked at Marina, who was sitting nursing her coffee cup pensively. Tonight wasn't turning out as he'd thought it would. Instead of showing her a good time she was having to listen to Jeff's troubles. Still the band was going back on to the stage. The saxophonist tootled experimentally and nodded to the others and they broke out into the 'Twelfth Street Rag'.

'You dancing?' Brian stood up as Marina nodded and he held out his hand to her. They threaded their way on to the floor. He glanced back at Jeff guiltily. 'Come on, there's plenty lasses dying to dance this one!'

His friend nodded moodily and Brian shook his head in exasperation, but the music was compelling and he whirled Marina round in a quickstep, making his way to the centre of the floor where a few other couples were starting to dance. Marina marvelled at how different he was on the dance floor. So much more confident.

'I can't do this,' she objected, though she was following him.

'Aye, you can,' he encouraged her, 'anybody can. Just let yourself go with the music, I'll guide you.'

They danced until they were out of breath. He was a natural, sure of his every move, different from the Brian she thought she knew and not in the least bit gauche. The music changed to a progressive barn dance and they stood in a big circle, going from partner to partner. She caught a glimpse of Brian holding a girl firmly in his arms and she was laughing up at him, saying something or other. He was popular with the girls, she realised, as a dancer at any rate.

'Now then, Marina, you glad you came?' It was Jeff bearing down on her, lifting her off her feet as he swung her round, smiling brilliantly, his depression seemingly forgotten.

'Put me down, you daft ha'porth,' she cried, and he laughed and was off to the next girl in line. Well, at least he seemed to have forgotten his troubles for the minute, she thought, hearing him laugh at something the girl said. But she couldn't forget the scene with Rose and her father and couldn't understand it either. It had really disturbed her. Maybe tomorrow she would call on Rose. Never mind what her friend's father said, he couldn't stop Rose being friendly with a girl, could he? Marina had a pang of doubt. Rose was so nervous of him, perhaps he could. Well, she'd see.

The next day there was a fall of snow and everyone began to talk about a white Christmas. Marina beat up Yorkshire pudding to go with the beef ration which was roasting slowly in the oven, a nice piece of brisket because you got more for your rations when you took a cheaper cut. And then she peeled the potatoes and mixed mustard and did all the other fiddling little jobs which went towards making a Sunday roast dinner.

'I'm just going to pop along to see Rose,' she said to her mother when everything was ready.

'Oh? I thought you two had fallen out,' Kate commented. For a minute it looked as though she was going to say something else, looking troubled, but all she did say was, 'Go on then. Mind, be back for two o'clock. You know the men will be home from the Club by then, wanting their dinners.'

Marina pulled on her coat, for there was a sharp nip in the air, and slipped along the ends of the rows to her friend's home. The house looked deserted somehow, the bedroom curtains above the yard drawn and the kitchen ones open only enough to admit the minimum of winter sunshine. Marina paused, uncertain, but then she lifted a hand and knocked at the back door. After a minute or two it was opened by Michael, who stood half behind the door looking up at her.

'Is Rose in?' she asked and he nodded.

'Who is it, Michael?' Rose's voice came from somewhere inside the house.

'Marina Morland,' he called, without taking his eyes away from Marina or opening the door any further.

'Well, can I come in –' she was saying when Rose came to the door.

'For goodness' sake, Michael, let her in,' she said and opened the door wide. Marina, whose imagination had been running riot since the scene at the bus stop the evening before, gazed anxiously at Rose for any signs that her dad had used her badly but there was no bruising, no black eye.

'Hi, Rose,' she said, and then, feeling that she needed to explain why she had come round, for after all relations had been somewhat cooler between them lately, 'I just thought I'd pop in to see you, see how your mother is an' all.'

'Michael, go on in the room, stay with Mam,' Rose said. 'And be quiet, I don't want her wakened.' The little boy trotted off obediently, though looking back at Marina as he did so, as if anyone being there was a novelty. Mary had come to the middle door and was standing silently, her thumb in her mouth.

'Sit down, Marina, I'm just making a bit of dinner,' Rose went on, going back to the enamel dish on the table where she was peeling potatoes before putting them into an iron saucepan.

Marina perched on the end of an old leather armchair by the side of the fire and watched her. She couldn't think what to say for a moment. It was as though she were a stranger to this house.

'I wondered if you were all right too?' she said at last, keeping her voice low.

Rose glanced sharply at her and back to the potato she was peeling. She cut it in half and dropped it into the pan. 'Why wouldn't I be?'

'Well, I mean...' Marina floundered. Because of last night, she wanted to say, because your dad had had a drop and was in a rage. 'There's your mam...it must be a lot of work. Me mam said she would help...' (She hadn't. What Kate had said was that she had offered twice, had taken along broth and had it refused by Alf Sharpe when he'd answered the door. 'We're not on the breadline,' he'd growled, 'so don't poke your nose in here, woman!' And she'd offered to do the washing but that offer had been refused too. 'I'm not one to go where I'm not wanted,' her mother had said to Marina when she came back, her face red with the snub.)

'I can manage, Dad doesn't like other folk in,' said Rose. She cast an involuntary glance at the ceiling as she spoke.

'But I'm your friend, Rose,' Marina protested, forgetting to speak quietly.

There was a noise from upstairs and Rose dropped the potato she was holding into the dish with a little splash.

'You'd best go now, Marina. I'll tell Mam you were asking after her,' she whispered urgently.

'But I've only just come. I –'

'Me dad will be getting up, and he'll want some breakfast,' said Rose. She was agitated, and Marina responded to her agitation though she didn't understand it. She got to her feet and walked to the door. 'Well, I'll see you one of these days,' she said vaguely. In her agitation, Rose had lifted a hand to her almost as though to hurry her on her way. Marina smiled again and went out. Normally the door would be held open until the visitor had disappeared through the gate, but when Marina looked round from halfway down the yard, the door was closed, the house as forbidding as ever.

'Well? Did you find out how Sarah Sharpe is getting on? Did you go in and speak to Rose? How are the twins – were their clothes clean? Are they being looked after properly, do you think?' Kate was waiting eagerly with her questions.

'Oh, Mam, of course they are. Rose looks after them, did you think she wouldn't?' Marina was disturbed enough by the atmosphere in the Sharpe house, her mother's questions irritated her. She wanted time to herself, time to puzzle out what was wrong.

'No, I know she's a good girl really,' Kate replied, then changed the subject. 'Come on, set the table, will you? The puddings are about ready.'

'Was that Marina Morland in the house?' Alf demanded. He walked into the kitchen from the stairs, braces hanging down, collarless shirt unbuttoned at the neck.

'She just called to see how me mam was,' Rose mumbled, bending her head over the turnip she was slicing. 'She wasn't here but a minute.'

'Eeh, our Rose, she sat down in Dad's chair!' Michael asserted and she shot him such a look he blushed and ran through to his mother.

'I had to ask her to sit down, Dad, it was common courtesy.' Rose finished cutting up the turnip and put it in a pan, carrying it through to the pantry for water. She ran the tap on it, working mechanically, all the time intensely aware that her father had followed her to the pantry door and stood barring her way out.

'Let me through, Dad, I have to make the dinner,' she said at last.

'I'll let you through in a minute,' he growled and caught hold of her chin with one rough hand, lifting it so that she had no choice but to look into his face. His pale blue eyes were bleary and bloodshot, there was a day's growth of stubble on his chin and his breath stank of stale beer so that it turned her stomach.

'Let me go,' she said, but quietly. She didn't want her mother to hear any of this, or the twins either come to that.

Alf ignored her plea, moving closer so that his body was just touching hers and Rose stood pressed back against the sink, feeling some of the water she had splashed soaking into her blouse at the back. 'Haven't I told you I don't want anyone in here?' he asked softly. 'I don't want your mother disturbed by anyone. I've told you that, haven't I?' He always used Mam for an excuse, thought Rose despairingly.

'She wasn't, Dad. Mam never woke up.' Her father

was only slightly taller than Rose and now he put a foot forward, trying to insinuate it between her two feet. She pressed her legs together. 'Behave, Dad,' she whispered. 'Behave yourself or I'll... I'll...'

'You've been naughty. Don't you think you deserve a good hiding when you've done something I told you not to do? Or will I punish you in some other way, is that what you want?'

'Dad!' She turned slightly and took a firmer grip on the pan handle. It shook and a splash of water came out and wet the front of her blouse. 'So help me, I'll hit you with this if you don't leave me alone!'

'No, you won't, you don't want to disturb your mam, now do you?'

He must still be drunk, she thought wildly. Oh, God, what was she going to do? He was edging into the pantry, trying to close the door behind him with one hand, but the place was so tiny there was hardly room. He pressed even harder against her and looked down to where the wet material of her blouse outlined the vee between her breasts. Rose tipped the pan and water and pieces of turnip cascaded down the front of his trousers. He still had one hand behind him, fumbling with the door, when suddenly it was pushed open so unexpectedly that he was taken off balance and fell past Rose into the tiny space before the end shelf.

'Alf Sharpe, you hacky, dirty, filthy, bloody man! What are you doing?' It was a screech rather than a shout and

neither Rose nor her father could believe it when they saw
Sarah standing in the doorway in her nightie, her hair in
grey wisps all around her face which was beetroot-red,
eyes almost popping out of her head, and all the while
the lump on her neck was swelling and pulsing, evil and
malignant. She was so mad with rage she had a strength
far beyond her normal powers as she caught hold of Rose
and pulled her out of the pantry and behind her.

'No, Mam!' cried Rose, starting back towards her. 'No,
it wasn't anything. We just had an accident with the water.
Come on back to bed, Mam, you'll catch your death!'
Behind their mother the twins were standing, clinging to
each other, screaming with fright. They jumped back, their
cries even louder as Sarah Sharpe suddenly collapsed on
to the brown polished linoleum which covered the floor,
head back and eyes rolling. Rose bent over her, lifting her
head and holding her fast. Her mother was breathing in
sharp, shallow gasps, her face had gone from red to a pale
parchment, but she was alive. She moaned slightly and
her head rolled into the crook of Rose's arm.

Rose looked back at her father. 'Help me get her into
bed,' she shouted at him. Alf, who had been standing with
his mouth open, seemingly numb with shock, came to her
and between them they carried Sarah through to her bed
in the other room.

'Get the doctor, Dad, go on!' Rose shouted as she
pulled the covers over her mother's rigid form.

'Yes. Yes, I'll go now,' he replied, a meek, frightened

little man now. He pulled a coat over his wet clothes and pushed his feet into his boots and fled out of the front door, across the garden to the path which was a short cut to the main road and the doctor's house.

Rose felt her mother's face with the back of her hand. Oh, God, it was so cold. She put coal on the fire from the scuttle by the side. The children crowded round her, crying softly now.

'Rose, Rose!' they cried, and after a moment she put an arm round them both and hugged them to her. All three of them stared at their mother's face, willing her to open her eyes.

'It's because she got out of bed, isn't it, Rose?' Michael said. 'She'll be all right when she's had a sleep, won't she?'

Chapter Six

'The poor woman's had a seizure,' Kate said to Marina. She lifted her half-eaten dinner out of the oven where Marina had put it to keep hot when Mary Sharpe had come running up the yard, crying her heart out.

'Rose says can you come, Mrs Morland?' she had gasped.

'Why, what's the matter?' Kate was rising to her feet even as she asked. 'Is it your mam?'

Mary had nodded, and wiped the tears and snot from her face with the back of her hand. 'Me mam...she's bad,' she had said, and hiccupped and sniffed together.

'I'll have to go.' Kate was already halfway to the door.

'Why, man, what about your dinner?' grumbled Sam. 'You'll make yoursel' bad next, running after folk.'

Kate ignored that as did Marina. 'I'll keep your dinner hot, Mam,' she said, and tried to persuade Mary to stay. 'I'll give you a plate, too,' she coaxed, but Mary didn't even hear. She was out of the door in front of Kate and away like the wind. Kate didn't even take off her pinny, but followed as she was, even to her house slippers.

Marina, her father and Lance were left to eat their meal and speculate on what was wrong.

'Mind, she must be bad for Alf Sharpe to let anybody in. The man's going off his head,' Lance commented. 'On the booze, no doubt.'

'Nay, he couldn't hold down that job if he was a boozer,' his father returned. 'I know he gets a skinful on a weekend but he doesn't drink when he's going to work. He'd soon get the boot if he did.'

'Aye, well, the day may come,' said Lance. 'But anyroad, if he ever treats me like he treats the young lads he has under him, he'll soon know the feel of my fist.'

'Don't talk so soft, lad –'

Marina's thoughts wandered off. Somehow she couldn't finish her meal. She got to her feet and took her plate through to the sink. She scraped the food into the scrap pail and rinsed the plate under the tap before going back into the kitchen and lifting the rice pudding out of the oven and serving it to the men. Afterwards she took the scrap pail down to the allotments to where 'Farmer' Brown, a neighbour and her dad's friend, kept a sow and litter. Farmer, as his nickname implied, loved working with animals and on the land. The fact that he dug coal for a living was some joke of the gods, according to Sam.

Peeping down John Street, she saw the doctor's car outside the Sharpe house. Should she go along after her mother and see if she could help? No, she'd only get in the way. But she felt so sorry for Rose, and after all she was her friend. Marina could think of nothing else for the next hour until her mother got back. By then the men had gone up to bed for their time-honoured Sunday afternoon nap.

'A seizure?' Marina said now. 'Is that like a stroke?'

'Aye. Just a fancy name for it,' said Kate. 'I offered to take the twins but Alf wouldn't have it. Said he'd telephoned the post office at Shotton, his sister lives near to it. "She'll be through on the next bus," he said. And practically pushed me out of the door.'

'I didn't know Rose had an aunt,' said Marina.

'Aye, well, she has evidently. Let's hope she's not as queer as her brother. After all, I helped Rose change her mother's bed, I combed Sarah's hair for her and plaited it out of the way, and I fed the bairns. And all that man could do when I'd finished was glower at me and push me out of the door. I tell you what, our Marina, he might be an overman at the pit but he's pig ignorant. Though I will say for him, he looked worried to death about Sarah. Kept standing right up close to her. The doctor had to tell him to move so that he could examine her.'

Marina nodded. 'Did the doctor say anything else? I mean, I thought he'd have sent Mrs Sharpe into hospital –'

'Not him. Says she'll be all right looked after in her own home. Though, mind, when I think about it, she'll likely be happier at home.' Kate looked sombre. 'If you ask me, she hasn't got long at all. That lump on her neck's getting bigger every day. I reckon the doctor thinks the same as me. Let her stop in her own home, like. Anyway he gave her an injection, though as far as I could see she was out like a light, wasn't feeling a thing.'

'That's a blessing then if she has no pain at least,' said Marina. Poor Rose, she thought, what must it be like to lose your mother? And poor twins an' all, they were only six.

Alf Sharpe certainly looked like a man frightened out of his skin. As soon as the doctor and Kate had gone he was back in the room by his wife's bed, muttering something to her even though she had barely opened her eyes and had failed to respond so far to anything anyone had said.

I'll tell him in a minute, thought Rose, I'll tell him to leave me mam alone. I know what he's doing and why and I'll tell him so. She had just come down from taking the twins to bed. Michael had cried himself to sleep and Mary was white-faced and quiet, too quiet. Rose went in and stood at the foot of her mother's bed. Her father was right by the pillow, head bent to Sarah's, whispering harshly. She just caught the words.

'You saw nowt, Sarah, nowt at all. What did you want to get out of bed for anyway? I tell you, you saw nowt and now look what's happened.' He was practically eyeball to eyeball with his wife.

She was staring up at him and as far as Rose could see there was absolutely no expression on her face at all.

'Oh, you agree now she got out of bed and came to see what you were doing, do you, Dad?' Rose asked acidly. 'I thought you told the doctor she just fell by the bed?'

'Well, it's all the same!' Alf twisted his head round and glared at her. 'An' don't you contradict what I say neither or you'll be sorry.'

'Well, come away from her now. You leave her alone, do you hear me? Because I might not have said anything to the doctor, but by heck I will say something to Aunt Elsie. I will, I'm telling you!'

'You'll say nowt!' snapped Alf. 'There's nowt to say. I don't know what you're talking about sometimes. Anyroad, I won't have her staying here. She can take young Michael home with her. You can manage Mary and your mother.'

'You're not going to separate the bairns?' cried Rose. 'You're not! I'll –' She stopped abruptly as something about her mother caught her eye. A flicker of ... was it consciousness? It was definitely something, a ripple of emotion, something, crossing Sarah's face. Rose rushed to the head of the bed and shoved her father aside.

'Hey, what do you think –' Alf expostulated, caught off balance for a minute. But she wasn't listening.

'Mam? Mam? Can you hear us?' cried Rose, taking hold of her mother's hand, so stiff and heavy it was and cold too, even though Rose had built up the fire and brought down an extra blanket from her own bed to pile on top of her mother's. She rubbed the poor hand and stared at her mother's eyes. The windows of the soul, they said. Did she blink just then? She had, *and* the blue lips moved. Rose could swear they had moved. 'She moved, Dad, she did!'

Alf Sharpe peered over her shoulder. 'Hadaway, lass,' he said. 'She's past talking, she's not budged a muscle.'

Rose stood up straight and glared at him. 'You don't care one bloody jot, do you?' she demanded.

'Aye, I do,' he asserted. 'She's me wife, isn't she? Me an' your mam, we used to have some good times, you know, years ago.' He dropped his eyes and rubbed his nose with his forefinger then walked from the room. Rose heard the armchair by the fire creak as he sat down in it. She pulled the bedclothes up to her mother's shoulders and dropped a kiss on her pale cheek then she too left the room. Her father was leaning forward, pulling coals down from the shelf at the back of the fire with the coal rake.

'We all used to have good times, Dad,' she said. 'What happened? Why did you change?'

'Me? I didn't change,' he replied. 'It was you, you and your mother, both of you. Neither of you want me now. You never touch me, you never run and give me a kiss when I come in from work, you never give me a bit of loving...'

Rose could only stare. He looked really badly done by, his tone pathetic. Good Lord, he really believed what he was saying. For the first time she had an inkling that he thought his attitude towards her was natural, not wrong at all. But he wasn't ignorant, he knew enough to be secretive about his ways, keeping folk out so there were no prying eyes seeing what went on. And he was frightened Mam would say something…

Rose shook her head to clear it of the dark images which crowded in on her. She opened the oven door and took out the two plates of dinner which Kate Morland had put in to keep hot for her and her father. The gravy was dried and the meat kizened and curled up at the edges but when she set it on the table for him, Alf ate his way steadily through it. Rose herself ate a few mouthfuls before giving up. They sat in silence, the door to the room open, Rose listening keenly, eager to hear even the slightest sound from the bed.

'We'll try to make a bit of Christmas for the sake of the bairns,' Aunt Elsie said to Rose. 'Have you got anything put away for them?'

'Oh, yes, what I could get. You know what it's like.' Toys and small luxuries were slowly coming into the shops, though the export drive took the best.

Aunt Elsie had arrived on the half-past-five bus, wasting no time when she got her brother's message. 'Well, you know how it is, I've nobody but meself at home now,' she had said when Rose had expressed surprise at her speed. Uncle Tom Brown had been killed in the pit before the war and Aunt Elsie lived in a council house on what the locals called the 'new site' on the edge of Shotton

Colliery. The family used to visit her there at one time, but during the war, when Elsie worked in the munition factory and Mam had begun to fail, the visits had dropped off, probably because of Alf. But here she was now and Rose was grateful for it. She felt as if the load she'd carried for weeks was at last being shared.

'Now then, our Alf,' was Elsie's only greeting to her brother. She made no attempt to kiss his cheek or anything like that.

'How are you doing, Elsie?' he responded and managed a thin smile.

'Champion,' she said. 'In the room, is she?' She had put her weekend bag on the table and gone straight through to see her sister-in-law. Rose followed behind her and watched as Aunt Elsie stood by the side of the bed and studied Sarah, before shaking her head. She looked round at her niece.

'By, Rosie, it's a bad do, this,' she said, and drew her lips down at the corners. Rose felt the tears suddenly prickle at the back of her eyes. She turned away, just in case her mother should be able to see from her blank, open eyes, and went out into the kitchen, empty now for her father seemed to have abandoned his responsibilities to his sister and gone out. Though where she couldn't think. He wouldn't be able to get a pint until the Club opened at seven o'clock. And it was Monday tomorrow, he had to work.

'Has she been like this since it happened?'

Rose jumped. She had sat down by the fire and was drying her eyes on the hand towel, which she'd pulled from the brass rail over the range, so she didn't notice Aunt Elsie enter the kitchen.

'Yes.'

'Come on, lass, bear up,' Elsie said bracingly, putting an arm awkwardly around her shoulders. 'Where's that brother of mine anyway?'

'Out.'

Elsie nodded. 'Aye, he would be. Well, never mind, let's have a nice cup of tea. Where's the twins?'

'Oh, I forgot. They were tired out, you know, they saw Mam fall. So I put them to bed. By, they've slept two hours, I'd best get them up.'

'No, leave them a few minutes, they'll take no harm. They can stay up a bit later the night,' said her aunt. Rose pushed the kettle on to the fire and set the table, bringing out bread and butter and sliced Spam. She'd been going to stew plums for tea and make custard but it was too late now. Instead she brought out a cake she had been saving for Christmas.

'I brought a few things and me ration book, of course.' Elsie said now. 'By, who'd have thought there would still be rationing two years after the end of the war? We all believed the Labour government would see things right, but now we're beginning to wonder. I know those poor folk on the continent are in a worse state than we are, or at least that's what we're told, but who *won* the flaming war?

That's what I want to know.'

Rose found to her surprise that she was hungry. She ate her way through the bread and butter (well, marge), and had a piece of cake, all the time listening to Aunt Elsie talk while keeping an ear open for her mother and the twins. And in spite of all her troubles, she was comforted.

Chapter Seven

There was a letter for Marina among the Christmas cards which came to the house on Christmas Eve. Kate picked it out and handed it over to her. 'Oh, look, this is for you,' she said. 'Who do you know in North Yorkshire? Apart from Hetty and Penny that is. This is a man's writing.'

Marina took the letter and turned away in case her face betrayed the rush of excitement she felt when she saw Charlie's narrow hand. 'I expect it's just someone from work, down there for Christmas,' she said. She felt wretched in a way. Why couldn't she acknowledge Charlie, tell her family all about him, be proud of her gorgeous boyfriend? After all, the family would have to know when they got married, wouldn't they? But still, she kept him a secret as he wanted her to, though she told herself she had no doubts about him, she loved him, didn't she? And here was a letter, proof that he couldn't get through the Christmas vacation without her.

'Well, go on, open it,' said Kate, who couldn't imagine that Marina could have anything which she wanted to

keep private from her. Reluctantly, she slit the top of the
envelope and pulled out the single sheet of paper.

It was a note rather than a letter. There wasn't even a
proper signature, just a *C*, and a sweeping line underneath
it. Very stylish, she thought.

'Meet me in the usual place in Durham,' it read. *'7 p.m.
Boxing Day. I have tickets for the concert at St Nicholas's.'*

Marina stared at it, a feeling of resentment beginning
to quell her excitement. Who did he think he was, not
even getting in touch for over a week and then summon-
ing her like this?

'What is it?' asked Kate. She peered over Marina's
shoulder and Marina let her. After all, there was nothing
suspicious in the note, nothing at all. 'Who is it? Why
didn't whoever it is sign his name properly? Affected, that
is.'

'It's not a man, it's a woman...Celia. You must have
heard me mention her? She works in the Surveyor's
Department. She's on holiday, comes back on Boxing
Day.' Even as she said it, Marina amazed herself with how
easily the lies rolled off her tongue. She didn't even know
why she was lying, or why Charlie wanted their meetings
kept quiet. In any case, she wasn't going to meet him, she
decided. To heck with him! She wasn't at any lad's beck
and call.

It was 7.05 p.m. on a cold and frosty Boxing Night when
Marina walked up Silver Street from the bus station to the

market place in Durham City. There were very few folk in the street; she had to stand to the side of the narrow thoroughfare only once as a bus lumbered down, bumping over the cobbles. In the market place there were more, a fair number of people making their way to St Nicholas's in the corner opposite. And under the statue of Lord Londonderry on his horse, their own special place, stood Charlie, his college scarf wound round and round his neck and chin, his hands thrust into his overcoat pockets. Her pulse quickened at the sight of him.

'There you are,' he said, and cupped her chin in his hand and kissed her lightly on the cheek. His lips were warm in contrast to the frosty air. 'I was beginning to think you hadn't got my note, that you weren't coming.'

'I nearly didn't.'

But Charlie hadn't heard, he was drawing her along to the church, eager to join the queue. 'Did you say something?'

She shook her head. He put an arm around her and bent his head closer. 'I'm sorry I didn't get to see you before I went home. It was difficult. You know what families are like.' He laughed deprecatingly. 'Did you have a nice Christmas?'

'Yes, thank you,' Marina replied like a polite little girl. It had been the usual family Christmas in the miner's cottage in Jordan; the government had allowed everyone extra rations and so Kate had made a fruit cake, even securing a covering of almond paste from the Co-op. There had been a duck, courtesy of Farmer Brown, a cock chicken and mounds of vegetables and gravy. Even a fruit-laden pudding and sauce, flavoured with a quarter-bottle of rum Dad brought up from the Club. And afterwards, tangerines and hazelnuts and presents from the family. 'You didn't send a card,' she said now and was immediately sorry, for it sounded like an accusation.

Charlie laughed softly. 'Neither did you. It doesn't matter, does it? It's a silly custom, I always think. I thought we would rather see each other, enjoy the concert together.'

Marina thought he could have sent a card anyway but her resentment was melting in the warmth of his presence. She didn't say that she didn't even know his address, so how could she have written to him or sent a card? They had reached the door of the church now and went in and found their seats, hard wooden chairs brought in from the Sunday School to augment the pews. There was an air of magic about the place today, the people talking in hushed tones, the vaulted ceiling darkly mysterious, a lighted tree in the entrance, a crib and gold-painted cardboard angels above it. The choir and orchestra were taking their places, the audience rustled as they settled down in their seats and looked expectantly towards them, talk trailing into silence. Charlie took her hand in a warm, firm clasp and the orchestra tuned up and finally launched into Handel's *Messiah*.

It was magical all right. Charlie leaned over to her in a

pause and whispered, 'You look rapt. You see, I told you you'd love it.'

She did. 'Oh, yes, it's grand, it is,' she assured him. 'Thank you, Charlie.' The evening passed in a haze of music and singing, low and reverent or sometimes unbearably sweet then swelling to a triumphant chorus which soared to the roof and beyond. And Marina's heart swelled with it, her hand still held in Charlie's firm grasp and her shoulder close against his and that was as sweet as the music. Too soon it was over.

Outside, balancing on cobblestones in the black strappy sandals she had got for Christmas from Kate, her toes curling up against the cold, Marina looked around the square at the coloured lights decorating the town hall and in Doggart's windows the reflections of the street lamps. They seemed to carry all the enchantment of the evening after the dark of the blackout years of war. She thought of news reels she had seen of London with the lights on again: Piccadilly, Shaftesbury Avenue, Oxford Street. No doubt Durham could not possibly compare but she would not change the little city for anywhere in the world, lit up or not.

'That's a faraway look you've got in your eyes,' said Charlie, coming out of the church behind her. 'What are you thinking about?'

Marina laughed and he tucked her hand into the crook of his arm. 'Oh, just that I haven't got used to the lights yet. Durham looks so lovely like this, doesn't it?' She lifted one foot off the ground as she spoke and shivered; the cold was shooting up her legs through the thin soles of the sandals.

He noticed the gesture. 'You're frozen!' he exclaimed. 'Why on earth are you wearing dancing sandals on a night like this?'

'I...they were pretty...' And her sensible brogues were shabby and scuffed and even if she had the coupons there was such a shortage of nice shoes in the shops, everything went to the great god export.

'Come on, we'll find a pub and warm you up,' he said and drew her down a street and into the Mitre. The place was full and so was the lounge, but Charlie left her and fought his way to the bar with the ease of long practice. Marina kept her head down, feeling abandoned. She wasn't used to pubs, wasn't even old enough to be in one, and she was nervous that if the landlord noticed her he would know that immediately. Laughing and talking went on all around her and people pushed past her. 'Scuse me, hinny, sorry,' someone said and put a large hand on her shoulder to steady her after bumping into her. Marina smiled shyly.

Charlie was soon back, though, and led her to a corner by the fire and thrust a glass of sherry in her hand. Not the sweet ruby wine they usually drank to bring in the New Year at home but a clear amber-coloured liquid which tasted acidic on her tongue. She could feel its warmth coursing down her throat and even her toes felt better.

'Charlie!'

Marina looked up to see a group of students carrying glasses of beer threading their way from the bar. They were talking and laughing together but their eyes were on her, speculatively.

'What are you doing here? I thought you weren't coming back until after the New Year,' one said. He stared at Marina. 'Still, need I ask, eh, old boy?'

She caught Charlie's look of annoyance before he quickly assumed a smile. 'Marina, these reprobates are friends of mine from college. Clive, John, and the other one is Scouser. Lads, this is Marina. She works at Shire Hall, in the Treasurer's Department. Processing all our grants, so be nice to her.'

The one he called Scouser made an exaggerated O with his mouth. 'Been robbing the cradle, haven't you, Charlie? Not that I blame you, lad.' His accent was thick Liverpudlian and Marina had some trouble in following him. When she did she blushed and took another quick drink, draining her glass.

'Shut up, Scouser!' said Charlie and took Marina's glass and put it down on a nearby table. He finished his own beer and took her arm. 'Come on, love,' he said, 'let's go. Goodnight, you lot.'

Marina was drawn out of the bar with unexpected suddenness. She called goodnight over her shoulder to the grinning students behind.

'Let's go to my place,' said Charlie, 'at least we can have some peace there.'

'Oh, I don't know...' said Marina, thinking of the bus journey home. She would have to get back to Bishop Auckland in time for the last bus out to Jordan.

'Don't you want to?' He was looking down at her, his face close to hers, one eyebrow raised. 'Of course, if you want to go straight home –'

'No. I'll come.' The hot denial came immediately.

Marina trembled, whether with cold or excitement she wasn't sure.

Charlie shared a house with other university men at the top of a steep hill near the main road out to Crook. Teetering in her high-heeled sandals Marina leaned against him for support and he put his arm around her and rushed her up the slope so that by the time they reached the top they were both panting and laughing. He took out a key and opened the door, ushering her into an untidy kitchen with a square hole where the range used to be and a gas cooker in its place. There was an old chipped sink and draining board with an assortment of cups and a couple of pint mugs up-ended on it. The deal table in the middle of the room was surrounded by a selection of odd chairs.

'Go into the other room, for God's sake, and take off those ridiculous shoes before they cripple you for life,' Charlie ordered, as she stumbled slightly on the worn lino. 'Not that they're not sexy, they are, but your legs don't need them.'

Marina blushed and, carrying her sandals, did as she was told.

It was the first time she had been here. She walked over to the window in her stockinged feet (precious nylons she had queued up in Woolworths to buy), and looked out at the city below her. The lights, strings of them. The looming cathedral, standing guard. That's what she needed: something to stand guard over her. What a fool she was! One part of her mind told her this but the other wasn't listening. Instead it was listening for Charlie's footsteps as he came through from the kitchen, and her blood sang. It was half-past nine, she saw as she looked at the watch on her wrist. Another Christmas present, this time from Lance. If she wanted to catch her bus and the connecting one in Bishop she would have to go in ten minutes.

Charlie came up behind her. 'You don't want your coat on in here, do you?' he murmured and slipped it off her shoulders. As he did so he buried his face in her neck. 'Mmmm, you smell delicious.' She turned to face him and he put the coat over a chair and took her properly in his arms and Marina melted inside, or felt that she did. He smelled delicious, she thought, of toilet soap and not White Windsor which Dad and Lance used because it was all they had in the war and before and they were used to it. 'Nancy boy soap,' they would sneer if they smelled this but it wasn't, it was lovely. Then all thoughts of soap and everything else were driven from her mind, she could think only of the way he was kissing her, his tongue driving into her mouth, tasting her, and she was tasting him and her mind whirled as her body tingled with the most tantalising sensations so that she hardly knew it when they sank down on to the tartan blanket which covered the sagging couch.

The feel of his hand on her breast gave her pause for a second only, it felt so *right*. Her senses whirled. When he slid his hand to the hem of her skirt she was incapable of stopping him. But then he lifted his head at the sound of a male voice going past the window.

'Come upstairs, my love,' he whispered. 'We don't want anyone bursting in on us, do we?'

Scouser, opening the front door, was just in time to see a female leg disappearing and Charlie's door closing softly. He grinned to himself. 'Good going there, Charlie,' he said but there was no one to hear.

Just for a moment Marina hesitated as she saw the bed. What was she doing here? But it was just a moment before she gazed up into Charlie's eyes. 'Do you love me?' she asked. Everything would be all right if he loved her, wouldn't it?

'Do you love me?' he countered but she heard only what she wanted to hear.

'Oh, yes!' she replied and stood passively while he took off her dress and never even considered enough to be thankful she was wearing her new undies, cami-knickers and bra, artificial silk and lace-trimmed. He pushed the straps over her shoulders and she stood there and let him look at her because, after all, they were committed to each other now. They had confessed their love to each other and one day they would be married. And, she admitted to herself, at the moment she didn't care if that fairy-tale future wasn't what he wanted. She loved him and was sure she could make him love her.

Charlie picked her up and laid her on the bed and kissed her lingeringly. Then suddenly he was transformed, shedding his own clothes hastily and abandoning them where they fell. Until he too was naked and springing into the narrow bed, perforce half on top of her, and she could feel his hardness against her belly.

Marina was a modern girl, a woman she would call herself, she knew what it was all about, didn't she? There had been lessons in school on human biology, occasions for tittering behind their hands and Miss Macdonald intoning solemnly on the need for adult responsibility, love and commitment.

None of it had prepared her for the surge of feeling which threatened to drown her or the pain which brought back some sense of reality as he drove into her. Charlie moved above her, mouth open, eyes glazed in a red face before shuddering and falling on top of her, his face buried in the pillow by her side. Marina lay quiet, waiting for him to recover.

So this was what it was like, married love. She felt a tenderness towards him, he seemed so vulnerable now. But was this all?

'Did you come?' asked Charlie. He lifted his head and kissed her gently on the lips before rolling off her carefully for it was a narrow bed. In the end he was balanced precariously on the edge.

Marina felt wet and sticky and muscles she hadn't known she had were protesting. 'Come?' she asked, not understanding.

'Was it good?' he asked, a little uncertainly now.

'Oh, yes, marvellous,' she said. 'Oh, Charlie, I do love you.' But he was asleep, one leg across hers, an arm over her chest and anchored on hers, a way of stopping himself falling out of bed. Well, she would have to stay now. But of course it was all right, they would be married. Maybe she was young to be wed, not yet seventeen, but after all, her own mother had only been eighteen. With Charlie she would have an introduction to the academic life of the university, she might even be able to take her Highers, go on and do other courses.

Marina eased her shoulder slightly, then in spite of the discomfort she fell into a deep, dreamless sleep.

Chapter Eight

'I had to stay with my friend, I missed the bus,' Marina said as she went in the door. 'I –' But there was no one there, the fire had burned down in the grate and the kitchen was chilly. 'Mam?' she called. 'Mam, where are you?' There was no answer.

It was the day after Boxing Day. Marina had caught the first bus out of Durham and rehearsed what she was going to say all the way home – and there was no one to tell it to. Of course, Dad and Lance were on first shift, they weren't in yet but they soon would be, she thought. Going upstairs, she found her mother's bed was unmade as though she had left it in a hurry; her own bed was smooth and obviously unslept in. Marina sat on it, mystified. She was tired and cold and her muscles were stiff and she felt she could smell Charlie on herself.

Well, she could hurry and wash and change before her mother came in, with any luck. She went downstairs and took a ladle of water out of the boiler which was part of the range; it wasn't hot but at least it was lukewarm.

She washed herself upstairs and dressed in her everyday clothes, coming down again to fill the boiler up for the men. They were going to build pithead baths at all the mines, or so the government said, but for the moment they still needed hot water and the tin bath which hung on the wall outside in the yard.

Mam often went out to help with a birth, in the middle of the night sometimes, Marina told herself. She could thank her lucky stars that this had been one of those times. She looked up at the mantelpiece and saw there was a note propped up against the tea caddy. Goodness, how had she missed it? What a relief! Mam must have been called out during the night and probably thought Marina was home and in her bed. She certainly wouldn't dream her daughter had done what she *had* done, would she? Marina was filled with guilt once again as she reached for the note and read the few words.

'*Marina. Gone to help with Sarah Sharpe, poor soul, she's dying. If I'm not back, make chips for your dad and Lance. There's some corned beef in the pantry to go with it and a new jar of pickles. Mam.*'

The tension flowed out of Marina. Her secret was still her own. And, after all, it wouldn't matter anyway. She and Charlie would get married and live in Durham...oh, the future was bright! She hummed to herself as she prepared the meal for Lance and her father. She was peeling a potato when suddenly she dropped the knife and clasped her hand to her head.

'What a selfish, unfeeling pig I am!' she said aloud. She had been so pleased that her parents weren't likely to get to know about her illicit night with Charlie that she hadn't given a thought to her friend or Rose's poor mother. As soon as the men came in and she had seen to their needs she would slip along there and see if there was anything she could do. Poor Rose, and poor Michael and Mary. What were they going to do now? How old were they? Six? For some reason she did not think of Alf Sharpe at all, nor of what he was feeling.

'What will we do now?'

Rose, Aunt Elsie and Alf sat round the kitchen table, drinking the tea which Kate Morland had made for them. Rose couldn't understand why she felt no grief. She hadn't cried, was simply numb.

'You should eat a bite of breakfast for a start,' said Kate. 'Howay now, just try a slice of toast. You'll feel the better for it.'

She didn't feel ill, Rose wanted to say. For a minute she wondered why Kate was here, making the breakfast, when she was perfectly capable of doing it herself. She looked at Aunt Elsie who was spreading dripping on the toast, offering some to Rose. She felt nauseous but took it and bit into it obediently, and was surprised to find she could swallow it.

Alf was munching steadily through his breakfast, spreading the precious butter ration on toast and covering it with plum jam. Men! thought Kate. Though, to be fair, her Sam wasn't like this one. He might be a gambler but he was a feeling sort of fellow. She stifled a yawn. By, she was getting too old to be up half the night every time something like this happened in the village. And all for the sake of a new pinny or suchlike. Not that she wanted any more...no, she didn't do it for any reward. But her mother had done it in years gone by and Kate had helped her and then when her mother got too old had carried on by herself.

'Don't worry about it now, Rose,' Alf's sister Elsie was saying. Mind, thought Kate, it was easy to see those two were brother and sister, they were so alike. In person that is if not in nature. Elsie was such a nice woman and obviously kind, her face open, no malice in her at all. Kate wondered why she had no family of her own. She had been a great help in laying out Sarah. Rose had wanted to help but Kate had banished her to the kitchen.

'Go and sit with your dad,' she had said. But the girl barely looked at him and when he'd tried to hug her she had pulled away and run outside to the yard gate. There she'd stood, staring out into the blackness, until Elsie had gone out to her and brought her in. 'You have a lie-down, pet,' her aunt had said as they came into the house, her arm around Rose's shoulder, and the girl had nodded and walked up the stairs though she hadn't stayed there for long before she was downstairs again, wandering from the kitchen to the room and back again, a bundle of nerves.

In the end, it was Alf who had gone upstairs to bed. Kate looked at him now. He'd finished his meal and was taking the cigarette stump from behind his ear, lighting it with a brass lighter made from a shell case. Most of the men had them; the soldiers had made them during the war and sold them to make a bit extra.

'You'll have to go to the register office in Bishop for the death certificate, Alf,' Kate reminded him sharply, for he was sitting back in his chair contentedly blowing cigarette smoke at the ceiling.

He frowned. 'What, now? Can I not do it later?'

'Best do it now, and don't forget to get a copy for the insurance,' Elsie joined in. 'And while you're about it, phone the Co-op Funeral Service and someone will come out and make arrangements.'

Rose looked down at the half-eaten toast on her plate. The funeral. Of course, that was what they had to do now, arrange the funeral. But first she had to tell Michael and Mary. She could hear them stirring and wanted to tell them herself.

'There's the bairns,' she said. 'I'll just go up to them.'

Kate looked at Elsie as Rose ran up the stairs. Neither woman tried to intervene though Kate cast an accusing glance at Alf. 'Poor lass,' she said and Elsie nodded.

'Look, Mrs Morland, if you want to get off now, do. I can see to everything else. You've been great, you really have, I don't know how we would have managed without you.'

'You'd have managed,' Kate replied. 'Still, I was glad to do what I could. But I don't deny, I'm ready for a rest now. I'll be off, if you're sure you don't need me any more?'

Alf looked up at her. 'Aye, thanks,' he muttered. Kate allowed herself a wry smile, thinking of the time when she had been ordered out of this house.

'Oh, I was just coming to see Rose,' said Marina as she almost bumped into her mother on the corner of the street.

'Don't bother Rose now, pet,' Kate advised. 'She has her Aunt Elsie with her so she'll be all right for the minute.'

'Was it awful, Mam?'

'It's never nice, pet.'

They walked arm in arm back to their own house. Marina's heart was full. She couldn't imagine what it would be like to lose her mother.

The wind whistled through the bare trees which lined the edge of the cemetery, drowning out the minister as he read the service. Michael and Mary started to weep as the coffin went down and suddenly, surprisingly, Alf picked up Mary and cuddled her and she put her thin arms around his neck and clung to him. Michael looked up at them bleakly and Rose put an arm around his shoulders. Snowflakes were beginning to fall. As they stood there everyone was covered in a light dusting of white. Rose pulled Michael's striped woollen pixie hood further over his head, shielding his face, and beside her Aunt Elsie took hold of his other hand in its striped mitten.

'Earth to earth,' said the minister. Marina struggled to control her tears for Rose wasn't crying and somehow it seemed presumptious to weep when her friend did not. Alf Sharpe's nose was red and he sniffled so perhaps he had been weeping? And Rose's Aunt Elsie...Marina forced herself to attend to the burial service, closing her eyes as the minister offered a last prayer.

It was the second of January and a working day, but Marina had taken a 'lieu' day for the funeral. Most of the women and even some of the men who were not working had attended the chapel service, some of them following the body to the cemetery. They stood around awkwardly, watching as Alf threw his handful of earth into the open grave, followed by his sister and eldest daughter.

Rose was the first to turn away after the minister had gone. At the gate she said, 'You are welcome to come back to the house for a bite,' in time-honoured tradition, to whoever might be listening. She couldn't afford to let go, she kept telling herself, not yet, not until the funeral tea was over and the house was their own once again.

Kate was back at the house, keeping the fire bright and the kettle boiling, and Marina had to hurry back to help her. She was glad to have something to keep her busy, offering cups of tea and plates of sandwiches and cake from the Co-op obtained with the extra ration points which were allowed for a funeral. She was glad that she really had no time to say more than a few words of con-dolence to Rose, stilted words which she could see meant nothing whatsoever to her friend. And the words had dried up in her mind anyway.

'The lass is still in a state of shock,' Kate whispered to Marina. 'She's not taking in what anyone is saying to her.'

In the event there were only a few neighbours present, those who had been friends with Sarah in the good days. It was barely five o'clock when Kate decided they could go, the other guests gone, leaving only Aunt Elsie and the family.

'Mind you,' she said as they hurried through the freezing slush of the dark January night, 'I feel sorry for the bairns but I'm glad to be away from there, I can tell you. There's something about that family...something I just can't put my finger on.' She shook her head. 'It never used to be like that.' And Marina knew exactly what she meant.

'Alf, I can take the twins home with me tomorrow. Now, it's for the best. Me and Rose have had a talk about it and we both think it's for the best. She's too young to have charge of their bringing up.'

'Have you quite finished, woman? *I'll* decide what's to be done.' Alf spoke very softly but his tone made the two women glance apprehensively at one another.

'It's the right thing to do, Dad,' Rose put in, though she couldn't imagine what it would be like in the house without Michael and Mary. Goodness knew how she was going to live without them. But it would only be for a few days (and nights, a persistent voice in her head reminded her), for though she hadn't told Aunt Elsie yet, she had every intention of following the twins just as soon as she could. She had tentatively suggested she might to her aunt but Elsie had been adamant that Rose should stay to look after her father.

'A man needs a warm house and a meal ready when he comes in from the pit, Rose,' she had said. 'Don't make it worse for your dad, hinny, don't let him think you can't wait to get away.'

Rose couldn't wait to get away and didn't care if her dad knew it. She almost blurted it out to Aunt Elsie but she didn't know how to put it. Elsie was Dad's sister after all. Rose considered what it would be like in the house alone with her father. She looked quickly across the kitchen to the door connecting with the room where her mother lay. 'Please, Mam,' she almost said aloud. And it suddenly struck her like a blow that her mother no longer lay there, she was gone, she was dead. And she bent her head and sobbed for the first time since the death.

'Now then, lass, bear up,' said Elsie, rising swiftly to her feet and going to her. She held Rose's head against her thin chest for a moment or two then offered a handkerchief.

'You've done so well up until now.'

With a tremendous effort, Rose controlled her tears, blew her nose and wiped her face. 'I'm all right, Aunt Elsie.' She looked across at her father who was staring fixedly at her. Oh, dear God.

Elsie resumed her seat. 'As I was saying, I think the

twins should come to me. I can look after them – I have a bit of money from your Uncle Tom's compensation. I can manage. And maybe you, Alf, can send some now and then, to help out like.' Her voice trembled as she gazed earnestly from Alf to Rose. She desperately wanted the twins. Michael had completely stolen her heart and, to a lesser extent, so had Mary. Surely they would be better off over at Shotton? They could go down to the sea sometimes, it was only a few miles, they could take a picnic, they would have some lovely times, she would be a mother to them...Elsie's runaway thoughts stopped abruptly. It all depended on Alf and there was no denying he could be...well, selfish. But then, their own dad had been so harsh with him. He'd beaten Alf mercilessly when he was a bairn. Many was the time she'd hidden him in her bedroom cupboard, away from her dad's rage.

'I want the little ones here,' said Alf. As if on cue, Mary crept downstairs in her nightie, her face rosy with sleep. And as she had used to do with her mother on many another evening, she went, not to Rose but to Alf. Rose could hardly believe it.

'Daddy, I can't sleep.'

'Come here, me bairn, come to your dad.'

As he took the child up on his knee her nightie rode up, showing the tops of her legs, and Alf put his hand there and hugged her to him.

A sense of horror took hold of Rose. She began to tremble. Not Mary. Oh, no, not Mary. The child had turned to him when he began to show affection for her, as a substitute for her mother no doubt. Rose vividly remembered how she herself had liked it when Dad had done the same to her. It was only later, and very gradually, that the caresses had changed subtly until they became uncomfortable and then worse. To be avoided at all costs. But she had been older, much older than Mary was now.

'Pull your nightgown down!' she said harshly, jumping to her feet and doing just that before Mary had a chance to do it herself. She bent over the child on her father's lap and Mary's lower lip trembled and jutted out and Alf bent and hushed her and kissed her on the cheek then looked straight at Rose and smiled. She couldn't believe it. It was such a knowing look, one that made Rose's insides churn and her head whirl until she thought she would fall over, she was so dizzy.

'Aunt Elsie!' she cried and clutched at Mary, dragging her from her father's grasp.

'What? What is it?' Elsie looked up quickly and Rose realised she hadn't seen a thing, suspected nothing at all. Mary was sobbing into Rose's shoulder and she automatically patted her back and stared at her father as he smiled up at them.

'Take her to bed, Rose,' he said kindly. 'Take her to bed, the bairn's worn out.'

Chapter Nine

'Let the twins go to Aunt Elsie's,' Rose begged her father. The two of them were on their own in the kitchen, Alf lacing his pit boots and Rose packing his sandwiches in his bait tin. There was a canteen in the pit yard now, but the miners still took their 'bait' for they didn't come out of the pit for their meal break.

He straightened up and walked over to her, standing right behind her. He slid an arm around her waist and she moved away quickly. She said nothing about it, even though she could still feel his touch burning into her after he had picked up his water bottle and the sandwiches and slipped them into his pockets. He walked to the door, not replying to her plea about the twins.

'Dad?' she tried again.

He turned back to face her. 'Rose, it would be a crying shame to send little Mary away. You know she's turned to me since her mam went. The poor bairn needs all the love she can get.' He knew all the right things to say, oh, yes. Even if it was all lies, just to cover up what he really wanted.

Perfectly reasonable words, Rose thought numbly. Or they would have been in any other father. She stared at him, her gaze hard and bitter. She had spent a sleepless night and now, after a day spent going over the situation endlessly, felt as though her head was filled with cotton wool. Then he grinned at her in exactly the same way he had grinned at her the night before as he held little Mary, and the thought of him with her sister filled her with terror and loathing.

'I'm going to tell Aunt Elsie about you!' she cried. 'Just you see if I don't!'

Alf walked back to the table and leaned on it, supported by his two fists, so that his face was within inches of Rose's.

'Aye? And what are you going to tell her? There's nothing to tell!'

'You're . . . you're evil, unnatural, that's what you are.' Rose stepped back from the table, away from him.

'You really hurt me, do you know that?' said her father in an injured tone. 'I haven't done anything wrong, you know I haven't, just showed a bit of affection for my lasses. And now you want to send my little one away. I tell you, it's you that's unnatural, Rose. You're a bonny lass, you are, especially when you get into a temper, but you're hard.' He turned back to the door. 'I have to go now, I'll be late for work if I don't. If you have anything more to say to me, you'll have to say it come the morning.'

Rose listened to his pit boots clip-clopping on the cement of the yard, heard the noise of them fading away as he turned out of the gate and went up the street. Then she sat down at the table and put her head on her arms and wept. She wept for her mother and for the twins and she wept for herself.

'Eeh, I say, lass, come on, bear up.' It was Aunt Elsie, Rose hadn't even heard her come in, the twins with her. 'Howay, I know it's hard for you, Rosie, but you have to think of the little ones, you know.' She laid an arm across Rose's shoulders and hugged her for a bare second before patting her head briskly and moving over to the fire. 'Come on, kids, let's have your coats off, boots an' all and slippers on. You'll soon get warmed up.' She talked away to Rose as she undid laces and buttons and helped the twins with their outdoor clothes. Michael and Mary stood quietly and let her do what she would, all the time staring solemnly at Rose.

She took a handkerchief out of the top drawer of the press and mopped her face, her back turned to them as she struggled to control her emotions. When Michael was ready he slipped over to her and put his hand in hers. 'I've been crying an' all,' he confided. 'Never mind, Rose, Mr Dent says Mam's in Heaven. She'll like it there, it'll be warm. You know Mam didn't like the cold.'

'Yes, she'll like it there,' Rose agreed, managing to smile. 'We'll set the table, will we? Are you hungry? I've got baked potatoes in the oven, and there's melted cheese and real butter, won't that be grand? Have you had a nice time out with Aunt Elsie?'

Michael's face lit up. 'Eeh, we did, Rose. We went to Rossi's and had ice cream then we went to see the castle and Aunt Elsie said it was Robin Hood's castle. By, Rose, it was this big!' He opened his arms wide. 'There's a park an' all and a deer house but I didn't see any deer. I expect Robin Hood was shooting his bow and arrow and they've all run away.'

Rose gazed at his eager little face, rosy with the cold and excitement. Had he never seen the bishop's castle before? Had she never shown the twins Auckland Castle or the deer park? She felt a twinge of guilt and looked across at her aunt. 'Thanks for taking them out, Aunt Elsie, you're ever so good to us,' she said.

'I enjoyed it.'

'Folks might be a bit surprised to know Robin Hood got so far north, though.' Rose grinned. 'Especially the bishop.'

'Well, nobody's to say he didn't,' asserted Elsie. 'Now, what do you say to us getting the bairns to bed and then we can settle down and listen to the Light Programme, how about that? A nice, cosy evening, just the two of us.'

The children were in bed and Rose and Elsie were sitting before the fire, mending and darning. *ITMA* had ended and Elsie put down the pit trousers she had been patching and turned off the wireless. She came back to her chair and gazed at Rose, the crease between her eyebrows showing she was worried. Rose looked up. 'What, Auntie? What is it?'

'That's just what I was going to ask you,' Elsie replied.

'You've been staring at that darn for five minutes without touching it with your needle.' She paused and bit her lip. 'I know you've had your share these past couple of years, Rose, and I know you were hit hard when your mam went, God rest her soul. But there's something wrong in this house apart from that. And it's not just because your dad wants to keep the twins here. That's his right, after all. He's their dad. Though I'm not saying I wouldn't love to have them,' she added wistfully. She stared into the fire, then got to her feet again and picked up the long steel poker and stirred the caked small coal until it burst into flames, sending sparks and smoke up the chimney. So she didn't hear the sharp intake of breath behind her, nor see the expression on her niece's face until she replaced the poker in its stand and turned away from the fire.

'Why, Rosie, what is it?'

'Auntie, you have to take Michael and Mary out of here. You *have* to!'

'Well, like I said, there's nothing I'd like better –'

'No! I mean, you *have* to, Aunt Elsie. I'm afraid for Mary, afraid of what me dad might –'

'What? Rose, what are you saying? Your dad? He's never hurt the bairn, has he? I don't believe it!'

No, he hadn't hurt Mary, thought Rose. 'It's what he might do, Auntie Elsie,' she said, and Elsie looked at her in disbelief.

'Look, maybe you feel like this because…because of

all you've had to put up with.' Elsie walked to the window and stared out at the rectangle of light illuminating the dark back yard. She folded her arms across her chest, her thoughts churning, not exactly sure why. She only knew she didn't want to hear this, whatever it was Rose was going to say.

'Aunt Elsie, he...touches me where he shouldn't,' Rose said to her back. 'I'm frightened for Mary,' she said again. Elsie swung round and Rose saw her face was red, whether with anger or deep embarrassment it was hard to tell.

'You wicked little cat! That's my brother you're talking about! Aye, and your dad!' She strode over to Rose and slapped her face. She was like a stranger to Rose, a completely different woman.

'But, Aunt Elsie –'

'Not another word, you little madam, not a word!'

Rose subsided. She sat forward in her chair and covered her eyes with her hands. She didn't know what she had expected but it wasn't this absolute refusal even to listen to her. She couldn't bear any more. If Aunt Elsie were not going to support her, what was she going to do? She fled upstairs to the dark bedroom and crawled into bed beside Mary.

Downstairs it was very quiet. Elsie was suddenly aware of the ticking of the clock on the mantelpiece, the sound of her own ragged breathing. She stood in the middle of the floor, staring at the wall, seeing nothing. It wasn't true, of course it wasn't true. Poor Alfie, he loved his children, she knew he did. It was hard for him after the upbringing he had had. Their da had been so much harsher with him than he had been with Elsie. Poor Alfie, poor little Alfie. Many was the time he had crept into her bed after a thrashing, just for a cuddle, just for comfort he'd said, and she'd been so sorry for him. She used to listen with dread to the sounds the leather belt made when Da sent her to bed with a look and started to unbuckle...

Elsie got to her feet and picked up the kettle, taking it into the pantry to fill it. No, she didn't believe it, of course she didn't, not of her brother. He was just a man who felt things strongly; demonstrative, that's what they called it. And anyroad, Rose was so upset, she wasn't thinking straight. She probably didn't meant to tell such lies, just got things exaggerated in her mind.

The kettle boiled and Elsie made cocoa, considering whether to take a cup up for Rose. No doubt she was sorry she'd said such things. But no, best leave her, she was probably asleep now and, Lord knows, she needed her sleep.

Mind, Elsie reflected as she sipped at the hot sweet liquid, she would still like to take the twins. As she thought about how it would be with children in the house, she was filled with a longing so strong it eclipsed all thought of anything else. She began her favourite daydream, the one about sitting on the sands at Crimdon, watching the twins build a sandcastle or paddling in the water. Or in

wintertime she would meet them out of school when it was
snowing and hurry them home and give them each a bowl
of broth and they would sit by the fire in their pyjamas –
oh, she could see it all, it would be lovely. And she would
look after them so well, buy them bicycles, give them so
much love it would make up for the loss of Sarah.

Rose, lying sleepless in bed, was also planning the future
but not a future she was looking forward to. She'd gone
over all the options, she told herself. She could try telling someone else. The police? Her mind shrank away
from the thought of the police. Everyone would get to
know, everyone in Jordan. And anyway had her dad even
done anything the coppers could take him for? Nothing
she could prove. The minister then? She pictured kindly
old Mr Mee. No, she doubted he would even understand
what she was talking about. In spite of her own state of
mind, she smiled. There was the time, years ago, when the
Sunday School class had recited the Ten Commandments
and Mr Mee had explained what they meant. But he had
glossed over *Thou shalt not commit adultery*, looking hard
at his Bible the while. No, not the minister then. And if
Aunt Elsie didn't believe her, who would? Maybe Marina.
But she could never tell her friend, the thought filled her
with horror.

There was only one thing to do and Rose knew what
it was. She didn't want to do it, no, she didn't, her very
flesh shrank against the horror of it. But there was no

alternative, not if Mary were to be saved. Beside her, the child whimpered in her sleep and turned towards Rose and cuddled in to her side. Rose put an arm around the small body, careful not to wake her. Then she settled down to wait for her father coming in from his shift. It would be the middle of the night but she would get up and put her proposition to him then, before she could change her mind. She absolutely refused to let herself think about how it would be afterwards.

Sometime in the early morning, Rose had fallen into a light doze but the sound of Alf's pit boots clanging against the cement brought her awake and she sat up with a start. Her head was thumping painfully and her mouth was dry as she heard the back door open and close quietly and footsteps as he walked over to the fire and stirred the cinders to get them to let out some heat. Now was the time; now, as he sat down by the hearth and took off his boots, but before he shed his pit clothes or filled the tin bath which had been left ready for him. Her heart beating as painfully as her head, Rose slipped out of bed and dressed quickly. She couldn't face him in her nightie. She had to be very quiet, didn't want to disturb Aunt Elsie who was asleep in the next room. As she went slowly down the stairs she tried to send a thought winging to her mam that was not quite a prayer. You know why, don't you, Mam? You understand.

Chapter Ten

Marina stood by the card-sorting machine in the office, staring out of the window rather than watching the cards slotting into the racks. Even then, she wasn't seeing the snow-whitened fields and dark river before her but Charlie's face when she had met him on her way to the bus the evening before. It had been an accidental meeting; he was with a group of students and she was hurrying down Silver Street to catch the bus, and as she dodged round a crowd of housewives gossiping in the narrow street there he was.

'Charlie!' she had cried, and the boy beside him who had been declaiming something in a loud, excited voice, stopped in mid-sentence. He looked from Charlie to Marina and back again, speculation dawning in his face, and for a split second she had thought Charlie looked embarrassed and irritated at the same time. Then she realised she was mistaken as he smiled a greeting.

'Hallo, Marina,' he'd said. It was a week into the new term and this was the first time they had met. He stood facing her and the group he was with moved on up the bank towards the market place, some of them glancing back to the couple standing still among the hurrying crowd.

'How are you, Marina? I was hoping to see you but you know what it is, the beginning of term and all that.'

'That's all right, Charlie,' she assured him, though of course it wasn't all right. It sounded as though he was making excuses. Why, even now he was edging round and glancing up towards his friends.

'Look, I'm in a hurry, I'll see you soon,' he said, and put out a hand and touched her on the cheek, smiling a cheery self-possessed smile now the encounter was almost over.

'Yes, see you soon.'

She had watched as he joined his friends and heard one of them laugh and clap him on the back before she turned and went on down to the bridge and then to the bus station.

There was a sudden change in the sound of the cards slotting away in the sorting machine and Marina's thoughts were dragged back to the present. A card had caught in the mechanism and others were piling up behind it, twisting and tearing. Hurriedly, she switched it off.

'Look here,' said Margaret and Marina jumped; she hadn't noticed the supervisor come up behind her. 'Don't you think you should be paying more attention to your work?'

'Yes, Margaret, sorry,' Marina mumbled and extricated

the spoiled cards from the machine, going over to a punch-ing machine to punch them again. Doris, feeding paper into the clanking tabulator, winked at her and rolled her eyes at Margaret's retreating form and Marina smiled rue-fully back.

Perhaps she had misread Charlie's expression, thought Marina as she took the newly punched cards to the sorter and ran them through. Perhaps he really was busy with the new term. He would get in touch with her as soon as he had the time, of course he would. They were practically engaged, weren't they? She looked up at the clock on the wall above Margaret's desk. It was almost five o'clock, Charlie could be waiting for her downstairs even now. The thought brought a little thrill of excitement with it. Of course he would be there. It was Thursday and last term he had always been there on Thursdays.

The noise of the machines stopped as the hands on the clock reached the hour and was replaced by girls talking and gathering up their belongings. If she rushed, Marina could catch the five-fifteen bus from the bus station as she normally did. Tonight, though, she took her time, calling goodnight to the others as they went. In the cloakroom she pulled a comb through her hair, clipping the sides back from her cheeks and turning the bangs on her forehead over her finger in the new fashion.

'Coming?' asked Doris on her way out.

'You go on, I have one or two things to do,' Marina replied.

As she descended the stairs, she felt her heart beat just that bit faster in anticipation so that when finally she got outside into the bitter wind which was sweeping down Old Elvet it was all the more disappointing when he wasn't there. Despondently, Marina started to walk to the bridge and on up the hill to the market place. The lights from the shops twinkled on the waters of the Wear and normally she would have paused to admire them but tonight she trudged on, not caring whether she caught her bus or not. He didn't say he would meet me tonight, she told herself. But the evening stretched ahead of her with nothing to fill it, nothing important anyhow.

The town hall clock was striking five-fifteen as she passed and went on down Silver Street so it was a waste of time even going into the bus station, she told herself. She would walk on. The air would do her good after that stuffy old office. She wound her scarf round her head and neck and began to climb yet another of the hills of Durham, not admitting even to herself where she was going until she stopped at the house and rang the bell.

'Is Charlie in?' she asked the scruffy-looking youth who answered. He looked uncertain.

'Er...I'll just see,' he replied and left her standing on the doorstep, wishing with all her heart she hadn't come. The door was slightly open and she could hear as he bounded up the stairs and knocked at a door at the top; she could even hear the sound of voices as he spoke to someone. She was being a fool, she knew she was being too forward, men didn't like to be chased, they liked to do the chasing. She would just go now, slip away before Charlie realised it was her. She was outside the gate and a few steps away when the door opened again.

'Marina? Where are you off to?'

Charlie's voice, cool and amused.

'I thought...'

'Come on in out of this wind, you must be frozen,' he said and smiled at her and all her doubts melted as she went into the light and warmth of the house. 'I meant to come and meet you out of work but then I got involved in something else,' he said as he took her arm and kissed the tip of her nose before leading her upstairs to his room. She wondered what else it was he had got involved in, what had made him forget about her. 'It's more private in here,' he said. 'You don't mind, do you?'

Marina shook her head. She could hear there were others in the communal sitting room, talking and laughing, and didn't feel like joining them, not tonight. She wanted to be alone with Charlie. Perhaps they would talk things out. He was smiling at her, his green eyes ringed with dark lashes a girl would have given anything for, and everything was all right, of course it was. Her barely acknowledged fears melted away.

'Come and sit in this chair. Take off your coat, I'll make you a cup of tea,' said Charlie. He shifted a pile of books from the only armchair and she unbuttoned her coat and hung it on the back of the door next to his. He went down to the kitchen and Marina sat back in the chair and looked around the room. There was a small electric fire so it was warm enough. The room smelled of books and ink and the mixture of Palmolive soap and young man and something else indefinable which was Charlie.

He sat on the bed and watched her as she drank the tea. (Too strong and too much sugar but she drank it nevertheless.) When she had finished he stood and drew her to her feet and put his arms around her and kissed her. Marina relaxed and kissed him back and after a moment they sat on the bed, still entwined in each other's arms, still kissing.

'I came to talk, Charlie,' she said breathlessly, not admitting even to herself that she had come for this. She leaned her head back and looked up into his face. His lips were reddened and moist and his eyes sleepy-looking yet intent.

'There's plenty of time to talk,' he murmured, and his fingers were under her jumper, cupping her breast, pulling down the bra. She could feel his thumb rub across her hardened nipple and felt a prickling deep down inside her.

I can stop any time, Marina told herself, but she was swept along in a tide of feeling which would not be denied and the moment for calling a halt just did not come.

'Charlie?' a man's voice was calling, dragging her back from the edge of sleep. She was lying in a curve with Charlie's body wrapped around her, his arm across her breasts.

'Charlie? Come on, we're going to be late.'

Beside her, he stirred and turned over on his back.

'OK, I'm coming. Give me ten minutes,' he called, and there was the sound of footsteps retreating down the stairs.

Ten minutes? thought Marina. She had nothing on, her skin felt sticky, and where were her clothes? She had to go. She sat up in bed, looking for her pants and bra. They were on the chair by the bed.

'Come on, love. I'm sorry to hurry you but I've made arrangements for this evening,' said Charlie. He was pulling on his trousers now, running a hand through his hair. She looked at her watch. It was only half-past six, they must have slept barely half an hour. She was suddenly angry with him. What did he mean by rushing her off as soon as he'd finished with her?

'I wanted to talk,' she said.

'What about? Oh, come on, love, we can't talk now. If I'd known you were coming...'

There was a tiny silence. 'I need the bathroom,' Marina said flatly as she reached for and fastened her bra. She pulled on her coat so that she was decent going into the corridor, bundled up her other clothes and went to the door.

'Don't –' he said, and stopped as she turned and stared at him.

'What?'

'Don't be long,' he went on, dropping his eyes, having

the grace to look sheepish. 'Look, I'm sorry, love. I really do have to go.'

In the bathroom Marina cleaned herself up and combed her hair. She looked at her reflection and took her lipstick out of her bag to outline her lips. 'I love him,' she said aloud, almost in apology to herself. She felt used.

Charlie was waiting when she got back to his room.

'Ready now?'

'Yes. When will I see you again?' She hated herself for saying it. How spineless she was.

'Oh, I don't know. Look, I really have to go now, I'll be in touch.'

'I love you, Charlie.' It was the first time she had ever said she loved anyone except her parents. He paused and looked over his shoulder at her, already at the top of the stairs.

'Don't be so intense, Marina. Look, I'll meet you after work tomorrow. In the cafe in the market place?'

She nodded and followed him out into the dark January night. His friend was waiting at the door and they went off together. She watched them go for a minute but Charlie didn't look back.

'I'm going to the pictures with the girls from work tonight,' Marina said to her mother in answer to Kate's raised eyebrows when she'd appeared dressed for work in her best blue tweed suit, the one with inverted pleats in the skirt. The jacket was nipped in at the waist and flared out over the hips.

'I don't know, Marina, you lasses are always gadding about nowadays,' grumbled Kate, and sighed. 'Still, you might as well enjoy yourselves while you can. Mind, I think you should spare a thought for Rose Sharpe. Weren't you two best friends for years? Now you scarcely have any time for her, and by the look of her she could do with a friend.'

Marina was smearing marmalade on a slice of toast. She stopped and looked over at her mother. 'Oh? I thought she had her aunt there?'

'No, Elsie's gone and taken the twins with her. There's only Rose and her dad. I don't know why she doesn't get a job, there can't be that much for her to do in the house, not with just the two of them. But she hardly goes out these days and you know what Alf Sharpe's like – he hates visitors.'

Marina felt guilty that she hadn't been to see Rose since the funeral. But Mam was right, Alf Sharpe was so awful, no manners at all, no wonder people had stopped going to visit Rose. No one liked to be insulted. 'I'll pop in to see her tomorrow, I promise.'

Charlie was not waiting in the cafe when Marina left work at five o'clock. Disappointment was like a great weight pressing down on her, even though in the back of her mind she had not expected him. She walked up to Elvet bridge, looking back every few minutes, and forward into the scurrying crowds in between.

'Hey there, I'll walk to the bus station with you,' a voice said at her side but it was only Doris.

'Sorry, I'm going the other way,' said Marina and sped off to the left and up New Elvet hill. She could catch the bus from New Inn at the top. It was further to walk but at least she would be on her own. Doris was left staring after her, mouth open in affront.

She wasn't going to go chasing after Charlie any more, Marina told herself. No doubt he had gone back to Yorkshire. After all, it was Friday. He'd probably intended to all along. He'd only said he would meet her to get rid of her. She burned with humiliation. And anger. She'd never speak to him again, she vowed. The bus came along on its way from Sunderland to Bishop Auckland and she climbed on to the top deck and went right to the empty seat at the front. Staring out into the dark night, she summoned up anger, wanting it to consume the humiliation. Oh, she would never, never speak to Charlie Hutchinson again, not if hell were to freeze over!

The bus stopped at Spennymoor and someone slid into the seat beside her. Marina hunched her shoulders resentfully and stared out of the window, to find herself staring into the grinning reflection of Brian Wearmouth.

'You not speaking to me now, Marina Morland?' he asked.

'Hallo, Brian.' She smiled brightly as she turned to him. 'Sorry, I didn't see you there. What have you been doing in Spennymoor?' She looked into his eyes as though he was the only boy in the world, and indeed, she realised, he was a good-looking lad now all right, with his dark eyes sparkling and his hair slicked back in a quiff. He'd become a man, in fact, broad-shouldered and tall, while his skin, the scourge of his schooldays, showed hardly a blemish.

By the time they had got off the bus in Bishop Auckland and were walking to the local stop for Jordan, he had told her how he had been to see Jeff who had gone to work at Easington on the coast because he couldn't get on with his overman at Jordan. 'Anyway, Easington's a big pit, a man has a future there.'

Brian took Marina's arm as they crossed the street and his grip was firm and warm and the way he looked down at her and smiled was balm to her rejected soul.

'How's he getting on?' she asked.

'Well, I think. He's got a good lodging with a nice family.' Brian pursed his mouth and shook his head slowly. 'At least...he's getting on all right at work and mixing with the folk there but he's not happy, Marina. He misses Rose.'

She was surprised. 'But I didn't know –'

'What, that they were a couple? They weren't. But Jeff would like to be. You know how it is, he's good fun, a right comedian, but he's always carried a torch for Rose. At one time I thought she liked him an' all.' He cocked an eyebrow at her enquiringly as though she knew the answer.

'Rose's changed, Brian, especially since she lost her

mother and then the twins having to go away like that. She never goes out, I don't suppose she has much time for boys.'

'And then there's her dad,' sighed Brian. 'Bad cess to him, that's what I say.'

Marina said nothing, there was nothing to say. They got on the bus to Jordan and after a while Brian enquired, 'Have you got a boyfriend, Marina?'

'No.' She immediately thought of Charlie. Oh, God, when was she ever going to get over him?

'I don't suppose you fancy going out with me, do you?' His voice was suddenly eager. 'I mean, we could go to the Majestic in Darlington tomorrow night. My dad has a car now and I've taken my test. He lets me borrow it sometimes.'

Marina started to shake her head then stopped. Why not after all? She was finished with Charlie, finished with men really. She was going to concentrate on work, better herself, aim for Margaret's job. But she could still go to a dance, couldn't she? Everyone needed time off.

'No strings,' she said, and Brian opened his eyes wide.

'Oh, no, no strings,' he replied, sounding light-hearted. He grinned at the conductor as they got off the bus and he looked after them speculatively.

'Mind, I didn't know those two were courting,' he remarked to Mrs Holmes as she followed them off the bus.

'Me neither,' that lady replied. 'But maybe they aren't. You know what the young 'uns are like nowadays. Some of these lasses go from one to another – shameless hussies they are.'

'Eeh, man, I think Marina Morland is a decent enough girl,' he protested.

'Hmm,' said Mrs Holmes, pursing her lips as she scurried off through the cold evening to the warmth of her kitchen fire.

Chapter Eleven

Brian was whistling to himself as he washed and shaved to go to the dance: '*Put another nickel in, in the nickelodeon.*' Annie, his young sister, popped her head around the door and sang along with him. The song was all the rage on the radio at the minute.

'Where are you going, our Brian?' she asked. 'All dressed up an' all.' He was. He had on his new blue suit with the narrow trousers and single-breasted jacket. As she watched he took up a comb and carefully smoothed back his quiff then eased it forward with his hand to just the right prominence. Putting the comb down, he checked himself once again in the looking-glass and turned to grin at her.

'Never you mind, little girl. You're too young to know.' He took her in his arms and whirled her round the tiny landing, Annie giggling as her thin little legs dangled in the air.

'Have you got a date?' she persisted when he put her down. 'Have you?' But he just laughed and ran on down the stairs and into the kitchen-cum-living-room.

'It's bed you should be going to,' his mother observed as she put a plate before him, piled high with sausages and potato and turnips. 'You were out all day yesterday, and only a couple of hours' sleep last night before you went on fore shift at the pit and then a couple more this afternoon.'

'I'll sleep tonight, Mam, don't fuss.'

'Brian's got a date,' Annie cried.

'Have you?' Mrs Wearmouth gazed at her son. He wasn't one for going out with the girls much and since Jeff had gone to live at Easington rarely went anywhere except the pictures now and then. She reckoned he'd always leaned towards Marina Morland though. She'd seen his face when he looked at the girl.

'Marina, is it?'

Brian looked up, startled. 'How did you – oh, Mother, I never said I had a date even. How did you know?'

'I have my ways,' she said and turned back to the oven to take out the rice pudding and stewed plums. She was smiling to herself. Oh, aye, her lad was growing up, he was a man now, taller than his dad. And he was quiet and manly and she was proud of the way he'd stuck up for Jeff when he'd had to leave Jordan pit and go over to the coast, especially with Jeff having no family of his own. He'd been brought up by his gran. Brian's dad had told her all about it. Apparently Alf Sharpe had needled Jeff all the time, goading him until the older men had taken it upon themselves to haul Alf into a corner and tell him to leave the lad alone.

'He's useless,' Alf had replied sourly.

'He's not, he's a good worker,' Mr Wearmouth had insisted.

'Well, he's after my Rose,' Alf had blurted out then and the men looked sideways at him. He saw it and knew they were thinking there was something funny going on...after all, Rose was of an age to go courting, it was only natural. Alf was a bit more careful after that but it was too late. Jeff gave in his notice and went to work at Easington. He fancied getting right away, according to Brian, joining the Air Force even. Some of the lads he had gone to school with were doing their National Service, quite a few of them as far away as Germany. They came home on leave with an air of new maturity. But the Coal Board wasn't too keen on letting a skilled miner go so for Jeff it had had to be another mine.

'You have a good time, Brian,' Mrs Wearmouth said now. 'Enjoy yourself.' She was thankful it hadn't been her lad who'd had to go away. Poor Jeff, what with his mother running off to London at the beginning of the war and then his gran dying last year.

'I will. See you later, Mam,' he replied, and dropped a kiss on her head and patted Annie's cheek on his way out.

'Well,' she said as the door closed behind him, 'he's with a nice girl, no complications with *her* family.'

'What do you mean – complications, Mam?'

'Never you mind.'

She was thinking of Rose Sharpe, of course, though

she discounted some of the whispers going about as being altogether too preposterous. Rose was all right, though she did seem a bit low these days. But that wasn't to be wondered at after losing her mother and the twins going away and that father of hers...Alf Sharpe was likely just too protective, that was all. Life hadn't been good to him lately either. Nothing had actually been said about him, or not openly. It was just the way people hinted at things unmentionable. She couldn't believe them, really she couldn't, felt guilty at her own dark thoughts. Maybe she just had a nasty mind.

'Come on in, Brian,' said Kate as she opened the door to him. 'Marina won't be but a minute or two. She's been visiting Rose Sharpe this afternoon and stayed on a bit. Rose misses the bairns, you know, and her mam.'

'Aye, well, she will,' said Brian. 'But how are you, Mrs Morland?' He was a little pink but quite self-assured and Kate smiled to remember him as a young boy. So painfully shy, he'd been.

'Canny,' she replied, then, courtesies over, motioned him to a chair and sat down opposite him, wiping her hands on her apron. She studied him frankly. He was all grown up now, she concluded, and a fine figure of a young man, clear-eyed and broad-shouldered. Their Marina could do worse than him. In fact she had been relieved when the girl had said she was going out with him. For a while there Kate had had a suspicion that Marina was up to something with someone she didn't want to tell her family about. Dark thoughts of married men had hovered to worry Kate, tell herself as she might that their Marina was a well-brought-up lass and had more sense than that. Yet sometimes when she came in late from work there had been a look about her. And there were all sorts of folk in Durham City, what with the university and all those office workers at Shire Hall.

Well, she needn't worry any more. Brian was a nice lad, she'd known him since he was a baby and he came from a clean-living family an' all. Kate watched as her daughter came down in a black taffeta dress with a velvet motif on the bodice covered with red and white sequins. Black! To go to a dance an' all. She opened her mouth to say something but stopped. After all, it was fashionable. She'd seen similar in the shop windows in Bishop Auckland. And judging by the expression on Brian's face, he thought her daughter looked a knockout.

He had risen to his feet and taken a couple of steps towards Marina as though drawn to her. Kate looked back at her daughter and frowned slightly. Marina was wearing a smile which didn't quite reach her eyes, rather like the day she had expected a pot doll from Father Christmas when she was little and had received a knitted one instead.

'Come on then, Brian,' she said. 'We don't want to miss the bus now, do we?' And he went to her eagerly.

'Put your big coat on, Marina,' said Kate. 'It'll likely

be cold when you come out. And mind, the eleven o'clock bus or your dad'll have something to say about it.'

'Oh, Mam, I was just going to wear me swagger,' Marina objected, but Brian picked up her top coat from the back of the chair where Kate had laid it ready and held it for her to put on. 'Come on now, Marina, your mam's right,' he said, surprising both women by his firmness. He *was* growing up, thought Kate. Marina wouldn't have it all her own way with him, even if she thought she would.

Marina wasn't thinking anything of the kind as she sat beside Brian on the top deck of the Darlington bus. She stared out into the night, unspeaking, and Brian was content to sit quietly by her. Neither he nor Charlie was on Marina's mind just then, she was thinking of the afternoon she had just spent with her old friend Rose. Alf Sharpe wasn't in when she called. Of course she hadn't expected him to be which was why she'd picked a time when she knew he would be down the Club.

Rose's face had lit up when she saw Marina, which made her feel guilty yet again for not coming more often. But the house was so gloomy somehow, even though Rose kept it spotlessly clean.

'Let's go for a walk,' she had suggested. Her friend had looked doubtful but Marina had persuaded her, and they had gone up on the fell beyond Jordan and walked along a deserted narrow road strewn with rocks from the outcrops which stuck through the bracken and dried yellow grass by the sides. Even Rose's pale cheeks soon glowed red as they walked in the teeth of a freezing wind until they came to an overhang; it was the place where they had always gone when they were younger and played house. Marina had sat down on the dried bracken, in the hollow which was sheltered from the wind and even warmed by pale afternoon sunlight, and Rose took the shelf of rock which stuck out unexpectedly about a foot from the ground. In the old days it had been their picnic table.

They had talked of those old days like two old women at a yard gate. Carefully, Marina skirted round the subject of Rose's home life though she was dying to ask why she didn't go out to work now she didn't have the twins to see to. Instead she told her about her date with Brian and about Jeff going to work at Easington Colliery.

'But why did he go?' Rose asked, and then suddenly, as if stricken, 'It wasn't because of me or my dad, was it?' She felt as though a great hole had opened up in her life. Even though she had seen Jeff so rarely since she left school, he had been *there*, and now he was not.

'No, of course not, don't be so big-headed,' Marina said lightly. 'Why would he go because of you? No, he wasn't happy at the pit...' Her voice faded away as she realised that she had revealed more than she thought, for hadn't Alf Sharpe been Jeff's overman? Marina gazed out over the wintry fields to where a group of jackdaws were squabbling noisily over something unmentionable in the grass. To her horror, when she looked back at Rose her friend was sitting with tears rolling down her cheeks, making no sound and no attempt at all to stem the flow.

'Here, Rose, don't take on like that. I didn't know you liked Jeff that much,' she said, and began rooting in her handbag for a clean handkerchief. When she found one she handed it over and Rose mopped her face. Marina put an arm round her shoulders and then Rose was hiccupping and saying she was sorry and crying some more until at last the tears stopped and she blew her nose and sat quietly, apart from an occasional sniff.

'Sorry,' she said again but in a more normal tone of voice. 'I don't know what came over me.'

'Well,' said Marina, 'I think I would be howling if I'd had to go through what you've been through. And the twins going away. I say, Rose, why don't you go back to your old job? You'd get out of the house –'

'Dad wouldn't let me.'

'Oh, rubbish! You're old enough to do what you like,' said Marina, the one who fibbed every day about her own movements in case her mam found out something she wanted to keep secret. 'Anyway, you could go and live with your auntie too. Surely she'd take you in? You don't have to live with your dad, you know, not when you're over sixteen, you don't.'

'I do. I can't get away.'

'But why?' Marina was genuinely puzzled, couldn't think what it was that was holding back her friend, when she was so miserable.

Because then he would bring the twins back. And Mary at least wouldn't be safe. Because he would do it to get at me, Rose thought. In fact the words seemed to ring in her head, but she couldn't say them. Instead she twisted Marina's handkerchief in her fingers.

'I'll wash this and give it you back.'

'No need. I've got loads. People buy me hankies for Christmas and birthdays when all I want is Chanel No. 5.'

Rose gave a watery smile. 'Oh, Marina, I'm sick of my life!' she burst out. And then, shockingly, for the first time confiding in another person: 'I hate my dad!'

Marina hugged her. 'Eeh, I don't know, pet, I don't. Does he hit you? Is that what it is? Is he cruel?' He would be cruel, vicious beggar that he was, she thought. Sometimes she felt she didn't like her own dad, especially when he gambled away his pay and made Mam miserably unhappy, but she couldn't hate him, the thought was shocking.

'No, he –' But Rose couldn't say it so she carried on: 'Yes, that's it. He hits me.'

'Bloody sod! And that's swearing.' Marina's own troubles seemed paltry compared with Rose's. Why, even if her dad found out about what she and Charlie had got up to, he wouldn't hit her, she was fairly sure. Though Mam might. Dear God, how could she even think of herself when Rose was in so much trouble?

'Listen, Rose, I think you should go and live with your aunt. Never mind what he says. If you tell her what he does she won't let him take Mary and Michael back. It'll be all right, you'll see.'

Rose imagined telling Aunt Elsie what her dad did to her. But no, her aunt hadn't believed her before so why should she now? To Marina it was all so simple. She saw what she should do and did it, or at least that was how it looked. Rose shook her head regretfully.

'No, I don't think that would work.'

Marina pondered, accepting what Rose said. After all, her friend knew better than she the situation at home. 'Well, I tell you what, you like Jeff, don't you? I'll get his address from Brian tonight and you can write to him. He doesn't live far from Shotton, does he? Easington isn't far from Shotton. Then when you go to see your aunt you can meet him. Isn't that something to look forward to?'

'Dad would go mad if I got a letter from a lad, Marina. Talk sense, for goodness' sake.'

'Yes, but he can address them to me at our house, can't he? And I'll give them to you. Isn't that a good idea?'

Marina was so obviously carried away with the idea that Rose smiled and nodded. She got to her feet and walked away to the edge of the fell, looking out over the rough grass and small hillocks which had once been spoil heaps for the bell pits which dotted the area in the eighteenth century. Now they too were covered in dead vegetation. As dead as she felt inside. It was no good, Marina could never understand. The winter afternoon was closing in, the jackdaws flying in a noisy black cloud towards the barn where they roosted. The wind was biting. Rose turned back.

'Well then, we'd better be off before we freeze to death, Marina. Thanks for coming with me anyroad. And for listening.'

Marina linked arms with her as they set off for the village. She looked at Rose from time to time, anxiety in her expression. No, Marina couldn't begin to understand and what was more it was unfair to ask her to try to.

'I'm all right, Marina. I just had the hump, that's all,' Rose assured her. And even though nothing was resolved she felt a little lighter of heart because she had talked with her friend, almost as they had shared their secrets when they were at junior school. Ever since the day they had both started in the infants' class they had done that. They had been seated next to each other then and had played together in the school yard. They would always be friends even though she would never tell Marina the whole truth.

'What are you thinking about?' Brian asked. Marina started. She had been so immersed in Rose's troubles that she had forgotten where she was. The bus was approaching Bondgate, she saw, on the outskirts of Darlington.

'Oh, nothing,' she said, debating whether to tell Brian all her worries about Rose. He was so sensible, surely he would think of something to help her? But no, she couldn't do that, it would be betraying a confidence. She smiled at him, trying to keep her mind on tonight and the dancing ahead of them. A good night out was what she needed.

Later, as they came off the dance floor and sat drinking coffee at the refreshment bar, thoughts of Rose returned to haunt her. How sad she was, and what a miserable life she was leading. Marina turned to Brian and asked, 'Do you think Jeff would like to write to Rose?' At his look of surprise she went on, 'I mean, she'd like to write to him and I know he likes her.'

'Yes, but there's her dad. He wouldn't like it at all, would he?'

Marina leaned towards him eagerly. 'Jeff could write to my house, I would give her any letters. Why not? Will you give me his address?'

'All right.' Brian made no further objection. It was yet another surprise to Marina that he had a pen and tiny note-book in his pocket. He tore off a leaf and wrote Jeff's address on it. Marina slipped it into her bag. There wasn't much she could do for Rose but this she could and would.

Chapter Twelve

Rose sat before the fire knitting pullovers for the twins, a deep blue one for Michael and a light blue one for Mary. At least the knitting was done, she only had to sew them up ready to take through to Shotton tomorrow. The twins were growing so fast now, or so Aunt Elsie had said in her last letter. Soon they would be seven. They had been gone for four months now, four months and eleven days. They went to school in Shotton and Aunt Elsie said they were on the Sunday School anniversary tomorrow. Rose wanted the pullovers finished to take with her, then if it was cold the children could wear them over their anniversary clothes. Mary had a pink broderie anglaise dress with a full skirt and Michael grey shorts Aunt Elsie had bought at the Co-op Store and a white shirt and blue dickybow tie. Oh, her aunt had told her everything.

Please God, let them stay at Shotton with her until they were grown. No, longer than that. Until Mary was married and out of her dad's reach altogether. Rose couldn't bear it if ... but her thoughts shied away from that.

She finished the seam she was working on and folded the work up carefully and put it aside. Dad would be in soon, she had to start the supper. She peeled potatoes for chips and sliced corned beef, all the time listening for his step in the yard. Let him be sober, I can handle him when he's sober, she repeated over and over, a silent chant in her mind.

Since that night after the twins went away, she had done it every night and sometimes it worked. She brought the chip pan down from the shelf and settled it on a bar of the fire to heat. The fat began to crackle and sizzle and she put the chips in the wire basket and plunged it into the fat. The sizzling heightened for a few minutes so that she didn't hear his steps in the yard, not until he opened the door and came in.

'Supper ready?' was all he said by way of greeting. Alf hung his overcoat on the hook on the back door and sat down on the chair by the side of the fire, crossing his legs, looking up at her as she bent over the chip pan to test a chip.

'Just a few more minutes,' replied Rose, keeping her back to him, watching the bubbling fat. He sat for a minute then began humming to himself and swinging his leg until it hooked under her skirt, lifting it. She moved sharply away and he stretched out his leg again, hooking the toe of his shoe just under the hem of her skirt and lifting it again. He giggled.

'Let me alone, Dad!'

Rose turned to face him. He smelled of beer, she realised, a sour repellent smell. The chanting hadn't worked this time.

'Oh, come on, Rose, it's only a bit of fun.'

She eased the chip pan off the fire on to the bar but kept her hand on the handle. She didn't look at him. 'Let me alone, Dad, or I swear I'll tip this over you,' she said evenly.

'No, you wouldn't!' he cried, but she could hear uncertainty in his voice.

'Oh, but I would,' she warned.

Alf got to his feet and went to the table. He drew out a chair and sat down, picking up the knife and fork she had set out for him. 'Come on then,' he said harshly, 'where's me supper? A man could starve waiting for you.'

She put his meal before him in silence. By, how she wished it was tomorrow and she was nicely away from this house, if only for one day.

'Rose! Look, Michael, Rose has come. I told you she would come,' shouted Mary as she met her sister halfway down the street and flung herself upon her. 'Rose, where have you been? You promised you would and we've been here *ages* and you didn't.'

'I'm here now,' said Rose, hugging the small body to her, burying her nose in Mary's nape and breathing in the clean little-girl scent of her, feeling the tickle of her fine straight hair on her face. Mary began to wriggle.

'Put me down, Rose, you'll crease my dress. Isn't it lovely? Aunt Elsie bought it for me. And look I've got shiny shoes to go with it.' Mary pirouetted on the pavement, delighting in the way the skirt of her pink dress swung out, showing the lawn petticoat beneath.

'Oh, it's grand, Mary, it really is. Pretty as a picture you are.'

'Like Shirley Temple?'

'Yes, just like Shirley Temple in *The Little Princess*.'

She did look lovely, and must have grown three inches, but the best thing was the way she chattered. No more shyness, no more fears and nightmares. She'd done the right thing for Mary, Rose told herself, and was thankful.

'But where's Michael?' she asked, looking along the street. There was no sign of him and she was struck by a moment's panic.

'He's not poorly, is he?'

Mary shook her head and the ribbon in her hair fluttered.

'No, he's not poorly. He's only hiding.'

Then Rose saw him, or rather his head, peeping round the door jamb of Aunt Elsie's house. She ran to him and swept him up in her arms, swinging him round too, but when she put him down again he stood still, gazing solemnly up at her.

'Aren't you glad to see me, Michael?'

He nodded, still unspeaking. His hair had been recently cut in a short back and sides style and the top was slicked back with a touch of Brylcreem. A schoolboy now, not an infant. His bow-tie was slightly askew and Rose squatted in front of him and straightened it.

'Michael cried for you,' said Mary.

'Didn't,' he refuted.

'Yes, you did, at first,' Mary insisted then dropped her eyes as he glared at her. 'Well, you did,' she muttered. 'You said we wouldn't see our Rose again.'

'Well, I'm here now.' She swallowed the lump in her throat. 'Are you going to let me in? These parcels are heavy.' Michael turned and walked ahead of her up the passage to the kitchen at the back where Aunt Elsie stood fussing over the range.

'Oh, you're here! I told them to give me a shout when they saw you. How are you, lass?'

Elsie moved forward to hug Rose; she was fatter, Rose realised, her cheeks rounded out, her voice softer than Rose remembered it. It was plain to see that she was happy, that she loved the children. Oh, yes, thought Rose as she returned the hug, she had done the right thing.

Throughout the day there were small, tell-tale signs that Mary liked it here, loved Aunt Elsie, had blossomed in this place. And Michael, well, he thawed a little, lost some of his initial stiffness, began to talk to her about his new friends and how well he was doing at school. They brought out pictures they had drawn to be admired, school books to show how they had both won gold stars for their work.

Rose sipped the tea Elsie had made, nibbled at Shrewsbury biscuits and made admiring comments on everything she was shown. But she saw how Mary leaned on Aunt Elsie; said, 'Didn't I, Auntie Elsie?' or 'Can't I, Auntie Elsie?' and in spite of herself felt tiny stabs of pain which she refused to acknowledge as jealousy. Yet she knew she was wrong to be glad that Michael stood by her side all the while, touching *her* and looking up into her face. One of the children at least still loved her the best.

They went to the Sunday School anniversary and the chapel was packed with proud parents. All the children had their 'pieces' to recite, of course. They sat in the choir stalls behind the minister and Mary stood forward when it was her turn and recited a poem based on Matthew, Chapter 19, Verses 13 and 14: 'Suffer the children to come unto Me'. She said it loudly and confidently and there were murmurs of appreciation and then it was Michael's turn and Rose trembled for him.

He didn't recite but sang a little song about God's love, in a high treble voice that was sweet and true, and Rose felt like crying because he never faltered once and held the tune perfectly, and most of all because she hadn't even realised he could sing. She found a handkerchief and dabbed her eyes and looked at Aunt Elsie and saw she was doing the same and they smiled mistily at each other. Michael bowed his head gracefully at the end and went back to his seat and the whole Sunday School rose to sing 'I've Found a Friend'. Soon they were spilling out on to the pavement, parents and grandparents waiting for the children to join them from choir stalls.

'Nice voice the little lad has,' the minister commented as he shook hands with them at the door. 'He'll be an asset to the choir when he gets a bit older.'

Rose swelled with pride and didn't even mind that it was Aunt Elsie he said it to, Aunt Elsie who said, 'Thank you, I hope he will be.'

Later, when the children were in bed, Rose said, 'Do you mind if I go out for an hour? I sort of promised to visit a friend.'

Elsie looked surprised. 'I didn't know you knew any-one over here, Rose?'

'This friend came to live here and we write to each other.'

'Oh, well, that's grand. I'm all right, I want to listen to the wireless anyroad. Shattered, I am. An hour on me own will just suit me.'

Dear Aunt Elsie, Rose thought as she hurried up to Front Street, she never pried, didn't want to know all the whys and wherefores but treated Rose as another adult. A small voice in the back of her mind said that Elsie didn't pry into her life since the one time Rose had tried to con-fide in her and she had been so horrified and disbelieving. No, kind as she was to the twins and Rose herself, she shied away from any such confidences.

Rose forgot all about Aunt Elsie as a voice hailed her from a car just pulling up beside her.

'Jeff! You never told me you'd bought a car. Here was I walking to the bus stop, expecting you to be on a bus.'

Jeff got out of the car with a flourish and bounded on to the pavement. For a moment she thought he was going to put his arms around her but he checked himself and took her hands in his.

'Oh, Rose, let me look at you. You're as pretty as ever, a sight for sore eyes,' he said, but his old bantering tone was gone. He looked and sounded so sincere as he gazed down at her. His voice had deepened and he tipped his head and smiled lopsidedly. His face was thinner than she remembered and a lock of fair hair fell over his forehead. He shook his head to throw it back. Impatiently, for his hands were still grasping hers in a strong, confident grip. She couldn't get over how he had changed, grown up, in the short time he had been in Easington.

'Aren't you going to tell me you're glad to see me?' he teased, and for a second the old Jeff was back.

'Oh, I am, Jeff, I am,' she said, and was surprised to find she was slightly breathless. His smile widened and he released one of her hands and led her to the car.

'It's a Morris. Do you like it? Only small, but it's a little gem. Come on, get in.' He opened the door and handed her into the seat with a flourish. Like a princess, she thought, and blushed as she noticed the queue at the bus stop staring with undisguised interest.

'But where are we going?'

'Just wait and see.' He drove off down Front Street,

heading towards the coast, and she wondered if he was taking her to Easington or even Sunderland. But no, he turned right down a small country road which wound round and back until she hadn't an idea in which direction they were heading.

She glanced sideways at Jeff. He was concentrating on negotiating the bends and looked serious. She noticed how strong his profile was, how fair his complexion apart from two tiny blue marks on his left cheek and a white scar over the bone. Marks of the coal miner. Had he been caught in a fall of stone? He hadn't told her if he had. She felt a quick spasm of anxiety. Was this pit more dangerous than Jordan? But she didn't ask.

He turned on to the main coast road. She saw they were on the edge of Horden or Blackball, one of the mining villages on the coast, she wasn't sure which.

'Are we going to Hartlepool?' she asked.

Jeff gave her a brief glance. 'Wait and see,' he said and turned left. They were driving on to the top of the cliffs at Crimdon, past the caravans until they were right on the edge. He parked the car and they got out and stood high above the sea. The sun was low in the sky and cast beams across the water, glistening gold and red. In the distance a ship, looking no bigger than Michael's toy boat, sailed south.

'Well, what do you think?' asked Jeff. He put an arm around her shoulders and she found the moment so magical she hardly dared breathe in case it was spoiled. But then his hand took hers and he was pulling her off to the side, down a steep grassy bank and across a wooden footbridge and they were in the dene, with woods to the side and in front of them a path leading down to the beach.

'Not so fast, Jeff!' she cried and he slowed as she took off her court shoes. He slipped one in each pocket and she ran with him to the sands in her bare feet. Rose flinched as she trod on the shingle and Jeff picked her up and carried her over it, putting her down on the soft sand. They sat with their backs against the concrete wall of a pill box left over from the war, saying little, content just to be there together.

'I watch for your letters all the time,' he said. 'Your writing to me is the best thing that's ever happened to me.'

'Me too,' said Rose. Every day she walked by the Morlands' house when she went to the shops. A roundabout way it was but her dad never questioned her route, which was one blessing. The days when Kate beckoned to her and gave her a letter ... oh, they stood out from all the rest. Those were grey, sometimes black days. Jeff poured out all that had happened to him in those letters, all his hopes and fears, his feelings for her. And Rose was beginning to reply in the same way. Sometimes she wanted to tell him all her troubles, her dark, dark secret. But of course she couldn't. She sighed and leaned her head against his arm and he kissed her lightly on the lips. And it was so different from the other, as different as ... as ... well, she just couldn't think of a strong enough alternative.

'Come on,' said Jeff, rising to his feet and pulling her

up too. 'Let's walk.' He had to move before his feelings got the better of him and he went further. He wanted their love to be perfect. What he didn't want was to make her do something for which she wasn't ready.

The beach stretched for miles, to Blackhall Rocks in the north and Hartlepool to the south. They ran to the edge of the sea and walked along the shore to where sea coalers were harvesting the thin line of sparkling small coal, ponies standing by patiently as the men shovelled it into bags and on to the cart, seeming to know just when it was time to move on, a split second before the men clicked their tongues and called, 'Gee up!'

'Wot cheor,' they said and nodded to the young couple as they went by, and, 'Now then,' Jeff replied.

'I was going to show you the fossils in the cliffs,' he said as they approached Blackhall Rocks. 'But the light's going.'

It was. A collier going north was lit up, and lights were appearing all along the shoreline.

'There'll be another time,' said Rose.

They turned and walked back to where a path led up the cliff, no doubt for the benefit of the caravanners. At the top they stood close together, catching their breath before making their way back to the car. Rose was filled with unutterable sadness because their time together was almost over.

'Why don't we have supper at the restaurant on the caravan site?' Jeff asked suddenly. 'Aren't you hungry?'

'Oh, can we?' Anything, anything at all, to prolong this magical evening.

'Well, they're bound to have something.' He had the keys to the car in his hand but gladly dropped them back in his pocket and they turned in their tracks and headed towards the barn-like building which housed the restaurant. There was a dance floor though no dance going on, for after all it was Sunday, but there was a man playing a piano and a few people singing along.

In one corner was the restaurant and they sat there and ate Cornish pasties, reminiscent of Lord Woolton's vegetable pie during the war, and drank hot strong tea. But it didn't matter what they ate, they were still together and Rose resolutely avoided looking at the clock on the wall. Though, of course, they had to go sometime.

At her insistence Jeff dropped her at the top of Front Street though he protested that no one would see them, no one knew them in fact, and what was more he didn't care if they did.

'We'll get engaged, Rose,' he said. 'Your dad can't stop us.' He leaned across her as they sat in the car and kissed her lightly on the lips, once then twice, lingering, and in spite of herself her mouth opened just enough for her to feel the tip of his tongue, to taste his mouth, fresh and oh so sweet.

'Yes. Oh, yes,' she breathed and leaned against him, allowing herself to believe it. Then he opened the car door for her and drew back.

'Go on then, sweetheart. I'll write tomorrow as soon as I come off shift. Go on before I change my mind and take you with me, kidnap you.' He laughed softly.

Suddenly, more than anything she had ever wanted in her life, she wanted him to make her stay, for him to take charge of her life, take her with him so she would never see her dad again. But instead she got out of the car and stood quietly on the pavement as he started the engine and put it into gear. He raised a hand, called, 'Ta ra, love,' and set off down Front Street. Rose watched his tail lights disappear into the dip in the road. When the sound of the engine died away altogether she turned away at last and walked to Aunt Elsie's house.

'Did you have a good time, pet?' her aunt asked, but didn't wait for an answer. 'It's been such a good programme on the wireless, you missed yourself, mind.'

She went on to tell Rose all about it but Rose didn't hear a word. As soon as Aunt Elsie paused for breath she intervened.

'I think I'll go straight up, Auntie. I'm tired and I have to take the early bus tomorrow.'

'But what about your supper?'

'It's all right, I had some with... with my friend.'

'Go on then, pet. I'll be going to bed myself in a minute or two.'

Monday morning, sitting on the number 18 United bus to Spennymoor where she changed for Bishop Auckland, it all seemed like a dream. It was a dream, thought Rose miserably. Unattainable. And even if her dad let her go, Jeff wouldn't want her when he knew what she had done. She felt dirty, her head ached, she was the lowest of the low, leading Jeff on to think she could marry him.

Chapter Thirteen

Sometimes Marina ached unbearably for Charlie. Every evening in fact, just like this one in late September when a few copper-coloured leaves were already drifting down from the trees. As she came out of work she would glance up and down Old Elvet, desperately hoping he would be there and would say, 'Marina, I've missed you!' Of course he would have to have an excuse for his absence and she invented possible reasons why he couldn't have come before now. A project at the university which couldn't be finished without his total commitment, or perhaps his mother was seriously ill, dying in fact. No, his mother was already dead, she remembered.

This evening, as every other, she went home knowing sadly that the reason he didn't come was that he'd had enough of her, was finished with her, had just faded out of sight instead of telling her. Well, she would simply put him out of her mind too, concentrate on doing well at Shire Hall. Doris was leaving to get married and Marina had been promised promotion to the tabulator. After that, who knows? She could become supervisor, Margaret wasn't going to go on for ever. She could take more night classes to qualify to work her way up the Treasurer's Department. Her prospects were good, very good.

So why did she not feel more excited about it? Oh, never mind, she told herself crossly. She wasn't alone, she still had Brian, faithful old Brian to go with to dances and the pictures. And she was fond of him too, liked going out with him, wasn't just making use of him. What's more, it was nice to have someone to go out with, someone she could rely on. They were going out tonight as it happened, they were off to the Majestic to see *Tom Brown's Schooldays*.

All thoughts of Brian or the picture or anything else were driven out of her head when she saw the letter on the side table as she went into the kitchen at home. Her eyes were drawn to it. At first she thought she must be imagining it, but no, there it was, a thick white envelope and Charlie's strong handwriting on it in black ink: 'Miss Marina Morland'.

'Hallo, pet. We've got some news,' said Kate. 'An invitation to a wedding no less. I bet you can't guess who from?' She was full of pleasure at the idea of a day out at a wedding and Marina's absent-minded response was disappointing.

'What?'

Her daughter wasn't even listening to her but staring at the letter which had come for her in the morning post along with the invitation.

'Oh, yes, there's a letter for you too. Looks like a man's writing. Mind, you've kept him dark, whoever he is. Does Brian know a man's writing to you?' Kate grinned then forgot about the letter. 'Don't you want to know who's getting wed?'

The letter was in Marina's hand, she was aching to take it upstairs to her room. Oh, it was all going to be all right! Charlie would never have written to her if it wasn't. Her heart pounded. She forced herself to look at her mother as the sense of what Kate was saying finally got through to her.

'Who?'

'Penny! Penny's going to marry that Charlie...emm, hang on a minute, I have the invitation here.' Kate reached up to the mantelpiece and took down a silver-bordered card. 'Oh yes, Charles Hutchinson. You know, I think we met him on Durham Day once. That time directly after the war.'

Marina snatched the card out of her mother's hand. Charles Hutchinson. Yes, it definitely said Charles Hutchinson. He was going to marry Penny two weeks come Saturday, the first Saturday in October. But it had to be another Charles Hutchinson, of course it had to! Marina stared from the card to the envelope in her hand.

'Don't snatch, Marina,' Kate admonished mildly. Then, looking puzzled, 'Aren't you pleased?'

She turned her back and fumbled with the buttons of her coat. She mumbled something which could have been a yes.

'Are you out of sorts, Marina? A bad time with your monthlies?' Marina shook her head. 'Well, come on and eat your tea. I've got a nice bit of liver –'

She hardly heard what her mother was saying, all she wanted to do was escape to her bedroom, be on her own.

'I have to get changed,' she said and fled.

Kate stared after her. She looked down at the plate in her hand; good food spoiling, that was what it was. She couldn't abide good food spoiling. Sometimes she didn't know what was the matter with her daughter, she was that temperamental. Maybe it was giving her such a posh name, but she'd taken such a fancy to Princess Marina when she'd married the Duke of Kent, God rest his soul. She put the plate back in the oven and hung the cloth on the rail. She'd just have to insist Marina ate it before she went out.

Upstairs, Marina opened the letter and drew out the single sheet. It was all a mistake, she knew it was. After all, Charlie had written this letter, hadn't he? She sat down on the bed and began to read.

Dear Marina,

How are you? I'm sorry I have not written before now, but the truth is, I've been so busy. Did I tell you I had secured a post at York University? Well, I start in October, we are very excited about it. By 'we' I mean your cousin Penny and I. We're going to be married at the beginning of October and then we are going immediately to York.

I will always think fondly of you, Marina. How sweet you are, and the good times we had together in Durham. But that is all in the past now. It has been understood ever since we were children that Penny and I would marry one day. Her mother was so good to me when I needed help. I know you will wish us every happiness, Marina, and be glad for us.

Yours affectionately,
Charlie

'Yours affectionately'. Marina ran her thumb over the words. Charlie didn't love Penny, of course he didn't. It was just that he had an obligation to Aunt Hetty, that was all it was.

'Marina? Are you coming down to eat this tea I made for you or not?' Her mother was becoming annoyed.

'Yes, Mam.'

Marina stuffed the letter in her drawer underneath a pile of clean undies and went down. She sat at the table and ate the meal which Kate put before her, every last scrap.

'We'll go into town on Saturday and buy dresses for the wedding,' her mother said happily. 'I have the money put away in the Co-op.'

'Always supposing Dad doesn't get to it first,' said Marina sourly. She felt scratchily irritable, ready to take on the world. But when the smile on Kate's face was replaced by a look of hurt reproach, she wished she had kept quiet.

'He won't do that, Marina. He's stopped gambling, you know he has.'

'Yes. And anyway, he can't get dividend money, can he? You have to sign for it.' Dad would never stop gambling, it was in his blood, a disease like the measles, she thought.

Why was she being so nasty? Marina pushed away her plate and rose to her feet. She put one arm around her mother.

'Sorry, Mam, I'm just in a bad mood tonight. Of course he won't touch the money. Look, I'm off to see Rose for a minute or two before I go out. I promised her I'd pop in and she hasn't been for that letter which came yesterday.'

That was true, there was a letter from Easington for Rose and it wasn't like her not to call in on her way to the shop on the off chance of there being post. It was safe enough, Alf would be at work.

'Your dad's not so bad,' said Kate. 'He's a sight better than some folks I could mention.'

'Yes, Mam, I know.' Marina tried to be conciliatory.

'He brings me his pay packet every Friday, unopened an' all,' she went on and Marina's nerves began to jump.

'I'll have to go, Mam. See you later.' She escaped into the street, calling, 'If Brian comes before I'm back, tell him where I am.'

'Aye, and I'll tell him you're getting letters from strange men.'

Marina turned back. 'Brian is not my boyfriend,' she snapped. 'It's none of his business who writes to me.'

Kate sighed. 'Oh, go on. I wasn't going to say anything anyway.'

Rose was alone, of course, she was mostly alone these days. The light was on in the kitchen and the curtains undrawn and Marina was jolted as she saw her friend through the window, sitting knitting by the fire. She looked so pale and wan. Not well at all. She was too thin and her dark hair needed washing and cutting. Marina doubted if it had seen a comb that day. Rose started up from her seat, dropping the knitting when Marina knocked and opened the door. She glanced about the kitchen as she came in, just in case Alf Sharpe was off work, ready to go in a minute if he was. But no, the house was empty. In the corner the wireless was on for the news. Rose walked over to it and turned it off.

'I can only spare a minute, I'm going to the Majestic with Brian.'

'But you can sit down, can't you?' Rose moved her knitting bag from a chair.

'Oh, yes.' Marina brought out the letter and handed it over and even in her own misery took delight in the way her friend's face lit up.

'It came yesterday. We thought you might have come round.'

Rose's expression dimmed slightly. 'I couldn't come yesterday, I was busy.'

Marina looked around the spotless kitchen, spotless and cheerless, not a thing lying about but the knitting bag. Rose may neglect herself but she never neglected the house. And she endlessly knitted for the twins. As soon as one garment was finished, another was cast on the needles. Rose clutched her letter, compulsively looking down at it every few seconds.

'I don't know what keeps you so busy,' Marina commented. 'You have an electric washer now, haven't you?' That was one good thing, Alf Sharpe never seemed to mind paying for things for the house. And he was making a lot of money now, of course.

'I had to go out.' Rose was staring at her letter.

'Oh, go on, open it. I know you can't wait.'

But she just held the letter so Marina waited for her friend to tell her where it was she had to go. Rose never went out, unless it was to the shops or on one of her rare visits to see the twins. She stayed silent.

'Of course, you don't have to tell me, I'm only your best friend,' said Marina, sounding huffy.

Rose thought of the doctor's surgery where she had sat on a form by the wall in the waiting room, then her humiliation as the doctor examined her.

'Haven't you brought a friend with you?' he had asked. 'I don't usually do this when a patient is alone.'

She almost poured out everything to Marina, felt she

would go mad if she didn't tell someone, and there was no one else but Marina, was there? Rose's joy in the letter was dead as darker things crowded in on her. She stared at it again and slipped it into her knitting bag. Jeff. For a minute or two when she had first seen the letter she had forgotten that he would not want her now. Definitely would not. So what was the good of writing? She would have to break with him, that was all.

'I'm so miserable, Rose!'

She looked across at Marina in surprise, the words mirrored her own thoughts so exactly. But what had Marina to be miserable about? She had begun to cry.

'Why? What's the matter? Oh, Marina, I'm so sorry! I'm a selfish pig, I am. I should have noticed how upset you were. I'm so full of my own troubles. Tell me all about it.'

'I've been such a fool, Rose. I –' Marina got no further for just then there was a knock on the door. 'Oh, God, it's Brian. We were going to the pictures. Oh, I don't want him to see me like this!'

'Go and wash your face, I'll talk to Brian,' Rose said, and waited until Marina was out of the room before answering the door. What she would do if her dad came home now she had no idea. She opened the door only halfway, holding on to the handle and peering out at Brian.

'Hallo, Rose. Mrs Morland said Marina was here,' he greeted her.

'She won't be a minute, Brian. Look, go and wait at the end of the street, will you? I'm nervous, me dad –'

He nodded, knowing what she meant immediately and backed off, but as he walked out of the yard his face was hard. That bloody man! What right had he to keep the lass in such a state that she was frightened of simple, everyday contact with a lad? By, one of these days that swine would get his comeuppance and he and Jeff might be just the ones to see to it.

'Come back and tell me all about it,' said Rose as Marina returned to the kitchen, looking pale but dry-eyed. And I'll tell you all my woes, she thought as her friend went off. She smiled wryly as she imagined Marina's face if she told her. What would she do? Run a mile, probably, horrified. Maybe she wouldn't believe it, would think it was all lies. Or maybe she would think it was Rose's own fault. After all, she had stayed with her father, hadn't she?

Rose picked up the knitting bag and took out the letter from Jeff. Before reading it she closed the curtains at the window and turned the key in the lock, just in case *he* came home.

'We're too late for the pictures now,' said Brian. 'Where shall we go?' He caught hold of Marina's hand and held it, his fingers warm and strong and comforting. 'There's the pubs,' he suggested. 'The Wear Valley Hotel is open.' So they sat in a corner of the almost empty lounge in the hotel opposite the railway station and Brian ordered brown ale for himself and a shandy for Marina. The publican looked sideways at her, unsure if she was old enough to be there, but he said nothing.

If Marina was unusually quiet, Brian didn't seem to notice, or if he did, he was too sensitive to say anything about it. He watched her as she sat, looking pensive, taking an occasional sip from her glass. She began to make an effort to be sociable, talk a little about the girls at work, how Doris was leaving to get married and she herself expected to be promoted to her place on the tabulator. How she was taking extra courses at night school.

'You'll get on,' said Brian confidently. 'You're clever, you can do anything you set your mind to.'

'Oh, you!' said Marina, but she smiled warmly at him and he was encouraged to say what was on his mind. This was a good place with no distractions, they could talk here.

'I'm going to night school too. I won't be a hewer all my life,' he said, and she gazed at him in surprise. Somehow she hadn't thought of Brian as being ambitious.

'Won't you?'

'No, I will work my way up. In good time take my under-manager's ticket – if I stay in mining, that is. I wish now I'd started in surveying. I could have done, you know.' He said it as though she might doubt him and impulsively she put her hand on his.

'I'm sure you could have, Brian.'

He sighed. 'Of course, it might mean I would have to

move away from Jordan.' The touch of her hand on his made him feel good, he never wanted to let her go. Yet for all they were going out together quite regularly now, there was still something elusive about her.

Marina wouldn't want to move away from her family, he knew that. And if she didn't marry him and go with him wherever he had to go, what was it all for?

'Would you like to get engaged?'

There, he couldn't believe he'd actually said the words. His heart beat faster in trepidation, he was sure he'd spoiled his chances now, she would refuse him, of course she would. The silence was broken by the clink of a glass as the barman put it down and crossed over to the juke box and put in a coin. Brian watched as the steel arm behind the glass moved and took a record and placed it on the turntable. Coloured lights flashed in the console. Frank Sinatra started to sing, albeit a little scratchily, a wailing love song.

'Engaged?'

Marina withdrew her hand and turned her head away from him, finding something totally absorbing in the juke box.

'Look, forget I said it. I know you're not ready. I –'

She turned back to him, her smile brilliant. 'When? When will we get engaged?'

Brian was nonplussed for a second or two. 'Tonight. Tomorrow. Oh, anytime you like.'

'Will I have a ring?'

'Why not?' He thought of his savings in the Trustees Savings Bank. Every week since he had been working the bank clerk had come to the pit office on payday. He'd had a pound taken from his wages at source and had never withdrawn a penny. He wondered how much a ring cost. What the heck did it matter? He was just beginning to realise that Marina had actually said yes!

Chapter Fourteen

'You're too young to get engaged, let alone married,' said Kate. 'Isn't she, Sam? You both are.'

'I don't know, you were just eighteen yourself when we were wed,' said her husband, and Kate turned on him in a fury.

'Aye, and look how that turned out!'

He looked shocked, turning first pale and then red as fire. 'It turned out all right, woman! Haven't we got three fine grown-up bairns? Haven't I worked for you and them all these years? Why, I bring my pay packet home every week wi' nowt out of it but me union dues, don't I?'

Marina blushed and looked sideways at Brian, ashamed he should hear her parents squabbling like this. He appeared to be absorbed in a calendar hanging on the wall.

'Oh, yes. Until the day you decide to bet all we've got on a dog or a horse or the cards. You're a gambler, Sam Morland . . .'

'Stop it, Mam, leave him alone!' cried Marina and Kate turned on her.

'Don't you tell me to stop it, young lady. You're the first one to moan about him when –'

'I think we should go for a walk, Marina,' Brian intervened. He took hold of her elbow and drew her towards the door.

'But it's late and we haven't settled anything yet,' she protested.

'Yes, we have, pet. Tomorrow we're going into Bishop to buy the ring. Now come on, put your coat on, it's a bit chilly out there. Just a turn around the streets. Goodnight, Mrs Morland, Mr Morland.' He nodded his head and they went out, Marina with barely time to fasten her coat.

There was a short silence in the kitchen. Sam reached up to the mantelpiece and took down a packet of Woodbines. He tore a strip of paper from the edge of his newspaper and twisted it, using it to light the cigarette. His fingers trembled slightly and as the first smoke entered his lungs he coughed, a harsh, laboured sound. Then he sat back and met his wife's gaze.

'You never back me up,' she remarked with the resigned bitterness she often used with him.

'Not when you're wrong I don't.'

'Our Marina's just a bairn. Only today she insisted Brian wasn't her boyfriend, they were just going out together sometimes.'

'Well then. She just fancies being engaged, the lad asked her and she thought she would like it. It'll all fizzle

out eventually. Marina's too sensible a lass to marry someone she doesn't care for.'

'But that's what I'm telling you! Why, do you know,
she had a letter from another chap only the day. She
doesn't know what she wants, that's the trouble.'

'It'll sort itself out, I tell you. Likely it's because her
cousin's getting married, did you think of that?'

Kate sighed. 'Aye. Likely.'

There was silence in the room, broken only by the
small noises of Kate tidying up for the morning and the
occasional cough from Sam.

'Well, remember, she's not said anything about setting
a date to be wed, has she? Getting engaged isn't final, is
it?' he said at last.

'No, you're right,' she acknowledged.

Sam threw the stub of the cigarette into the fire and it
flared up briefly. 'That's what you think, is it?' he asked.
'I mean, about you and me? You're sorry we got wed?'

Kate looked down at her hands. What could she say?
She didn't know if she loved him still, didn't know now if
she ever had. At first perhaps, in the good times, when she
had believed him when he'd said he would never gamble
again. But always the good times had been followed by the
nightmares. The mountains of debt which had to be paid
somehow, the humiliation of knowing other people knew.

Then she looked up into his face and couldn't bear to
see the hurt there. 'No, I'm not sorry,' she said and moved
briskly to the bottom of the stairs. 'Well, I'm going to bed,

I'm dog-tired. An' you'd better come an' all. Just leave the light on for Marina, she'll be along in a minute.' As they were climbing the stairs, she remarked, 'I tell you what, that lad's got more to him than you'd think. I suppose it wouldn't be a bad thing at all if they did marry. But mind, not for a long time. I expect it to be a long engagement.' As she undressed in the cool of the bedroom she chuckled suddenly. 'A ring no less! Things have changed since our day, Sam. We were lucky to get a wedding ring, never mind an engagement one.'

The ring was a three-stone row of tiny diamonds, set on the slant in platinum to make them look bigger. The gold was eighteen-carat and the whole thing cost £25. Daft, Kate called it.

'You could buy a lot for the house with £25,' she said to Marina. 'You'll find out, my girl. A little house has a big mouth, my gran always used to say.'

'Oh, Mam,' said Marina. She held up her hand under the overhead electric bulb and the ring sparkled satisfactorily. That would show Charlie Hutchinson next Saturday when they went to the wedding.

Oh, Charlie. Marina felt as though she was weeping inside but smiled brightly. 'I'm going write to Aunt Hetty and ask if Brian can come with me to the wedding,' she told her mother.

'It's a bit late for her to alter the numbers,' Kate objected.

'Well, all right, I'll phone. I'll go down to the phone-box now.'

Marina swathed her new dress in tissue paper and hung it carefully in the wardrobe. She gazed critically at her reflection in the mirror on the wardrobe door. Did she need a haircut? She swung her head slowly from side to side and her brown hair, styled in a long bob which turned under on the shoulders, swung too. Pity about the colour but her mam would go mad if she bleached it. Still, she'd be looking her best, done up to the nines and with a handsome lad hanging on to her arm, when she faced Charlie.

'Marina! It's time you were going over to the Wearmouths',' Kate called up the stairs. 'Get a move on, girl, you don't want to be late. I don't know, you'll be late for your own funeral.'

Marina pulled a face at her image in the glass and took out her good blue costume and a white blouse. Smoothing the pencil-slim skirt over her hips, she cast one last glance in the mirror and went downstairs. Tonight she was invited to the Wearmouths' for her tea and to show off her ring.

The wedding reception was held in Fortune Hall, now a hotel, one of a string owned by Aunt Hetty and her second husband, Richard Fortune. At least Marina had always assumed he was her second husband for the other hotels all had Pearson in their names and Penny was called Pearson-Fortune. Or had been before the ceremony. Now she was called Hutchinson.

Marina felt a peculiar stab of pain deep inside her. She took a long drink from the glass of champagne she was holding and smiled brilliantly at Brian.

'Steady on, love,' he said. 'You'll be tipsy if you drink it too fast.'

'Well, it doesn't matter. Aunt Hetty has booked us rooms. We don't have to get home tonight, do we?' She waved at someone on the other side of the room. Brian glanced over but could see no one he knew except the bridegroom who was talking animatedly to his new father-in-law.

Brian pursed his lips and gazed at Marina thoughtfully. She was on top form, eyes sparkling, had laughed at every joke the best man told. When they had entered the reception room to be greeted by the bride and groom and the bride's parents, she had kissed Penny effusively and blushed a pretty pink when the bridegroom had bent and kissed her cheek.

Then she had taken Brian's arm and drawn him forward. 'We'll be next!' she had cried, and flashed her left hand with the ring on the fourth finger, looking sideways at Charlie as she did so.

'Oh, how lovely!' Penny had cried. 'Congratulations to you both. We hope you'll be as happy as we are, don't we, Charlie?' Her white satin wedding gown clung to her figure and fell straight from the hips. Her veil was of beautiful lace with a headdress of seed pearls, its centre in the shape of the rose of York.

'Yes, indeed.'

But Brian had observed something, some constraint between Marina and Charlie, and even as they moved down the line she had been glancing back at him. Oh, come on, he told himself, you're imagining things. Marina can barely know him. Wasn't he a Yorkshire man? Anyway, she loved him, Brian. Wasn't she wearing his ring?

Marina had cried in church, trying to hide it, pretending she had something in her eye. He had looked but there was nothing and he grinned.

'Come on, Marina, all women cry at weddings, it's expected,' he had said, and she had sniffed and turned away. Looking at her now, as she turned to speak to Hetty Fortune who was going round the room having a word or two with all the guests, he still felt slightly uneasy yet wasn't sure why.

'Penny and Charlie are going to Venice for their honeymoon,' Hetty said.

'Venice? How gorgeous!' cried Marina. Suddenly a wave of pure jealousy swept over her, enveloping her in dark misery. She looked about her. The feeling was so strong she was sure other people must notice it, she had given herself away. She looked down at the ground and managed to say, 'Excuse me a minute. I must go...' And fled into the hall and looked round desperately for the toilets.

Locating them in one corner, she ran in and hid in a cubicle until the black wave receded and she felt able to come out and splash her face with cold water. She patted it dry with a fleecy towel from the pile by the basins and gazed at herself in the mirror. She was a sight, she decided ruefully. At least she had her pancake stick with her, and her lipstick. Sitting down in a pink upholstered chair, she took out her make-up bag.

Five minutes later, Marina felt ready to face the world again. Of course she hadn't betrayed herself. Why should anyone suspect anything anyway? Here she was with her own fiancé, and mind, she acknowledged to herself, Brian could hold his own in any company. She had felt quite proud of him as she walked beside him up the path to the church. He was tall and dark and handsome, and yes, sometimes when he held her and kissed her she hadn't to pretend a response at all, it came naturally.

'How are you feeling now, pet?' asked Brian, who was hovering in the hall when she came out. 'Maybe you'd better not have any more champagne? I told you you were drinking it too fast.'

'I'm fine. Don't go on at me, Brian!' she snapped. 'You're not my keeper.'

'OK.'

To her astonishment he turned on his heel and went out of the front door of the hotel, disappearing in an instant. She looked out of the side window but he had gone. Now what was he playing at? she thought, exasperated.

'All alone?'

Marina spun on her heel at the unexpected sound of his voice. It was Charlie. She looked around and behind him but Penny wasn't there. In fact, for the moment there was no one else in the hall but them.

'I was just going in,' she said stiffly, and made to pass him.

Charlie took hold of her arm. 'Oh, come on, wait a minute. I'd like to know how you've been getting on,' he said, smiling down at her. Marina's heart began to thump.

'You can see how I've been getting on. I've got engaged to a lovely lad and we're going to get married.'

'Pretty quick, wasn't it?' Charlie lifted an eyebrow. 'Are you sure you want to marry what's-his-name?'

'Brian, Brian Wearmouth. And why shouldn't I want to marry him? You didn't think I was still pining for you, did you?'

'Well...'

At that moment Brian was walking past the window, regretting his abrupt departure. He glanced in and there she was, still in the hall, and with her Charlie Hutchinson. He was saying something to her and leaning forward, looking at her in such an impudent way that Brian wanted to punch his nose. And surely Marina was returning the look... Brian turned and strode off again.

'Charlie? Who are you talking to? Oh, it's you, Marina. Are you having a good time?'

It was Penny, the train of her wedding dress hooked over her arm. She walked up to Charlie and linked her free arm in his, not waiting for Marina's reply. 'I'm going up to change now, Charlie,' she said. 'We have to be at York station by four or we'll miss the train. Are you coming?'

'Yes, of course, darling.'

Marina watched as they went up the curving staircase; she wondered what Penny would say or do if she called them back and described the mole Charlie had high up on his thigh – no, of course she couldn't do that. She swallowed hard. The sound of the wedding guests laughing and talking inside the reception room was suddenly very loud. Someone was playing the piano, an old Ivor Novello ballad – she couldn't remember the name – but whoever it was began to swing the tune, making it ridiculous, robbing it of its beauty.

She couldn't go back in there and wondered if she would be missed if she went up to her room. But no, she might bump into Penny or Charlie there and she couldn't bear that.

'Can I help you, miss?' A barman paused as he crossed the hall, struck by her lost air and pale face. He wondered if she'd had too much champagne and hoped she wasn't going to be sick, not on the polished oak floor.

'No, thanks, I'm just going outside for some fresh air,' she replied, to his relief, and went out into the garden. She walked rapidly around the old house, to a cobbled yard with outbuildings, garages and stables. There she leaned against the wall and fought for control of herself.

Here Brian found her as he returned from a brisk walk through what seemed to be an old orchard and beyond on the moor. He had been ready to carry on until he came to the village. Maybe he could catch a bus or something, find his way home.

But that impulse had soon passed. After all, he was probably making something out of nothing. He had no real reason to believe there was anything between Marina and her cousin's new husband. Just the way she had looked at the man...and that was probably the champagne. He owed it to her to stay, he wanted to stay. Oh, God, he thought, jealousy was the very devil.

'Marina? Marina, love? What is the matter, for goodness' sake?'

'Nothing. Well...I thought you'd gone.'

'Of course I hadn't. I wouldn't leave you here to go to the dance on your own, would I? Too many other chaps about. You might get snatched away from me and I'm not having that.'

She looked up at him and smiled. He put his arms around her and held her to him. She was trembling.

'Let's go for a walk together, Brian,' she said. 'I think I just had too much champagne, I need to walk it off.'

'You should have listened to me, pet, shouldn't you?' Their arms around each other, they strolled through the orchard.

'We'll miss the bride and groom going off,' he said as, round the corner, they saw the best man and a few of his companions attaching tin cans and old boots to a car.

'I don't care,' said Marina. And found that she meant it.

Chapter Fifteen

'What was the wedding like, then?' asked Rose, and Marina looked at her. Rose was not herself, Marina thought anxiously. She spoke jerkily, not making eye contact, as if she were simply making conversation, saying something, anything.

They had walked up to their favourite spot on the moor and were seated under the overhanging rock, sheltered from the ever-present wind. Marina had at first demurred when her friend had suggested they should go up there. After all, Rose's dad was just at the Club, it being Sunday afternoon, and could be home at any time.

'I don't care,' she had said as she banged the door to behind them and set off into the clean, cold air. The children were reciting the Lord's Prayer as they passed the Methodist Sunday School and a little further on the Anglican vicar was standing at the church door shaking hands with his flock as they came out of morning service. Looking back as they climbed the bank away from the village they could see the smoke from all the chimney pots rising in a straight line to the pale blue sky as ovens were heated ready to take the Sunday joint.

Marina glanced surreptitiously at her friend. Rose seemed so calm, unnaturally so. She didn't seem to care that she also should have been preparing the dinner for her dad when he came out of the Club. She had plucked a dry, brittle stalk of grass and was breaking tiny pieces from it almost as though she didn't realise she was doing it.

'The wedding?' Marina remembered Rose's question. 'Oh, you know, it went like all weddings do. The hotel was nice, though, very posh.' She wasn't ready to discuss the wedding, not yet. Her mind shied away from it.

Rose nodded, not really interested. She hadn't even heard the reply.

'What is it, Rose?' Marina asked abruptly. 'Come on, tell me. I know there's something, you're different today somehow.' Rose dropped the grass on the ground and straightened her shoulders as though facing up to something. Her voice, perhaps sharpened by her state of mind, came out aggressively.

'I've fallen wrong.' The words hung on the air. Rose could hear her own voice saying them but they didn't sound real.

'What?' Marina was sure she'd misheard.

'I'm going to have a baby.'

'Are you sure? I mean... well, you can't be, you never go out with anybody. Oh!' Light dawned on Marina. 'Have you been meeting Jeff on the quiet and never told me?'

'No.' Rose shook her head. She began playing with her skirt, pleating it and smoothing it, over and over again, with quick, nervous fingers.

'Why, then you must be mistaken. You can't be. What was it – as immaculate conception?' Marina grinned at Rose, trying to jolly her out of her strange mood. She must be going a bit doolally with being on her own in that blooming house so much, that was it. She had a sudden frightful thought herself. By, what if she had got pregnant when she was with Charlie? It didn't bear thinking about.

'I'm not, I've been to the doctor. I'm expecting, I tell you, I'm four months on.'

'Rose!' Marina was jolted out of herself to the point where she was almost speechless.

'I don't know what I'm going to do,' said her friend, not sounding distraught, no emotion at all in her voice now that she had told someone at last.

'Well.' Marina found her tongue. 'You'll have to marry Jeff, won't you? Never mind what your dad says.'

'It's not his baby.'

Marina started. 'Well, whose is it?'

Rose got to her feet and walked off towards the path. After a moment Marina followed her. 'Wait a minute, where are you going?'

'Up to the top of that rock,' Rose replied.

'Whatever for?' But realisation dawned even as Marina spoke. 'You're not going to throw yourself off? You're not trying to kill yourself? Rose!'

She stopped and looked squarely at Marina. 'No, I won't kill myself. If I did, who would protect Mary from him? It's not high enough to kill me anyway, but it might get rid of the baby.' She began to climb the grassy slope at the back of the rock.

'Stop it! Behave yourself, Rose, you're talking like a loony. I don't know what you're on about!' In the urgency of trying to stop Rose, the bit about protecting Mary didn't register on Marina properly. She scrambled after her friend and managed to grab hold of Rose and force her to a halt, though in the ensuing struggle they both fell on the steep ground and rolled over a couple of times, almost to the bottom. A grouse flew up in startled flight right by their feet; the wind blew remorselessly. The girls lay on their backs, panting. Marina was the first to get to her feet. She took hold of Rose's forearm and hauled her upright too.

'Come on, you're shivering,' she said, and Rose went with her docilely enough, the fight knocked out of her for the moment. They returned to the shelter of the little dell.

'Now then, madam,' said Marina, and all of a sudden she sounded exactly like Kate. 'I want the whole story.'

'You won't want to know me if I tell you.'

'Don't talk so daft, it can't be that bad. Howay, out with it.'

Rose looked away from Marina into the middle distance where there was a stand of trees, grown lopsided by the force of the prevalent winds. Well, she thought, I have to tell someone and Marina might believe me when some folk won't.

'Do you remember, years ago, when we were about eleven? We were walking to school with June Simpson and that girl passed us, the one that used to live on the farm up the road?'

'Now how would I remember one single day out of all the days we walked to school?'

'Yes. But June Simpson said, if you remember, "That girl's da is her granda".'

Marina's brow creased in puzzlement then cleared as the memory returned in a flash. 'Oh, yes! And I said June Simpson wasn't talking sense. We didn't know what she meant, did we?'

'I knew. And it frightened me. That June Simpson always knew too much about other folk.'

'But what has that to do...Rose Sharpe, you don't mean...' Suddenly the hints and innuendoes about Alf Sharpe which periodically went around the village came back to Marina. Bits of gossip, not actually saying anything outright, things she'd discounted as malicious rubbish. 'Do you mean what I think you mean?'

Rose looked down at the ground, her face flushed a dull brick red. 'Yes,' she whispered.

'And the baby? The baby's father is...no, it can't be true!'

'I knew you wouldn't believe me.' Rose stared at the ground, pale now.

'Oh, yes, I do, Rose,' Marina answered. She couldn't bear to see such misery in her friend's face. Impulsively she put an arm around her, shocked to feel how bird-thin she was. Dear God, Rose was skinny as a TB victim. 'I'm sorry, of course I believe you. You're my friend, aren't you?'

Rose began to sob. 'I don't know what I'm going to do, Marina, I don't! I thought if I threw myself off the rock I would get rid of it. I thought if I hurt myself and you were here you would look after me. I'm sorry, I shouldn't have brought you into it.'

'Rubbish! But I don't think it would have worked, and anyway you might have broken your neck, man.' Marina paused for a minute, horrified by what might have happened, what she might have had to do if Rose had succeeded in her plan. Poor lass, she must be out of her mind with it all. That rotten excuse for a father! But why had Rose let it happen, especially as she grew older? Marina stopped herself from asking.

She sat holding Rose, rocking her gently as Kate had done with her when she was younger and had hurt herself or was full of some childhood misery.

'You have to get away,' she said. 'I don't know why you didn't go when the twins went.'

'I had to stay otherwise – well, Mary –'

'No!' So that was why. My God! 'Is that what you meant about protecting the bairn? Rose, no, he wouldn't... A little lass like Mary. No!' A new world was opening up for Marina, a dark, horrible world she could barely believe existed. Yet here was Rose to prove it did: all the mystifying changes in her over the years, her dad's attitude to her friends, and especially to boys. She'd thought Alf Sharpe was being protective, albeit obsessively so, when all the time it had been him from whom Rose needed protection.

'Rose, no matter what, you have to go now. Surely you can see that? It's all going to come out anyway if you stay.'

'He'll bring the twins home, he's said he will, and he's their legal guardian. How can I risk that?'

'No, he won't, Rose. Can't you see? You can threaten him with the law.' That was Marina, always going straight to the heart of the situation, always jumping straight to the obvious remedy. And this time she was probably right.

'But everyone would know –'

'Oh, for God's sake, Rose, everyone will know if you stay. Don't be so daft!' In her agitation, Marina jumped up and strode about the fell, backwards and forwards, backwards and forwards. 'Listen, I tell you what. We'll go back now. Your dad won't be in for an hour or two yet, I'll bet. Get your things and I'll go with you to Shotton, how's that? You tell your Aunt Elsie, I'll back you up.'

'She didn't believe me, you know, when I tried to tell her before.' Rose was doubtful.

'Did she not? The stupid cow! Everyone knows you don't tell lies. Well, she'll believe you now, I promise you she will. I'll drum it into her.'

'I'll have to tell him.'

'Leave him a note then. Tell the truth. He won't dare follow you.'

Something about Marina's certainty was beginning to make Rose think her friend could be right. Slowly, she nodded her head. They linked arms and walked down the path. Marina was a tower of strength to Rose. She had to be, couldn't let her change her mind now.

Back at the yard gate, Rose turned to Marina. 'Listen,' she said, 'it's good of you to offer but I think I'd best go on my own. Aunt Elsie won't thank me for bringing in someone outside the family, d'you see? She'd be mortified. Even worse than she's going to be now.'

'You sure? Look, you're going to go, aren't you? Well, I'll go to the bus with you.' Just in case Rose got cold feet, she told herself.

But Rose packed her things, throwing her clothes higgledy-piggledy into a cheap cardboard case, the only one in the house. 'I'm ready,' she said. Now she couldn't wait. Her nerves were screaming and she wanted to scream with them: *Let's go! Let's go!* He could come home any minute, there was no telling.

'Oh, for goodness' sake, do something with your hair first,' Marina said, looking her up and down. 'And look, you've got your coatbelt twisted. The bus doesn't go till one o'clock anyway.' It was a quarter to the hour. She fiddled with Rose's belt, waited while she combed her hair.

'Hang on a minute,' said Rose at the last second and found a scrap of paper in the press and wrote a note: '*Gone to Aunt Elsie's.*' That was all. Her heart beat painfully in her chest so that she felt it would burst.

'I know I said leave a note but why bother? He doesn't deserve it,' said Marina. Rose shrugged. Within ten minutes of entering the house, they were on their way to the bus stop. As it chugged up the bank towards them, the two girls hugged each other.

'You'll write?' Marina felt like crying now the moment of parting had come.

'Of course. And you'll come to see me later, in a week or two?' The conductor helped Rose on with the case.

'A bit late to be going on a holiday, isn't it, love? Blackpool, is it?'

Rose mumbled something in reply, managed a smile. She found a seat near the front. The bus was half-empty, it being a Sunday. Marina was fluttering her handkerchief outside as the driver set off, Rose too full of suppressed emotion to wave back.

Chapter Sixteen

'You look like death warmed up, lass!' Aunt Elsie exclaimed after she'd greeted Rose. 'Come on in and I'll heat you some dinner up, we've had ours.' She opened the door wide for Rose to bring in the suitcase, dripping wet it was now and looking in imminent danger of falling to bits. The day had darkened with a sudden autumn storm. On the way from the bus stop at the Throstle's Nest, on the edge of the village, the rain had sheeted down. Everything about Rose was soaked.

Elsie eyed the case but said nothing about it. 'If I'd known you were coming I would have kept the twins in. They've gone to a party, one of their friends has a birthday today. Now come on, get those wet things off and dry yourself in front of the fire, you're shivering like a jelly.' She paused and looked sideways at her niece. 'There's nowt the matter at home, is there? Alf's all right, I mean?'

'He's OK.'

Rose stripped off her things and nothing was said for a while as Elsie bustled about putting a plate of dinner to

warm in the oven, pushing the kettle on to the glowing
fire, spooning tea into the brown betty teapot. It was only
when Rose was once again in dry clothes with warmth
seeping back into her bones and was seated at the table
before the steaming food that her aunt poured herself a
cup of tea and sat down opposite her.

'What's wrong, then?' she demanded. 'Come on, out
with it!'

'I've left home, Auntie. Can I stay with you for a bit?'
Rose turned her fork in a pile of mashed potato, making
a channel as she used to do when she was little, watching
the gravy run into it like a miniature river. She didn't look
at her aunt. She was dreading Elsie's asking the reason;
now that moment was near she didn't think she could tell
her. She might not believe her, might send her away. Rose
rushed into speech to hold off the moment.

'I can get a job – there's clothing factories quite near
here. I won't be a burden, Auntie. I can help you with
Michael and Mary, too.'

At the mention of Michael and Mary, Aunt Elsie
relaxed. Her expression softened. 'You miss them, eh? Of
course you do. I know I would.'

'That's it.' Rose seized on it as the perfect reason for
her coming. It was true, too. 'I miss them an awful lot. I
do, Aunt Elsie.'

'Aye. They're little angels, they are. Well, sometimes
they're little demons but there would be something wrong
if they weren't, wouldn't there?' She laughed, leaning

back in her chair, her delight in having the twins shining out. Then her manner changed. She put her cup down on its saucer and leaned her elbows on the table.

'But what about your dad? Who's going to look after him?'

'I have a right to a life of me own!' Rose burst out, her lip quivering. 'He earns enough money, he can afford a housekeeper. I want to be with the kids!'

Aunt Elsie sighed. 'I know, I know. Don't think I haven't seen how unhappy you are. I noticed the last time you were here. You've changed, lass, turning into an old woman before your time. And so skinny . . . you were such a plump, jolly bairn.'

'Can I stay, Auntie?'

'We'll see, we'll see. Now howay, stop playing with your food, I don't make a good dinner for it to be wasted.' She poured a cup of tea for Rose. 'By the way, I expect you told your dad what you were doing? Did he say it was all right?'

'I left him a note.'

'Hmm.' Aunt Elsie looked sceptical but she held her peace.

Rose felt as if a load had been lifted from her shoulders. Aunt Elsie hadn't said she could stay but she hadn't thrown her out either. At the very least it was a breathing space. What she would do when she found out about the baby was another thing.

Later, with Michael and Mary home, the evening passed

in seeing to them, giving them supper, getting them ready
for bed. In the way of children they didn't question Rose's
presence, just accepted her with joy, both trying to climb
on her knee at once. And afterwards, when Michael and
Mary were in bed, the women busied themselves laying
out their school things before settling down before the fire
to listen to the Light Programme on the wireless.

'You'll have to sleep with Mary the night,' Aunt Elsie
said. 'Tomorrow I'll seek out the camp bed from the attic.
It'll do until we manage to get a better one.' And Rose felt
a surge of gratitude to her. She was going to be allowed to
stay. What would she do without Aunt Elsie? Tomorrow
would be soon enough to tell her aunt the truth. Or even
perhaps later, when she had found a job, was at least earning her own living.

Then there was Jeff. The thought of him hurt her inside.
How could she possibly tell him? Yet how could she not?
There was one thing for sure: he would be finished with
her altogether when he learned the truth. Of course he
would, what lad wouldn't? She was dirty, used, soiled.

'A good thing an' all,' said Kate when Marina told her that
Rose had gone to live with her aunt in Shotton Colliery.
'Why she didn't go when the twins went mystifies me.'

Marina gazed at her mother. What did she know? What
did the rest of the folk in Jordan realise about Alf Sharpe?
All of it. Or if they didn't know, they had suspected the
truth. Everyone but herself. So why hadn't they done

something about it? Marina's childlike faith in her elders had taken a blow. In the ordinary way it was natural for a girl to stay at home and look after her father if he was on his own, that was what usually happened. She put the question to her mother.

'Isn't a girl expected to look after her father if he's on his own? After all, Rose isn't the only one in the village.' She wasn't, there was one other girl at least in that position, living on the other side of Jordan.

'Not if the dad's like Alf Sharpe, they're not,' snapped Kate.

'How?'

'For goodness' sake, lass, stop going on! You've got eyes in your head, haven't you?' And she would say no more.

There was a letter for Rose from Easington on the following Monday.

'What are you going to do with that?' asked Kate, scrutinising the envelope. 'I suppose you have her address?'

'Yes.'

'That's all right then, you can send it on.'

Marina had other ideas, though. She was owed a lieu day at work, she would go in tomorrow and ask if she could take the afternoon off at least. Shotton wasn't far from Durham City, no more than half an hour on the bus, she reckoned. And she couldn't wait to see how Rose was getting on; if her aunt had believed her and taken her in.

*

Alf Sharpe took a taxi to Shotton. It cost half a week's wages and was the highlight of the week for the taxi driver who came out from Bishop Auckland to pick up his passenger. Alf had drunk a bottle of cheap whisky on Sunday afternoon after he came in from the Club already half-cut and found no dinner ready and the fire out. After a few minutes yelling for Rose, he found the note she had left on the kitchen table but which had been brushed to the floor as he walked past.

He had lain for twenty-four hours on the mat before the range, waking up stiff and cold, with a mouth like a cesspit and a black fury inside him that couldn't wait for slow buses to get him where he wanted to go.

It was a messenger from the manager of the pit who had knocked and knocked and finally woken him, for Alf had missed his shift.

'Mr Harris wants to know what's the matter, Mr Sharpe?' It was a young clerk from the colliery office, trying not to gag at the stench of stale whisky. Alf stood in the doorway, holding the door and swaying slightly.

'I'm bad. Can you not see I'm bad?' Indeed he was red-eyed and unshaven and looked like a tramp, thought the boy, who was from a Primitive Methodist teetotal family and shocked to the core. He stepped back from the door out of range of Alf's breath.

'Yes, I can, Mr Sharpe, but the manager'll want to know what's the matter.'

'I've got the flu,' he improvised, then, noticing the

boy's instinctive recoil, 'I've taken a drop to ease it, like. Now damn well get out of here, that's all you need to know.'

'But Mr Harris'll want to know when you're coming back.'

'When I'm better!' Alf slammed the door and leaned against it, fighting the waves of nausea which threatened, the deafening pounding in his head. The din receded at last, his stomach settled and he tottered to his chair by the empty grate and lit a cigarette, drawing the smoke deep into his lungs so that the cigarette burned down half its length in one drag.

Rose wasn't going to get away with it, the bitch was his! He would go to Shotton and bring the kids home, the kids or her, he swore he would. He'd told her he would, that night she'd come into the kitchen and offered the deal, and he would do it, she'd better believe it. And Elsie would make her come home. She was besotted with those two brats, would give up anything but them. Even Rose.

That morning, Rose had dressed in her good suit and announced she was off to the Labour Exchange as soon as Michael and Mary had left for school. She felt a rush of optimism. This was the start of a new life. She'd had a good night's sleep, free from the worry of waiting for *him* to open her bedroom door, and the shadows under her eyes were lessening already.

'There's no rush, Rose,' Aunt Elsie said, 'give yourself

a few days' holiday, pet. You look as though you could do with it.' She had the oilcloth cover off the kitchen table and was sorting clothes on the white-scrubbed wood. In the yard, the setpot boiler was just beginning to emit little puffs of steam as the water heated up.

Rose hesitated. Maybe she should stay and help her aunt with the week's washing. She offered but Aunt Elsie would have none of it.

'No, no, I didn't mean that. I can manage fine. No, if you want to go now, that's all right by me,' she said. 'Mind, I'd look in the *Echo* first if I was you. The Sits Vac column.'

'I did that. There wasn't anything.'

Rose had more luck at the Labour Exchange. She was there for half an hour and when she came out had a card in her hand for a job at the raincoat factory, Ransome's, on the newly built industrial estate near the colliery.

'West Auckland Clothing factory you worked at? Have you a reference?' The personnel officer looked over his glasses at Rose.

'No. Well, I left a while back. My mother died and I had to look after the house,' she replied.

'I see.'

He glanced at her application form but hesitated for only a minute; he was chronically short of machinists. And he knew Elsie Sharpe, who was a respectable woman.

When Rose came out of Ransome's, she had a job on the sewing-machine belt, earning two pounds a week basic and more if she was fast enough. The machinists were on piece work.

'I start tomorrow, Aunt Elsie, making raincoats at Ransome's,' she cried as she came in the back door, flushed with success. And stopped dead, the smile wiped from her face when she saw who was standing in front of the fire, his hands folded in front of him, face red and blotched with anger.

'No, you bloody well don't,' said Alf, his voice not raised but harsh with the strength of his rage.

'Your dad's here for you,' said Aunt Elsie, coming out of the pantry, wiping her hands on a tea towel. She looked anxiously from one to the other. 'Now, Alf, don't be hard on the lass,' she said. 'She missed the bairns, that was what it was.'

'I'll not be hard, I'm a reasonable man,' he replied, not looking at his sister but at Rose. 'She said she would stay wi' me, see to my needs, and I let the twins come to you. It was agreed.'

'I cannot stay any longer, Dad,' Rose managed to say, though her throat felt as if it was closing up. She was strangling with fear and revulsion. Waves of heat washed over her. For a while, a very short while it had turned out to be, she had thought he wouldn't have the nerve to follow her in case she told and someone believed her. But that was only a dream, she saw that now.

'Can you not? Well, then, mebbe the twins can't stay here any longer either. What do you think of that?' Rose sat down suddenly, before she fell.

'Alf! What do you mean? You can't take them back now, they've settled in, they go to school here. Alf, be reasonable, man!' Elsie paled and screwed up her face in anxiety.

'Aye. But I'm their father, Elsie. I'm their legal guardian. I'll take them if I damn well want to.'

'No, you won't, Dad,' Rose said, lifting her chin, the dizziness receding.

Alf nodded. He scratched his stubbly chin and smiled, and somehow his smile looked far worse, Alf smiling looked far more menacing than Alf in a rage.

Rose looked down at the cheap linoleum with which Elsie had covered the cement floor, tracing the abstract pattern of red and blue on brown to where it disappeared under the clippie mat. She tried to gather her resources. She had to win this one, she *had* to.

'You won't take the twins,' she said. Her voice sounded strong and calm in her own ears which was strange because she was quaking inside.

'No, of course he's not going to take the twins,' said her aunt. 'They're far better off here. They've made friends, they're happy here. Alf?' It was a plea.

Her brother looked at her. 'Pull yourself together, woman,' he snapped. 'If you want to keep them, talk to little Rosie here, it's up to her. Well, Rose?'

'Aunt Elsie, I'm sorry. I can't go back, really I cannot.'

'But why not? He's your dad, for goodness' sake. You owe him something, don't you?'

'Nothing at all. Nothing but misery,' declared Rose. She folded her arms in front of her, holding herself; she was as tense as a coiled spring, her mouth dry.

'What are you talking about?' Aunt Elsie's mouth was slack, the question came out in a wail.

'I think you know what I'm talking about.'

'I don't! If you're talking that filth you said when your poor mam died, I don't believe you. I don't believe a word of it! I told meself it was because you were so upset over your mam but if you start saying such things again, I'll never forgive you, I'm telling you!'

'Whether you believe it or not, it's true,' Rose said and stared grimly at her father. All the times he had threatened her, all the times he had used her, even when her mother was in the house, all the misery she had undergone because of the evil that was her father, *her own flesh and blood*, the hell of it, the thought that it could all happen again with Mary...it all came to a head. She got to her feet and screamed at him, screamed at them both, brother and sister.

'He wouldn't leave me alone, not even when Mam was there! He still won't, can't you see? I only stayed because he said he would take the twins back. Dear God, Aunt Elsie, can't you see what would happen to Mary if he did? I thought you loved her.'

She was standing now, legs astride and hands on her hips, her head thrust forward as she shouted at them both, for Elsie Sharpe had run to her brother, both of them braced as though facing an enemy. Alf was panting, fists opening and closing at his sides, Elsie as red-faced and furious as her niece. Then she spoke, or hissed rather, through her teeth.

'Nothing is going to happen to Mary – nothing, I'm telling you. Nowt will happen because she's staying here with *me*, isn't she, Alf? Not that I'm saying anything would happen if she went back with her dad, because it wouldn't. You're a filthy-minded little bitch, Rose, and I wouldn't mind betting you're not Alf's bairn at all, if the truth be known! You don't take after the Sharpes, that's for sure. I always wondered about your mother –'

'I wish to heaven I wasn't his!' cried Rose. 'Especially now. Most especially now. I cannot go back, I tell you, I cannot! I'm going to have a baby!' She raised a finger and pointed it at Alf. '*His* baby it is. Ask him. If he denies it, he's lying in his teeth.'

'Oh, so that's it, is it? You're going to have a nameless brat and think you'll blacken your dad's name by blaming it on him? My God, you're pathetic' Elsie stepped forward and slapped Rose across the face so that her head rocked over to one side and her ears rang. When she'd recovered slightly, Rose turned to her father, filled with despair now. She had only one course left to her.

'I'm going to the Welfare,' she said. 'I'll tell them – I will. I swear I don't care any more who knows. I don't – I only care about the twins!'

Alf Sharpe stepped forward. He had said little so far

and nothing at all to Rose; he now simply drew back his
fist, hardened by years in the mines, and drove it into her
stomach. She fell to the ground and her head hit the brass
rail of Aunt Elsie's fender and she was out like a light.

Chapter Seventeen

'We don't usually allow personnel to take an afternoon like this, especially at such short notice,' said Mr Brown. He was manager over all the accounting machine offices in the Treasurer's Department, the comptometers and the Burroughs, accounting machines besides the office where Marina worked.

'But I'll take it as a lieu day,' she said. 'And the work is up to date.'

'Well, as Tuesday isn't a particularly busy day,' Mr Brown conceded, 'go on then.'

Anyone would think he was doing me a special favour, thought Marina as she hurried into her outdoor things and raced along Old Elvet to the bus station. She hardly felt the sharp wind as she climbed the hill and on, down Silver Street. Her thoughts were of Rose and how she had got on.

Rose's aunt would be sure to take her in, Marina told herself. Of course she would. She shuddered with revulsion as she thought of Alf Sharpe. The piece of slime!

He wouldn't have the nerve to go after Rose, of course he wouldn't. Dad had said he was off work, but that was probably because he'd been on the beer last Sunday. Marina checked in her bag to make sure she had the letter from Jeff. It was her excuse for coming, really.

She ate the sandwiches Kate had prepared for her lunch as the bus ambled slowly through Sherburn and out into the country. The autumn sun shone through the window and warmed her and Marina began to feel quite optimistic. Rose was going to be all right. But, mind, if only there was some way of seeing Alf Sharpe got his just desserts without spreading Rose's name all over the *Northern Echo*, Marina would be even happier.

Getting off the bus on Front Street, she easily found 14 West Row, the address Rose had given her. The back street seemed to be the best way in and she walked up the yard to the back door and knocked. There was no reply. Marina stepped back and looked at the window but the curtains were drawn. The upstairs window was the same, nothing to see there. She knocked again. Perhaps they were at the front. After a moment or two, she called through the letter box. Still no response. There was a string hanging inside, she felt its weight with two fingers, but there was no key hanging on it as surely there would be if Elsie and Rose had just slipped out to the shops.

Disappointed, Marina walked back to the gate before looking behind her at the house. There was no smoke from the chimney, it looked as though it was empty. Was it the wrong house?

'Marina! Marina!'

As she stepped through the gate there were the twins, Michael and Mary, coming down the road hand in hand. Of course, it was half-past three. The infant schools would be finished for the day, she realised with relief.

'Hallo, loves,' she cried, stepping forward to meet them and kissing them both on the cheek, a gesture which Michael at least found not to his liking. He rubbed vigorously at the spot with a decidedly grubby fist. 'I'm looking for Rose, but she doesn't seem to be in.'

'Why, no, she's not, she went back to Jordan,' said Mary, the smile leaving her face. 'She didn't even say goodbye, Marina. When you see her, tell her we're not speaking to her for not saying goodbye.'

'You might as well have stopped at home!' chortled Michael. 'Did you not see her? She went yesterday – last night after we'd gone to bed.'

'But where's your Aunt Elsie?' asked Marina. Before the twins could answer a woman came out of the next-door house. 'Come away in wi' me, pets,' she called to the twins. 'I'll give you your teas. Your auntie had to go somewhere.' She was a tiny, thin woman, hardly up to Marina's shoulder, her greying hair scraped back into a bun, nose red and sore as though she had a cold. 'An' who are you?' she asked, looking Marina up and down. 'You're not from round here, I'll be bound.'

'No, she's not, Mrs Todd,' cried Michael. 'She's come from Jordan to see our Rose but she's too late. Rose went home.'

'Aye, well, you two'd better get in by the fire, it's a cold day.' She waited until they had disappeared into the house. 'You might as well go home, lass. Like they said, there's nobody in next door. An' I cannot stand here, I'll catch me death of pneumonia.'

'But didn't Elsie say where she was going? I have come a long way,' Marina protested.

'I'm not one to pry,' Mrs Todd said. She pulled the grey cardigan she was wearing tighter round her thin frame. 'By, I'm nithered an' all. I'd ask you in but it's better you should go home, the nights are drawing in now, aren't they? It's a long way to Bishop Auckland. That's right, isn't it? Where the bairns come from?' She turned away into her own yard but then came back. 'Elsie's brother was here last night, I saw him turn in to her gate. Mebbe your friend went back wi' him.'

No! No, she didn't, she wouldn't, Marina wanted to shout, but she only stared at Mrs Todd in disbelief. After the woman had gone into the house Marina hung about irresolutely. Should she go on home as Mrs Todd advised? Or should she wait for Elsie Sharpe to come back from wherever she had gone, as she surely would? After all, she had the twins to see to. Mrs Todd didn't look the sort to mind them for very long at a time. What a waste of her lieu day this was! And if Rose had gone back with her dad, she was no further forward. But no, she never would. Marina pictured the struggle on the fell on Sunday morning and shuddered. Dear Lord, don't let her do anything silly.

Sitting in a cafe on Front Street as she waited for a bus, Marina sipped strong milky tea and tried to eat a tasteless scone with half a dozen currants in it and spread with lumpy yellow margarine. She took a couple of bites and then stared out of the window at the darkening street, crumbling the scone between her fingers, hardly knowing she was doing it.

Miners were walking past on their way home from the pit, their faces and clothes clean and shining, unlike the 'black boys' of home. Of course, there were pithead baths here, had been since before the war. There were at Easington too, she remembered Brian saying so. The pithead baths at Jordan were under construction at last, the men had even been issued with cheap bath towels. Her thoughts ran on inconsequentially, anything to ease her worry about Rose for a few minutes. She never realised that she hadn't thought of her own troubles for days.

A bus drew up to the stop opposite and people got off and walked across the road, women with shopping baskets mostly and one or two children in school uniform – grammar-school kids, she judged. Looking up at the destination plate on the front of the bus, she read 'Easington Colliery' and on impulse jumped up and ran across to it, dodging a car which honked angrily at her, thinking the bus would set off without her if she didn't hurry. She needn't have bothered, there was a queue at the stop which had been hidden by the bus; it was slowly filing aboard.

She had to stand for most of the way, hanging on with one hand as they lurched around corners on the narrow roads, awkwardly looking for pence for her fare. When she finally got a seat she drew out the letter from Jeff to Rose. There was no address on the back, she hadn't thought there was but checked just in case. Should she open it? She grinned at herself. No, of course she shouldn't, but she was going to, she needed Jeff's address.

Briefly she considered changing her mind and finding her way back to Jordan. Brian had Jeff's address, she could get it from him. But she would have to tell him something of what was happening, he would wonder why she wanted it otherwise. Anyway she was practically there now, it would be daft to go back. She opened the envelope: 9, Greenwood Street. Well, that should be easy to find. She resisted the temptation to read further, though she couldn't help noticing the beginning: 'My Dearest Rose'. It made her feel better about what she was doing somehow. Jeff thought the world of Rose, always had, even at school. He would help her.

When Marina eventually found the house it was Jeff himself who answered the door and stared at her in surprise.

'Marina Morland! What on earth are you doing here?'

'Hallo, Jeff. I'm looking for Rose. Is she here with you?'

'Rose? My Rose? Why should she be here?' He stepped forward on to the step, sudden anxiety sharpening his voice. Drops of rain fell on to his head and trickled down his face unheeded.

'Can I come in, Jeff?' asked Marina, dispirited. She began to realise how wet she was herself. The walk from the bus stop was quite long and had been made longer by her losing her way once or twice despite getting directions from people passing by. She shivered, feeling that if she didn't sit down in the warm soon she would fall down.

'Eeh, I'm sorry, come on in,' he said and stood aside to let her pass. 'The landlady's out tonight, I have the house to myself. Come away into the kitchen, there's a good fire on.' He ushered her into a room very similar to her own mother's kitchen, A range polished to a shine with black lead, the brass fittings twinkling in the light from the heaped-up fire. There was a bright flowery wallpaper on the walls and a settee with plump cushions. And either side of the fire, a pair of armchairs, deep and soft.

'Now what's this all about?' he asked as soon as she had removed her soaking wet coat and sat down before the comforting blaze. 'What made you think Rose was here?'

'I didn't really, it was just – well, I thought she might be.'

'Come on now, tell me what it's all about.'

And so Marina told him, not the whole story, not about what Alf Sharpe had done, not about Rose falling wrong.

But how unhappy she had been living with her father, how she had cried about it on Sunday when they went up the fell, how she herself had advised Rose to go to Shotton. 'She missed the bairns such a lot you see,' she said.

'But surely, she'd been there all this time since her mother died, she never told me she was that unhappy,' said Jeff. 'I mean, for her to up sticks and leave, without speaking to Alf, I don't know.'

'Yes, well, there was more,' said Marina. But she couldn't say it. In the end she simply added, 'She missed you though, Jeff, you being so far away. And Shotton's only a few miles from here, isn't it? Likely she thought she would be near you.'

'Did she? Did she really?' He sounded delighted but only for a few seconds. 'Aye, but she went back, didn't she? When Alf came for her, you said.'

Marina bit her lip, looking puzzled. 'You know, I can hardly believe it. If you'd seen her on Sunday...she was so upset, vowing she couldn't stay in Jordan. And besides, what about Elsie? Where is she? The house is empty, like I said, the twins are being looked after by the neighbour.'

Marina sat back in the chair. It was *so* comfortable, and what with the heat from the fire...she felt suddenly exhausted, exhausted and despondent and filled with worry for her friend. She glanced at her watch. Eight o'clock already, the time had flown by and she hadn't discovered a thing.

'I'll have to go, Jeff,' she said, forcing herself to sit

upright. 'I'll have to catch the number eighteen bus from Easington Lane, I'm not even sure how to get there. But if I don't, I won't catch the last bus to Bishop Auckland at Spennymoor.'

'No, no, you don't have to do any of that,' he replied. 'Sit a minute, I'll make you some Ovaltine or something, it'll make you feel better. Then I'll take you home. I've got a car now.' He said it all as if his mind was on something else, though he got to his feet and filled a pan with milk and put it on the bar. He brought a couple of cups from the dresser by the side of the fireplace and spooned Ovaltine into them, all the time working automatically but efficiently. 'I'll go to see Alf Sharpe,' he said abruptly. 'I'll get to the bottom of this.'

Marina sank back into her chair, grateful for someone else to take over. She looked at Jeff, doing a small domestic task, but obviously a man she could depend upon. Like Brian, she thought suddenly. Jeff would find Rose. She drank the Ovaltine when he handed it to her, felt her eyelids drooping. Next minute he was shaking her gently by the shoulder.

'Come on, lass, wake up, we're on our way,' he said and she stumbled to her feet. They set off on the thirty-or-so-mile journey to Jordan, taking the Spennymoor road rather than that to Durham. At Shotton Colliery they did a short detour into the village to look again at Elsie Sharpe's house, leaving the car at the end of the row and both of them walking down to the gate and looking in. The rain had stopped and moonlight lit the yard but there was no light from the windows. Jeff went in and knocked at the door but there was no response.

Marina stood at the gate, her arms folded together against the cold. She had hoped Elsie and Rose would be there, and have some simple explanation of where they had been earlier in the day, but there was no one. At least . . . she thought she saw a shadow move at the upstairs window, a flicker of something. But, no, it must have been a trick of the moonlight, the house was empty.

'Howay, lass, back to the car,' said Jeff. 'You look absolutely nithered.' He took her arm and hurried her down the back street.

'The twins must be sleeping with Mrs Todd,' Marina said thoughtfully, and Jeff nodded.

'Very good of a neighbour to go to such trouble, isn't it?'

It was too, thought Marina. Unless something terrible had happened, like someone in the family being carted off to hospital or dying. She didn't mention her fears to Jeff. After all, he probably had his own.

They were very quiet as they drove on, through Coxhoe and Spennymoor and on to the Bishop Auckland road. It was almost ten o'clock when Jeff drew up before the Morland house.

'Mam's going to be furious at me being so late,' said Marina, thinking of it for the first time. 'She'll be stotting mad.'

'I'll come in with you, if you like?' Jeff offered. 'I'll explain.'

'Oh, no, I'll be all right. But what about you? Are you going straight home?'

'I'm going to call on Alf Sharpe first,' he replied grimly.

'Look, come back here later, Mam'll give you supper,' Marina suggested. 'I'd like to know if Rose is there, and what happened. Besides, it's a long way back to Easington.'

'Yes, I will. Thanks.'

Just as Marina had thought, Kate was stotting mad.

'Why didn't you say where you were going? You know how I hate to waste food and I'd made you a hot pot. It'll be ruined now. I've been sitting here, with your dad at work on night shift and Lance goodness knows where... I think he's got a lass by the way... and I've been worried to death about where you were... By, our Marina, how could you be so thoughtless?'

'I'm sorry. I am, Mam. But I thought I'd be back sooner.'

She hardly had the story told when there was a knock at the door and Jeff was back and if anyone looked worried to death it was him.

'Alf Sharpe's not there, Marina,' he said after greeting Kate. 'No one's there at all. The house is as empty as his sister's.'

'But Rose *has* to be there!' cried Marina. 'Where is she, Jeff?'

Chapter Eighteen

There is someone knocking, the sound is very faint but insistent. Rose struggles but no matter how hard she tries she cannot move. She must move, she must get to the door to let him in, the children are depending on her. Mary is in terrible danger; Rose knows it but Mary doesn't. She is in the corner cupboard, playing with her dolly. The door is slightly open and she looks through the gap at Rose then scrambles to her feet.

'No! Don't come, stay there, Mary,' Rose is shouting but no sound is coming from her. Dear God, help me, she prays. Don't let them go away. Michael... where are you, Michael? Answer the door, Michael, please. But Michael isn't there, he is in the cupboard with Mary. He pulls the door to. Yes, that's right, Michael, hide.

Rose struggles to move, to get away from the figures hovering over her. If she could only move her little finger, that's it, concentrate on moving a finger, a hand, anything.

'God in heaven, why did you do that?'

A woman's voice, she knows it, it's... no, the

knowledge of who it is is elusive, on the edge of her mind, but whoever it is, it's not the woman who is threatening her, Rose is sure of that. Help me, please, she begs silently, and a pain rips through her body, a pain such as she has never experienced before, a sharp, burning pain. The man leans forward. He has a knife, that's what it is, he's cutting into her stomach, killing her, and after that he will kill Mary...

Rose screams, the sound loud and shrill in her ears, shocking in its terrible intensity. But it won't go past her mouth, except for a low moan. The man puts a hand over her mouth, she can't breathe, she is slipping away. A nightmare, that's what it is, only a nightmare, a voice inside her head is saying, calming, peaceful. Sleep now.

'She's dying,' said Elsie. She was weeping and staring at her hands in horror. They were covered in blood. There was a terrible mess in the bed, great clots of blood and a watery substance. 'Alf, Alf!' she sobbed. 'Go away and let me clean the poor lass up. You should have let me get the doctor –'

'Don't be so flaming soft! We can't have a doctor poking his nose in here. You'd lose the bairns then, I can tell you. We'd both likely end up in Durham gaol an' all. You can see to her, can't you? You've had plenty of miscarriages in your time, you know what goes on.'

'She's lost too much blood, Alf, I'm frightened. What am I going to do?'

Elsie was shaking but she scooped the mess on to newspaper with her hands, trembling as she touched the slimy stuff, bundling it quickly into a parcel, glad to have it hidden from her sight.

'Give it here, I'll put it on the kitchen fire.' Her brother took his hand away from Rose's face and snatched the bundle and headed off down the stairs. As he did so Rose's head dropped to the side, her mouth fell open and Elsie jumped back as a low sound came from deep in her niece's throat. The figure on the bed was still, quiet, the eyes not quite shut.

'I'm sorry, Rose,' said Elsie. 'I am, really. But I *have* to do it. I have to for the sake of the bairns, you know that.'

She started to change the bed then stopped and drew the covers up over Rose. She hardly knew what she was doing. This was the second night of horror. People had been knocking on the door, she was terrified Mrs Todd had heard something. Elsie had had no sleep for almost forty-eight hours and felt as though her head was about to burst but she knew she wouldn't be able to sleep again. She stood by the bed, her hands hanging by her side, the stench of blood and urine in her nostrils. Everything was unreal, she thought, she was floating, swimming in a dark, murky nightmare. But it was all for the twins, she had to remember that. It was all for the sake of the twins.

How long ago was it that she had seen them, sent them off to school? It seemed like years. She marvelled at how they had stayed asleep through all the long night before, not hearing anything, accepting the story she told them of how Rose had gone home with their father. How normal she had been when she had asked Mrs Todd to see to them, said she had to go to visit a dying relative, a cousin, see to her. Well, it was true in a way, wasn't it? The twins had accepted that story too. They had gone obediently to Mrs Todd, it was a small adventure for them. She had kissed them goodbye, the skin of their cheeks warm and soft on her lips.

She and Alf had been lucky so far. Of course, the luck might not last. How could it? There was still Rose, though there was no longer the shame of a baby coming. Rose wouldn't tell, even if she lived.

Elsie looked at her, lying there, white and still. There was no more bleeding. Did that mean she was dead already? She bent to the bed, her ear to Rose's lips. Could she hear anything, feel breath on her cheek? If Rose was dead and they were found out and she and Alf went to gaol, what would happen to the twins? It would be all for nothing, then!

'Alf, Alf, why did you have to do it?' she moaned and began trembling again.

'Pull yourself together, Elsie. You're standing there like a gormless fool! Come on, I've worked out what I'm going to do. Howay now, you have to help me.'

Elsie jumped, her heart beat wildly, painfully, in her chest. She hadn't heard him come back into the bedroom.

'What? What do you mean? Oh, Alf, I think the poor lass has gone. Eeh, you shouldn't have done it, Alf, you shouldn't have. What did you hit her for? Alf, Alf...' Her voice was rising out of control and he grabbed her by the upper arms and shook her until she broke off and stared at him, frightened for herself now, eyes large and uncomprehending in her white face.

'Stop that. Damn well stop it! Now!'

'Don't hit me, Alf,' she whimpered, shrinking.

'I'm not bloody well going to hit you,' he snapped impatiently. 'Now come on! Wrap her up in an old sheet or something. No, I've changed my mind. Put her clothes on, her coat an' all. We're taking her out of here.'

'But someone will see!'

'No, they won't. The night-shift men are home by now, the fore-shift ones already away. The place is quiet, this is the best time to do it.'

Between them they struggled to dress Rose's unresisting body. Her head sagged on her chest; her arms flopped like a rag doll's, would go in any direction but the armholes of her coat. Alf swore.

At last she was ready. He crammed her shoes on to her feet and picked her up in his arms. She was light as a doll too, thin and bony. Her shoulder bone stuck uncomfortably into his chest. He hoisted her higher.

'Why, aye, look,' he said to his sister, 'I can manage her fine. You stay here and clean up. I won't come back, it'll be dawn in an hour or two.'

'But, Alf, what am I going to do? What if someone asks...'

'Flaming hell, woman, you always were a bloody fool! Say nowt! Didn't you tell that woman next door that me and Rose had gone home? Then why is anybody going to ask you anything?'

'But, Alf –'

'Buck up, will you? I can't stand here all morning holding her. Get out of my way!' He shoved her aside with his free shoulder and went down the dark stairs, surefooted, used to the dark of the pit. She followed him, weeping quietly, stood with the door open looking out, long after he had disappeared down the street.

It was very dark now, the few street lights out. Suddenly a light appeared at the bedroom window next door.

'Who's that? Say who you are now or I'll get the polis!'

Elsie froze, unable to speak, her tears turned off like a tap.

'George? George? Run for the polis, now. There's a burglar next door.'

'No, Mrs Todd,' Elsie found her voice. 'No, it's me, I came home early, me cousin's better.' She scrabbled around for a reason why she should come home so early in the morning. 'I'll be here to make the bairns their breakfast, Mrs Todd, I won't have to bother you with that. Thanks for everything.' She sagged against the door frame.

'Eeh, I'm glad it's you! I was getting worried, I thought I heard something before. It would just be you coming in, was it? Well, I'll get back to bed. There's two hours yet before I have to get up.'

'Yes. Sorry I woke you,' said Elsie, and forced her reluctant legs to carry her inside. Shutting the door behind her she leaned against it and closed her eyes for a minute. Then she gathered up a bowl of hot water and some cleaning rags. She would concentrate on that, keep her mind off whatever Alf was doing.

Rose was cold, very very cold. She turned over on to her side. The bed was hard, that was the trouble with camp beds. Aunt Elsie still hadn't got her another bed. She must have lost her pillow and there was a dull throbbing ache at the pit of her stomach. A period pain? A bad one. She turned over on to her back and a sharper pain shot through her. She cried out and a weight landed on her. She caught her breath in agony.

'Get off, Michael,' she tried to shout but it came out in only a whisper. A tongue licked her cheek. She opened her eyes in shock. An inch or so from her face a pair of large brown eyes looked into hers, a silky ear brushed against her cheek. She flailed weakly with her arms and managed to dislodge the spaniel from her stomach. Where on earth was she? Bewildered she tried to sit up but to her surprise found herself unable to. Weakly she tried to push herself up on her elbows but her arms wouldn't work properly, they wouldn't hold her. The effort exhausted her she felt herself sinking into a black hole.

'Come here, Trix. Here, I'm telling you!' a man's voice shouted from a very long way away. 'What's that you've found?' The light returned temporarily. There was a man and he was right beside her, a grey-haired man with a white scarf tied round his neck. He leaned over her.

'Bloody hell!' he exclaimed. And, 'Get off, Trix, get back, I say! Eeh, lass, what the heck happened to you?'

Rose opened her mouth to tell him she hadn't the slightest idea but the blackness was coming back, drowning out the sunshine which was filtering through the leaves of the tree above her.

'Hang on, lass, hang on,' said the man, though she didn't hear him. He slipped the lead on his dog and tied her to a bush then took off his mac and wrapped it round Rose. His white scarf next. He folded it and put it under her head, careful to move her as little as possible. He was a deputy at the pit and a member of the St John's Ambulance Brigade, with medals and bars to his credit, trained to deal with accidents. Though the lass didn't seem to have broken anything so far as he could tell. Had she lain out here all night?

'Stay here,' he ordered the dog, and she gave a small bark and sat down obediently. Satisfied he'd done all he could for the minute, the man got to his feet and ran up the side of the wooded incline of the dene, panting as he reached the top. Too many tabs, he told himself. He would have to cut down on the cigarettes, that was for sure.

It was a fair way along the path to the road but he didn't have to go all the way. A mate was just turning into the dene with his whippet.

'Call an ambulance, Jimmy!' the first man shouted. 'There's a lass here, and mind, she's in a bad way an' all.'

He hardly waited for an acknowledgement, was well acquainted with the owner of the whippet who would waste no time in getting to the phone box. He hurried back to the girl and bent anxiously over her.

It was warm in the bed; deliriously, gorgeously, luxuriously warm. It was the first thing Rose was aware of as she dragged herself out of the blackness. Through her eyelids she saw the brightness of the sun above her. No, that couldn't be right, how could she be in bed and under the sun? She struggled to open her eyes.

The bright light was electric. There was a row of them, stretching away down a ward. Her arm was tied to a board and there was a needle in it. It pricked when she moved.

'Keep still now,' a soft voice warned and she turned her head and there was a nurse in a navy-blue dress and white apron, one of those funny caps on her head. Rose stared at her, speechless.

'Would you like a little drink?' the nurse asked, and Rose nodded. The nurse held her head up from the pillow with one hand and a glass to her lips with the other. Rose drank greedily until the glass was taken away. It was orange juice, reconstituted like the 'baby' orange which was issued to infants since the National Health came in.

'Where am I?' Rose asked, her voice coming out croaky. She cleared her throat weakly.

'The Cameron,' the nurse replied. 'Lie quiet now, I'll fetch the doctor.'

The Cameron? What and where was the Cameron? Rose wondered. But she didn't really care. She was here in a warm bed and the drink had been delicious. She had an ache in her stomach but it wasn't too bad. It had been worse, much worse when...Weak tears ran down her cheeks. She rubbed at them with her free hand. She stopped thinking about then, now was all right. Now she was safe and warm and there was the nice nurse to help her.

'So you've decided to join us, have you, young lady?' The voice was young and jolly and kind. Oh, yes, the doctor, she remembered. The nurse had said he was coming.

'I'm Dr Morris. How do you feel now?' he asked, automatically feeling her pulse, looking at the drip in her arm, making notes on the clipboard he held.

'Better,' she said and he nodded, smiling professionally, and hooked a foot under a chair and pulled it to the side of the bed so he could sit down. A nurse came hurrying up with a screen.

'Never mind that now,' said the doctor, 'I'm just taking notes.' Rose watched him. He was shining clean, red hair brushed back from his freckled face, nails manicured short, white at the edges. She curled her own uneven nails out of sight.

'First of all, we need to know who you are. You hadn't an identity card on you when you were found.'

'Found?'

'In Shotton Dene. Can't you remember?'

Oh, yes. The grass, the spaniel, the grey-haired man.

'I didn't know where it was.'

'What do you remember?'

Rose was silent. She remembered her dad. Oh, yes, she remembered him hitting her in the stomach and the pain. She remembered Aunt Elsie's white face, staring as she fell.

'Your name then, that'll be a start.'

'I don't remember.'

Dr Morris sighed. 'Come on now, I know you hurt your head but it's not too serious. Are you sure you don't remember?'

'I don't. And my head *is* aching, there's a bump here, look...'

'I know. You were examined thoroughly when you were brought in.' He decided on a more direct approach. 'You know you have lost the baby?'

The baby! Her hand went to her stomach. It felt sore, tender. Rose turned her eyes away from him. All she could feel was an overwhelming relief. Instinctively she knew she shouldn't let him see that.

His voice hardened. 'Did you do something to yourself, is that it? You know it's an offence to try to abort a baby?'

Tears began to roll from her eyes silently and he stood up immediately, changing tactic again.

'Look, I don't think you did but I had to ask, it's the law. Lie quiet now, you have a bad bruise in the abdominal area. Staff Nurse will bring you some broth shortly. It's past suppertime but I'm sure she'll find some in the kitchens. Then you can have a tablet and get some rest. That's what you need now. We'll talk in the morning.'

She watched him disappear down the corridor, go into a room to one side, heard his voice faintly. He was talking it over with someone. If they thought she'd done it herself, the police would come, she knew, and she would be arrested. Maybe that was right, she should be punished.

The nurse brought chicken broth. Rose didn't think she would be able to take any but it was delicious. The nurse was cheerful, eyes full of sympathy when Rose could bring herself to look her in her face, for she'd expected condemnation.

The nurse spooned the broth into her mouth, talking softly all the time. The lights in the rest of the ward were already dimmed, the patients quiet under the covers.

'My name is Staff Nurse Benton. Rosalie Benton,' she said.

'Oh! I'm called…emm, Lily.' Now why did she say that? It was stupid. But she had to give some name and Lily was as good as anything. The staff nurse looked pleased.

Rose took all the broth, and a cup of tea afterwards with a small pink tablet. Her head throbbed, her abdomen hurt, her arm ached. But she lay down on the pillow and gradually everything faded away and she slept.

Chapter Nineteen

'I don't know, Brian, I really don't know what to do,' said Marina. 'If she's not at Shotton and she's not here in Jordan, where is she?'

'We'll find her. Girls don't just disappear, not in this day and age,' he replied. 'Jeff had to go back to Easington, but you know him. He won't rest until he finds her.'

Brian put an arm around Marina's shoulders and hugged her comfortingly. 'Did you ever think maybe she just wanted to get away by herself? You know what Alf Sharpe's like, the slimy toad! You couldn't blame any girl for wanting to lose herself if she had him for a father.'

She knew what Alf was like all right, better than Brian did. If he knew just what Alf had done . . . Marina shrugged away his arm and got to her feet. She walked to the window and looked out at the tiny garden. The flower bed under the window was bare so late in the year, except for a clump of Christmas roses just coming into bud. It would soon be Christmas, she thought. Rose had been gone for over a week now. Where was she? Marina asked herself for the thousandth time. Surely if she was all right she would have got in touch by now?

'Will you come with me to see Alf Sharpe again?' she asked.

'Oh, I don't know...' Marina turned round sharply and frowned at Brian and he changed his mind abruptly. 'All right. But it won't make any difference. You know what he's like.'

They had gone with Jeff to Alf's house on the Wednesday night. At least Alf was at home then, the light was on in the kitchen, though the curtains were drawn and they couldn't see anything. He didn't answer their knock at first but Jeff persevered, thumping with his fist on the wooden panel of the door.

'Come on, answer the door!' he shouted. 'We know you're in there, Alf Sharpe!'

There was an exclamation from inside and eventually the door opened. Alf stood in the doorway, barring their entrance.

'It's you, you young buggers, is it? And what the hell do you want? I don't know how you have the nerve to come round here, disturbing a man's peace,' he snarled.

'We want to see Rose,' said Jeff. 'Where is she?'

'You do, do you? Haven't I told you not to come sniffing round my lass?'

'Stand aside, we're coming in,' said Jeff. 'I'm not prepared to have this out on the step.' He shouldered the older man to one side and marched into the kitchen. In the short time since Rose had gone, the appearance of the room had undergone a dramatic change. There were dirty cups on the table, spilt grease on the bar of the range. To one side was a tin bath holding cold, black, scummy water. A pile of pit clothes was laid over the white cover on the back of the couch, specks of coal which must have fallen off them glistened there. He must be going to work then, surmised Marina. Yet he stank of spirit, his face covered in stubble and his eyes bloodshot. Surely not even Alf Sharpe would go down the pit drunk? And him an overman.

'Where is she?' demanded Jeff.

'Well, she's not here, is she? What did you think, I had her tied up somewhere?' Alf was looking even shiftier than normal, Marina reckoned. He didn't meet Jeff's eyes when he answered but hawked and spat into the fire, then lit a cigarette with trembling fingers, drawing hard on it so that it burned halfway down its length.

'I wouldn't put it past you,' growled Jeff. 'You made the poor lass's life a nightmare.'

'Go on then, have a look,' Alf snarled. 'Gan on! I'm not stopping you.' He gestured with the hand holding the cigarette, dropping an arc of ash on the mat.

'I will,' said Jeff. 'Come on, Marina, come with me. You stay there, Brian.'

Marina followed him up the stairs, though she had a fair idea Alf was telling the truth. Rose wasn't here. And so it proved. The only signs of her were a few clothes hanging in a wardrobe.

'What did I tell you?' Alf said truculently when they returned to the kitchen.

'Well, she's somewhere, Mr Sharpe,' said Marina. 'And she's not at Shotton, I went to see and she's not there. And your sister's neighbour said she had come back here with you.'

'You're a sight too interested in our business!' Alf flared up suddenly, rising from his chair and taking up a threatening posture over the girl.

Brian stepped in front of Marina protectively. 'Don't you bully her!' he said. 'She's only trying to find out where her friend is. Anybody would think you'd be worried about Rose's whereabouts too.' He turned his head to Marina. 'Go on, go outside, pet. We won't be but a minute.'

'Aye, you can all of you get outside. Go on, I'm going to work, you're holding me up. If our Rose has gone off, what can I do about it? Here, look about you. She's left me in a right mess, hasn't she? No one to see to the place –'

'Aw, shut your mouth!' snapped Jeff contemptuously. 'We're going anyway.'

Outside Marina couldn't help breathing a sigh of relief. Since Rose's revelations she hated to be in the same room as Alf Sharpe. Her skin had crawled in his presence. For the first time she realised what the saying meant. It literally felt as though it was crawling. She shuddered and Brian took her hand.

'Never mind, pet,' he said. 'Rose must be all right or we would have seen something in the paper.'

They walked up the street to the end where Jeff's car was parked. 'I have to go, I'm on fore shift,' he said, but was reluctant, they could see. He kept looking back towards where Rose had lived.

'You'll let us know if you find anything out, won't you?' Marina asked.

'I will,' he promised. They watched as he climbed into the car, started the engine and set off, waving as he went.

Now it was Friday teatime and Marina had persuaded Brian to go with her to visit Alf Sharpe once again, see if they could find out something, anything, about where Rose was and what was happening to her. But after all it was a waste of time for the Sharpe house was empty.

'He might have had to go into the pit early,' said Brian. He glanced at Marina, could tell she had built herself up to confront Alf again and now was disappointed that he wasn't there.

'Never mind, love,' he said. 'I'm sure she's all right.'

'How can you be? Anything could have happened to her.'

'Well, we can't do anything about it now, can we?'

'If you had a car like Jeff's...'

'Yes, there's something to be said for having your own transport,' Brian said, rather wistfully.

'Can you afford a car?' asked Marina, rather startled at the possibility.

'Not really.' He grinned. 'Not if we're going to get

wed. But maybe a motorbike...' He watched her face for her reaction.

'A motorbike! By, Brian, that would be grand,' she exclaimed and they walked off down the road, arm in arm.

'I've seen a Norton I could afford, I think,' he confided. 'Come with me on Saturday, it's in Morrison's in Bishop.'

Later, as she lay in bed, Marina was horrified to realise she had almost forgotten about Rose for the remainder of the evening. Kate had commented that probably she had simply run away to be on her own. 'The lass is entitled to a life,' she had declared. 'Stop worrying about her all the time. She'd want you to get on with your own life, our Marina.'

Maybe that was true, she thought. But, by heck, she hoped and prayed that Rose hadn't come to any harm. Maybe she'd gone into one of those mother and baby homes which they'd heard about during the war and after. And if she needed help she would surely get in touch. She knew where they were, didn't she? But if Alf Sharpe brought the twins home to live with him, she, Marina Morland, wouldn't keep her mouth shut, no she wouldn't. She'd lay him in to the police, she would.

'How would you like to go home today, young lady?' Rose's face must have shown her dismay for Dr Morris stopped smiling and looked concerned. 'What's the matter? Don't you want to go home?'

'I can't, I'm never going home,' she said flatly. 'Anyway,

I can't recall where home is,' she added, remembering she
was supposed to have lost her memory.

He looked at her impatiently. 'Nonsense. Come on
now, Lily, we know you're putting it on. It often happens
with girls in your position. You don't think you're the first
to be afraid to tell your parents you've made a mistake,
do you? I'm sure your mother will be only too pleased to
have you back, she must have been worried to death.'

'My mother's dead.'

'Oh. Oh, I'm sorry, stupid of me.' He patted her hand
awkwardly. 'Your father getting married again, is that it?
I know that sometimes girls can't accept a stepmother,
sometimes they run wild. Is that what happened?'

'No, it isn't, Doctor. Please don't ask me.' Rose had
to accept that her story had worn far too thin to hold up
now but she certainly wasn't going to tell him the truth.
'Don't worry about me, Dr Morris, I'll be fine. I'll find a
room somewhere. And a job. I'm a sewing machinist, you
know. I can get work in a clothing factory, there are plenty
of them around here.'

Well pleased with the way he had got her thinking and
planning for her future, Dr Morris smiled. These silly
girls! How easily they were led astray by a man. No doubt
she had thought herself in love. He had a sudden idea and
made for the door. 'I'll be back in ten minutes or so,' he
said and went off down the ward.

Rose looked around her. Though the ward was spar-
tan with its worn furniture – shabby lockers by the iron

bedsteads standing in regimented rows down the sides of the ward, a steel cabinet at the end with a sink and boiler for sterilising instruments and such – it was bright and cheerful enough. Flowers stood on most lockers, and by the table in the centre patients who were mobile moved about chatting to those in bed. A cleaner was buffing the shining floor, a nurse pushing a trolley from bed to bed.

Rose liked it here. These few days had been a haven for her, she had felt safe. No one had actually pestered her to find out who she was, just a gentle questioning which she had resisted easily. She was grateful that she hadn't been reported to the police, accused of aborting her baby. She supposed it looked as though she had simply fallen on something and hurt herself. Her baby. The phrase sounded strange in her ears. She felt no distress at losing it, only relief. Was she unnatural? No, never, of course she wasn't. Instinctively she denied the thought.

The door at the entrance to the ward opened and Dr Morris came in, his open white coat flying behind him, stethoscope swinging from side to side around his neck.

'Just having a word with Lily, Sister,' he said as she looked up at him enquiringly and he walked over to Rose's bed.

'How would you like working in the sewing room here?' he asked. 'Just plain sewing, I know, but it's a job. It will help you get on to your feet.'

'Oh, could I? Is there a vacancy?'

'I saw it among the job opportunities in the main

entrance this morning. When you said you'd worked a sewing machine, I thought of it.' He smiled down at her. 'Of course, you'll have to have an interview but I'm sure it will be OK.' He walked to the end of the bed before turning back. 'And you'll have to give them your real name. And if you don't know where your identity card is, then you will have to apply for another.'

Rose had to give a sample of her sewing but she was good and fast from having to do piece work in the factory at West Auckland when she'd first left school. When she left the hospital, clutching a piece of paper with the address of what the almoner called 'a good, clean lodging house', she had the job.

'Start next Monday, nine o'clock sharp,' Mrs Timms said. She was the housekeeper, or domestic supervisor. 'It's mainly plain work, mending sheets and pillowcases and such, and keeping the uniforms in good order. We have a nice set of women here, friendly like. Two pounds ten shillings a week and your dinner.'

She had looked Rose over, noting her pale face, the shadows under her eyes. But Dr Morris had assured her that there was nothing really wrong with her, she just needed time and good food to build her up.

'Mind, don't you go gadding about this week, take it easy,' she advised. 'Some walks by the sea, that's what you need. I'm a believer in good sea air. Well, I'll see you next week, I haven't time to be standing here talking.' She had bustled off, keys jangling by her side, a round little woman with iron-grey hair pulled back in a bun that was fashionable three decades before.

Rose found the address on the paper easily. The room in the lodging house was tiny, up in the eaves of the old house near the docks, but it was clean and the narrow bed comfortable. The almoner had arranged for her to have an advance on her wages to be paid back at five shillings a week.

These first few weeks were going to be hard but she would manage. She had to. If only she had some assurance that Michael and Mary were all right. She felt so betrayed by Aunt Elsie, so alone. Yet surely her aunt wouldn't let anything bad happen to the twins? She loved them, didn't she? In bed that first night, in the strange room with the strange sounds from the sea and the docks, Rose cried a little. Then, determinedly, she wiped her eyes, blew her nose and turned over to sleep. Worrying would get her nowhere and she needed her health if she were to be able to help the twins at all. But inside she couldn't help weeping for them.

Chapter Twenty

'There's a letter for you,' said Mr Brown. 'Though why you should have your personal mail sent here I do not know.' He pretended to be stern but Marina knew him well by now, he was just a softie underneath. Besides, now she had the job on the tabulator and already had her sights on the next rung up the ladder, she was becoming quite an important cog in the accounting-machine department at least. After that, who could tell?

He picked up the letter and looked at the stamp. 'London, eh? Who do you know in London?' He caught her expression and, smiling, handed over the card. 'None of my business, eh? No, of course it isn't. Now we'd better get started – there's a lot to do today. Salaries, grants for university...' He sighed in mock sorrow. 'No one ever gave me a grant. Money for nothing, eh?'

'Yes, Mr Brown.' Marina's answer was mechanical. She was staring at the handwriting on the envelope, not taking in what was written at first. Waves of relief swept over her. Oh, thank God, Rose was all right, she was fine!

She had to be or she couldn't have written a letter, could she? Sometimes in the night when Marina woke or when she was feeling down, she had wondered if Rose was dead. Something could have happened to her. In the light of day she agreed with what Brian said must have happened: Rose had simply gone away, she was getting on with her own life. And here was proof. Marina tore open the envelope as she walked to her locker.

'*I'm OK, Marina,*' Rose had written. '*Living it up in London. I'll write again.*' Nothing else. No mention of Jeff or her baby or anything. No address. But she was all right, she said she was. Oh, praise be! Though as time had gone on the worry about Rose had faded into the background somewhat, it had still been there and now Marina felt as though it had rolled away. She couldn't wait to get home and see Brian.

'We'll go through to Easington and tell Jeff,' was the first thing he said. 'We'll go tomorrow. See, I told you she would be fine, didn't I?'

It was Friday evening and the couple were in Kate's kitchen. As usual Brian had called for Marina. They were off to the Majestic picture house where *The Greatest Show on Earth* was showing. The summer of 1949 was a warm one and Marina was wearing a starched cotton dress, white with red sprigs on it, and a red cardigan to match. She looked a picture, Brian thought proudly, her brown hair shining and healthy, cut in the shorter style now coming in with a fringe across her brow. She was so happy about Rose and it was good that she felt like that for her friend. Like himself and Jeff it was.

'Have you thought of telling Alf Sharpe?' asked Kate, and at Marina's blank look added, 'Well, don't you think he would be interested? He is her father, after all.'

'We should tell him, Marina,' said Brian quietly.

'Oh, you tell him if you like, I'm not going near the old toad,' she said flatly. 'Now, are you ready?'

'You're not going on the back of the motorbike dressed like that, are you, my girl?' demanded Kate, and Marina pulled a face but caught up her duster coat and took it with her.

She loved riding on the Norton, her arms around Brian's waist, her head pressed into his back and her hair wound up in a scarf against the wind. Passing the bus as it trundled its way into town was great. And it felt like they were flying down the last hill and then up again the other side, the engine loud in her ears as Brian revved up to reach the top.

They parked opposite the cinema and he took her arm as they crossed the road. He bought her Maltesers at the kiosk inside the foyer for at last sweets were off the ration. They sat in the back seat of the balcony and Brian put his arm around her shoulders and Marina felt warm and happy as they watched the main feature and ate the chocolates.

'We would have had to walk home if we hadn't had the bike,' she remarked as they came out into the moonlight. 'The last bus will have gone by now.' She lifted her wrist and peered at the watch which Brian had bought her for Christmas.

'It would have been great walking through the fields,' he said, grinning. 'No one else about. We could have got up to all sorts of things...'

'Oh, you!' said Marina and felt that familiar pang of excitement mixed with apprehension. Brian must have guessed there had been something between her and Charlie when he saw them together the afternoon of the wedding; that she and Charlie had gone 'all the way' as they said. Surely he had? But nothing had been said about it since then. Would he care that she was no longer a virgin? All the girls said a man could tell... Sometimes it had been hard to resist Brian when he kissed her, put his hands on her. Her body had leaped in response. But she had always managed to stop him before things went too far, fearful he would realise she was experienced. Experienced! She didn't feel experienced, it was a daft word to use.

Oh, what the heck! she told herself. She wasn't going to think about it. Brian started the bike and waited for her to climb aboard and she threw her leg over and tucked her skirt in decorously before leaning in to his back, hugging him to her. And away they went down Tenters Street and along the main shopping street to the road for Jordan. Brian stopped the bike at the yard gate and kissed her goodnight. Both of them had work to go to in the morning.

Marina hummed to herself as she ran up the yard to the back door, pulling off her scarf as she went. 'Hi, Mam,' she cried, in the manner of the actors she had been watching on the screen, 'it was a great –' She broke off as she saw her father sitting in his fireside chair, head bowed, and her mother standing over him, her hands balled into fists. Kate was shouting something at him, her face red with the exertion.

'I told you, Sam Morland, I *told* you!' Her voice was hoarse with shouting.

'What, Mam, what? What's the matter?' asked Marina, the fresh colour in her cheeks from the wind in her face beginning to drain away. Her heart began to thump as she looked from one parent to another. She hated these scenes which had occurred too frequently when she was younger.

Kate turned to her daughter. 'What do you think is the matter? What is it always with your father? It's the bloody gambling! Well, it's done for us this time. I'm telling you, the last straw, that's what it is. I'll never be able to hold me head up in Jordan again. Never, I tell you!'

'Oh, Mam, it cannot be that bad,' said Marina, desperately hoping it wasn't. 'Come on, what have you been playing at, Dad? Pitch and toss behind the slag heap, was it?' She gazed at him. He was sitting in a clean shirt, fresh from his bath. It was collarless and unbuttoned at the neck and his Adam's apple was bobbing convulsively.

He avoided her eye, moved automatically to get a cigarette from the mantelpiece, changed his mind and sat still, staring at the slippers Marina had bought him for

Christmas. He curled his toes up in them, forming bumps in the plaid wool tops, straightened them, curled them again almost in a reflex action.

'I'm sorry, lass,' he mumbled, a picture of humiliation.

'Sorry? You'll be sorry all right! I'll make you sorry.' Kate leaned towards him, almost spitting out the words.

'I'll tell you what he's done an' all.' She turned to Marina. 'He's been betting on the horses again. We've had a visit tonight from Johnny Green and that runner of his. Lives over the other side, hangs about the street corner – you know him, the long string of nowt! On the doctor's panel he is, supposed to have hurt his back. No doubt getting compensation for it too. Anyway, they reckon your dad owes them a hundred pounds. A hundred! It might as well be a thousand for all the chance he has of paying it! An' that's not all! He owes half the village, that's what Johnny Green says. "So what were you doing letting him get in that deep?" I asked. Not that I got an answer but I'm not letting that nowt talk down to me.'

The long speech seemed to have drained Kate. All the anger went out of her. She sat down at the table and put her head on her arms. 'Never be able to hold our heads up in this place again,' she muttered.

Johnny Green, thought Marina. The bookie from the town. If it was bad enough to draw him out to the village to seek out her dad then it was very bad.

'Mam, it'll be all right,' she said, feeling that it would be anything but. She cast around in her mind for something comforting to say. 'What about Lance? Can he not help?' She thought of her own savings. She had forty-eight pounds towards her wedding.

'Lance? There's no help there. He's off to Australia. At least that's what he said tonight. I'll never hear from him again. Following our Robson he is, and you know we haven't heard from *him* for years. On a ten-pound assisted passage Lance is going. Him and that lass of his, Joan. They're getting wed and then off to Australia he said, only tonight. That was the first blow. Seems she's in the family way. Lasses these days have no sense of shame...I blame the war, it changed everything.' Kate held her head in her hands, rubbed her eyes. 'Australia. It just swallows them up, it does.' She sat up and wiped her eyes with the bottom of her apron. 'Aye, well, they're best out of it. Let them make a life of their own, I say. I'll just have to get on with it, won't I? Mothers don't count for nowt, not when a lad gets wed.'

'Oh, Mam, stop feeling sorry for yourself. Lance isn't like that. He'll write, you'll see,' said Marina, though she wasn't too sure herself.

'We'll see, all right,' said her mother, then turned round and caught Sam looking at her. 'And now this. Oh, Sam, will you never, ever learn?'

He bent down suddenly and changed his slippers for the highly polished boots he always wore to go out in.

'Where do you think you're going?' she demanded.

'Out.'

He wrapped his white scarf round his collarless neck and pulled on his old jacket. 'I'm off, I cannot stand this.' And he went.

Marina and her mother looked at each other. 'Just like him. Spineless,' Kate commented bitterly. 'It's me has to clean up the mess, always me.'

Marina shook her head. 'I don't know, Mam,' she said. 'You're too hard on him. I think he was really upset.'

'So he should be,' her mother replied bitterly. 'Well, I'm going to bed. I'm not waiting up for him.'

Someone was knocking at the door. A loud 'ready money' knock as Kate would call it, and on the front door, the one which was never used. Marina tumbled out of bed and groped for the light switch. She pulled a kimono over her pyjamas and put on her slippers.

The knocking came again, loud and insistent. 'Are you in, missus?' came the shout. Marina went out on to the landing, almost bumping into Kate as she came out of her bedroom.

'It's the polis,' she said, eyes wide with fear. 'Oh, my God, what has he done now?'

'I'll go, Mam,' said Marina. 'It's probably nothing. Or nothing to do with Dad anyway. Where is he anyway? Is he not back yet? What time is it?'

'Half-past four. No, he's not back. Where can he be, Marina?' She shook her head and headed down the stairs. Sam had gone off on other occasions similar to the one last night. He always came back in the end, when he thought the flak would have died down.

'I'm coming, I'm coming,' she called as she went through the front room and tugged back the bolt of the door. It was indeed a policeman standing there.

'Mrs Morland?' he asked, stepping forward. 'No, I can see you're not. Is your mam in, ninny?' he asked in a strong Geordie accent.

Wordlessly, Marina ran to the bottom of the stairs. Her mother had already come down, had heard every word.

'What is it? Don't keep him standing on the doorstep, our Marina, all the neighbours will be listening. Come on in, constable, and shut the door behind you.' Kate led the way through the front room to the kitchen before turning to face him. 'Well?'

'Take a seat, missus.'

'Never mind that. Just tell us what has happened, will you?'

The policeman cleared his throat and glanced at Marina before opening his notebook. 'Are you Mrs Kate Morland?' he asked. Kate opened her mouth to tell him to get on with it but he was before her. 'You husband is – was – Sam Morland?'

'Yes.'

The single word came out in a whisper for now Kate knew for sure what was coming. Marina moved to her and put an arm around her shoulders.

'I'm sorry to have to tell you he was knocked down by

a bus at half-past twelve this morning. He was killed outright, missus, wouldn't have known what hit him.'

'There aren't any buses at half-past twelve, the last bus would go ages before that!' Marina burst out.

'I'm sorry, pet, but there was. It was the fore-shift bus taking men to Fishburn. If someone could come down and identify him for us...'

After the policeman had gone Lance came in, still in his pit clothes where they had called him out of the pit. Marina saw to his bath, made him some tea, did all the small homely tasks necessary. She felt numb and went about them in a daze, startled from it only when she came out of the pantry and heard what Kate was saying to him.

'You won't be going now, will you, son? To Australia? Not now this has happened?'

Lance didn't answer directly. 'We won't talk about that now, Mam,' he said. 'Plenty of time for that. Howay now, you'd be better in bed and I have to go down and identify him. Come on, Mam, it'll be a long day tomorrow.'

'Aye,' his mother said and stood up obediently.

'I'll go up with you, Mam.' Marina moved to her side and put an arm around her mother's shoulders, but Kate shrugged it off impatiently.

'I can go by myself. I'm not senile, you know,' she snapped. Marina and Lance looked at each other as she went out and up the stairs, talking as she went. 'What a day this has been! Eeh, could anything else happen, do you think?' She sobbed suddenly. 'Aw, Sam, Sam! You

know I didn't mean it. Why did you have to throw yourself under a bus?'

'He didn't! It was an accident. Dad didn't!' Marina
shouted, almost in unison with Lance. They had both
jumped to their feet in shock. Marina ran to the bottom of
the stairs. 'It was an accident, Mam!' she shouted again
and Kate turned on the landing and looked down at her.

'Aye, mebbe,' she said. 'Mebbe it was.'

It was a full week before the funeral could be held. There
had to be a post-mortem and an inquest. 'Accidental
death' was the verdict. 'I told you,' Marina said to Kate.
'The coroner said it was an accident.'

'Aye,' said her mother. 'But him saying it doesn't make
it so.' She sat in the corner of the fireplace, saying little
and eating less. In the week since Sam had died, the flesh
looked to be falling from her. Marina worried about her.
She knew her mother was still blaming herself, going over
and over that last scene with Dad.

'It's the shock, that's all,' Brian tried to comfort her.
'She'll come round, you'll see.' He was a rock in all this,
Marina thought, and found herself leaning on him more
and more.

The funeral was small and private. Kate had insisted
on that even though Sam had been a popular man in
the village in spite of his propensity for gambling and
borrowing money. Normally every man off shift would
have gone to the chapel service at least. Marina knew

why, though. Her mother was worried he had owed more money to the neighbours; it wasn't just sorrow which kept her head bowed; she was ashamed. At the chapel service she looked neither to left nor right, acknowledging none of her neighbours or friends, imagining they were pointing the finger at her and her family. She barely answered the minister's condolences. And afterwards she sat by the fire, eating nothing, occasionally wiping her eyes with a handkerchief which she had rolled up in her hand.

That night, Marina and Brian were sitting quietly in the front room, Kate had gone to bed and Lance had disappeared – to his girl's or to the Club, Marina didn't know or care. Before he went he'd confided his plans in Marina.

'I haven't told Mam yet,' he said, 'but we're going the week after next. We decided today. Just a quiet register office wedding next week then we're away, out of here.'

'You decided today, when it was Dad's funeral?' Marina was shocked into saying. Sometimes she felt Lance was not her brother at all but a stranger. She couldn't understand him. Not like the big brother who had looked out for her when she was small, almost a second father to her.

'Don't look at me like that, you know we can't put it off,' he retorted, and a minute or two later he had gone out.

Marina leaned her head against Brian's shoulder and sighed. 'You know, I wish I could just leave everything, forget all about Jordan, get away to a place where everyone doesn't know our business,' she cried. 'We could make a fresh start just like Lance and Joan. I don't blame him when I think about it, he does right to get away from here. It's horrible, full of busybodies, always talking about us.'

'Aw, come on, it's not so bad,' Brian protested. 'The folk aren't so bad either.' He grinned, trying to lift her out of her mood. 'At least, me and my family aren't bad, are we?'

Marina leaned back against his arm. She felt so tired. The emotions of the last week had drained her, the tiny surge of resentment which had given her the energy to say what she did had died. 'No. But you know what I mean,' she said weakly, and stared into the fire.

Aunt Hetty and Penny had come to the funeral. Aunt Hetty was Mam's cousin, family, but somehow Marina hadn't thought of them coming. When they had walked in the door her heart had jumped in anticipation of seeing Charlie and this in spite of her misery over Dad. But he wasn't with them and she was glad, she told herself now. She couldn't have coped with seeing him, not today. She could hardly speak to Penny, but thank goodness her cousin had smiled in understanding, obviously thinking it was because Marina was so upset over Dad's death. They had gone straight after the service, kissing Kate and Marina and promising to keep in touch. No thanks, Marina had thought.

She closed her eyes and Brian, ever observant, saw and eased his arm from under her.

'Come on, bed for you,' he said. 'It's been a hard day for everyone. I'll go now.' They got to their feet and he kissed her gently. 'Tomorrow is another day,' he whispered in her ear. 'I'll see you then. I'll always be here for you. I love you, Marina.' She had never doubted that.

Her mother called out as she trailed wearily up the stairs, 'Brian gone home?'

'Yes, Mam.'

'He's a lovely man, our Marina,' said Kate. 'And you're a lucky girl to have him.'

'Yes, Mam,' said Marina. And she was, yes, she knew she was.

'Sam was a lovely man an' all,' said Kate and choked on a sob. 'Your poor dad.'

'Yes, Mam.'

Marina paused on the landing, wondering whether to go in to her mother but Kate called, 'Goodnight, pet,' and Marina went into her own room and closed the door. That wasn't what her mam had called him only a short week ago.

Chapter Twenty-one

The work was easy, that was one thing about it. Oh, the sewing room was busy enough, always bed linen to mend, uniforms to alter to fit as staff came and went in the hospital. But there was no piece work, nothing driving her to go faster and faster all the time. Not as there had been in the factory. Rose would have been contented enough in the small world of the sewing room were it not for the worry about Michael and Mary always nagging at the back of her mind.

'Another batch for you, Lily,' said Alice, dumping a pile of torn sheets on the table by her side. Alice was the boss of the sewing room, under Mrs Timms of course. She was a bustling, middle-aged woman, always cheery, working alongside Rose and the other girls.

'Thanks, Alice,' said Rose, and picking up the first item began the meticulous patching and mending for which she was beginning to get a reputation among the sewing-room staff. She applied herself to the job, taking pride in the neat patching and darning, and by elevenses had a good pile on the table of neatly mended and folded bed linen.

The other women gathered in a bunch but Rose sat on alone by her machine. As she drank her tea she reflected that Marina should have got her note by now, so at least she would know Rose was doing OK. It had been a good idea when one of the girls had been going to London last week to ask her to post the letter for her. If Marina let it out to Dad he would never dream she was so close, only twenty-odd miles away, and only about five miles from the twins and Aunt Elsie.

Aunt Elsie...Rose couldn't think of her without feeling betrayed. But Aunt Elsie wouldn't hurt the twins, no, she loved them too much for that. But did she still have them with her? Oh, dear Lord, let it be so.

'Lily?' At first Rose didn't answer. She was thinking about the past and didn't realise Alice meant her. She had to repeat herself. 'Lily? Now then, stop your daydreaming, it's time we were all back to work. Besides, Mrs Timms will be in any minute.' Alice put a hand on her shoulder, kindly but firm, and Rose put her cup back on the tray and switched on her sewing machine.

Of course Rose had had to get a replacement identity card and the hospital authorities, including Mrs Timms presumably, knew her correct name. But it was assumed that Lily was the name Rose went by, for whatever reason, and no one commented on it. And she was grateful for their lack of curiosity. She was even becoming used to being called Lily. Most of the time, anyway. Were it not for Mary and Michael...An idea occurred to her. She would ring the junior school at Shotton. Surely they would tell her if the twins were still pupils there? Of course. Why hadn't she thought of it before?

The time dragged after that, but at last it was one o'clock and dinnertime and she could slip along to the telephones in the main entrance and for once her luck was in. There was a directory hanging by a string from the shelf in the booth.

'Shotton Colliery Junior School. Head mistress speaking.'

For a second or two Rose couldn't speak. Her throat closed up, her pulse began to race.

'Hallo? Can I help you?'

'Emm...Can you tell me...I think you have Michael and Mary Sharpe in the school?'

'Well?'

'I mean, do you have Michael and Mary Sharpe as pupils there?'

There was a brief silence. 'Who's speaking? Who wants to know?'

'I'm a relative, I –'

'I'm afraid I can't give out information about the children on the telephone, especially when I don't know who you are.' The voice was hardening, becoming suspicious, Rose could hear it over the wire. She bit her lip, not knowing what to say.

'Well, if that's all, I have work to do. Goodbye.' The line went dead. Rose stood there, tears springing hot to her eyes. She had really banked on finding out where the twins were this way, or at least if they had left Shotton and Aunt Elsie.

'Are you finished, caller? I'm afraid the party has hung up. Do you wish me to try again? That would be another fourpence, please.' The operator's voice was bright and impersonal.

'No, thank you,' Rose blurted and hung up. She leaned against the wooden partition of the booth and closed her eyes.

'Are you finished? Come on, don't hog the phone.' A second-year nurse was banging on the door and Rose swallowed and came out, muttering, 'Sorry', not looking at the nurse. After buoying herself up she was all the more down at this disappointment.

'Lily? Are you all right?' Rose jumped. She had almost bumped into Dr Morris as she turned a corner in the corridor leading to the sewing room. 'Oh, yes. Thank you, Doctor.'

Dr Morris studied her pale face and suspiciously red eyes. 'Well, you look a bit under the weather to me,' he observed. 'Where are you off to now? Have you had lunch?'

'I wasn't going to bother, there's a lot of work waiting –'

'Nonsense, girl, you have to eat,' he said tersely, though his hazel eyes were smiling. 'Look.' He glanced at his watch. 'It's my half-day. So go and get your coat, there's a good girl. We'll go to the cafe over the road. I'm a bit peckish myself.'

Rose blinked. Doctors just didn't go out with domestic staff. If anyone saw them the hospital would be buzzing with it, making a mountain out of a molehill too, no doubt. But it would be nice, he was such a kind man. And she did need something to cheer her up. Oh yes, she did indeed.

He saw her indecision and took her arm. 'Come on, I'm going to see you get some good food into you, do you hear? You're far too thin anyhow.'

Sitting opposite Dr Morris in the cafe, eating corned beef slice and chips and limp bread and margarine, Rose had to grin at him. 'I bet you'd have eaten better in the doctors' dining room,' she remarked. 'I would have, even in the canteen.' They were both of them a little damp as it had begun to rain outside. He had laid her old coat over the back of an empty chair carefully, as though it were a Dior model. It was all very strange to Rose, his manners, everything about him.

'Call me Bob, you're not a patient now,' he said. 'Anyway, it's good to get away from hospital food some-times, even if it is just across the road here.' He speared a chip on the end of his fork and dipped it into a blob of brown sauce on his plate and chewed it thoughtfully, watching her as he did so.

Rose put down her knife and fork and took out her

hankie and patted her mouth. This wasn't the sort of place where there were napkins or even paper serviettes. She glanced up and saw he was still watching her.

'What?' she felt compelled to ask, his expression was so quizzical.

He shook his head. 'Nothing. At least not if you don't want to tell me.'

It was warm in the cafe and Rose put a hand to her forehead. 'Would you like a glass of water?' he asked immediately and jumped up and went over to the counter and came back with some. 'You looked so worried, I was alarmed,' he said.

He was so kind her resistance was worn down, and she had to talk to someone, she told herself. Except about *that*, of course. 'It's the twins, you see,' she said, and then it all came out in a rush. How she didn't know if they were with her aunt, how she couldn't go and see, couldn't let her aunt know where she was...

'Why?' he asked bluntly. 'Why can't you?'

'I just can't,' she replied.

'They're yours? The twins, I mean.'

'No, Michael and Mary are my brother and sister. They're eight years old.' He leaned his elbow on the table and put his chin in his hand, listening intently as she went on, and inevitably he realised it was the father who was the cause of her fear. How she couldn't bear it if the twins were to go back to him. What was she going to do? If only she knew they were safe in Shotton...

'Shotton? Shotton Colliery? Only as far as that? Why, that's no distance away!'

'I know.'

How could she tell him that it might as well have been a thousand miles, she daren't go there, she was so frightened of her father. And she knew it was silly. Her father wasn't even there, or at least she hoped he wasn't. Oh yes, indeed, she hoped and prayed he wasn't, for the sake of the twins. And yes, she was a coward, that was it, an out and out coward.

'Do you not want to go on your own? Look, I have a free afternoon –'

'No!' She almost shouted the word and he was startled, it showed in his expression. 'I mean, I have to work this afternoon. In fact, I must be getting back.' She made to rise then sat down again. 'How much do I owe you for the meal?'

He dismissed the question with a wave of his hand. 'I can pick you up at five o'clock. I'll go with you, Lily, be your moral support, if you like?'

'No, I'm not going today, I have things to do…'

'Come on, I'll walk you back.' He held her coat for her and she felt cherished. It was a rare feeling for her. The only other times she had felt cherished had been when she was with…Jeff. There now, and she had sworn to herself that she was not going even to think of him again. It was no good, he wouldn't want her now. He would find another girl, one from a proper family, not a twisted one like hers.

'Go today,' Bob said as they stood on the pavement waiting for traffic to pass. 'Come on, it's the only way you'll find out how the twins are. And surely, no matter what you have done, your aunt will not throw you out?'

'But she will,' Rose said. 'I couldn't go to the house. Oh, no.' She was weakening though, he sensed it. But then she shook her head. 'I might be seen.'

What had she done that she felt she couldn't let her family see her? he wondered but asked no more questions. Time enough, he thought.

'Think about it,' he urged her. 'I'll meet you here at five. All right?' He turned away and walked to his car which was parked at the other side of the hospital, before she could put forward any other objection.

'Hmm,' said Alice suggestively later as she paused by Rose's machine. 'I saw you and Dr Morris, sitting with your heads together in the cafe. Your secret is out, my girl.'

'There is no secret,' said Rose. 'There's nothing between us, he's just interested in me as a patient.'

'Is he now? But you're not his patient, are you? If you were he would have to pass you on to someone else, the way he was looking at you...'

'There's nothing! Nothing!' Rose was vehement in her denial and Alice backed down at once.

'Nay, I was only funning,' she said. 'I meant nowt, lass. Take no notice of me. Not that I would tell a soul if there were something. Not if you didn't want me to.'

Rose picked up a pillowcase which was torn down the seam and turned it inside out to mend. As if she didn't have enough to worry about! Dear Lord, why didn't *anything* go the same for her as it did for other girls? She thought of Marina. If her friend were here she could talk to her. Marina was the only one in whom she could confide. But she had effectively cut herself off from her friend now. Rose mentally shrugged her shoulders, recognising the mood as pure self-pity. And that was going to get her nowhere, nowhere at all.

Bob Morris wasn't waiting at the gate when she came out at a few minutes after five and she was disappointed. Well, she had no right to be, she told herself, and decided she would walk to the lodging house. It was a lovely evening and she might as well save her bus fare.

'Lily, come on, I'm here, get in.' Bob was sitting in his car a short way up the road. He leaned over and opened the door on the passenger side. She looked quickly about her before climbing into the car.

'You shouldn't have done this, not so close to the hospital. People will talk,' she said, thinking of Alice. Luckily there was no one around she knew but what about him?

'Why? Do you think it should be kept a secret? Or that I should have met you in some out of the way place?'

'No, not that.' They shouldn't have met at all, she thought. She would just tell him she couldn't let him take her to Shotton, not let him get involved with her, it was all too nasty, too dirty. Oh, God, what would he think if it all came out? He wouldn't be able to look at her then, would be horrified. That she had let her father...No, she wasn't going to think of *that* again.

'Well, then,' he was saying as he started the car and set off along the road inland. 'I was thinking, you see. If you're absolutely sure you mustn't be seen, and you're absolutely sure you must check if the twins are all right...You are, aren't you?'

She nodded. She couldn't look at him.

'Well then. I thought you could sit in the car, perhaps a little way away from the house, and I could go there and ask after them. Don't you think that's a good idea?'

'I...I don't know.' Why was he doing this for her?

'Or I could ask after you, could say I was a friend of yours. That would be the truth, wouldn't it?'

A friend. Heaven knew she needed a friend. 'But what if I was seen?'

'You won't be. Or if you are, well, I've got sunglasses here, you can wear them. And pull your headscarf over your face. Oh, come on, you want to find out about the children, don't you?'

Oh, yes, she wanted to know about the children. She was desperate for news of them. Her heart ached every minute of the day and she cried every night before going to sleep. The twins were her reason for living, the only reason she felt she had left.

'But why? I mean, why are you doing this?' she asked.

'Let's just do it.' He leaned across her, still looking

out of the windscreen, found the sunglasses in the glove compartment and handed them to her. He was turning into the Shotton road, now past old Shotton village to the later pit village of Shotton Colliery. And then they were running by the ends of colliery rows, past the street when Aunt Elsie had moved to from the new site because she liked the friendliness of the old rows. Rose looked down the back street eagerly but there were no children outside playing kicky off chock or chanting skipping games. The brick-lined alley was deserted. Of course, it was teatime, the main meal of the day. The twins would be sitting up at the table, eating. Corned beef hash if Michael had his way, that was his favourite. A lump formed in Rose's throat.

Bob was parking the car further up the road, round a corner, out of sight. He turned to her. To lighten the atmosphere, he said, 'My, you do look strange in that get-up! Like a character from a murder mystery.'

She glanced in the mirror. The glasses and headscarf obscured most of her face. Rose huddled down in her seat, feeling more confident.

'Righto then,' he said. 'I'll go. Just sit tight, I won't be long. What number did you say?'

'Fourteen,' she whispered.

'Fourteen it is. See you in a minute.'

Chapter Twenty-two

Elsie had the pan in her hand, all ready to serve the hash to the children, when the knock came at the door.

'Heck!' she said, exasperated. 'Who can that be now?'

'I'll go and see, Aunt Elsie,' said Michael, sliding from his chair at the table. A knock at the door was exciting, it meant it was a stranger for the neighbours usually called out, 'Are you there, Elsie?' and walked right in.

'Go on then, pet.'

Michael opened the door then stood tongue-tied, staring at the tall young man standing there. He hung on to the doorknob, unsure of himself, and it was Mary, looking over his shoulder, who said, 'Hallo. Do you want Aunt Elsie?'

Bob smiled widely. One of Lily's problems was solved already. Here were the twins, gazing up at him with Lily's eyes, and as far as he could tell at first glance, both fit as fiddles.

'Yes, please,' he said. 'May I come in?'

They stood back from the door wordlessly and he

walked into the kitchen-cum-living-room, which was typical of most of the miners' cottages in the area. This one was spotlessly clean and shining, he had time to register. The woman was in her forties, he surmised, standing with a pan in her hand almost as though she had forgotten it was there. But the thing he noticed most about her was her expression. Apprehension, it was, rather than surprise. And, seeing her attitude, the two children stood closer together and gazed at him with big, solemn eyes too.

'Hmm…good evening,' he said, kicking himself mentally for he realised he couldn't address her properly. Had forgotten to ask Lily for her surname. Was it the same as Lily's? Her real name was Rose Sharpe, he had found that out from the office. 'I hope you don't mind my coming in. Miss Sharpe, is it?'

'My name is Mrs Brown.' It was just above a whisper. Elsie was still holding the pan and now she turned and put it down on the bar of the fire. She stood for a second or two with her back to him then turned round to face him. 'What can I do for you?'

'Oh, I'm sorry. I didn't introduce myself, did I? I'm Dr Morris, how do you do?' He held out his hand and after a slight hesitation she responded; her hand was limp and cold despite the heat in the kitchen. Something wrong here.

'And these are?' he asked, indicating the children.

'I'm Mary and me brother is Michael,' the little girl piped.

'Hallo, Mary. Hallo, Michael.'

'I asked if I could help you,' said Elsie, sounding a little less frightened.

'I hope so. I'm looking for a Miss Sharpe. Rose Sharpe?'

'Our Rose? That's me sister, mister!' said Mary. 'She doesn't live here any more.'

'Mary! Michael! Go on into the front room. Go on now, play with your toys.' Elsie was white and pinched-looking, her voice urgent, almost a shout. Michael's lower lip trembled but he took his sister's hand and pulled her away.

'I haven't had me tea,' Mary protested as she went.

'Go on now, you'll get your tea in a minute,' insisted Elsie. After they had gone she turned back to Bob. 'Why? What do you want with her?'

'Oh, nothing for you to concern yourself with, Mrs Brown,' he said smoothly, watching her with a doctor's eye. She was frightened and there was something else – defensive, that was what she was. She had a guilty look to her.

'Well, I don't know where she is. Rose went off on her own. Just left, without a word.'

'I wonder why?' he asked, as though to himself. He pursed his lips and played with his driving gloves, smoothing them over his hands.

'Well, I don't know, do I?' Elsie suddenly flared. 'I have enough to do looking after those two bairns, haven't

I?' Her eyes narrowed. Now she was over her shock she was becoming suspicious of him, he realised. 'Where do you come from anyway? Bishop Auckland, is it? Jordan? Why have you come all this way?'

Bishop Auckland? And Jordan was a village near Bishop, he knew that. Well, he'd found out something at least.

'Yes, that's right, Bishop Auckland,' he fibbed. 'Look, it was nothing important. I was just passing by and I knew Miss Sharpe had come over this way to live so I thought I'd call... Well, goodbye, Mrs Brown, I'm very pleased to have met you.'

He was out of the house in a minute, before she had time to ask any more questions. He practically ran down the back street and along the road to the car. He passed Mrs Todd, on her way to the fish and chip shop for a piece of haddock for her supper, almost bumping into her as he rounded the corner, avoiding her at the last minute.

'Hey! Watch where you're going!' Mrs Todd shouted after him. She followed him with her eyes, saw him get into a car parked just inside the alley of one of the rows. As she passed the end of the alley she had to stop as the car pulled out and she glared into it. There was a woman sitting in the passenger seat wearing dark glasses and a headscarf. As the car pulled away she took off the glasses and turned to the young man.

'Do you know,' Mrs Todd said to her husband as they ate their fish and chips later on, 'I thought I saw that Rose

Sharpe tonight, in a car.' She shook her head as she picked up the teapot and poured the tea.

'Did you?' he asked absently, uninterested. 'You forgot to get mushy peas, lass.'

'You can do without mushy peas for once, can't you?'

Mrs Todd put a piece of crunchy batter into her mouth and chewed thoughtfully. Rose Sharpe. She hadn't seen her since that night she went off with her father, back to Bishop, she supposed. She and the father had just left those two bairns to be looked after by their aunt. Funny family. Mrs Todd shook her head and reached for the jug she'd brought the brown ale in from the back door of the pub. 'A drop more, Matt?' she asked, the jug poised over her husband's glass.

'They're there. The twins, I mean. Michael and Mary.' Bob watched the woman teetering on the kerb, just in case she decided to cross in front of the car, decided she was waiting for him to go, and set off for the Hartlepool road.

'Oh, thank God,' whispered Rose, and took off the glasses and closed her eyes for a minute.

'Put them back on, we're not out of Shotton yet,' Bob admonished, and she hurriedly obeyed. Then she sat forward and peered at him through the dark glass. The sun had gone down and evening shadows were adding to her difficulty in seeing.

'Are they all right? Michael hasn't got a summer cold, has he? He had a terrible one last year –'

'He looked fine to me.'

'Oh, good. And Mary? Was she all right?'

'Mary too. They look fit and healthy and just about the right height and weight for eight- or nine-year-olds. And that's a professional opinion. That enough for you?'

'Oh, yes, thank you, Bob. Oh, thank you. I'm ever so grateful, I am.'

'That's all right, R— Lily.' He caught himself almost saying her real name and glanced at her but she didn't appear to have noticed.

Rose was happy. The twins were still with Aunt Elsie. No matter how rotten Elsie had been to her she would never hurt the twins, Rose told herself for the thousandth time. No, never.

She felt quite light-headed with relief. Until she thought, suddenly, suppose her dad was there? Suppose he was living with them? Suppose he was at Shotton, had left his job at Jordan? Suppose...

'Was there anyone else there? Their father, I mean?'

'No, no one else.' Not her father, Bob noted, the children's father.

'He could be living there, though, couldn't he? I mean, if he was out at work or something.'

'I don't think he is, Lily, really I don't. There would have been signs, something belonging to him, if a man was living there.'

Rose sat back in her seat, relieved. Then he hadn't carried out his threat to take the children home with him.

That was something to be thankful for. But she was still hungry for news of the twins.

'Tell me what happened. What you said?'

He was driving into Hartlepool by now, the street lights coming on. Bob glanced at her, the light illuminating her pale face, then fading, then lighting it up again. She looked eager, her eyes sparkled in the lights. A lock of dark, almost black hair had fallen over her forehead. She brushed it back impatiently.

'Everything?'

She nodded. 'Everything.'

So he recounted it all, from the door being opened by Michael to his hurried getaway, careful to leave nothing out.

'You called me Rose,' she commented. 'You knew all along, didn't you?'

'Just your name, from the hospital records. It's difficult to change your name with identity cards. If you want me to call you Lily, I will.'

'It was my grandmother's name.'

Rose became silent as they turned into the street where she lived. He pulled up at her door and she turned to him.

'Thank you, Dr Morris, for taking me. On your afternoon off an' all.'

'My pleasure. It was an...interesting evening. If I can do anything else to help, you only have to ask.' A polite exchange, creating a slight distance between them.

'Don't get out, I can manage. Goodnight, Dr Morris.

Bob,' she added as he made to protest. She opened the door. Then, as though on impulse, she turned and kissed him lightly on the lips and whispered, 'Goodnight,' again. She'd slipped out of the car before he could respond and disappeared into the house.

Bob was left with a tingling sensation on his lips where hers had touched him in a sweet, soft as gossamer touch. He sat for a moment or two before starting the car and driving off. He was expected at his friend's house for dinner.

There was something about the girl, something in her past, something more than she had told him earlier that day. There was such an air of tragedy about her, appealing yet unconsciously so. Some tragedy...what had her father done to her? Oh, Bob could take a guess. He had not worked in a large hospital without finding out a thing or two about the darker side of human nature. But his mind shied away from any of that. Not Lily...Rose. Oh, surely not?

Rose slept through the night for the first time since she'd come to Hartlepool, her anxiety over the twins appeased, at least for the time being. So instead of waking with a thick head and ten minutes late so that she had to rush breakfast to get to work, she was half an hour early and could take her time.

She turned on to her back and stretched luxuriously. She had dreamed she was in a car and the man driving had bent and kissed her just as she had kissed Dr Morris last night. A presumptuous kiss of gratitude which she regretted now. What must he think of her?

In her dream the man had not been Dr Morris, oh, no, she only ever had good dreams about one man. Jeff. The man had been Jeff and he had turned to her and kissed her and it had been just like that night, which seemed ages ago now, on the sands at Crimdon Dene. That magical night. She was in love with Jeff, she admitted to herself. She loved him, but it was hopeless, for even if he loved her now he wouldn't when she told him how things had been for her. No man would, it stood to reason. She could never marry anyone, she knew that. She was soiled, tainted, filthy.

By, but it had been good, the dream. So sweet. She yearned for it to become reality even while she was telling herself it couldn't happen. She wondered what Jeff was doing this morning. Coming home from fore shift or going down in the cage on back shift. He would be laughing, joking with the other men, helmet pushed to the back of his head, Davy lamp in his hand.

'*My lad's a collier lad*,' she sang under her breath. How did it go now? '*He brings the bright siller to me, to me!*' And she would be taking the children to school, a boy and a girl just like Michael and Mary, and maybe one in a pushchair, a baby...No!

No, she was a fool. The daydream faded, leaving her with an awful sense of loss. Rose pushed back the bedclothes and got out of bed, pulled on the dressing gown she had bought with her last week's wages, a soft, white, candlewick dressing gown with roses on the breast. If she hurried she would get to the bathroom before the others, have time for a quick bath.

She should have been so happy this morning, she told herself. Why had she let herself dream about Jeff? Normally she wouldn't, had schooled herself not to think about him. But today she couldn't seem to help herself. Did he still write to her? Was he hurt that she didn't write back? Had Marina told him she was in London?

Rose had an overwhelming urge to write to Jeff, keep the link with him, no matter how tenuous. Even though she had decided to cut him off completely, let him get on with his life. He could meet another girl, a girl who could love him as he deserved, a girl he could love wholeheartedly.

What a fool she was, causing herself pain thinking like this, wallowing in it. Pull yourself together, Rose Sharpe, she told herself. There's nothing to be done so you might as well get on with it!

Chapter Twenty-three

'I can get a transfer to Easington Colliery. Jeff's there, it's better than going where we know no one at all,' said Brian. He and Marina were walking on the fell. He had his arm around her and she was leaning in to him as though for support. He felt ten feet tall.

'But what about Mam?' she asked. 'I can't leave her here, Brian, not now Lance has gone.' He had gone as surely as her dad had gone, hadn't he? Marina thought miserably. Australia was the other side of the world, it wasn't very likely they would see him again. Dad. At the thought of him tears prickled at the back of her eyes. She hadn't realised just how much she'd loved him until he was gone. Small episodes from her childhood kept coming back to her.

'Take me to the rec, Dad,' she had demanded so often when she was little, knowing he would put down his book and lift her on to his shoulders and take her to the recreation ground built by the Miners' Welfare and kept in order by a retired miner, the grass cut, the swings oiled, even the toilets kept clean by the old man. And he had stood at the bottom of the great slide and caught her as she came down, swinging her into the air, and, oh, she'd thought he was the best daddy in the world. Funny how such long-ago episodes had come back to her lately. The later ones, the rows about money and gambling, had faded from her memory somehow.

'Marina, are you listening to me? I said, we could take your mother with us. I'm sure I could get a house – they're building them all the time now, Jeff tells me. He's buying his own, did I tell you? Just an old colliery house, but he's doing it up.'

'Is he?' Brian had caught her attention now. It wasn't a common thing for miners to buy houses, though some had moved out of colliery houses into the new estates of council houses which were springing up all over the place.

'He says we could move in with him until we get a place of our own. And then we could send for your mother.'

'Oh, Brian, could we?' She turned to him, her eyes shining. It was an escape route. Away from the curious eyes she saw, or imagined she saw, looking at her and her mother in Jordan; the constant whispers.

They had come to the overhanging rock, the place where Marina and Rose had sat so often and talked; the place where Rose had told her that awful secret, the one Marina couldn't divulge to anyone, not even Brian. Even in her excitement the place reminded her vividly of Rose. Where was she now? Why didn't she write? Was she still in London?

But thoughts of her friend were driven from her mind the next moment as Brian drew her into the shelter of the overhang and pulled her to him.

'We could get married next month,' he said. 'Jeff has already asked about a job at Easington. He says the manager will be pleased to have me. It's a big pit, Marina, going right under the sea. Under the North Sea waves. You like the seaside, don't you? Easington beach is spoiled but it's close to Crimdon. There are lovely beaches all up the coast of Durham.'

Brian was excited, eager to get her to agree. His arms around her were strong, his eyes loving. Marina felt a stirring deep in her belly, her heartbeat quickened.

'We'll go to see the minister tomorrow, will we?' he asked and she nodded. If an image of Charlie flitted through her mind it was blotted out by the surge of feeling which threatened to overwhelm her as Brian bent his head and kissed her on the lips, gently at first, then more demandingly. Her mouth opened under his, his questing tongue was tasting hers. They slid together to the grass, brown now at the end of the summer, brown and dry and warm in the shelter of the rock.

His hand was on her breast under her coat, her bra and even the thin cotton of her blouse an intolerable barrier. He slid his hand beneath to cup and hold it, rubbing his thumb over the swelling, erect tip.

'Marina, Marina,' he groaned and pulled the blouse aside, bending his head to reach the white skin with his

lips. She strained towards him, her woman's body automatically turning to submit to the man, and his hand
strayed to her thigh where her skirt had ridden up. He
touched the bare flesh above her stocking. His hand moved
of its own volition to the wide leg of her lacy panties as
a mist swam before his eyes. There was nothing, nothing
in the world for him or her in that moment but the need.
A need which, he realised triumphantly, was going to be
assuaged at last.

Next moment he was being pushed in the chest and,
caught off balance, was thrust easily to one side as Marina
struggled to sit up. 'No! No, I told you, Brian Wearmouth,
not until we're married!' she shouted.

'But...but, darling, we'll be married within the month,
won't we?' he asked helplessly. The mist before his eyes
was clearing but his heart still pounded, the urge to finish
what they had started insistent, demanding satisfaction. He
could take her now, he knew he could, her resistance as
nothing, she'd tantalised him enough, hadn't she? But he
couldn't do it, no, he couldn't, it wasn't in him. Not when
he looked at her lovely face, her bright and sparkling eyes –
whether from passion or anger he was not quite sure.

Brian's heart melted for her. His love, she was. He
would never do anything she didn't want him to. Not even
that, no matter what the provocation, though it was hard,
almost more than a man could stand. Her expression was
becoming contrite too.

'I'm sorry, Brian, I led you on,' she admitted. 'But

honestly, love, I want to wait. It's not long now, is it? We'll get married and go to live in Easington. But are you sure it's all right for Mam to come and live with us? You're sure you don't mind? Oh, Brian, I do love you – I do! You're so kind to me, so kind.' She leaned against him and he almost groaned aloud. Didn't she know what she was doing to him? He held her away from him, did his best to think sensibly.

'Come on then, let's break the news to the folks,' he said, getting to his feet and straightening his clothes. He brushed bits of grass from her back, turned so she could do the same for him. They stood for a moment, arms around each other, the only people on the wide sweep of the moor, just sheep cropping among the fading purple heather and dying bracken. Clouds were gathering above them, soft and reaching to the rim of the moor in the hazy distance, lying there like fleecy blankets. They began to walk home, arms around each other. From the side of the track a grouse rose into the air, startled at their approach. It would soon be the shooting season, Marina thought sadly, the young birds were grown. Poor things. And then the winter, the dead season, when the snow poles would come into their own, outlining the edge of the road in the snow.

Surely it was right to make a new beginning in a new place? she thought as they turned into the colliery rows of Jordan. As they reached the street where the Wearmouths lived, they saw Jeff's car parked by the gate and Brian quickened his pace.

'Come on,' he said, eagerness lighting up his face. 'I bet Jeff is here to tell me what the manager said.'

'Are you going away, our Brian?' Annie burst out as the couple went through the back door. 'Jeff says you've got a job at Easington, are you going?' Her small face was eager, alight with the news Jeff had brought.

He was sitting on the settee with a cup of tea in his hand. Everyone who came into the house had a cup of tea given to them in the first five minutes and perhaps a piece of Yorkshire parkin or Victoria sandwich.

'Sorry, Brian, didn't realise you hadn't said anything,' said his friend.

'Oh, don't mention it, Jeff,' said Mrs Wearmouth, her voice tight. Brian shot her an apprehensive glance. She was red in the face and her eyes were bright with what looked like unshed tears.

'Sorry, Mam, I was going to say but there wasn't any point if I didn't get the job, was there? Come on, I'm only going over to the coast, aren't I?'

'I'm sure I wouldn't stop you.' She sniffed and glanced behind him at Marina's uncomfortable-looking face. It was because of the lass, she knew that, and she felt a moment's animosity. But after all she wanted her lad to be happy, didn't she? And that meant she had to be nice to Marina.

'Cup of tea, pet? It's just mashed.' It was an attempt to appear as though the news that her son was leaving home made no difference to her whatsoever. Jeff at least was deceived and felt relieved, though Marina knew better.

'Only thing is, Brian, you have to start the week after next. You'll have to give in your notice today. But it's all right, you can stay with me. Why not? I have a spare bedroom.'

Mrs Wearmouth sat down suddenly, as though her legs wouldn't hold her. She looked to Marina for support. 'But what about you, lass? You don't want him to go so quickly, surely?'

Marina smiled. 'We're going to see the minister tomorrow, Mrs Wearmouth. I'm going to Easington with him, as soon as we're married. I can get to my work at Shire Hall just as easily from that side of Durham City as this, can't I?'

'You're going to work? After you're married?' Now her future mother-in-law did look shocked, but Brian laughed.

'Oh, Mam, all the women work nowadays. Unless they have bairns, that is.'

His mother closed her mouth in a thin line. Young 'uns these days! her expression said as clearly as if she had spoken the words aloud. Still, in her day there had been no work for women to do, not paid work that is, and certainly not in the pit villages.

The wedding was in the chapel at Jordan. Marina had wanted a small wedding. She felt she couldn't bear to have folk commenting spitefully on the cost of the celebration when her dad had died owing money to so many men in the village. But Kate had been against its being too small. A 'shabby wedding' it would be called then, and contemptuously too, by the folk there about.

'Get away!' she had said. 'You ask your mates from work, and Brian can ask his friends an' all. I'll not have it said my daughter had a shabby wedding. No, I will not.'

Where she got the money from, Marina didn't know. Kate refused to allow Brian or his family to contribute except in the traditional way of buying the bride's bouquet and paying for the taxi which was to take them on their honeymoon, a week in Scarborough. Fifteen shillings each per night, in a boarding house on the edge of Peaseholme Park, full board of course.

'Honeymoon, is it!' Kate had said. 'By, things have changed all right from my day. But there, if Brian has the cash . . . still, it would make more sense to put the money to some decent furniture. But I reckon you'll take no notice of me.'

Marina was quite looking forward to it, though she wasn't looking forward to the wedding night. She still had a dread that Brian would find out she wasn't virgin and turn nasty. Though she couldn't really envisage him ever being nasty, he was so even-tempered normally. But goodness knows how a man would react if he found out someone else had been there before him.

She was so nervous about it that she left her bouquet on the bed at home and the service was held up while Jeff rushed away to fetch it for her. In the vestibule she kept glancing at the minister, sure he must be annoyed about the delay. After all, he was going straight to another wedding in the chapel in the next village. But he had seen it all before and his kind smile never left his face. He smiled down at her, patted her shoulder.

'Don't worry, Marina,' he said. 'Everything's all right.' Then, before him at the communion rail, she trembled and almost ran out of the chapel but Brian had hold of her hand and it was too late. Afterwards, when Alice and Mr Brown and the other girls from the office were throwing confetti, and Mrs Wearmouth, who cleaned the chapel, was saying, 'Not on the chapel grounds, *please*,' with no effect whatsoever, she knew it was indeed too late. The ring was on her finger, feeling strange. She couldn't forget it was there.

It was when the reception in the schoolroom was over and Marina and Brian had wandered around the room and had a few words with all the guests, and the dainty white court shoes which she had bought in Doggart's in Bishop Auckland were nipping her toes something awful so that she couldn't wait to get home to change them, that it happened.

The bride and groom had left the guests to themselves, Jeff running them over to the house so Marina could change. As they got out of the car Alf Sharpe, drunk as a scuttle and twice as smelly, appeared from nowhere and put a hand on Marina's arm.

'Get off! Get your filthy, mucky hands off me!' she shrieked and Brian pushed her behind him protectively.

'What the hell do you want?' he demanded, strong language for Brian, who never swore.

'What's the matter with her? I was just going to wish her happy, that's all. Why does she have to go on as though I was something that just crawled out from under a stone? I've seen the way she looks at me.'

'You are! That's exactly what you are – something from under a stone!' Marina shouted, trembling with disgust and hatred. 'You drunken, filthy pig!'

'Nay, lass,' he whined. 'You an' my lass were pals when you were bairns...' at the same time as Brian protested, 'Hey, you're going a bit too far, Marina.'

'I'm not.' She rubbed her arm where he had touched her as though she were rubbing away filth.

'An' now my lass is dead and gone,' Alf was quavering, drunken tears starting to his eyes and threatening to overflow.

'Dead? When? Who said she was dead?' Jeff stepped forward, his face suddenly white, eyes blazing black as coal.

'Oh, it's you, is it? I thought I'd got rid of you altogether,' Alf snarled, and Jeff stepped forward and caught hold of him by his lapels, bringing him up off the ground until he was on tiptoe. Alf looked startled, frightened out of his drunken haze.

'What's the matter with you, man? Leave me alone,

don't you touch me!' he blustered. Jeff, a grown man now and strong, was very different from the boy he used to bully.

'Who told you she was dead?' Jeff repeated.

'I mean,' Alf quavered, 'she must be. I haven't heard a thing from her and she would have got in touch wi' me. Her dad, I am. We were close, me and our Rose –'

'Close? *Close!* She hated you!' Marina shouted.

'Hang on, hang on,' said Brian. 'Marina, go on inside, you're upset and I won't have it on our wedding day.' He watched as she turned wordlessly and ran up the yard to the door, banging it shut behind her. Well, he would follow her in a minute, make it all right, he thought.

'I should have told you. I forgot,' he said, turning to Alf. He had too, in the excitement of the wedding and going over to Easington, his new job and everything. 'Rose isn't dead, Marina had a letter from her. She's all right.'

'She's not – she's dead!' Alf cried. He had gone as white as a sheet, staring at the two younger men, his face working, spittle at the corners of his mouth. 'I know –'

Jeff let go of him and Alf slumped, just catching himself from sliding into the gutter.

'Aw, get lost,' said Jeff. 'You know nothing of the sort.' He and Brian turned their backs and went into the house. After a minute or two, Alf walked unsteadily away. At the bottom of the street some children were playing hidey-go-seek but they stopped and stared at him.

'Hey, look, that old geezer's blubbing,' one shouted

and they followed him along the rows, shouting out, 'Lassie lad, lassie lad! What's the matter, mister? Lost your dummy?'

Alf hardly heard them. He arrived at his own door and fumbled for his key, finally managing to let himself in. The kitchen stank but he didn't notice that either. He sank down into a chair and stared at the empty grate. Rose wasn't alive, she couldn't be! Why, she was almost gone when he'd left her in the dene, it could only have been a matter of a few minutes. The fumes of alcohol were clearing from his brain. He should have buried her there he realised. No one would have known, not if he'd covered the place over with branches and such. No, she couldn't be alive, of course not. But why hadn't there been a report of a body being found in the dene? He'd scoured the *Echo* every day but there was nothing. Mebbe she hadn't been found yet, that was it.

'Eh, man,' he said aloud to the blank walls, full of self-pity. 'What a bloody life this is! She turned on me and now I daren't even get me own little 'uns back. Mary now, she would be a comfort. I have the right to Mary.' Especially when he couldn't have Rose any more, he thought dimly. And sniffed. Mind, she'd brought it on herself, none of it had been his fault.

I'll go to Shotton the morn, his thoughts ran on. I will, I'll go and see the bairns and have a word with Elsie. That bitch isn't going to keep my bairns! Oh, no, she is not, I'm their father and I want them back.

Chapter Twenty-four

'That nice Dr Morris is keen on you, Lily,' Alice observed with a knowing smile as she took the pile of mended linen which had kept Rose's head down over the sewing machine for the whole of the day.

'Don't talk daft,' she said easily, careful not to sound embarrassed though she turned her face away to hide the heightened colour in her cheeks. She had seen it with the other young girls. They were teased unmercifully by the older married women in the sewing room and she wasn't going to let it happen to her.

Alice laughed, not easily put off. 'I know what I saw,' she said.

'He's just a friend, that's all,' said Rose, though she knew she would do better to keep quiet.

'Oh, aye?' Alice sounded sceptical. She looked round at the other women, all of them now beginning to finish up their work ready for a quick getaway at five o'clock. Lily was the only one not in a rush to get off, she was often the last to go.

'What do you think, girls?'

There was a general chorus of laughing agreement.

'You'd better not let my boyfriend hear you say that,' said Rose, inspired, thinking that would shut them up.

'Ooooh!' said Alice, a long-drawn-out sound. 'You have a boyfriend, have you, Lily?'

'Yes, I have. Now will you shut up? I want to finish this theatre gown,' said Rose, bending over her work.

'Aw, leave it, it'll be here tomorrow,' said Alice.

'You'd best not let Mrs Timms hear you say that.'

'Oh, and are you going to tell her?' Alice's tone had changed, it wasn't friendly any more.

'No, of course not,' Rose said, but Alice was obviously not mollified. Nor was she ready to give her victim a rest.

'Lily has a boyfriend, girls, did you hear that? What's his name, Lily?'

'Jeff.' Now why did she say that?

'Jeff, is it? Did you hear that, girls? His name's Jeff.'

But wishing it wouldn't make it true.

It was five to five and the machines were all shut down except for the one Rose worked. The women wanted something to amuse them while the hands on the clock went slowly round to the hour.

'Jeff, eh? With a G or a J?' one of them asked.

'Jeff with a J.'

Rose sighed as she finished the seam she was sewing and deftly cut the threads. She might as well shut down now, she thought. Then it was back to her single room in the lodging house. The evenings could be long and lonely and her library book was finished. But Alice wasn't finished with her yet.

'Does Jeff with a J know that Dr Morris is dangling after his girl then? Does he, Lily?'

Rose put the cover on her machine. She didn't answer Alice. It was five o'clock anyway, the other girls had lost interest and were going through the door. There were just she and Alice left in the room and Alice was moving to the door too. But slowly, glancing back at Rose, who took her time about putting on her coat, taking a comb out of her bag and running it through her hair, all the time hoping the other woman would just go for she felt that Alice was going to probe and pry until her curiosity was satisfied. In this Rose was right.

When she could dally no longer and left the sewing room, Alice was dawdling outside in the corridor. 'This Jeff then, tell me about him,' she said, falling into step with Rose.

'No!' she was stung into replying. 'It's none of your business, Alice.' She began to walk faster but the other woman simply adjusted her stride to suit.

'Oh, hoity-toity, eh? What's the matter, don't you want Dr Morris to find out about him?'

Rose stopped and turned to face her. 'Look, Dr Morris has nothing to do with it, I told you.'

'I bet you haven't told the good doctor about this Jeff,

though, have you?' Alice could read the answer in Rose's
face. 'I thought you hadn't.'

'There was no reason to tell him. Alice, please leave
me alone,' said Rose. They were outside now, walking
down the drive. Why had Alice turned on her?

'Oh, leave me alone, is it? Little miss put-upon, I suppose. Well, was it because you were put upon that you
ended up on the gynae ward...was it? Was it this Jeff that
put upon you, or should I say put it in you? Is that what
it was?'

Rose gasped. She stopped walking and swung round to
face her tormentor. 'What are you talking about? What?
What do you mean?' Her insides were churning up and
she felt sick. The palms of her hands as she clenched her
fists were damp and clammy.

'Aw, come on, man, what do you think I mean? Do
you think a lass can do what you did and it not get about?
Especially in a place like a hospital. Why, man, it's a little
world on its own.'

'Shut up!' Rose said, her voice hoarse with emotion
and Alice's face went red, eyes closing to mere slits as she
glared at the younger girl.

'Oh, shut up, is it? Oh, aye, it would be. Getting off
with a doctor now, aren't you? Too good for the likes of
us. But I know what I know an' I'm telling you – you're
a nowt, that's what you are. A bloody nowt! You should
have been in Durham gaol, that's where you should have
been, doing what you did. You dirty little hoor!'

Rose started to run, rushing for the gate. For minute of absolute panic she imagined that Alice had found out about her and her dad, that that was what she was talking about, that was why she had changed towards Rose. Then reason told her that Alice must have heard why she had been in hospital, but how?

There were people around them hurrying down the drive, rushing for buses, anxious to get home before it rained, for the sky was overcast and lowering. But they paused in their hurry, mouths opening in surprise, gazing at the two women obviously having a row. Rose couldn't bear it. She felt like a sideshow. Her run turned into a sprint.

Alice was close behind her, though, that hateful voice still in her ear. 'Think you're somebody, don't you? Think if you get off with a doctor, folks will forget you mucky past. Well, I'm telling you, madam –'

What it was that Alice was going to tell her was blessedly lost to Rose, for as she ran along the road a bus came and she jumped on it, caring not at all where it was going, wanting only to get away. She didn't look back to see Alice standing on the pavement, mouth open, watching her prey escape.

Rose sat down on the first empty seat on the road side, away from the pavement, her shoulders hunched, staring unseeing out of the window. Someone sat down beside her but she barely registered the fact.

'Fares, please!'

She heard the conductress but didn't react.

'Come on, I cannot stand here all night.' The conductress was impatient now. Leaning over the person sitting beside Rose, she shouted in her ear, 'Where do you want to go, love?'

It brought Rose out of her stupor. She turned and saw the woman, hands ready on the machine clipped to her belt.

'Sorry! Emm...how far do you go?' Rose hadn't an idea where the bus was going. A quick look out of the window showed her that the street they were on was strange to her.

'Blackhall. Ticket to Blackhall, is it?' The conductress wasn't even looking at Rose but leaning over to ring the bell; the bus slowed to a halt and the girl next to Rose got off. Rose fumbled in her bag and took out her purse, handed over half a crown. 'Yes, Blackhall, please.' Though for the minute she couldn't even remember where Blackhall was.

Grumbling about change, the woman took her money anyway and handed back a handful of pennies and one sixpence. 'You should try to have the right change next time, lass,' she said, and went off down the bus.

They were out of Hartlepool now, trundling along the coast road. Looking out of the window, catching glimpses of the sea, Rose suddenly knew where she was and that she must get off. Oh, yes, she wanted to get off here. More than anything else in the world she wanted to, yearned for it.

She pushed her way out of the seat and hurried to the front, searched for a bell and rang it. The bus slowed and pulled into the stop by an underpass under the railway.

'Hey, you said Blackhall –' the conductress shouted but Rose had the door open. She jumped down on to an asphalt path and stood for a moment in the drizzle of rain before walking off through the underpass. 'Some folk don't know where they want to be,' the conductress grumbled and rang the bell for the driver to set off. The bus was half-empty now and she sank down in the front seat, resting her weary feet. Only the journey back to the depot and her shift was ended, she told herself thankfully.

Rose passed a noticeboard. She could just make out the words. 'Crimdon Caravan Site' and in capitals above 'EASINGTON DISTRICT COUNCIL'. She passed by mostly empty caravans, lined up along deserted roads. A few were occupied. It was getting to the tail end of the season, she realised, the end of September. The site probably closed in October, after the school half-term holiday.

Rose wasn't really interested in the caravans, however; she was making for the edge of the cliff at the other end of the site, the steps leading down to the sands. The sea was loud in her ears, waves crashing angrily on the shore when she got down. It was going to be a stormy night, she thought dimly, but it didn't give her pause. She walked on.

When her shoes sank into the heavy sands she took them off and pushed one in each pocket of her coat, walking on in her stockinged feet. In her mind she was with Jeff, going along the shoreline to Blackhall Rocks. As the light disappeared her eyes became accustomed to the dark.

She held Jeff's hand. He smiled down at her, face full of love. She could see that plainly even in the dark. The water lapped at her feet, and over them. Unconsciously she was moving closer and closer to the bottom of the cliffs for the tide was half in, not half out. She moved towards him, put her other hand to his. She could feel the rough tweed of his jacket against the back of it.

She told Jeff about Alice. How nice she had been to Rose when she first went to work there only a few short weeks ago; how nasty she had turned out to be now because she was jealous. That was it. Oh, yes, Rose knew why it was, should have realised it earlier. Alice didn't like the fact that she was friendly with a doctor.

'Oh, no, Jeff,' she said aloud, in case he misunderstood. 'I'm not so friendly as all that. I don't want any lad but you.' And she smiled up at him as the waves crashed and thundered by her side.

She had no hat or scarf, her hair was dripping and the rain was coming down in sheets now, running into her eyes so that she could hardly see where she was going. But she was happy, walking with Jeff, her love. Then gradually instinct for self-preservation made her aware of how cold she was, bitterly cold, and soaked to the skin. She looked around her. Jeff wasn't here, how could he be? She felt bereft, as though he had been with her at least in spirit and now had gone. She was going wrong in her mind, she told herself dismally.

Rose pulled her coat close around her body. The strip

of sand between her and the rocks was narrow now. She looked for a way up the cliff but she couldn't make one out. There were caves, or at least indentations in the rock, but she couldn't be sure the tide wouldn't go that high. She had to make it to the top of the cliff.

She began to hurry. What a fool she'd been, letting Alice get to her like that. As though she didn't have enough to worry about. She must not be very well, she told herself, starting the flu or something. Bob Morris had told her she would have to be careful for a while, her body had been through a traumatic experience when she lost the... No, she wasn't going to think about that either.

At last she found a path, water lapping around the bottom now. Her feet were soaked. She began to climb the steep cliff, the rocks slippery with rain. She reached a patch of grass and stopped, catching her breath in deep painful gasps, and sat down precariously to stare out to sea. There were gaps in the cloud layer now. The moon came through for a fraction of a second, moonlight glinting on the pounding waves below, her own heart pounding with them. But she was almost at the top. She managed to scramble the last bit on her hands and knees and lay there panting, her eyes closed, the pain in her chest so bad she felt it would burst. She felt dizzy and fought to hold on to her senses. She had to get to shelter, get out of these wet clothes, drink something warm.

Her heartbeat slowed. At last she was able to sit up, then stand. She looked about her but the night was black again, there was nothing to see except a string of lights in the distance. She made her way cautiously towards them, stubbed her toe on a stone and even though her foot was freezing cold the pain stabbed up to her knee, making her hop on one leg, holding her foot. The stocking was in shreds, of course. She remembered her shoes but there was only one in her pocket. She must have lost the other in the scramble up the cliff.

Rose limped painfully on, once having to climb over a fence, towards the lights. It was the caravan site. She might find shelter there. But the line of caravans were all dark and empty, their windows shuttered. Spent, she leaned against the nearest, sheltered from the wind. The rain had stopped though there was a steady drip-drip from the sloping roof above her, hitting the steps before the door. She moved to them shakily and sat down, wet though they were. She couldn't get any wetter than she was, she told herself wryly, and her legs were about ready to give out.

Leaning back against the door, she closed her eyes and lifted her face to the sky. The water dripped on her cheek and she moved her head to the side, leaning against the edge of the door and its jamb. Next minute she was sprawling back on a prickly doormat. The door lock must be faulty, she thought dimly, but what she mostly felt was a vast relief to be inside, out of the weather.

The caravan was dark, she couldn't see a thing, but she crawled inside and pushed the door to with her feet.

She would pay the owner, of course she would, tomorrow. Surely he would understand, whoever he or she was?

Magically, there was a carpet, quite a thick one. She felt her body sink into it. There would be a bed, she thought, or a bench at least. She tried to pull herself up, intending to explore with her hands, perhaps find a blanket, the prospect of warmth drawing her on. But she couldn't, her legs were leaden and her arms collapsed under her. She lay down again on the carpet, the blessed carpet. Anyway, she was warm now, was her last thought. It was quite hot in fact, heat washing over her. Rose slipped into the blessed dark.

'Geordie? Geordie! Have a look here, this van's been broken into. The door's not shut properly. Geordie!'

The voice invaded her dream, her lovely dream where she and Michael and Mary were at the seaside, sitting on the sands listening to the sound of the sea. Michael had a shell to his ear. 'I can hear the sea, Rose,' he was saying. He held the shell out to her and she put it to her own ear but she couldn't hear the sea or anything at all except for a man's voice. He was shouting but she couldn't make out what it was he was saying.

'Shut up, will you?' she said to him. 'I want to listen to the sea.' But somehow her voice didn't come out right.

'Hey, Geordie man, there's somebody here,' said the voice. 'It's a lass by the look of it. She looks drowned. I hope to hell she's not dead.'

'Be quiet!' said Rose. 'I'm listening!' This time she was heard.

'Nay, lad, she's not dead,' Geordie observed. 'But I reckon she's not far off it. Run along to the office and telephone for an ambulance, will you?' He went down on his knees beside Rose, felt her head, and she muttered something again. She was cold, dangerously cold, he thought, yet her forehead was hot. 'Can you hear me, lass?' he asked. 'Are you hurt?'

She didn't answer but turned full on to her back, and threw her arms out at him. He caught them and held them.

'Hey now, pet, hold still,' he said, more to himself than her. 'I'll lift you on to the couch.' He gathered her up and she fought him or tried to, her arms and legs going wildly.

'Get off me, Dad!' she cried.

'I'll not touch you, lass,' the man said mildly. He found a blanket in the wardrobe and wrapped it round her, then stood watching her, waiting for the ambulance. She was just a young lass, he thought, not much older than his own Jenny, at school the day. This one was as white as snow and he could hear her breathing, laboured and rasping. How in the world had she got into this pickle?

Chapter Twenty-five

'I can take them back with me any time I bloody well like!' Alf thumped his fist on the table and his teacup jumped in its saucer. He glared at his sister who had risen from her seat opposite him, features working in agitation.

'Oh, no, you cannot!' she said.

'An' who's going to stop me, eh?'

'*I* am.'

Alf laughed. He picked up his cup and took a swallow of the dark, strong tea, then wiped his lips with the back of his hand. Elsie stared at him. She had gone white when he said it but now she was more in control of herself and her lips were set in a thin line as she waited for what he would say next.

'They're my bairns, I can do what I like.' He thought of Mary. By, she was the image of her sister, she was, and growing up as straight as a ramrod. She was just of an age now an' all...

Elsie did not reply at first. She had been prepared for this day for weeks, had rehearsed what she would say

to him over and over when the twins were in bed in the
evenings. Ever since that dreadful night, the one when
Rose had gone. That was the only way she allowed herself
to think of that night; she had blocked out the worst of it.
At first she had had nightmares and woken up in a turmoil,
shaking and sobbing. But gradually they had stopped.
Elsie had told herself every day that it hadn't been her
fault, none of it had been her fault. Anyway, everything
she had done had been for the sake of the twins. And
besides, she hadn't really *done* anything, it was all down
to her brother. She had only tried to help Rose when she
lost her baby; that and protect the twins from what was
happening, of course.

'If you take Michael and Mary away from me, I'll tell
the child welfare people what happened. The police an'
all.'

There, she'd said it aloud. She'd said it in her mind
often enough. Elsie got up from the table and moved a few
steps towards the door almost without thinking. Alf could
be violent, oh, yes, she'd seen that even when they were
children together. And then, that last horrible night – an
image of Rose falling, her hands to her stomach, came
unbidden, but Elsie closed her mind to it.

'No, you would not! You were in it up to your neck.
You helped.' Alf glared at her but he wasn't seriously disturbed by her threats. He could control their Elsie, he was
sure of that. Always had. A weak woman was his sister.

'I'm taking them and be damned to you,' he said. 'You

might as well get their things packed. Where are they anyroad?'

'At school. Where else would they be at this time of the day? An' why aren't you at work on a Monday?'

'I've taken a shift off to come for me bairns,' Alf said comfortably. He sat back in his chair and gave a superior smile.

'Pity you're not getting them then, isn't it?' Elsie flared, reacting immediately. 'You stink of rum. Do you think if I call the polis he'll let you take two canny bairns with you? If you're not careful you'll be losing your job an' all. If you went down the pit smelling of drink like that you'd be out on your arse before you knew what you were at. You an overman too. The bosses wouldn't stand for it.'

'I know what I'm doing. I don't drink when I'm going to work, never you fear!' Alf was stung into replying. The grin had left his face and he jumped up from his chair and took a step towards her. 'And you'd better watch what you're saying, our Elsie, or I'll bat you one!' He was angry because he had twice gone down the pit this last week with drink in him. Luckily he had not been caught nor had he made any serious mistake, but he knew the risk he had run.

Elsie cringed back towards the door. 'Don't you dare lay a hand on me!' she cried. 'I'll have the polis here so fast you won't know what's hit you – I'm telling you!' And looking at her determined face, he knew she meant it.

'Don't be so gormless, Elsie. You know as well as I do

that if you go to the police we'll both be had up for murder. You're as guilty as I am, don't you forget it, and you'll hang along o' me, see if you don't.'

'Do you think it'll make much difference to me, Alf? If you take the twins away, I'll have nothing left to live for. An' at least I'll have got it off me conscience. I tell you, if it wasn't for those two I'd do meself in. They're all I've got, they're everything in the world to me now.' Her voice was hard, bitter, he knew she meant every word she said. They stood face to face, glaring into each other's eyes, and his were the first to drop.

Alf changed abruptly then. He stepped back to the fireplace and took a cigarette butt from behind his ear. 'Aw, howay, our Elsie, I'm not going to hit you. You just get me all riled up, that's all.' There was a brass holder on the hearth, kept filled with rolled newspaper spills by Michael. Alf took one and lit the cigarette butt from the fire. He inhaled deeply, then cupping the butt in an open fist considered what to do.

He didn't know what had got into his sister, she was putting up more of a fight than he'd expected. But he wanted the twins. Mary in particular. So he tried another tack.

'Elsie, you don't know what it's like for me, coming home to an empty house all the time,' he said, full of self-pity. 'Now my Sarah's gone –'

'Aw, go on, don't come the old soldier with me,' said Else, completely unmoved. 'I know you were only too glad when Sarah died, got out of your road. And God only knows what you got up to with Rose.' This was the first time she had admitted, even to herself, that there had been anything unnatural in his relationship with his eldest daughter. This row had brought it all to the surface from where it had been buried deep inside her. She'd let the lass down, she knew that all right. For the sake of the twins.

Alf was staring at her open-mouthed, she noticed. He began to bluster.

'What do you mean? I haven't –'

'No, of course you haven't,' she broke in contemptuously. 'Never touched me when I was a little 'un either, did you? You forget how well I know you, Alf Sharpe.'

'Eeh, Elsie, you want to wash out –' he tried again.

'Shut your mouth!' she shouted, shocking him into doing just that. 'You can get out of my house too. Get out now and don't you ever come back or I swear by God in Heaven I'll have the law on you. And don't think I won't!'

'Now, Elsie, don't be hasty. Consider what you're doing,' he said, trying to calm her down. But she was in the grip of a turmoil of emotions, past considering anything except that she wanted him out, and before the twins came home at that. Never wanted him back either. She was close to breaking point, he realised. Alf was not a clever man but he was not slow either. He saw that if he persisted with his claim to the twins now he wouldn't be able to stop her from going to the police.

'Calm down. Calm down, man. All right, I'm going,'

he said urgently. He moved towards the door and she stepped out of his path. He glanced at her warily as he did so. Her face was a blotchy red, her eyes wild. She was panting as if she had been running.

Alf opened the door and went out into the yard and she followed him as though she didn't trust him not to turn back as soon as she looked away. They were both silent but the silence between them was more eloquent than the row they had just had and fraught with danger.

At the gate he paused, was about to say something more when they were hailed by Mrs Todd. She was leaning on her own gatepost, watching out for what she could see. 'Catching a breath of air' she called it.

'Grand day, isn't it, Elsie?' she remarked by way of a greeting, though she was looking curiously at Alf. Elsie agreed that it was, though her eyes hardly left her brother.

'I see you have a visitor again,' Mrs Todd went on and smiled at Alf.

'Yes. You know my brother Alf, don't you?'

'Oh, 'course I do. It's not that long since he was here. Come to see the twins, have you, Mr Sharpe? Pity they're at school the day.'

Of course they were at school, Elsie thought savagely, wishing to high Heaven that the woman would go inside and mind her own business. Some of her feelings must have communicated themselves to Mrs Todd for she shifted her stance and folded her arms in front of her, the smile slipping.

'Well, I'll have to be getting the washing in,' she said, and even took a few steps into her yard before turning back. 'By the way, Elsie, I meant to say before – was your Rose visiting the other day? One day last week it was I thought I saw her. I remember thinking, done well for herself has Rose. She was in a handsome little car an' all and with –'

'You saw our Rose? You couldn't have done!' The breath was knocked out of Elsie, the words hardly louder than a whisper. Alf had gone white. He had been showing his impatience with the women's chitchat but now he was all attention.

Mrs Todd shrugged, pleased she had remembered. 'I'm sure I did,' she insisted. 'I was going to the fish shop. Me an' the old man likes a nice bit of haddock for supper now and then, you know, and I had to stop at the top of the rows for this car and when I looked in there was Rose, as large as life. Do you mean to say she didn't come to see you? Mind, nothing those young 'uns do surprises me these days. Are you all right, Elsie? You've gone a funny colour. There's a lot of that flu about these days –'

She broke off as Alf took hold of his sister's arm and hustled her up the yard and back into the house.

'How bloody rude can you get?' Mrs Todd asked herself crossly, and went back into her own yard and began feeling the washing on the line to see if it was dry enough to iron.

Inside the next-door kitchen brother and sister stared at each other.

'I thought you said she was dead when you left her in the dene? Hidden, you said she was, covered over. It would be weeks before anybody found her. That's what you said, wasn't it?' Elsie's voice was rising out of control. She was shaking with fear. He caught hold of her by the upper arms and shook her roughly.

'Pull yourself together, woman, you're hysterical. What the hell's the matter with you?' He pulled her over to an armchair, pushed her into it and stood over her. 'Keep your flaming mouth shut, do you hear me?' For Elsie had started to moan. She was rocking herself backwards and forwards in the chair, hands clasped in her lap, fingers working convulsively against each other.

'At least if she's not dead we cannot be had up for murder,' she said, almost to herself. She took not a bit of notice of Alf. It was as if he wasn't there, so he pulled back his arm and slapped her hard across the face. Her head went right over the arm of the chair with the force of the blow. She stopped moaning and stared up at him, eyes wide, her hand held to her face.

'Now you listen to me,' snapped Alf. 'The old biddy couldn't have seen Rose, could she? Because, like I told you, she's dead. Dead and gone. I left her hidden in Shotton Dene, didn't I? An *nobody* could have found her. If they had, it would have been in the paper, wouldn't it? Stands to reason.

'Now, go and wash your face before the bairns get in from school. And don't you ever forget: if you breathe a word of anything that happened, you'll lose those kids as sure as eggs is eggs. They'll go into a home, and you and me, dear sister . . . you and me will hang in Durham gaol.'

Alf stood back, his hands on his hips, breathing heavily. All the effects of the rum he'd drunk earlier were gone now, and he was as sober as a judge. Gradually Elsie took hold of herself. She took a hankie out of her pinny pocket and blew her nose, then felt her cheek gingerly with her fingertips.

'There was no call for that, Alf Sharpe,' she said. 'You hit me that hard it's a wonder you didn't break my jaw. Now I suppose there'll be a bruise and I won't be able to get out at all for what people will say.'

'Well, you brought it on yourself,' he replied. Now that she was calmer he could afford to relax a bit. 'I'm telling you – go on as though nothing has happened. Nothing *has* happened anyroad. Say you fell against something if anyone asks about your face. And think yourself lucky you can keep the twins. At least for the time being. I'll be going now. I might as well go to work the night.'

The slap, the worry about Rose even, were forgotten. Elsie smiled, albeit painfully. 'Eeh, thanks, Alf. You know they're better off here with me anyway.'

He went to the door then turned and said, 'Aye, well, you think on. Keep that bloody trap shut. If you don't, you'll get more than a slap in the gob.'

'An' I'm telling you – you touch me again and I *will*

have the law on you,' she retorted. 'I don't bloody care any more.'

Alf grinned in disbelief. As he walked out of the gate Mrs Todd was there once more. 'Not waiting to see the twins then, Mr Sharpe? I'm sure they'll be sorry to have missed you. They must look forward to seeing their dad, poor, motherless bairns that they are.'

'I have to go on shift, woman,' he snarled and strode off down the street. Sniffing, she started after him. 'That fella has something on his mind,' she said to her husband later in the day. 'Something bad an' all, I'll be bound. He cannot look a body in the eye.'

'You're imagining things, woman, as usual,' he replied. 'Is this all I'm to get for me tea?' He eyed the two boiled eggs on his plate with disfavour. 'Mebbe if you took less notice of other folk and more of me you'd have time to make a man a nice meat pie when he's had a hard shift underground.'

'It's washing day! I've been grafting all day. If you'd dig deep in your pocket and buy me one of them new electric washers I'd have time to bake. 'Til then, you'll get what I've time for!' she replied tartly.

Chapter Twenty-six

'Brian's gone to hospital,' said Jeff as he came into the house he had shared with Brian and Marina since they came back from their honeymoon.

'What?' Marina's heart jolted. She turned from the shiny new gas stove where she was frying liver and onions, the pan in her trembling hand, fat spattering on to the blue and white linoleum.

'Hey!' said Jeff. What a fool he was, coming out with it just like that. 'Only Outpatients. He's all right, just a cut on his head. There was a fall of stone but it was a little one and it nearly missed him altogether. A bit of stone flew up, that's all, and cut him.'

Marina put the pan back on the stove and turned off the gas, her hand still shaking. 'Jeff, man, you gave me a fright there.'

'Aye, I should have had more sense,' he said. 'Me tongue's quicker than me brain. I'm sorry, lass.'

'Are you sure he's all right? Maybe I should go down there. Easington, is it?' Marina was already untying the apron she had donned when she came in from work.

'No, the Cameron. There was a few hurt, none badly like, but they sent some of them to the Cameron. Spreading the load, I reckon.'

Marina hesitated. The Cameron was in Hartlepool and a bus journey of a few miles. 'Come on, I'll run you down,' Jeff offered, looking regretfully at the pan of liver from which there was a gorgeous smell, enough to entice any man, let alone one who'd been hard at it cutting coal all day. That was one of the good things about having his friend and his wife living in with him. He hadn't to eat in the colliery canteen all the time if he wanted a decent meal.

'Will you? Do you mind?' But Marina was already pulling on her coat, pushing her feet into knee-high boots. 'Do you not want to eat first?'

'I'd only get indigestion, rushing it,' said Jeff. But he took a piece of liver from the pan, dark brown and glistening and piping hot. He juggled it in burning fingers but managed to convey it to his mouth, chewing appreciatively. 'Ooh, scrumptious,' he said when he was able.

'It'll soon warm up when we get back.' Marina was apologetic. 'Anyway, we can give Brian a lift home. If there are a few of them and they have to wait for an ambulance...' She went to the door and looked back at him. Jeff followed, taking out his car keys as he did so. At least he wasn't in his black, having washed at the pithead baths.

When they arrived at Outpatients there were only a couple of miners left waiting, one with his arm in a sling which looked startlingly white against his jacket still black with coal dust. The other had a bandage round his head, a few spots of blood mixed with the black on his cheek. Marina flew to him and flung her arms around him, careless of the coal dust which flew up and would almost certainly mean her light brown coat would have to go to the cleaner's.

'Brian! Are you all right? I was so worried,' she cried.

'Of course I'm all right,' he said. 'Get off me, Marina, you'll be filthy.' He looked sideways at the other miner who was all grinning interest. Brian was embarrassed that one of his new workmates should see the fuss his wife was making. Newly married men had enough ragging to put up with in the pit without Marina giving cause for more.

He was blushing, she realised, though it was difficult to see through the coal dust on his face. 'But are you sure you're not badly hurt?' she asked anxiously, though she stood back from him and brushed ineffectively at the marks on her coat.

'No, I'm fine. Did Jeff not tell you?' He looked accusingly at his friend who shrugged and glanced at Marina. Women! his glance said eloquently. 'I'm just waiting for the doctor to look at my X-ray, then we can be off. Just a few stitches in my head, that's all I've got. If I'd ducked a bit sharper the blooming stone would have missed me altogether.'

'Too slow to catch cold,' Jeff commented, and turned to the miner with his arm in a sling. 'How about you, Bert? Can I give you a lift?'

'No, thanks, lad. Broke me wrist,' he replied. 'I have to wait for the plasterman, they've called him in.' He gazed at the sling. 'Flaming nuisance it is, I was going to have the garden dug over this weekend, give the soil a chance to break up before the winter.' Bert was a champion gardener, Jeff remembered; he had an allotment at the other end of the colliery. He'd won first prize at the leek show at the Club a few weeks ago: twenty pounds and a chiming clock.

'Never mind, you'll get a few weeks off now while that mends,' Jeff said by way of consolation, but Bert looked anything but consoled. He grunted and pulled a face. Jeff remembered then that Bert's missus was notorious in the colliery for being a nag, perhaps one of the reasons he spent so much time on his allotment.

'Brian Wearmouth?' A nurse had appeared at a door to one side and Brian started to get to his feet. She saw him and came over to them. 'Your X-ray was clear, Mr Wearmouth.' She smiled brightly. 'You must have a hard head, that's all. Now you can go, but first of all take this to the office over there, you'll get a note for your doctor. And come back in ten days to have the stitches out.' She nodded and went over to Bert, the last customer of the day by the look of things.

'Thank the Lord it's nothing worse,' Marina said to Brian as the three of them trooped over to the window of the office. Two doctors were in there talking and a man was sitting at the desk before the window, putting a letter in an envelope and sealing it up.

'Won't be a minute, Mr Wearmouth,' he said, then his attention was distracted as another doctor came into the office and began to talk to him. Jeff heard something one of the doctors said, something about Rose Sharpe. He could have sworn the man said Rose Sharpe...

'Rose?' he said aloud, leaning into the window. The two men in white coats looked up, startled, the older man frowning irritably.

'Pardon me?' he said haughtily.

'I'm sorry, I thought you mentioned the name of a friend of ours.'

'This a private conversation,' said the doctor and turned his back, but by now the younger one was only half attending to what he was saying. He stood gazing after the two miners and the girl, obviously the wife of the one who had been hurt. They were going out of the door.

Perhaps they had been talking about the same Rose Sharpe, thought Bob, and as soon as he could he broke off the conversation with a hurried apology and went after them. They must have gone for the bus, he reckoned, all three wouldn't be allowed in the NCB ambulance. He ran down to the gates but the bus stop was empty. There was a tooting behind him and he stood aside automatically as a car went out of the grounds. He didn't notice the occupants; for some reason it didn't occur to him that they might be in a car. Oh, well, it probably wasn't even the same Rose they seemed to know.

Jeff parked the car outside the house and Marina and Brian went inside, Brian looking pale and tired now under the layer of coal dust. He was glad to go upstairs and lie in the steaming hot bath which Marina ran for him in the newly installed bathroom which had been taken off the spare bedroom.

She warmed up the liver and onions and sliced fresh bread she had bought on her way home from work. Ages ago now, it seemed. Both she and Jeff were quiet as they ate, Marina because of the events of the evening. She couldn't help thinking of what could have happened. Only a fraction of an inch and Brian would have been dead or at least badly injured, despite his miner's helmet. She shivered and put down her knife and fork, suddenly not hungry any more.

Jeff, though concerned for his friend, was thinking of other things. He wished he had kept quiet and listened to what the doctors were saying about Rose. It wasn't so common a name that there could be two of them, was it? Was she in Hartlepool? Was she ill or hurt, was that why the doctors were discussing her? He resolved to go there the following Saturday and look around a bit. Maybe, just maybe – and he knew it was a chance in a million for the twin towns of West Hartlepool and Hartlepool must hold thousands of people – he might find her. And he could always go to the hospital, keep a lookout for that young doctor. He might know where Rose was. For Jeff felt in his bones that she was near, certainly not as far away as London.

Brian came down, his face now almost as white as the bandage round his forehead apart from an angry red graze on one cheek. Marina fussed around him, bringing him his dinner which had been keeping hot in the oven. But he ate little and after a while went up to bed, saying he had a headache.

'Not surprising if you persist in standing under falling stones,' joked Jeff. He was grinning but his eyes showed his sympathy.

'I won't be long coming up,' Marina promised. 'I'll just clear this lot away and set the breakfast things.' She bustled about the kitchen, her expression thoughtful. It had jolted her all right, the accident. What must it be like for women who had their men killed in the pit? She thought of the disasters she had been told about, so many in the past. But surely it was different now? The mines were nationalised, there were proper safety measures, of course there were. Yet a fragment of an old song, a lament, ran through her head as she dipped the plates in soapy water and rubbed at them with the dish cloth.

> *Let us think of Mrs Burnett,*
> *Once had sons but now has none,*
> *In the Trimdon Grange explosion*
> *Joseph, George and James are gone.*

Trimdon Grange. That wasn't so far away from here, was it? Fire damp it was that had ignited and killed so many men and boys. Marina shook herself mentally. It had been long ago, she was becoming morbid. She rinsed the plates and put them in the rack above the gas stove. By, it was nice having all these new conveniences. She didn't know how she could go out to work if she didn't have them.

'Jeff, is there fire damp in the pit here?'

She had not intended to ask the question, it just seemed to pop out, as it were, surprising her as much as it did Jeff. He had been staring into the fire, feet stretched out to the blaze.

'Fire damp?' he asked. 'The gas, do you mean?' He looked up, thoughts obviously still far away. She nodded.

'Well... we always have to be on the watch, you know, that's why the rules are so tough. No smoking down the mine, you know that. "Contraband" they call it.' He looked at her properly, realising she was really bothered. 'Hey now, what's up? Why are you asking questions like that?' But he knew. The poor lass had got a shock tonight, the dangers of the pit brought home to her.

'Oh, I just thought...' said Marina vaguely.

Jeff sat up straight. 'Now look, I told you, the safety

men look after everything. There's no need for you to worry your head. Come on now, get off to bed. A night's sleep will do you the world of good.'

He had been going to ask her if she'd taken notice of what those two doctors had been talking about, but tonight was not the time. She was too upscuttled by what had happened to Brian. Or what had almost happened to Brian. It could have been so much worse.

'Goodnight then, Jeff. Thanks for taking me in to the hospital.'

'Goodnight,' he echoed.

Upstairs she undressed in the dark so as not to disturb Brian then slipped into bed beside him. Marina lay quietly on her back for a moment or two then automatically turned and put her arms around him, lying close, drawing up her legs to fit the curve of his, resting her head against the hollow between his shoulder blades. He moved a little, settled himself more comfortably against her, took her hand in his and held it to his chest yet didn't seem to wake.

Marina's thoughts ran back over the last few weeks. Their honeymoon in Scarborough...the first night she had been so scared of. What a fool she had been! she thought, smiling to herself. Brian had noticed nothing, she was sure of it. That story about a man knowing if a girl was experienced was just an old wives' tale, it must be. And he was a good lover, a gentle man, careful to please her, anxious that she should be satisfied. Oh, yes, indeed he was. Warmth spread in the pit of her stomach as she thought of it.

They had lain in bed in the tiny room of their board-ing house – obviously originally one large bedroom now partitioned into two for one wall was flimsy and thin. She had been worried they would make too much noise and whoever was next door would hear it all. But none of that mattered really. All that did was that Brian loved her and she loved him and their love was growing every day.

Soon they would have their own house, she thought drowsily. She was saving every penny of her own salary for a deposit on a house. They had their eyes on a semi-detached on the outskirts of Easington village, still close enough to the colliery for Brian to get to work without too much trouble.

Her thoughts drifted, soothed by the warmth of the bed and the proximity of her man. Before she slept she murmured a prayer for Rose as she did every night. That she should be kept safe, that Rose's father should get his comeuppance, that... what was that the doctor had said tonight? It was on the edge of her consciousness, some-thing about Rose... But Marina was asleep before the memory came back properly to her.

'I'll ring and tell Mr Brown I can't go in today,' she said to Brian next morning. 'He'll understand, of course he will. I'll tell him you've had an accident and...'

'No, you don't have to stay at home for me. There's

nothing at all the matter with me now. I haven't even got a headache,' he replied, smiling. 'Tell you the truth, I'll just wander away down to Bert's allotment for a chin-wag. We'll both be glad to have a bit of time away from the women.' He ducked as she aimed a blow at him then winced as the movement gave him a twinge of pain. The bandage was off now, the doctor having told him to leave the stitches open to the air. There was going to be a scar across his forehead, Marina thought. Thank God there was nothing worse than that.

'Sure?' she queried, still anxious.

'Oh, go on. Jeff will be in this afternoon, won't he? He'll keep me company.'

On the bus in to Durham, thoughts of Rose kept coming back to Marina. She couldn't get her friend out of her mind. It hadn't been like that all the time since Rose had disappeared, especially since her own marriage with so much else to think about. Was something wrong? Was Rose in trouble? Perhaps she wasn't in London at all, perhaps she was somewhere near. That doctor last night, had he been talking about her friend?

Marina shook herself mentally as she descended from the bus in the market place at Durham and walked briskly down over the bridge to Old Elvet. She was being silly. She remembered her gran going on like this. She'd had a bit of a name for the second sight, always knew when anyone was ill or in trouble. Or at least she'd insisted that she did; Marina was always slightly sceptical. Deliberately she turned her mind to other things. Shivering, she huddled her chin into her collar, there was a sharp wind blowing up the Wear. It was almost Christmas, she thought, looking in a shop window as she passed. A girl was decorating a tree with shiny baubles and coloured lights. Something to look forward to, her first married Christmas. Next year they could be in their own home. Not that it was bad living with Jeff, he was a sensitive soul and tried to give them the privacy they needed. She would buy him a nice present, she decided, talk it over with Brian first to see what he might want.

It made no difference how she tried to keep her mind on other things, though. Thoughts of Rose persisted all through the day.

Chapter Twenty-seven

Rose lay against the pillows in the hospital bed, her face almost as white as the linen. She was wearing an oxygen mask, she knew. In her time at the hospital she had come to recognise a lot of the equipment. Her chest hurt. In fact, she was sure there must be a knife cutting into her side. She tried to move out of its way, but that only made the pain worse, much worse. She was desperately hot and tried to push back the bedclothes, let some air get to her fevered skin.

This is a dream, she told herself. In a minute I'll wake up and everything will be all right. She remembered the beach at Crimdon, how cold it had been, how icy the sea water when the waves washed over her feet and legs. She longed to feel the waves again, hear Jeff whisper to her...I'm in a caravan, she told herself, lying on the floor and it's hard as rocks. I'm hot because the sun is shining in through the roof light. I must stir myself, I must. I have to get out of here before someone finds me. By a tremendous effort of will she opened her eyes fully, forced herself awake.

She was wrong about the caravan, right about the oxygen mask. The sun was coming through a window opposite, beaming across the floor of the ward and landing on her bed. A hospital bed, hard and unyielding though the pillows were soft.

Oh, God, here I am again, she thought despairingly. Back in the Cameron. This time she was on a medical ward. Sister Macpherson was coming towards her, and she was on the medical side, Rose was sure of it.

'Oh, good, you're awake,' Sister remarked and smiled her professional smile. With cool, capable hands she removed the oxygen mask and turned off the cylinder, wheeling it away into a corner. Rose breathed a sigh of relief. She had felt the mask was choking her though she knew it couldn't possibly be.

'Good morning,' said Sister Macpherson. 'Welcome back.' She smiled at Rose, watched her chest for a moment or two, checking on her breathing.

'How... how did I get here?' she managed to croak.

'By ambulance,' replied Sister Macpherson. 'I understand the caretaker at Crimdon Dene caravan site found you. And lucky for you he did! If you went any longer without treatment you could have been a goner. Pneumonia, my girl. You ought to be taking better care of yourself, you know. As it is, you can thank your lucky stars for penicillin.' She stuck a thermometer in Rose's mouth and placed cool fingers on her pulse.

'What day is it?' Rose asked when Sister had removed

the thermometer and written something down on the chart on the end of Rose's bed.

'Tuesday. You've been here four days.' Sister called to a junior nurse walking by and together they lifted Rose gently forward, shook up her pillows and laid her back. Expertly they stripped the bed, rolling Rose about as though she were a parcel. They pulled the draw sheet through so that she was lying on a cool part. The bed was made up in double quick time and then Sister was on her way. 'Doctor's round in half an hour,' she said over her shoulder.

Rose felt as though a hurricane had gone through the ward; she was exhausted. She closed her eyes, hearing the distant voices of the patients and nurses, the rattle of cups on a tea trolley, the everyday sounds of a full ward. How stupid she'd been, going down on to the beach like that. See where it had got her. But she had felt close to Jeff there, beside the waves of the North Sea, and it had been so sweet. Too fanciful, that was what she was. Jeff wasn't at Crimdon, not unless he was working hundreds of feet below the North Sea waves. Was Crimdon close enough to Easington for that? No, of course not.

Her meandering thoughts were interrupted by a familiar voice.

'Here we are again then, Rose Sharpe.'

Rose opened her eyes. Bob Morris was standing there, looking grim. 'What did you think you were doing, girl?'

She looked at him, weak tears pricking her eyelids. He

had been her only friend since she came to Hartlepool, for that last afternoon in the sewing room had shown her that she had no friends there. A tear squeezed out of the corner of her eye and she dashed it away angrily.

'Come on now, none of that,' he said, his voice softening. He went over to the screens at the end of the ward and pulled a couple over, placing them round the bed. Sister appeared, popping her head through the screens, looking disapproving.

'Can I help you, Dr Morris?'

He smiled apologetically. After all, he was technically a visitor to the ward and should have asked her permission, but she had been out of sight when he came in and he had been so relieved to see Rose awake.

'No, thank you, I'm not examining the patient, I can manage on my own,' he replied smoothly, and Sister ducked out of sight again.

'Did something happen, something to make you take off like that?' he asked. 'You might as well tell me, Rose.'

'Lily,' she protested but Bob shook his head irritably.

'We'll have no more playing silly buggers, Rose. That's your name, there's not a thing wrong with your memory.'

'Are you doctor on this ward?' she asked. That was something else she'd learned since working in a hospital, that doctors had their own areas.

'No, you know that,' he replied. 'I just came in to see how you were. What did you think you were doing, out at Crimdon that night? I came to pick you up, you know, take you out to supper, and when the landlady said you hadn't been home, well...'

Oh, yes, thought Rose, he had said he would do that. But it had been driven out of her head along with everything else after the encounter with Alice. The animosity, not just from Alice, she'd felt from the others in the sewing room. What had she done to deserve it?

'I'm sorry,' she whispered, and looked up at him with great dark tragic eyes which were further accentuated by the translucent white of her skin. He was moved to compunction for badgering her. How could he have done? But he had been so worried about her. If she'd lain undiscovered in that caravan down by the shore for much longer, not even the wonder drug, penicillin, could have saved her.

He coughed behind his hand to mask his emotion. 'Well, never mind now,' he said, taking her hand, feeling the fragile bones of her wrist. Dear God, she was so painfully thin. What on earth was it that haunted her so?

'Dr Morris, the rounds are about to begin.' Sister poked her head through the screens yet again and he withdrew his hand from Rose's quickly.

'Yes, Sister. I'm going now.' He began to push the screens back from the bed but she waved a hand imperiously. 'We'll do that, thank you, Doctor.'

Bob cast a wry smile at Rose. 'I'll see you later,' he said in an undertone. He passed Dr Wray, the medical consultant, as he went out of the door and exchanged greetings with him. The other doctor looked slightly puzzled, but he was a mannerly man and asked no questions.

Walking over to the doctors' rest room, for he had been called out in the middle of the night to yet another poor woman who had been bleeding heavily after a botched back-street abortion, Bob pondered on his own mixed feelings for Rose. He had truly thought he was only interested in her history but there was something about the girl which he couldn't get out of his mind. Her love for her young brother and sister, her parent anxiety for them... yet when he'd gone to see them they had shown no signs of being anything but healthy. He would also say they were happy with their aunt. But he wondered about the father, brooded over it in his spare moments, hating to think the problem was what he suspected it to be in his darker moments.

Bob longed to chase away the shadows which were so evident on Rose's face. He was falling in love with her, he realised it now. She had crept inside his heart. He poured himself a cup of coffee from the pot keeping warm on the hotplate, added sugar and took it to a worn leather armchair. He sat down, leaning his head into the hollow in its back made by generations of young doctors before him. Rose, he thought. How shocked he had been when she had been brought in unconscious. What a relief it was now she had come out of her coma. Of course it would be weeks before she was fully well again, but at least the first step had been taken.

He drank his coffee. It was strong and sweet yet left a bitter taste on his tongue. But he needed it, had a ward round with his consultant in half an hour. And then, if the woman brought in during the night should have a relapse...

'Damn those back-street butchers to hell,' he said savagely to the empty room. 'With their knitting needles and crochet hooks, their slippery elm bark. A filthy trade altogether.' The clock on the mantel above the gas fire ticked away, the only answer to his tirade.

He thought again of last evening when he had spoken to Dr Wray in the office in Outpatients, asking his opinion on Rose and why she had taken so long to respond to the antibiotic.

'She was a patient of mine,' he'd explained. 'So I'm interested in her condition.'

'Rose Sharpe? Coming along. I'm sure the penicillin will do its work. Just as well, she would have stood a poor chance –'

'Rose Sharpe?'

The question had interrupted the two doctors and Dr Wray, a physician of the old school, had been outraged. Bob himself had been taken aback too, but only for a second or so. The question had come from one of the group of miners injured in a mine accident or maybe it was his friend. As was always the case, doctors in the hospital not busy at the time had been called into Outpatients to deal with the influx expected when they were warned a mine accident had happened. But there had only been a few miners, their injuries slight, thank God.

Bob could kick himself for not catching the two miners and the girl before they left the hospital. There had been an opportunity there to solve the puzzle and he had let it go. Too slow by half, he'd been. Impatiently, he pulled himself up out of the armchair and, running a hand over his hair, straightening his tie and checking his white coat in the mirror, for his consultant was a stickler for the niceties, went back to the wards.

It occurred to him as he strode along the corridor that of course the miners had come from Easington Colliery, and the addresses of those injured would be on record in Outpatients. He might be able to find out something there. Though he would have to be very, very careful. He didn't want to distress Rose further. Not for the world.

'What a foolish young woman you are,' observed Dr Wray. 'You almost died, did you know that?'

Rose lowered her eyes to her clasped hands, lying on a white sheet turned over the regulation ten inches on to the green cotton counterpane. Her straight black hair, longer than she normally kept it, was combed back from her face and tied at the nape of her neck with a piece of ribbon one of the nurses had found in the odds and ends box in the linen cupboard. Her black lashes fanned out over her cheeks, which were stained a delicate pink now as she blushed slightly at his mild reproof.

'I'm sorry to put everyone to such trouble,' she mumbled.

Dr Wray softened. This girl was just about the age of his own daughter, now at Newcastle Medical School, studying to be a doctor like her father. Crossed in love, he supposed. Ah, the agony of being young. He sincerely hoped his Janet didn't get into a state over some young fool, or at least not before she finished her training. But then, Janet was a level-headed sort of a girl. Her great passion was medicine and he was very proud of her progress. He turned his attention back to the girl in the bed. She'd do, he reckoned.

'Ah, well, let it be a lesson to you,' he droned, and even to himself sounded like an old fogey. He looked at Sister Macpherson, standing respectfully beside him with the pile of case notes. He took up Rose's file and wrote something in it, then nodded and prepared to go on his way.

'When will I be able to go home, Doctor?' Rose asked, though her small bare room down by the docks could hardly be called a home, she thought.

'Don't be in such a hurry, young lady,' he admonished, hardly pausing in his stride, so well used was he to that particular cry from patients. 'You've been seriously ill, remember.'

It wasn't that she particularly wanted to go, Rose thought to herself as she watched his stately progress up the ward amidst his little court of junior doctors and Sister. She fingered a neat machine-done darn in the sheet under her hands, one of her own stitching very likely. But neither did she want to see Alice or any of the other women in the sewing room, not yet, not until she felt stronger. And Mrs Timms was bound to find out where she was. No doubt she had been informed already.

At the moment Rose felt like nothing so much as crawling off into a hole and not seeing anyone, anyone at all. Not even Dr Morris. All she wanted was a bit of peace, as her mother used to say. And almost immediately her peace was shattered by Sister's voice.

'Now then, Miss Sharpe.'

Rose sighed and opened her eyes. Sister had drawn a chair up to the bed; she took a pen out of her breast pocket and held it poised over a paper in Rose's file.

'I see you didn't give the name of your next of kin the last time you were in the hospital. I'll have it now, please. It's essential we have it, one of our rules.'

Rose stared at her. The Sister's determined expression made it plain she intended to receive answers to her questions. Dad was her next of kin, thought Rose. Her dad, and he had left her to die. She hadn't realised it at first but she did now. She would never give his name, never. Nor Aunt Elsie's. She had helped him, hadn't she? That nightmare scene in the bedroom flashed through her mind, making her tremble.

'Miss Sharpe? Rose?'

The Sister's voice was softer. She had seen that fear, and was almost ready to admit defeat before she had begun.

Her questions could wait for a few days, she reasoned. Rose Sharpe was still very weak. Sister got to her feet and hovered over the girl in the bed, putting one hand to her brow. It was clammy.

Rose looked up at her. 'Marina Morland,' she murmured. 'Marina Morland. She lives in Jordan, near Bishop Auckland. She's . . . she's my cousin.'

They only needed it in case she should become seriously ill or die. They wouldn't get in touch otherwise, she was sure. But even if they did, Marina wouldn't tell Alf Sharpe where Rose was, of course she wouldn't. She was perfectly safe.

It was another two weeks before Dr Wray decided that Rose might go home. By that time she had progressed from sitting out of bed in an armchair to being able to go to the bathroom by herself, to walking shakily round the ward on the arm of a nurse until her legs no longer felt as though they belonged to someone else and she could manage by herself.

'You must have at least a month away from work,' he told her. 'Are you sure you have someone to care for you?'

'Oh, yes, Doctor,' she replied, crossing her fingers behind her back. Well, her landlady was there, wasn't she? In any case, she was better now. All she needed was a quiet rest, something which was impossible on the busy ward. She would be fine.

Jeff cared for her, she thought. All she needed was him.

Oh, Jeff! If only she could see him. She thought of going to him anyway, for surely he still loved her? Of course he did, she'd never doubted it. He loved her as she loved him, for their lifetime. In her weakness she was tempted to go to Easington and find him. He would keep her safe from her dad. But he would hate her, despise her if she told him the truth, wouldn't he? And she couldn't bear that. Oh, Lord, why couldn't she stop thinking of him all the time?

The one thought that didn't occur to her was the contradiction inherent in being so sure of his love yet sure also that love would turn to hatred if he knew about her and her dad.

Dr Morris came to see her just before she left the ward. But she was guarded with him, remembering how he had so innocently provoked jealousy among her workmates. She couldn't help feeling a sense of relief that she had not to go back to the sewing room. Not at least until she was stronger.

It was a few weeks later, when Bob Morris happened to be in the hospital records office, that he thought of asking to see her file and there, in the next-of-kin slot, was a name. One which evidently Rose was not afraid to give.

Chapter Twenty-eight

Kate was excited as she dressed in her best black costume and combed her hair, now more grey than brown, into a roll around her head, fixing it in place with kirby grips. She glanced in the mirror above the fireplace. Though she said it herself she still looked handsome and the white frilly blouse she wore to lighten the mourning outfit looked very pleasing. She fixed a tiny hat over the roll, securing it with a pearl hatpin at the back. There, she was almost ready to go.

She smiled at her reflection. Marina had said there was a nice surprise waiting for her when she last wrote, and Kate had a fair idea what it was. Her daughter and son-in-law had been talking of buying a house ever since they were married and when they did, she, Kate, was invited to live there with them. By, she would be glad to be shot of Jordan! All the heartache she'd had here. She looked around the room. To her it was full of ghosts. A new house, with no associations with the past, that was just the ticket, she told herself. And she would never interfere with the young couple, never be a burden either.

A knock at the door made her frown in irritation. Who the heck was that? She'd paid the milkman only five minutes ago and the insurance man had been the night before for his money. She couldn't afford to miss her bus, she thought, as she went to open the door.

'I'm so sorry for disturbing you,' the stranger standing on the step said politely. 'But I wonder, is it possible for me to speak to Miss Morland? Miss Marina Morland?'

He was well dressed in a gabardine coat open over a good wool suit. Quite young, Kate saw, and mannerly. He held his trilby hat in his hand before him, a spotlessly clean hand, the nails well tended and cut short. All this registered in the first few seconds as she stared at him, unsmiling. What was he doing chasing after their Marina and her a respectable married woman? But the young man was looking at her enquiringly.

'I'm sorry, it isn't,' Kate collected herself to say. Short and to the point, she thought.

'Oh? But I understood this was where she lived.' The young man looked at a loss for a moment. Kate was about to close the door in his face, for after all it was Saturday and she was getting ready to go through to Easington to visit Marina and Brian, wasn't she? A happy feeling ran through her, a rare thing for her these days.

'An' who might you be then?' she asked instead of putting him straight as to the whereabouts of her daughter.

'Oh, I'm sorry. My name is Dr Morris, Robert Morris. I came here in the hope of having a word with...your daughter, is it?'

Kate shivered. The cold was seeping into the house and she had banked down the fire in preparation for going out. She opened the door wider.

'You'd better come in for a minute, Doctor,' she said. Though there was still a touch of impatience in her voice, she had an inherent respect for medical men. 'There's a gale blowing through here with this dratted door open.'

'Thank you.' He followed her into the kitchen-cum-living room and sat down in the chair she indicated.

Sitting down opposite him Kate gazed squarely into his face. 'Now then, I haven't much time, I've a bus to catch,' she declared.

Bob cleared his throat. 'I'd like to have a word with your daughter,' he said. The woman, Mrs Morland he presumed, said nothing, simply gazed at him then glanced at the clock on the mantelpiece. 'I...about her friend, Rose Sharpe.'

'Rose Sharpe? It's no good asking our Marina where that girl is. She took off, you know. Rose went over to her aunt's place in Shotton then took off. For London, I believe.'

Then they *did* know Rose, Bob thought to himself. He was going to get to the bottom of the mystery at last.

'London?'

'Yes. Our Marina had a postcard from her a while ago. Not a word since so far as I know.'

'When exactly did your daughter receive this card, Mrs Morland, can you remember?'

'Oh, man, it was months ago.' Kate got to her feet and pointedly put on her gloves. 'Now I have to go. Sorry, but I told you I was on my way out.'

Bob stood too and gave what he hoped was a winning smile. 'Will you give me your daughter's address, Mrs Morland? I really do have a good reason for wanting to talk to her about Rose Sharpe.'

'I told you, I haven't time,' she replied as she walked to the door. 'Anyroad, why do you want it?'

'Well, it's confidential, you know. I am a doctor . . .'

'She lives on the coast, Easington Colliery. I'm just off there now.' Kate gave in. If she didn't go now she really would miss the bus. By this time they were out of the house and she had locked the door and set off down the yard.

'She does? Oh, I'm going over that way myself, can I give you a lift?'

Kate's attitude changed immediately. 'Are you sure? I wouldn't be taking you out of your way?' She was beaming as she reached the gate. There were one or two women about, all of them casting curious glances at the Rover drawn up close to the gate in the narrow back street.

'I'm going to Hartlepool at least. I can easily make a small detour and take you to Easington Colliery,' said Bob and his smile showed amused understanding.

'Morning, Jessie,' said Kate to her nosy-parker neighbour who was standing there with a couple of friends, 'having a natter' as she would call it. Gossiping about folk more like! Bob opened the door for Kate with a flourish. 'Just off to see our Marina and her man.' She settled herself on the leather seat – real leather, she could tell good stuff when she saw it – and as they departed waved casually to the open-mouthed women.

As they drove along the ends of the rows they had to pause then overtake the bus standing at the stop. Just getting in was Alf Sharpe.

'That was Rose's father there,' commented Kate.

'Where?' Bob slowed and looked about him.

'Oh, he's gone now,' she said hastily. She definitely didn't want to waste time talking to Alf Sharpe. Bob picked up speed.

Now he knew where he could find Rose's father he could always come back if he needed to. But he remembered Rose's attitude towards her father. She wouldn't like it if he did contact the older man. No, any enquiries he made in that direction would have to be discreet.

'Mrs Morland, come on in,' said Jeff as he opened the door to Kate. He looked at the man behind her, a young man who looked familiar somehow.

'Hallo, Jeff. By, it's parky this morning. That wind's enough to take your ears off,' said Kate by way of greeting. 'This is Dr Morris, he wants to talk to our Marina,' she added, nodding over her shoulder and walking on down the passage leaving the others to follow.

'Mam! You're early. I wasn't expecting you yet,' Marina exclaimed. She was in the kitchen, her face flushed, her brown hair in wisps about her forehead. She had an apron tied around her waist and there was a smell of baking scones heavy on the air.

'Just as well I am early then. If you leave those scones in the oven much longer they'll burn,' said Kate. Still in her coat and hat she whipped a cloth off the line and opened the oven door. 'Done to a turn. You're improving, pet,' she went on as she took out the tray and tipped the scones on to a wire rack on the kitchen table.

'Marina, there's someone here to see you,' said Jeff, ushering in Bob. 'Dr Morris did you say your name was?'

'That's right. You're Marina Morland?' Bob held out his hand to Marina and, looking surprised, she took it. 'I wonder, can we go somewhere where we can talk?'

'Use the sitting room, I'm off now,' suggested Jeff. He was wearing a Sunderland supporters' scarf, red and white with a touch of black, and everyone supposed he was going to the match early. In reality he was earlier than he had intended to be for his expedition but it was nowhere near Roker Park or anywhere else in Sunderland he planned to go.

It was cold in the sitting room for the fire wasn't normally lit except on high days and holidays but Marina switched on a tiny two-barred electric fire. They sat opposite each other, Bob thinking she looked a nice, ordinary girl, obviously newly married, and Marina completely baffled as to what this good-looking young doctor wanted with her. Had she seen him before? She waited for him to explain what he wanted, thinking that if he didn't hurry up her mother would come bursting in asking did he want tea or something, but in reality because she couldn't contain her curiosity.

'I am making enquiries about Rose Sharpe,' he began, and light dawned for Marina.

'Oh, yes, you were one of the doctors talking about her the other night, weren't you? In the hospital, I mean,' Marina said eagerly. 'Do you know where she is?' She frowned as an alarming thought occurred to her. 'She's all right, isn't she? Nothing's happened to her? Or the baby –'

'You do know her? And you knew about the baby?'

'Yes, of course, she's my best friend.'

'And yet you don't know where she is now?'

'She went to London,' said Marina, on the defensive against the implied criticism. 'Oh, please, tell me, is she all right?'

'She is now. She lost the baby.'

'Oh, thank God!' Marina gasped and meant about the baby too, Bob could have sworn. 'Where is she?'

'She's in Hartlepool.'

Marina jumped to her feet and ran to the door and out on to the street. 'Jeff! Jeff!' he heard her calling. 'Rose is all right! She's in –' But her voice trailed away and after a moment she came back into the sitting room and sat down. 'He's already gone,' she said. 'But Hartlepool...I can't believe she's that close. Tell me about her, please. Did she speak to you about me?'

'She gave your name as next of kin.' Bob had to be careful now, felt he couldn't give away anything that Rose wanted kept a secret, but she had given Marina's name, hadn't she? In the end he told her about Rose and her coming into the hospital, about her attack of pneumonia and how ill she'd been. And how she seemed to be terrified of her father and her aunt, worried for her small brother and sister. And Marina in her turn told him about Alf. All about Alf. It was such a relief to say it to someone.

'You won't repeat this to anyone, will you?' she asked anxiously when she'd finished, half wishing she hadn't said anything about it all but there was something about this young doctor that made you want to confide in him. There was something so honest and trustworthy about him.

'No, not while Rose doesn't want anyone to know, I won't,' he said, and his voice sounded amazingly normal in his own ears for inside he was blazingly angry, truly blazing. There was such a fire of rage within him that it threatened to consume him altogether. He couldn't sit still. He got to his feet and walked over to the window, looking out on to the street and the row of houses directly opposite, all exactly the same with their white-stoned steps and gleaming windows shielded by dolly-dyed net curtains. And by the side of each front door a slate in the wall for the lady of the house to chalk the number of bottles that were needed from the milkman.

Of course the slate had originally been for the knocker-up to know which houses need a rap on the window for fore shift but now in the time of alarm clocks...Bloody hell! That poor girl, his poor darling. Damn and blast the man to hell and eternal damnation!

Bob fought to control his emotions in the way he had used ever since he'd first been confronted with the misery and human agony he encountered in his work: by thinking of mundane things. And usually he was fairly successful, but not today, not when it was his Rose. Oh, dear God, no. He remembered with heartaching clarity her face when she was brought into the hospital the first time, how her poor bruised body was so lifeless, so cold, after lying out in that dene for so long in the icy early morning dew. How he and the nurses had worked over her, trying to bring life back to the poor young thing. And had succeeded at last. When she had opened her eyes the fear lurking in their depths had struck him like a blow. All he had wanted to do was gather her to him, keep her safe from the world, from whoever or whatever it was that had brought her to this state.

And then the second time. Dear God...

'Dr Morris?'

He turned from his unseeing survey of the row of houses opposite to the young girl, Rose's friend. 'I'm sorry.' He went back to his seat and sat down, even smiled at Marina.

'I'll come to see her. That will be all right, won't it, Doctor?'

'I'm sure it will. She needs a friend, it will do her good,' he said. Heavens, he was repeating phrases he used about any and all of his patients.

'No one else knows what I've told you, Doctor,' Marina said, anxiety returning. 'Not my family, not a soul, not even Jeff. Oh, they know her dad was rotten to her, mean and violent at times, but they don't know about…about…' She could not quite say it, not again, it had been difficult enough the first time. But, looking up at Bob, she saw him nodding in understanding.

Jeff must be Marina's husband, he surmised, that young fellow who had hurried off to the football. They hadn't been introduced. 'Don't worry, I won't mention it to anyone, I told you.'

'She's left the hospital, you say? Do you have her address?' Bob took out his notebook, wrote the address on it and tore off the page. Then he got to his feet. He had to get out in the open air, would take the car up to the moors and get out and walk and walk until the fresh, clean air blew away some of the filth he felt he was steeped in.

'Thank you, Marina,' he said, holding out his hand to her, 'for being so straight with me. You will go to see her, won't you? On your own. I must stress that I don't think she could face –'

'On my own, Doctor.'

He nodded, satisfied, and they were going towards the door when Kate knocked and put her head round. 'You'll have a cup of tea, Doctor?' she asked, face alive with curiosity.

Drat the woman! he thought, he couldn't wait to go out. But Marina butted in smoothly, 'The doctor is just off, Mam. He has to get back.'

Bob hardly knew whether he mouthed the usual platitudes on leaving or not. His one thought was to get out on to the open road and vent his rage and love and great burden of pity for poor, damaged Rose out of sight of his fellow men.

'Well? What did he want?' Kate asked after the door had closed on Dr Morris and they had the house to themselves, at least until Brian came in. 'Has something happened to Rose? Where is she?'

'I don't know, Mam,' said Marina, feeling the piece of paper in her skirt pocket and lying in her teeth. 'He thought we might know, he'd met her ages ago.'

Kate glared at her daughter. She knew full well that this wasn't the truth. What fellow would come searching for a girl he'd met ages ago and hadn't bothered to keep in touch with since? 'By, our Marina! The day was when you used to tell me everything, we were that close,' was all she said, however, her voice full of hurt.

Marina decided it was time to change the subject. 'Come on, Mam,' she said. 'Brian will be in soon and we're all going to see the new house. Eeh, Mam, it's grand, and there's a lovely room for you. You'll think it's great, I know you will.'

And Kate was instantly diverted. This was what she had been looking forward to ever since Brian and Marina were married.

Chapter Twenty-nine

Jeff drove to Shotton Colliery, his thoughts so full of Rose he could think of nothing else. She wasn't in London, of course she wasn't, that had been a red herring. He had known it at the time. She would have written to him if so. No, something had happened to her, she was in trouble, he was sure of it. Felt it in his very bones.

But that woman in Shotton, her aunt, she must know where Rose was. She *must*. She was Alf's sister, wasn't she? Of the same blood, touched with the same rotten nature? Of course she was. Well, he was going to find out about Rose. He'd had all he was going to take of not knowing, this time he was determined to find her.

Jeff drove along Front Street then pulled into a side street. He would walk from here, he thought, calm himself. He had been letting his thoughts run riot and that was no good. He had to do this right if he was to find out anything at all. Getting out of the car, he turned back into Front Street, looking about him, fixing in his mind the direction to the house he wanted.

Passing the cafe, he glanced in the window, almost without thinking. And stopped and stared. He was hallucinating, he must be. The blood rushed to his head, his vision blurred. For God's sake, it wasn't her, it couldn't be her. He wanted her so much that he was seeing her now when of course she wasn't there at all. He put out one hand to support himself on the window frame, shook his head to clear it. Mind, if any of his friends saw him now they would laugh their caps off, they would. Him, Jeff, champion hewer and a strong man, a *miner*, weak and faint because he thought he saw a woman in a cafe.

Rose sat at a table back from the window, holding the handle of her cup with one hand. With the fingers of the other she crumbled a cream cracker on her plate. She had come back to Shotton, drawn to the place, yearning to catch a glimpse of Michael and Mary, her feelings so strong she felt sure they must know and would come along Front Street. To the sweet shop surely? It was Saturday morning and they would have pocket money to spend. But she had sat here for an hour and hadn't seen them so far. She was just fooling herself.

Dr Morris had been going to drive her here in his car but at the last minute he'd said he had something important he had to do and that was just as well because she had to tell him that it was no good, she was no good to him, there was no future in a relationship between them. Nor ever had been, she thought guiltily. She knew she had been weak, letting him help her. In these last few weeks especially she had needed a friend so badly and he was there, whenever he could get time off from the hospital, bringing her flowers and chocolates, easing the terrible loneliness of her single room in the boarding house down by the docks in this old seaport, so battered by the war.

She was strong enough now to come to Shotton on the bus, she'd told herself. But then she had had to stand all the way and when she had alighted had felt so weak and dizzy that she had come into the cafe and ordered Bovril and crackers for she'd had no breakfast. That was the reason, of course, just plain hunger. She had to be better because Dr Wray had said to her when she saw him in Outpatients yesterday that she could start work on Monday. Oh, Jeff, she thought sadly. Jeff. Sometimes she thought she would never, ever see him again and she couldn't bear it. And his name, the memory of his face laughing into hers, the clean smell of carbolic soap and something else, the essential *Jeff*, kept returning to her at times when she was thinking of something else altogether, and the sense of loss which followed then left her desolate.

She had to think of something else, she thought desperately. Had to eat for a start. But she was having trouble getting the cracker down. The hot Bovril was nice, comforting, reminding her of the times during the war when the rations had almost run out, the night before the Co-op store waggon came round with Mam's order, and they'd had Bovril and bread for supper. She put a sliver of cracker in her mouth and washed it down with the beefy drink and then she looked up at the window again and Jeff was there, leaning against the side of the window, staring at her.

He straightened up, his vision clearing. It *was* Rose, it was! His lovely Rose here in Shotton Colliery on a Saturday morning, not in London, nowhere but here, and he knew that it was this that had drawn him here, the presence of his love. He drank in the sight of her. She was gazing at him now, her lovely dark eyes enormous in her white face, her soft mouth slightly open as she started to rise from her chair to come to him.

Suddenly he moved, pushing the door open, and in two strides was by her side, taking her in his arms and holding her, kissing her, drowning in the total and absolute joy of it. And she was holding him, clinging to him, murmuring his name against the crisp hair at the nape of his neck.

Around them there was an astonished silence lasting for all of ten seconds, then someone chuckled and the cafe owner said, 'Hey, what do you think you're doing? Not in here, if you please.' But he was shouted down by his customers and subsided behind the counter as they began to clap and cheer.

'Come on, my love,' said Jeff and took her hand and walked her out of the cafe and round the corner to where he had parked the car. They got in. It was their own private little world. He took her in his arms again and murmured to her, disjointedly.

'Where have you been? Not a letter . . . you should have written . . . I've been out of my mind . . . Oh, my love, my precious love. Thank God, thank God, thank God...'

Rose couldn't speak, lost in the incredible sweetness of being here, in his arms. In any case there was no need, not yet, for he wasn't waiting for an answer. His lips were on hers, his body pressed against hers and a clamouring was rising within her, a great surge of feeling that refused to be denied.

Someone was knocking at the window, giggling and chattering, sounds which at last penetrated through the haze of Jeff's love. He looked up. There were boys outside the car, young lads of ten or eleven, all grinning and pointing at them, eyes old and knowing, nodding to him to go on; it was a show to them.

'Come away from that car!' a male voice shouted and over on the other side of the road there was a policeman wheeling his bicycle, propping it up against a wall, preparing to come over.

'We have to go, flower,' said Jeff, disengaging himself tenderly. Putting the car into gear, he set off, leaving the boys and the policeman staring after them. He drove up Front Street and turned left, not making for anywhere in particular, just getting away to somewhere, anywhere where they would not have an audience to their love. Rose sat beside him, glancing up at him every few seconds, reassuring herself it was really Jeff and often he caught her glance and they smiled into each other's eyes for a fraction of a second because he had to keep his attention on the road, had to force himself to for he was carrying a precious load now, he was driving his Rose.

She turned to look out of the window, hardly knowing what she was seeing but then with a jolt realising they were driving along the end of the colliery rows and suddenly the brightness they were enveloped in fell away and dark horror filled her.

'Stop!' she cried, one hand scrabbling at his arm. 'Oh, stop!' And he braked hard and pulled into the kerb while behind him someone pipped angrily and held up two fingers to him which he never even saw.

'What? What's the matter? Tell me –' But he broke off as he realised that she wasn't even listening to him, she was fumbling with the door catch, sobbing in frustration because she couldn't get it open. He leaned across and opened it for her and she tumbled out and ran down the road, with Jeff close at her heels though at first he didn't know why they were running.

Then he saw them. For a second only, Rose's Aunt Elsie sobbing and crying, her mouth slack and ugly, her nose running, her hair wild in the wind. And Alf Sharpe pushing Michael and Mary into a car – Michael shouting and screaming at his father, Mary white-faced and quiet. And then they were gone, Rose only a couple of yards behind them, running after the car as it picked up speed and took off for the main road.

'You let them go! You let them go with him and you knew what would happen...what he would do...'

Rose was screaming at her aunt. She brought her arm back and slapped the older woman hard on the face, making her reel against an end wall. Elsie stayed there, no longer sobbing, just staring at Rose in ashen-faced horror. Jeff caught up with Rose and pulled her to him, holding her close, pinioning her arms so that she could not use them on Elsie again, for the rage and hate on her face showed that she would kill her if she could.

Dear God, he thought, what was it all about? What? Surely Elsie had not done anything to warrant this? He dragged Rose back towards the car and she was still screaming at the woman. 'Why? Why did you let them go? Why?' But her voice was lower now, failing, her face breaking up in the throes of extreme distress. He pulled her to him, turning her face into his jacket to screen her from the curiosity of the folk now standing around, attracted by the fuss, the unexpected sight of one woman attacking another in the open street on a cold Saturday morning.

'Go after them, Jeff, please! Please, go after them. Stop him, Jeff,' Rose cried after he finally got her into the car. She was fighting for self-control, taking great gulps of air into her lungs.

'I will, of course I will, but where will he be taking them? Jordan?'

'Jordan, yes, he'll be taking them there.'

'But why is it so urgent? What –'

'Don't ask questions Jeff, please, just go,' she said, clutching at his arm.

'All right, I'm going, don't worry. I'm sure I'll catch them up. That was a hired car, the driver won't put up any speed.' He really didn't know what the urgency was but he trusted Rose implicitly. He started the car and was away immediately, touching the speed limit, but when he got out of the village and on to the main road he opened up and the little car ate up the miles.

In the back of the car he had hired at Heatley Hill, only a couple of miles from Shotton Colliery, Alf sat with the twins on either side of him. He was filled with a sense of triumph. By, he'd got one over that bitch of a sister of his, hadn't he? And he didn't believe for a minute she would go to the polis, of course she wouldn't. She was as guilty as he was, wasn't she? He looked down at Michael, sitting at the extreme end of the seat, as close to the door as he could possibly get, determined not to touch him, his own father.

A wave of irritation went through Alf. He caught hold of the boy's arm and pulled him over bodily, forcing him to look at him. He twisted the boy's arm, making tears start to his eyes, but Michael stared at him bravely. Cheeky fond the kid was, he'd have to knock that out of him. No doubt Elsie had been too soft with the little bugger.

'Don't you be so flaming cheeky, lad, or I'll give you what for when we get home,' snapped Alf.

He caught the driver of the car looking at him in disgust. 'What the hell's the matter with your face?' Alf snarled.

'A bit rough with the lad, aren't you?'

The driver was a family man himself; he knew how bairns could get on your nerves, how at times you could murder them, but he didn't hold with actually hurting them, especially a little mite like that young 'un.

'You mind your own business. When I want your advice I'll ask for it,' said Alf, but he loosed the boy's arm. The driver said no more but turned his whole attention to the road ahead. He could have turfed the fellow out at the roadside but he could do with the fare, and anyway, how would that help the kid?

Alf looked down at Mary on his other side, and felt the surge of triumph again. She was really turning into a nice plump little thing. She hadn't made a fuss either, actually liked her old dad, he was sure of it. He put an arm around her and she looked up at him, eyes large in her face. They were so like Rose's and her hair was already darkening to black too. She had her thumb stuck firmly in her mouth, though, wasn't saying a word. He squeezed her to him.

'Daddy's little pet, aren't you, Rose?' he said and she never moved to release herself, just stared up at him, her arms forced forward before her body, her face becoming red.

'It's Mary, not Rose,' said Michael beside him. 'Let her go, Dad, will you? She's frightened.'

'No, she's not. She likes me to cuddle her, don't you, Mary?'

He glanced up at the driving mirror and *saw* that the

driver's eyes were once more fixed on him. The car had slowed down too; they would never get to Bishop Auckland at this rate. Alf released Mary and leaned forward to speak to the man. 'If we're there before one I'll give you a good tip,' he said. 'I . . . we have to meet someone.'

The man looked at him, his face unreadable, but he picked up speed. Alf sat back, satisfied. It was marvellous what the promise of a bit of extra money would do, he thought smugly. Well, the driver was in for an unpleasant surprise when they got there. Alf would burn in hell before he'd give him a tip.

There was hooting behind them. Alf turned round. What was the matter with the car behind? There wasn't a soul on the road apart from the two of them. If he was in such a hurry why didn't he just overtake and get on his way?

It was a young fellow with a girl beside him, showing off no doubt . . . Alf stared, his mouth open. It wasn't true . . . it couldn't be. But yes, it was, it was that lad Jeff, the one who had sniffed after his Rose. What did he think he was doing?

Jeff swung out into the road, pulling alongside the hired car for only a moment. He was making gestures to the driver to stop and the damn fool was doing just that. The other car had dropped behind again, evidently confident Alf's driver would do as he asked. Alf leaned forward.

'Don't you stop! Drive on. Go, I tell you – what do

you think I'm paying you for?' He looked furiously back at the other car. Who the hell did he think he was, forcing them to stop?

The girl beside Jeff. Alf hadn't looked at her properly until now, in fact she had been half hidden, holding her head down. Now she leaned forward and stared at him and suddenly he knew why they were doing what they were doing. But it couldn't be, no, it couldn't be! He leaned suddenly on the driver and the car bucked and jumped and swung round to the side and there was a crunch and Alf was thrown forward, his head and shoulders going through the windscreen, his body shielding that of the driver who was pinned in his seat by it. Behind them, the two children were thrown forward too, Mary hitting the back of the driver's seat and falling to the floor.

Michael went flying slightly to the left where the front door had swung open and was catapulted out, going over the parapet of the bridge they were on, out into the empty air above a slowly flowing, six-inch-deep tributary of the River Wear.

Chapter Thirty

'I'm their sister, let me go!' Rose shouted, and the ambulance man hesitated and glanced at his colleague who nodded. He released his hold on her and she climbed in and sat between the stretcher beds. Michael lay, white and quiet. Oh, God, he was dead and it was her fault, all of it. If she hadn't got Jeff to race after them the twins would be alive and well, both of them.

'Auntie Elsie?' On the other side Mary moved, moaning a little, asking for her aunt, and the ambulance man moved to check her, feeling her pulse, his eyes going over her.

'Lie still now, petal,' he said, his voice calm, cool. 'Don't move, there's a good girl.'

'How is she?' Rose whispered anxiously.

He smiled in a way meant to comfort. 'Don't worry,' he said. 'We'll soon be there. We're taking them to Hartlepool, it's nearer than Durham.'

He moved to Michael, feeling for the pulse in his temple, pulling the red blanket more closely round his body. Michael looked so small lying there, small and vulnerable, and Rose felt her heart dissolving into tiny bits. But there was whimpering coming from the other side now. Mary was moving her head from side to side.

'Auntie Elsie? Auntie, where are you? My shoulder hurts, Auntie Elsie.'

'I'm here, Mary. I'm here, pet. It's Rose. Don't you know me, Mary?'

The child opened her eyes fully. 'Rose?' she asked, uncertainly, but at least she knew her and Rose breathed a prayer of gratitude. 'Rose, it hurts,' her sister said, the high thin thread of her voice sounding so pathetic Rose felt she couldn't bear it. She put out her hand and Mary clung to it, her fingers tightly wrapped around hers.

'I know, love, but we'll soon be at the hospital and the doctor will make you better.' Please God, and Michael too. The journey seemed to be taking for ever, though in fact, when she glanced at her watch, it had only been five minutes. The longest five minutes of her life. Rose hardly dared look at Michael's face now, terrified she might see that the tiny thread which was holding him to life had been broken.

She held Mary's hand, stroking it gently, and her mind went back to the series of horrifying images that had gone before. Never would she be able to erase from her memory that image of Michael suspended in the air above the burn. It would be her everlasting penance. She had raced up to the bridge, to the broken wall and the car crumpled into it,

Jeff close behind her, calling, 'Rose! Rose, don't...' But
she had to see for herself, only she didn't know where to
look first.

'You stay here, I'll see about Michael,' said Jeff. He
put a hand on her shoulder to make sure she had heard
but it only galvanised her into action and she was round
the wall – the wall which stretched for no more than six
feet. Six feet of wall in all that long stretch of road with
nothing else at the sides but grass and wooden fences
and hedges, and they had had to hit the wall. She was
over the fence and down the grassy slope, pushing cows
out of her way. They took fright, already startled by
the commotion in their midst, and ran clumsily up the
bank, away from where they had been drinking at the
burn.

Barely looking at the figure of Alf, slumped over the
seat and still over the wildly cursing figure of the driver,
she dared to look at Mary, sitting on the floor in the back
of the car, her shoulder at a strange angle, her little head
swaying backwards and forwards, saying nothing, eyes
closed. She was at least alive. But Michael couldn't be,
could he? Of course he couldn't. No one could be alive
after falling over a wall and down into a burn filled with
boulders and rocks and pebbles, all so hard.

Rose was aware of them yet not aware as she reached
the saturated bank by the side of the burn, mud all churned
up for a depth of some inches so that she slipped and fell
and struggled through it on her hands and knees to where

the limp figure of her brother lay. So still. Oh, dear God, so still.

'Don't move him, Rose! Don't move him!' Jeff was waving his arms and shouting from the top of the bank. 'An ambulance is coming.'

But she had to move Michael's head, turn his face to the side for it was in the mud. She moved it gently then pulled at her skirt to wipe his face but it too was smothered in mud so she tugged impatiently at her coat buttons and found the tail of her blouse and used that. She hooked her finger in his mouth to clean it of mud. Oh, God be praised, there was but a tiny amount on his lips, none deep inside, he could breathe. She tore a piece from her blouse and dipped it in the stream and used that to clean his lips and teeth.

The cows were coming close again, curious as only cows can be, wary of her, their large brown eyes questioning, dropping their heads to within an inch of Michael's face. 'Get off! Get away!' Rose shouted furiously at them and waved her arms and they turned clumsily and splashed off, over the stream to the other side. And then the ambulance came, two in fact, and the ambulance men had taken charge.

But now they were entering the gates of the hospital, speeding up to Outpatients and Emergency. 'We're almost there, darling,' she said to Mary. 'The doctors will make you better.' Her sister looked fearfully at her, frightened of the unknown. Then the ambulance man was at the door and suddenly there were nurses and doctors bustling about. One of them had taken hold of her and was leading her out, sitting her down, taking the children away and Rose cried out, 'I want to go with them!' But hands were restraining her and a calm voice was saying something to her.

'It's all right, they're in safe hands now. Sit quiet a minute, will you? You're suffering from shock.'

She watched numbly as the adult-sized trolleys were wheeled away with the children looking smaller than ever and forced herself to stay calm. She had to keep a hold on herself. She had to, had to, had to. And then Jeff was there, sitting beside her, putting his arm around her, holding her to him.

'They're not dead, Jeff. They're alive, both of them, they are, aren't they?' For suddenly she had a terrible fear that it was an illusion, all of this, that the twins were dead, their battered bodies lying out there on that road. The waiting room didn't even look real to her.

'No, they're not dead, Rose,' Jeff confirmed. Her father was. Oh, yes, Alf Sharpe was dead all right. And Jeff couldn't find it in his heart to be sorry, either. He had only been stopped from immediately following Rose down the bank to the burn as he suddenly realised that the driver of the crashed car was pushing Alf's body off him.

'Get off me,' he was saying, 'bloody well get off me! Look what you did, you bloody fool –' And Jeff had seen what was going to happen in that instant and managed to open the back door of the car and catch Alf Sharpe's dead body before it fell on Mary where she sat on the floor between the seats, moaning now, her head not swaying any longer as she rested it on the back of the driver's seat.

The driver himself was completely unhurt so far as Jeff could see. He had got out of the car and lurched across the road where he stood quietly vomiting over the fence.

'Sit still, ninny,' Jeff said to the child. 'It'll be all right soon, I promise you.'

He darted over to the wall and saw Rose as she put a hand out to the mud-covered body of the little boy. 'Don't move him,' Jeff shouted urgently. 'Don't move him, Rose. Don't – don't move him.' The first aid training he was undergoing for use in mining accidents was taking over.

Dear God, she loved those bairns, he thought. And he…had he been the cause of the accident? He didn't truly know but even the thought was an agony to him. He heard a car approaching and ran out into the road, waving his arms.

'An ambulance – call an ambulance!' he cried, and the driver, taking in what had happened at a glance, hardly stopped but nodded his head and sped on to the village just visible in the distance.

'Watch the bairn here, will you?' he called to the driver of the hire car and the man nodded and came over, looking white and shaken but otherwise in one piece.

'It wasn't my fault, you know,' he said. 'She's not badly hurt, is she? I've never had an accident in my life. That bloody man's an idiot…if I'd known I'd never have driven him, I wouldn't.' But he was talking to thin air for Jeff was vaulting over the fence and running down the bank to where Rose crouched, touching Michael's face gently with her fingertips, moaning softly, 'I'm sorry, Michael, I am. I'm that sorry. Oh, God, I didn't want you to be hurt.'

'Michael knows that, Rose,' said Jeff. 'It wasn't your fault. I don't think it was my fault either. I didn't crowd the car, I was careful not to.' And it was true, he realised. In fact it had all been the fault of Alf Sharpe, just like everything else that had happened to Rose and her brother and sister.

Jeff followed the ambulances to the hospital, hardly noticing they had turned off the Durham road and were heading into Hartlepool, driving almost on automatic pilot yet safely and surely until they turned into the hospital grounds. He lost some time finding the private car park and all the time he was thinking: suppose Rose turned away from him, suppose she blamed him for what had happened, how could he bear that? And then feeling ashamed that he could even think of himself at such a time.

But Rose, when he found her, was sitting in a chair all by herself in Outpatients, looking so tragic and alone that it was something else he found hard to bear. And she allowed him to put his arm around her and comfort her at least.

*

'There's a nasty accident just in,' Sister Smith, the new young sister on Gynae, commented as Bob, now back on duty, sat in her office and drank a cup of milky hospital coffee. It was that period on a hospital ward when the rounds were over and lunches had been served and cleared away and the patients settled down for a sleepy afternoon. Half the staff had gone for their own break and Sister had been sitting at her desk, struggling with the off-duty rota, trying to see that the ward was covered at all times with her depleted staff as two of the nurses were down with flu. She had welcomed the arrival of Dr Morris with relief, her chance for a break.

'Is there?' he responded then recollected. 'Oh, yes, I heard something about it. Two children and their father, wasn't it?'

'Two children anyway. Twins. The father is dead.'

'Oh, poor kids.'

Bob wrote something down in the patient's notes he had been reading, closed the folder and slapped it on the pile on the desk. He was late today, what with going out to Easington to see that friend of Rose's. But it had been a good opportunity, the ward was quiet, his colleagues were there to deal with any emergencies.

He finished his coffee and got to his feet. 'Thanks, Sister, lovely coffee,' he lied. 'I'll get out from under your feet now. I know you like the afternoons free from being pestered by doctors.'

'Not at all,' she murmured politely.

Bob walked round the outside of the buildings on his way back to the doctors' rest room. Normally he would have taken a short cut through Outpatients and Emergency but today was glad of the fresh air, it helped him think. For all he had had his suspicions about what it was that had really happened to make Rose as she was, it was still a shock to realise all was as her friend had told him. Poor darling Rose. All his protective instincts came to the surface. He would look after her now, do his darndest to make sure nothing hurt her ever again.

In the rest room he changed out of his white coat and washed his face and combed his hair. It was his weekend off, really, even though he had felt the need to come in again this morning, to finish writing up the notes he had been too tired to do the evening before. He felt buoyed up by the thought that he had a whole afternoon and all day Sunday to devote to Rose. She would be expecting him. He had promised to take her to the cinema, the first house, and then on to dinner at a little Italian cafe he knew in Old Hartlepool.

Putting on his overcoat, for it was cold out today, a stiff wind coming over the North Sea, Bob walked down the corridor, past the entrance to Outpatients and Emergency again, and out to the doctors' car park. As he drove he thought again about the accident which had happened on the Durham road, evidently. Funny, that road was quite straight. He wondered about it. Poor kids, being hurt and losing their father like that.

Bob showered and changed, ate a late lunch and set off for Rose's boarding house. It was a while since he had been to the pictures and he was looking forward to it. He didn't care which picture it was, Rose could choose. No doubt she'd pick the costume drama which was on at the Odeon, *Jassy,* that was the name of it. Women liked costume dramas. With Stewart Granger, of course, and Margaret Lockwood.

Rose wasn't in. The disappointment he felt was out of all proportion, he knew, but he couldn't help it. 'Have you any idea where she went, Mrs Dash?' he asked. The landlady shook her head.

'I don't enquire into what's none of my business,' she said tartly. 'I've other things to think about.' She began to close the door then opened it again. 'An' you're the second person to come looking for her an' all. There was a young woman not five minutes since.'

Bob thanked her automatically and turned away. He walked to the end of the street and stood on the corner undecided. He was filled with fears for Rose, remembering the time she had been found on the caravan site at Crimdon. Had something happened to her? Oh, surely not again? No, she was quite fit now, she would be all right. A girl her age had probably been bored and just gone to look at the shops.

He thought of what the landlady had said. A young woman? Who could it be but young Mrs Wearmouth? Yet she had said she was busy that weekend. He glanced across the road and saw Marina sitting in the window of a coffee shop. Bob hurried across and went in, bought a cup of coffee and sat down opposite her.

'May I?'

'Oh, it's you, Doctor! Yes, of course.' Marina was stirring her coffee absent-mindedly. She put down her spoon.

'I thought I'd come today after all. Jeff didn't come home, you know, and Mam didn't mind. She's making the meal for tonight. In her element, she is. I thought I'd see Rose, be able to tell them how she is and everything. No luck, though. She's out, according to her landlady.'

'I know, I've just been here myself. I can't understand it, she knew I was coming.'

'She might have forgotten.' Marina rose to her feet, leaving her coffee untouched, and he did too. 'Look, I'd better be getting back. It was daft me coming out when me mam's there and Brian coming in and all. I'll get this bus.'

'Look, I'll give you my telephone number, you can ring me tomorrow. Will you do that? I'm sure she won't be long. We were going to the pictures.'

Marina took the slip of paper on which Bob had jotted down the number and put it in her bag. 'If I don't hurry I'll miss my bus,' she said. He didn't offer to take her home, wanted to stay close to the boarding house in case Rose came back. He had a sense of foreboding which was growing stronger by the minute.

Chapter Thirty-one

'You are the boy's sister?' the doctor asked. 'Are you his next of kin?' They were still in the waiting room. Both Rose and Jeff had risen to their feet when the doctor appeared.

Rose's heart thumped painfully against her ribs. Oh, God, he was going to say Michael was dead and she couldn't bear that. She held out an unsteady hand and Jeff stepped swiftly forward and took it.

'She is, Doctor,' he said. 'Their mother passed away about three years ago.'

'Oh, I'm sorry. And the father was killed...' He looked down at the notes he was carrying. 'Will you come with me?' he said. 'Somewhere more private, I think.'

Now he was going to say it, Rose thought. She followed him into a small office, Jeff close behind. The doctor glanced at him.

'And you are?'

'Her fiancé,' Jeff said firmly.

Rose heard the words but nothing was really registering

with her, her mind was fully focused on the children. Why didn't he say it?

'Well, Miss Sharpe,' said the doctor, after she had sat down in the chair he offered, Jeff beside her. 'I'm pleased to tell you that the girl, Mary, is not too seriously injured. She has a dislocated shoulder and we believe there is some concussion. We would like to keep her in for a few days at least, but she should make a full recovery.'

'Thank God. Oh, thank God,' Rose breathed. 'But Michael? What about him?' Her voice rose when the doctor didn't answer immediately and Jeff pressed his fingers into hers.

'Steady, lass,' he said, and amazingly her panic subsided slightly.

'Michael also is suffering from concussion. There are abrasions on his legs too. I understand he was thrown out of the car and over a bridge. He is a very lucky little boy in that case. We will be keeping a careful eye on him, though. There is a hairline fracture of the skull. Not too serious –' He stopped suddenly, cursing himself for not seeing how close the girl was to collapse. She had slumped in her seat, her face deathly pale, a pulse beating wildly at the base of her ear. Oh, dear, what a day this was turning out to be.

Rose opened her eyes to find herself stretched out on an examination couch, a blanket covering her. A nurse was holding a glass to her lips. It tasted vile and she struggled to get away from the colourless liquid.

'Now then, it won't hurt you, it's just to calm your

nerves. You've had a bad time, haven't you? Come on now, the little ones need you, don't let them down. You've been a brick, haven't you? The ambulance man told me...'

'Drink it, Rose, it won't hurt you,' said Jeff and she saw him hovering near, looking so desperately anxious she obeyed him at once and drank the foul stuff. And she had to admit she felt better. When she sat up the world had stopped spinning.

'Can I see the children?' she asked the nurse. She had to see for herself that they were going to be all right, she had to.

'Are you sure you're up to it?'

Rose got to her feet and held her head up high. She was determined to show that she was in full control of herself now, wasn't going to collapse again. 'Is there a cloakroom? If I could just make myself presentable, comb my hair...'

'Yes, of course.' The nurse looked at Jeff. 'You'll be with her?' she asked and he nodded.

'All the time.' For ever, he thought. He was not going to lose her again.

Rose walked up the corridor of the children's ward, outwardly composed and with an expectant smile on her face, but her hand was clutching Jeff's tightly and he could feel the slight tremor she was fighting to subdue. The twins were in a small two-bedded room adjacent to the main ward, both lying flat, their bedheads padded with pillows.

'Five minutes, that's all,' said Sister firmly. 'They need to rest after that ordeal.' She left the door ajar, just in case. She had been Sister on this ward for a long time and was well aware that relatives of the tiny patients often burst into tears when they saw them, causing more upset than good for her patients, in her opinion at least.

'Rose!' Mary, looking almost her old self except for her arm being bandaged close to her side, tried to sit up and had to be shushed. And, thank God, Michael was awake too, his dark eyes, so like Mary's and Rose's own, looking up solemnly at her.

'There were cows, Rose,' he confided when his sister had kissed them both carefully, hardly daring to touch them. Rose was surprised he remembered. She cast a startled glance at Jeff, standing just inside the door. 'I fell right among the cows,' he went on. 'Black and white, they were. Aren't cows big, Rose?'

'They are,' she agreed. 'Hush now, Michael, my pet. You're going to be fine.'

'Where's Auntie Elsie?' asked Mary, suddenly fretful. 'I want Auntie Elsie. My shoulder hurts, Rose.'

Rose stared at Jeff. She had completely forgotten about her aunt, and what was more, her first instinct was to leave Elsie to stew. But she could see that Mary at least had grown fond of her, naturally enough as she'd had been the mother figure in their young lives since their own mother died. If Rose felt a tiny pang of jealousy to find that Mary wanted Aunt Elsie rather than her when she was hurt, it was quickly stifled. Of course Elsie had to be told and brought to see the children.

'I'm sorry, you'll have to go now,' said Sister from the doorway, and Rose opened her mouth to protest but one glance at the other woman's determined expression convinced her it was a waste of time. She kissed the children, whispered she'd be back soon and went out.

'And Auntie Elsie?' asked Mary, inclined to tears now. Rose was forced to nod.

'Visiting two until four tomorrow afternoon,' Sister stated. 'Only two visitors, mind.'

'Dragon,' said Jeff with feeling as they walked out into the fresh air, and they smiled at each other. When they got to the car, instead of getting in they stood close together, arms around each other, her head resting on his shoulder, not needing to say anything. The relief and relaxation of tension had given Rose a feeling of deep lethargy. She felt she could never worry about anything ever again. For the time being, especially after the terrible events of the day, it was enough that they were together, the twins were going to recover, and she and Jeff were as deeply in love as they had ever been.

There was a sweet communion between them, the fear all gone. Rose felt as though a great burden had been lifted from her, an impenetrable cloud had rolled away from the sun and let the light shine through. Its golden light was wrapped around the two of them, enveloping and warm.

Bob Morris saw the couple as he turned into the hospital

grounds, two people, standing as one, so obviously deeply in love. Rather, he saw the shape of them for the light was rapidly fading. His heart went out to them. Their very bearing expressed his own deep feeling for Rose. He realised he was in love with her and decided he would ask her to marry him soon. A twinge of anxiety shot through his mind. Where was she? There must be some simple explanation for her disappearance. He couldn't think what it could be but there had to be something. She would come back.

For now, however, he had been called to the hospital. Yet another young girl had put her faith in the hands of a back-street abortionist and he was required to repair the damage. He parked the car and walked back to the main building of the hospital, having to pass the young couple, still standing so still, so close, so united. He couldn't help glancing at them as he passed then felt as if a great cold hand had taken hold of him and squeezed, forcing the breath out of him.

'Rose?' Someone said the name, he wasn't aware that it was himself. The couple didn't move for a moment. He felt as though he were watching the three of them, all so still and silent, the young couple and himself. He couldn't believe it, no, this couldn't be Rose. It seemed an age before she lifted her head from the man's shoulder, and indeed it was Rose, his lovely Rose.

'Bob? Dr Morris?'

A car drove past, headlights illuminating the scene,

and his disbelieving eyes recognised the man. It was her friend's man, her friend's husband, the girl he had been talking to only a few hours ago, the one who had told him the dreadful story about Rose and her father. A tale of incest and degradation. And here Rose was, with that girl's husband, the newly married husband. 'Blood will out.' That was a phrase his mother was fond of using but he had never believed it. Not until now.

Suddenly, he collected himself. Muttering something inarticulate, he started to walk rapidly away. By the time he got to the corner he was almost running.

Rose gazed sadly after him. That one look into his eyes had shown her the shock he had suffered, and it was all her fault. He was in love with her, she realised, something she had refused to consider until now. But she had used him, she knew that too, and acknowledged it. He had been there and she had needed someone. She had had nowhere to turn, no one to turn to, and she had missed Jeff so.

'Rose? Come on, love, get in the car, it's growing cold. Come on now, sweetheart, I'm going to look after you.' She turned to see Jeff holding open the door of the car for her to get in. Oh, Jeff, her dearest Jeff. Somehow she couldn't think about Bob Morris, not now, not tonight. Tonight she was going to be steeped in Jeff's love, the love which had been denied her for so long. Tomorrow everything might be different, tomorrow she would have to tell him the truth, but not tonight.

'Let's go home, love,' he said and it was the sweetest

sentence there had ever been in the English language. Tomorrow she would think about Bob and what she was going to say to him. Tomorrow she would think about Aunt Elsie. Both of them would have to be faced. Yes, there was a lot to be faced tomorrow. But not tonight. She was so tired, deathly tired, she couldn't even think how she was going to tell Jeff about her father, what he had done, what he had been.

Jeff also had things he didn't want to go into tonight, not least the chap who had called to Rose as they stood by the car. He could have sworn it was the same one who had come to the house early this morning. But nothing else mattered to him very much now except that he had his Rose and that devil, her so-called father – for what real father would torture a girl as he had done – that demon from hell, was dead and Jeff couldn't find an ounce of pity for him in his heart.

'Is this yours?' asked Rose as they drove up to the terraced house in Easington Colliery. The curtains of the front room were drawn together but chinks of light were showing, reminding Jeff that he had company. He groaned inwardly. The last thing he or Rose wanted now was to meet Kate Morland. They might have managed Brian and Marina at a pinch but no more. He restarted the car.

'Where are we going?' asked Rose, not really minding, trusting him completely.

'On our honeymoon,' he said. 'We're going to be different, put the cart before the horse.'

They didn't go far away. Rose wanted to be near the children so they took a room in an hotel in Seaton Carew on the outskirts of Hartlepool. It was nine o'clock on a cold winter's night but the room was cosy with the curtains drawn and an electric fire on the wall. The bedside lamps cast a rosy glow over the room; the bed with its covers turned back looked clear and fresh against the old furniture. It looked comfortable. The bed...A niggle of worry intruded on Rose's happiness but Jeff had his arms around her. He was drawing her to him and she was lost in the golden haze once again.

'Let me look at you,' he whispered and began to take off her twinset, fingers fumbling over the buttons of her cardigan so that Rose laughed softly and helped him. He took off her skirt and folded it carefully over the back of a chair, pulled down the straps of her bra, kissed the tops of her gently swelling breasts. At last she was fully undressed and he stood for a moment, drinking in the sight of her.

'I'm too thin,' Rose murmured, suddenly shy, and he laughed softly and scooped her up in his arms and laid her in the bed.

'You're perfect,' he said.

She watched as he threw off his own clothes and stood before her. And, oh, *he* was perfect, he was, his shoulders broad with rippling muscles, his stomach so flat, and below his manhood stood erect and proud. He was trembling with his need for her yet he lifted the covers and got into the bed beside her carefully. Gently he kissed her eyelids, her lips, the nape of her neck, and brushed his tongue over the rosy tips of her breasts which sprang up in instant response.

Rose stiffened once, a trace of panic on the edge of her mind when his hand strayed to her secret place, the urge to freeze, to get away, striking with a sudden image of her father, the hated feel of *his* hands. But this was Jeff, not Alf Sharpe, this was her beloved, her Jeff, her own lovely man and the image fled, lost in the overpowering sensations which Jeff had aroused in her. Jeff, her love.

He had stopped instantly as he felt her stiffen, her instant of withdrawal, though his own needs were causing a clamouring in his blood that took all of his will to control. 'Rose,' he murmured. 'Rose. My own darling Rose.' His head against her breast he could feel the panicky quickening of her heartbeat but then she relaxed, moved against him and he knew it was going to be all right.

It was in the early morning that she awoke, filled with a sense of contentment, happiness singing in her veins as she felt the length of his body so close to hers, his arm flung across her, his head snuggled into her shoulder. There was a grey light filtering through the curtains. Rose looked sideways down at his beloved face, breathed in the essence of him. A tiny blue scar marked his left temple. In this light it looked darker against his skin. She placed a forefinger against it, ran the finger gently along. He'd been hurt sometime, she thought, and she hadn't even known. How could that be?

She shivered but not with cold. As she came fully awake she began to feel a terrible sense of foreboding, of guilt... she didn't know what it was. Sliding her arm carefully from under Jeff she moved away to the edge of the bed. He murmured in protest, flinging the bedclothes back to his waist and turning on his back. Carefully she pulled up the covers, tucking them into his neck as she would with one of the twins.

A terrible feeling of desolation was creeping over her, all the more intense for the joy and happiness which had gone before. There was a spare blanket on a chair. She wrapped herself in it and went to the window. Pulling the curtain back so that she could see out, she stared out over the sands to the sea. She had cheated him. Only now did she realise how badly she had cheated him. She should have told him. She folded her arms before her, holding on to the blanket, head bent as she stared out, seeing nothing at all.

Jeff woke with a start and instantly felt bereft. Where was she? He had been having a bad dream, had dreamed that Rose was going away yet again. 'I have to go, I have to,' she was saying in the dream and she was crying, great teardrops rolling down her face in hopeless abandon. 'Don't go! Don't go, darling,' he called. He was racing after her, calling her name, and when he woke the euphoria of the night before was gone.

Rose was standing by the window, the picture of

dejection, tears rolling down her cheeks as they had in his terrifying dream. He jumped out of bed and hurried to her, gathered her in his arms, held her to him.

'Don't go,' he said. 'Don't go. I won't let you, Rose, do you hear me?' He picked her up and carried her back to the bed where she lay listlessly in his arms. 'Tell me what it is? Tell me!' he said. 'Rose, there's nothing you can say that will ever turn me from you. Nothing.'

It was her father. He saw now what it had been with sudden clarity. It had to be her father. She must have had some feeling for him, he thought, and now Alf was dead. But, no. Everything bad in her life had been due to her father, he knew that. How could she miss him? 'Tell me,' he insisted again; he was not to be denied. And Rose began to speak. Slowly, it all came out: the years of growing to be a teenager, the way it had caused her mother's death earlier than need be, the fears she had had for her little sister Mary, the infamous bargain she had made with her father because of it. And last, worst, the dead baby and her father's callous treatment of her, even to leaving her in the dene to die.

'I had nowhere to turn, no one to turn to,' she said, dry-eyed now. 'Aunt Elsie helped him, Jeff. She was so terrified that he would take the twins from her.' She was silent now, reliving the awful sense of betrayal when her aunt did what she had.

'You had me,' he said. He could hardly speak, filled with such a sense of loathing for Alf Sharpe. And self-loathing too. Oh, he had heard rumours when he lived in

Jordan, talk among the men at the pit about Alf Sharpe's unnatural obsession with Rose. He had been on the receiving end of the man's hatred when he had thought Jeff was too fond of his daughter. But he hadn't wanted to believe it, couldn't bring himself to believe it. And he could have done something! Anything. He could surely have got Rose out of that hell. But he'd been so young, had had nothing to offer her, had thought he was doing the best thing by getting away out of Alf's sight. But he had let her down. She had said it herself. She'd had nowhere to turn, no one to turn to. He had been useless to her. Holding her to him Jeff began to cry himself, for the first time since his mother had died when he was a youngster.

That was it, thought Rose, her happiness was gone for ever. It had lasted for a few short hours only. Jeff didn't speak, he was holding her but lying so still he seemed to have forgotten that he was. He must be full of disgust for her, she thought dumbly, but couldn't summon the energy to leave his arms, get out of bed, go. He should be free to find a normal girl, not someone tainted as she was. She opened her mouth to speak but the words wouldn't come. It was when she felt the wetness on his cheek that she forced herself to say them.

'I'll go now, I won't bother you again,' she said and was amazed at the steadiness of her own voice. Jeff's arms tightened around her convulsively.

'You will not,' he said. His voice was husky from tears but strong. 'You won't leave me ever again.'

Chapter Thirty-two

'Jeff's been out all night.' Marina, frying pan in hand, was dishing out bacon and eggs to Brian and her mother. It was Sunday morning, early, for today they were going to the new house again, Sunday being the only day Brian had free to help with the painting and wallpapering.

'Hmmm, I wonder what he's up to.' Brian looked speculative but unworried. After all, Jeff was a single man and if he wanted a night out on the tiles...well, then. He himself was more interested in the smell of the bacon and breathed it in with pleased anticipation. The bacon ration only ran to one breakfast a week so Sunday mornings were a treat.

Marina finished dishing out and brought her own plate to the table. She too had her mind on things other than Jeff's absence. She sighed. 'At least we know where Rose has been all this time,' she said pensively.

'An' she might have let us know an' all,' said Kate. She put down her knife and fork and lifted her cup of tea, leaning her elbows comfortably on the table while she sipped from it. By, she thought, she was enjoying this weekend and it was going to be lovely when the three of them were in a house of their own. No more lonely evenings spent listening to the wireless on her own. She'd always been used to a full house and being lonely was a new and unwelcome experience for her. And thinking of the wireless ... 'Put the news on, will you, pet?' she asked Marina. 'I like to keep up with things.'

Obediently, Marina rose and went to the side table where a new wireless stood, Jeff's really, but he never minded them using his things. She glanced at the clock. Ten-past eight.

'It'll be nearly over, Mam.'

The BBC announcer was coming to the end of the news but he was followed by bulletins from the regions, in their case from Newcastle for the North East. Nothing very interesting to them except that Easington Colliery had exceeded its production target for the month yet again. Brian nodded his head and grunted his approval. But then there was an item of traffic news which knocked them all sideways.

'A fatal accident occurred on the road between Shotton Colliery and Durham City yesterday at about one o'clock in the afternoon. A car collided with the parapet of a small bridge over a stream. A man was killed and two children injured and are now recovering in the Cameron Hospital, Hartlepool. The children, eight-year-old Michael Sharpe and his twin sister Mary, are understood not to be seriously injured. Their father, Alfred Sharpe, was killed instantly. If anyone saw the accident, will they please get in touch with their local police.'

There was stunned silence in the kitchen. After a while Brian got up and turned off the wireless. Marina stared down at the congealing fat on her plate. She felt sick.

'Those poor bairns,' said Kate, breaking the silence. 'Those poor little mites. Orphans now.'

They would be better off without their father in Marina's opinion, but she said nothing. Rose must have known about this, she suddenly thought. Was that where she had been last night, at the hospital? Oh, she must go to her, never mind about Mam being here.

'I'll have to go,' she said aloud and began clattering dishes together, thinking only of getting off.

'Why, Marina, what about the house?' asked Kate. 'Why do you have to go, anyway?'

'I just do.'

'I'll run you through on the motorbike,' suggested Brian. Kate opened her mouth to protest again but just then they heard a key in the front door. 'Jeff!' said Brian. 'I wondered...' His voice trailed off as Jeff came into the kitchen, ushering Rose before him.

Marina flew across the kitchen and flung herself on her friend. 'Rose!' she cried. 'Oh, my God, Rose!' She was practically weeping with relief at seeing her. The two girls hugged each other, making small exclamations, laughing, crying, then standing back and gazing at each other.

'Blooming heck, Rose, you're as thin as a lathe,' cried Marina. 'Where in the world have you been? Why did you say you were in London? By, I've been that worried, I have –' She broke off, remembering the news item about the car accident. 'Eeh, Rose, I'm sorry about the bairns, I am.' She dropped her arms and stood back a pace. 'How are they, do you know?' She didn't mention the death of Rose's father. There was nothing to say about that.

'Let us get in, eh, Marina?' Jeff was grinning widely. He put an arm around Rose's shoulders and led her to the fire, sitting her down on an armchair and settling her as though she were made of glass. And, gazing at her, it was all too evident to Marina that she was fragile, or 'femmer' as her mother would say. She looked as though she couldn't tip the scales at more than seven stones. Marina was filled with guilt. Oh, she should have made more of an effort to look for Rose, she should have sought until she found her. She wondered about the baby Rose was carrying when she had gone, remembered that Sunday when her friend had confided in her. And she, Marina, hadn't been equal to it, she had failed her friend. Yes, indeed, she'd been too wrapped up in her own concerns. Rose had obviously been through so much since then.

'Are you not well, hinny?' Kate was asking, forgetting everything but concern for Rose. But she smiled brilliantly, her face alive with happiness. She looked over at Jeff and her white cheeks became suffused with pink.

'I'm fine, Mrs Morland,' she said. 'I have been poorly but I'm over it now. Oh, yes, I'm very well now.'

'Well, are you? You look as though you could do with a good feed to me,' pronounced Kate, folding her arms. 'Is there any of that bacon left, Marina? Enough for these two?'

'We've had breakfast, thanks very much, Mrs Morland,' said Jeff. He stood by Rose's chair, his hand on her shoulder as though he couldn't bear to be separated from her by even an inch or two, and she put up her own hand and laid it on his and he grasped it, holding it close.

'And what about the twins, are they all right? I mean, it said on the wireless they were recovering,' asked Brian.

'We rang this morning,' said Jeff. 'Michael had a good night, Sister said, but Mary was restless though she wasn't hurt as much as Michael.'

Mary had been calling for Aunt Elsie, the Sister had told Rose, and had asked who Aunt Elsie was. Could she come to see the child and then she might settle down? 'It's not good for head injuries to get emotionally upset,' she had added.

'We're on our way to Shotton to see Rose's aunt, she hasn't been told what's happened yet,' said Jeff. 'But Rose wanted to come here first.'

She and Marina exchanged a long look of understanding. There was a lot to be said between the two of them but somehow explanations didn't seem so important to

Marina as she had once thought they would. They could wait. For the moment Rose was thinking apprehensively of her meeting with Aunt Elsie. She had no idea how she was going to react when she saw the woman she felt had betrayed her. But the bairns loved her, Mary especially, and now they needed her.

'Well, have a cup of tea before you go at least,' said Kate, taking charge as it seemed no one else was. She picked up the kettle and took it to the sink to fill but Rose was rising to her feet.

'No, don't bother, Mrs Morland,' she said. 'We're going now and after we've been to Shotton we'll go on to the hospital, probably take . . .' She swallowed, it was a hard thing for her to say even though she had been thinking it. 'Probably take Aunt Elsie.' Mary was calling for Aunt Elsie, she reminded herself yet again. Mary loved her aunt. It didn't matter that if Rose had only herself to consider she would never speak to the woman again.

'Just you go on with your own plans,' said Jeff. 'We'll see you later.'

'Well, that was a brief visit,' commented Kate after they'd gone. 'An' after all that time too, I must say.'

'Oh, Mam,' said Marina. She was so glad that Rose was back, that she was well and at last with her beloved Jeff, that she had no patience for her mother's carping.

'So long as Rose is all right,' Kate said quickly, realising she had sounded somewhat uncaring. 'Look, let's get the breakfast things washed up and then we'll get along to the house. The sooner it's done, the sooner we can move in, isn't that right?'

Jeff drove into Shotton and along the end of the rows, parking on the street where only yesterday they had witnessed Alf Sharpe take the children, Elsie's distress and the neighbours gawping. Rose sat still, gathering her reserves of strength to get out of the car and face Aunt Elsie.

'Howay, flower.' Jeff's heart turned over in love and pity for her, his lovely Rose. But why should she have to do this? Hadn't she been through enough? 'I'll go myself and tell her, if you like.'

'No. It's up to me,' she said, and managed a tiny smile for him. Her eyes followed him as he got out of the car and walked round to the passenger side of the vehicle, opening the door and helping her out tenderly.

'Well, remember I'm right here beside you.'

'I know, Jeff. I know, and I'm grateful.'

They walked close together up the yard to the door of Elsie's house where Jeff knocked. There was no reply, just a silence, and Rose let out the breath she hadn't realised she had been holding.

'She's not in,' she said, relief flooding through her. 'Come on, Jeff, let's go.'

But he was trying the handle and the door opened, it wasn't locked. And directly in front were the stairs Rose only vaguely remembered being carried down on that awful night. The pain, the terror...she felt it rising up again in her throat.

She forced herself to look up and there was Elsie, standing on the tiny landing at the top, a dishevelled, half-undressed, wild-haired woman, face red and swollen from many hours of weeping.

'Rose? Is that you?' And from standing frozen to stillness at the top of the stairs, Elsie came suddenly to life and rushed headlong down, slipping on a step and righting herself somehow until she was there, standing before her niece. 'Have you brought them back, Rose? Are they here? Oh, thank you, thank you –'

'They aren't here, Aunt,' said Rose, and surprised herself by the calm tones she used.

'Where are they? You didn't leave them with Alf? You didn't, did you? No, of course you didn't.' The woman was frantic. She peered round Rose, ignoring Jeff altogether. She couldn't believe it, she had been so sure Rose had the children with her.

'Go and put something on, Aunt,' Rose commanded and Elsie glanced down at herself.

'Oh, yes, but tell me –'

'When you're dressed, Aunt.' Elsie didn't argue. She ran back up the stairs and they could hear her pulling open drawers and cupboards.

'Are you all right?' Anxiously Jeff gazed at Rose. Her calm seemed unnatural somehow.

'I am.' Her chin was set, her teeth clenched together.

Elsie came clattering down the stairs and into the kitchen. Wringing her hands, she bent over Rose where she sat in a fireside chair. 'I didn't want to hurt you. You know that, Rose, don't you? Afterwards I would have sought you out but Alf said you were dead. I was so frightened, so scared, I didn't know what to do. I –'

'Never mind that now,' said Rose. 'Haven't you heard the news? It was on the wireless.'

'The news? No, I haven't had the wireless on, I'm not interested in the news.' Elsie shook her head impatiently, she could think only of what she wanted to say to her niece. 'Rose, I wasn't going to let Alf have the bairns, I wasn't, I swear it. I said I would lay him in to the police. I did my best, Rose. You know I would lay down my own life for them, you know it –'

'And mine too, I know that.' Rose couldn't help the comment.

'No, I told you . . .' Elsie dried up at last, unable to think of any more excuses. She gazed in mute appeal at Jeff.

'Rose,' he said, 'tell her.'

'Tell me what?' demanded Elsie.

Rose glanced at Jeff and he smiled encouragingly. She looked so strained, he thought, was keeping such a tight rein on her emotions.

'There was an accident yesterday, it was on the news,' said Rose. 'In fact I'm surprised Mrs Todd didn't tell you about it if you didn't hear it yourself.'

'She came to the door but . . . an accident? Rose, what's

happened? For God's sake, tell me!' Her voice was rising in panic.

'It was Dad. Dad and Michael and Mary. The driver of the car was unhurt.'

'WHAT? Don't tell me they're dead? Don't tell me – don't!' And Elsie began to moan, her mouth slack.

Her cry was so anguished that remorse struck Rose. She had intended to make her aunt suffer, drag it out, had thought she would enjoy her revenge, but seeing Elsie's distress she couldn't do it. No, she couldn't do it to any human being.

'The twins are in hospital, Aunt Elsie,' she said, her voice softening, and Jeff breathed a great sigh of relief. 'They're recovering, the doctor said.'

'Oh, thank God for all his goodness,' breathed Elsie, sitting down abruptly opposite Rose. Then she lifted her head and looked squarely at her. 'And your dad?'

'He was killed.'

Elsie bowed her head. 'My poor brother,' she whispered. 'My poor tortured brother.'

Rose stared at her in blank disbelief. Elsie felt it rather than saw it. 'You don't know, Rose, you don't know... When he was a bairn –' She broke off, and so low they barely caught it went on, 'No, you don't want to hear it, not now, not ever.' The room became quiet, a cinder settling in the fire the only thing to break the silence.

'We're going to the hospital now,' said Jeff, his words dropping into the quiet.

Elsie shook her head. 'Rose won't want me to come,'

she said sadly. 'But you'll let me know how they are? Please?'

Rose stood up. Suddenly she was desperate to get out into the fresh air, out of this house. She looked at her aunt's ravaged countenance. 'Go and wash your face, Aunt Elsie,' she said gently. 'You don't want Mary to see you like that, do you?'

A look of hope blazed on Elsie's face. Tremulously she stared at her niece. 'I can come?' she whispered.

'Go on, wash your face, we'll be waiting in the car,' said Rose. Elsie ran to do as she was bidden, pausing only at the bottom of the stairs to turn, suddenly doubtful.

'You won't go without me?'

'We won't go without you, Aunt Elsie. We'll be waiting in the car, I promise you.'

As Elsie ran upstairs Jeff put his arms around Rose and kissed her tenderly. 'I'm proud of you, you did the right thing,' he said. 'Oh, Rose, everything's going to be all right, you'll see.'

'Well, the children love their aunt,' said Rose, accepting it. They went out to the car to wait. There was no sign of Mrs Todd, thank goodness, thought Jeff. Just at the moment they could do without having to handle a nosy neighbour.

Chapter Thirty-three

'Morning, Dr Morris. You look as though you could do with your bed,' Sister said briskly. 'I gather it was a busy night?'

Bob glanced up from her desk, where he was sitting writing up notes on the three patients who had come in during the night, all emergencies. 'Morning, Sister,' he said and looked at his watch. Dear me, it was eight o'clock already and here were the day staff.

Sister Stewart picked up the book with the reports written by the night staff. 'Goodness,' she said, scanning it. 'You really have been busy. Three, eh?'

'Yes. One still under observation and the other two back from theatre and doing nicely, thank you. Mrs Gray, a ruptured ectopic. Ethel Burns, abortion. And the one under observation. But you'll have it all down there. I won't be a minute longer then you can have your desk back.'

A long night indeed, he thought bleakly. Being on call, he had slept in the doctors' quarters at the hospital, or at least had lain down on the bed between cases. The longest period had been for about fifty-five minutes. Even then he had not been able to sleep at all, no matter how he had tried to empty his mind of anguished thoughts of Rose, so that he had almost been glad of the diversion when the telephone summoned him back to duty. What a fool he had been! Why hadn't he realised a girl such as Rose would have a boyfriend already?

He sighed, closed the folder and added it to the pile, deciding he would go home, have a bath and shave, try to rest for a while. His chin felt scratchy, his head ached dully. Maybe then he would feel able to join the rest of humanity.

'I'll be back for the rounds, Sister,' he said and left the ward. As he went outside the hospital buildings the fresh air hit him. He felt almost drunk with weariness and depression. The weather matched his mood. Clouds were gathering overhead, it looked like being a wet day.

Jeff and Rose, with Aunt Elsie accompanying them, entered the children's ward a couple of hours later.

'It's not visiting hours, you know,' said Sister, looking severely at them over her spectacles. 'And it's not as though either of the children is on the critical list.'

'Well, thank God for that,' breathed Jeff. 'Anyone would think it would be better if they –'

'What?' Sister glanced at him suspiciously and he smiled beguilingly.

'I mean, it's great news, Sister.'

'Oh, please,' begged Elsie. 'Please, I haven't seen them since the accident.'

This is the aunt Mary was fretting for,' Rose put in swiftly. Sister pursed her lips. 'Oh, well, just for a few minutes then. Only two of you, mind. No more than two visitors at once. But it's almost time for Matron's round. If she comes you'll have to go.'

'I'll wait outside,' said Jeff.

It had been worth it, thought Rose as she saw Mary's face when Auntie Elsie walked into the ward. Worth putting her own resentment behind her, putting the children first yet again.

'Auntie Elsie!' cried Mary, sitting up in the bed and holding out her arms to her aunt. And Elsie had clasped the child to her, hugging and kissing her until Sister spoke disapprovingly from the doorway.

'Mary Sharpe! You must lie down, how many times have I told you?' And reluctantly Mary did as she was told.

'See, Auntie Elsie, my arm's in a sling. I can't move it, I hurt it, but the doctor says –'

Auntie Elsie was 'oohing' and 'ahhing' and nodding her head as Mary's words tumbled over each other in her haste to tell her tale. Rose smiled and turned to Michael's bed. He was awake, pale and fragile-looking but awake and smiling even.

'Did you see the cows, Rose?' he asked quietly, his

smile widening. 'I wasn't frightened of them at all. I wasn't, honest, Rose.' His brows knitted for an instant. 'How did we get there?' he asked. 'I can't remember.'

'Oh, never mind, pet,' she replied and kissed him gently on the cheek, taking his thin wrist in her hand. He was growing up, she thought suddenly. His face wasn't a duplicate of his sister's any more but a proper boy's face.

'When I'm big I'm going to be a farmer,' he told her. 'We've been reading all about farms in school and I wrote a composition. I got a star an' all, did Auntie Elsie tell you?'

Rose looked across at the other bed. Elsie was perched on the side of it now, one hand on Mary's dark hair. Elsie was unable to contain her happiness, couldn't stop herself from smiling, almost laughing when she spoke.

'I haven't had time yet, son,' she said. 'But I was going to, I'm so proud of you.'

'And me too,' put in Mary.

'And you too,' agreed Auntie Elsie, laughing outright, and Rose laughed too, their eyes meeting over the beds in perfect understanding.

'I'm afraid you'll have to go now,' said Sister and Mary began to whimper. Elsie bent over the bed and brushed her lips across the little girl's cheek.

'I'm coming back this afternoon at two o'clock,' she whispered. 'Will I bring Rosalie?'

'You won't forget, will you?' Mary asked anxiously and lay back on her pillow, satisfied when Aunt Elsie assured her she wouldn't. 'You too, Rose? You'll come, won't you?'

'I will.'

As the two women walked down the corridor, Rose asked, 'Who's Rosalie?'

'A doll. I bought it for her when she was crying for you last year,' Elsie added, looking sideways at her niece.

I've missed a huge slice from the children's lives, Rose thought sadly. But the sadness slipped away quickly enough. There was no place for it today.

Jeff had gone outside to wait. It was marvellous, he thought, how kind and understanding nurses could be with relatives when the patient was seriously ill yet how distant and forbidding when there was no danger. He'd noticed it before. He leaned against the wall and whistled softly, an old tune from the war, 'We'll Meet Again'. The rain which had threatened in the early morning had moved on. The air was fresh and cold but dry and full of promise.

He felt supremely happy, remembering Rose in the hotel during the night, how loving and generous she had been, his lovely lass. And now the twins, the children she had sacrificed so much to protect, were out of danger, and things were at last going their way. Even the clouds were dispersing, it would be a sunny afternoon. It would be great in the front room this afternoon, just him and Rose. The room faced south-west and would be filled with sunshine and they would sit close together on the couch and talk about the future which stretched ahead of them, the lovely future.

They would get married as soon as possible. Why wait? Rose needn't come back to Hartlepool at all, he was earning enough for them both. And the twins too if need be.

Jeff was distracted by a figure in a white coat coming out of the door opposite. Of course, it was that same doctor who always seemed to be about, he didn't know why. But it didn't matter, he could hear footsteps behind him, Rose was coming, Rose and her aunt. They could go home now, start their future.

'Bob!'

They stood for a moment, a tableau of four, looking at each other. It was Rose who spoke first. 'Bob, I'm sorry I missed you yesterday evening.'

'That's all right, think nothing of it,' he replied, unsmiling, his whole body stiff. 'I'm glad you found your friends.' He made to move on but she put one hand on his arm.

'No, wait a minute. Please, Bob.' And he looked down into her great dark eyes, seeing the concern in them. 'I want to tell you, explain...'

'No need.'

'Yes, there is,' she insisted. 'We've been visiting the twins. I couldn't meet you yesterday because of the accident.' Beside her, Aunt Elsie looked puzzled. She had seen this doctor before, she was sure of it. Jeff too was puzzled but the male in him recognised a rival. He was aware without being told that this man loved his Rose. He stepped closer to her, put an arm around her shoulders, showing in the age-old way that she was his. But Rose seemed to want to speak to him.

'Oh, you mean the car accident?' Bob was startled into asking. 'That was your father? Oh!'

'Yes. He was killed,' she said, and glanced up at Jeff who was waiting, very still now, wanting to know what this was all about. 'Bob, this is my fiancé. I just met him again yesterday.'

'But I thought – Oh, well, never mind what I thought.' He gazed at Rose with Jeff's arm still around her shoulders. So obviously in love they were and his hope died. He began to walk away from them, backwards. 'I...er...I have to go now. I...I'm sure you'll both be very happy,' he said and disappeared into a ward.

'Who *is* that, Rose?' asked Jeff. 'He came to the house yesterday, spoke to Marina. I was in a hurry to get to Shotton so I didn't wait to see what he wanted.'

'He was a good friend when I needed one,' she answered softly. 'One day I'll tell you all about it. But not now, Jeff, not today.' They walked on in the sunshine, holding hands, Aunt Elsie walking quietly behind them. She spoke once in the car.

'We have the funeral to think of, Rose.'

'I can't think of it, Aunt Elsie,' Rose replied sadly. 'I just can't.'

'Well, I was his sister. I'll see to it.'

So Alf Sharpe was laid to rest in the cemetery at Jordan

after a brief service in an almost empty chapel and only Elsie, his sister, wept for him. Rose was reluctant to go.

'You must,' insisted her aunt. 'He was your father.'

'Well, maybe you should have reminded him of that fact,' Rose replied. So hard and bitter she sounded, Jeff thought, not at all like his Rose. He had done all the running about in preparation for the funeral, collecting the coroner's report and the death certificate, arranging the ceremony with the minister, the memory of his grandmother's funeral returning to haunt him. Not that he could speak of his grandmother in the same breath as that man...

'You must go, Rose,' he'd said when they were alone. 'The children too. They must be allowed to think of him as...as...'

'Normal?' she asked acidly. But he was right, she knew it, and so for the sake of the twins she attended the ceremony and, surprisingly, felt her heart soften towards the dead man as she gazed at his coffin standing at the front of the chapel. She held Mary's hand and the little girl cried because her auntie was crying but Michael stood as straight as a soldier and dry-eyed.

The chapel was almost empty. Alf had lost any friends he had had in the early days. It was a sad end.

The wedding was to be held at the Methodist Church in Easington Colliery at 3 p.m. on the Saturday after Christmas. There were only a handful of guests invited. After all, both bride and groom had been brought up on the other side of the county, Easington was a new beginning for them. Jeff's grandmother had been his last relative. And Rose had only her Aunt Elsie and the twins.

The morning of the wedding, Rose sat at the dressing table in the spare bedroom of Marina and Brian's home, gazing at her reflection in the mirror. She could hardly believe it was actually happening. Marina stood behind her, brushing her dark, lustrous hair into shining waves before pinning on the circlet of pearls and satin leaves which held the gauzy veil.

'It was good of you to lend me your dress and everything,' Rose murmured.

'Oh, go on, don't be soft,' said Marina. 'It suits you better than it ever did me anyroad. And I think it's nice, us sharing like this. After all, it's too nice a dress to be worn only once, isn't it?'

Rose gazed once more at her reflection. The dress was of stiff, figured taffeta and in reaction to the war years was cut on generous lines with a full skirt, long sleeves and a heart-shaped neckline. It was a new fashion after the clinging satin which had been all there was available a year or two before.

Marina herself was to be matron of honour and her dress was a deep blue taffeta, unusual for a wedding but her idea was that it could easily be turned into a dance dress. 'Just the thing for the New Year's Eve ball at the Institute,' she reckoned, and Rose agreed with her.

'Though Brian's worrying on like a hen with one chick

since I told him I was expecting,' commented Marina. 'I told him, why shouldn't I dance? I'm no more than four months gone after all, my waist's hardly thickened yet. Here, what do you think?'

She turned sideways and looked into the mirror, and Rose obligingly got out of the way so she could see. 'I'm sure you're right,' was her judgement. Marina seemed to have forgotten her ambitions to rise to the top of the Treasurer's Department at Shire Hall. Now all she could think of was her Brian and the new baby. She had turned into a model housewife.

'The car's here,' Brian called from the bottom of the stairs. He was going to have been Jeff's best man but in the end had decided that Rose's need for someone to give her away was more urgent.

The two girls smiled at one other. 'Eeh, pet, I wish you all the luck in the world,' said Marina, eyes suddenly bright with tears. 'The Lord knows, you deserve it. You haven't had much luck so far.'

'But I have,' Rose replied, her voice so soft it was almost a whisper. 'I have Jeff, don't I?'

'You do indeed,' Marina agreed and kissed her lightly on the cheek. 'Howay now, time to go.'

Jeff had asked his marra from work to be his best man. Dan Murray was a tall, gangling sort of lad with a freckled face and hair somewhere between blond and ginger. He stood beside Jeff, beaming at everyone in the chapel, obviously delighted to be asked. There were plenty of people to smile at too. It seemed to Jeff that half his shift and their wives and girlfriends had come to see him wed, all of them dressed in their best: the women in wispy hats; the men with their hair slicked back with a quiff at the front in the mode of the day.

The organ struck up 'Here Comes the Bride' and Dan nudged Jeff. 'Now then, lad, here we go.' They stood and took their places before the communion rail, Dan fumbling in his pocket in a sudden panic that he had lost the ring. But Jeff was watching his Rose, his lovely flower, walking down the aisle on Brian's arm, her smile the most beautiful he had seen in his life.

Behind her Marina stepped forward to receive the bouquet. The twins looked unnaturally solemn as they stood behind her, Michael's hair slicked down with water and Mary's tied up in pink satin ribbons.

From a side pew, Auntie Elsie watched them proudly, her habitual anxious expression completely gone, for hadn't Rose promised the children could stay with her in Shotton, so long as they were happy there? And Elsie was well aware what heart-searching had gone into that decision. She turned her attention to the bride and groom as the service got under way.

'Dearly beloved...' the minister began. Jeff looked down at Rose, who had taken her place beside him, catching her glance up at him, and the two of them were once again wrapped in that precious golden haze of love.

Also by Maggie Hope:

The Servant Girl

**She is the downstairs maid
He is the Master's son...**

Forced to become a kitchen maid at Fortune Hall, Hetty Pearson strikes up an unlikely friendship with the younger son of the house, Richard.

But Hetty is just a poor servant girl: what hope does she have of either winning Richard's heart or escaping his older brother's more base attentions?